The Forgotten Folk
Vol I
Four Wishes

The Forgotten Folk Vol I
Four Wishes

First published in Great Britain 2023 by Lockwright.

A CIP catalogue copy of this book is available from the British
Library

Artwork by dariakupchus-photography

ISBN: 978-1-7384510-0-5

For my two tawny-headed sons Lawrence and Adam
With love.

Inspired by the late Elaine Kirsch-Edsall
An antiquarian and friend to all creatures.

*Folklore means that the soul is sane, but that the universe is wild
and full of marvels.*

Contents

Four Wishes

Chapter 1 The Book

By the time Ben got to the small independent bookshop, the queue outside was like an unnatural plant, extending shoots down side streets and across roads. He couldn't even see the end of it, and the people at the end couldn't see the beginning of it at least judging by the way heads bobbed around to gauge the distance between them and the shop. The rain hammered down upon them all. Nobody seemed impatient though, because the bookshop was in a small town named Dorchester, in southern England, and British people are notorious for loving to stand in an orderly line. In fact, there was an air of festivity with people gossiping with their immediate neighbours.

The reason for the prolonged queuing was quite surprising, considering the focus of all the effort was a rather dirty-looking shop front door, with bottle base mullioned windows on either side. The faded display posters from a previous promotion and a poorly positioned pile of books gave the premises a disreputable look, as if the whole set-up was a front for something else. A handmade sign attached with a drawing pin explained the direction deliveries should take.

A swell of laughter near the front of the queue caused a gap to open behind two girls as people craned forward. Ben slipped in unnoticed, resentful, but at the same time thankful for his learned ability to blend in and deflect attention. Ben often reflected on how he had achieved the invisibility most people acquire with age. Chameleon-like, he could merge into the scenery, often for inclusion, and sometimes for safety. He was a delicate-looking young man, and in his neat shirt, linen jacket and skinny jeans, he had contrived a subdued definition of maleness for everyday use. The girl in front to the right of him was complaining bitterly about the cost of the text they were obliged to purchase.

"I mean, Sarah," she said to her friend, "A hundred quid for a book!"

"Yeah!" said the other. "What a con. And," she continued, in a higher register, "You can't even get in without buying it."

Ben couldn't help himself. He blurted out, "It is a very special book, though, isn't it?"

"A book's a book," said the right-hand girl, turning to face him momentarily before phone alerts caused her to face back the other way. The two backs together formed an impenetrable wall.

Suddenly, Ben's own phone bleeped. It was a message from his boss, stark and impatient. 'Where are you?' it demanded. Ben panicked. Another message swiftly followed it: 'Your client's already here.' Some people can bring in excuses smoothly, like un-liked relatives at a wedding, but Ben had a problem with lying. His mind went blank and he stared at the message before realising his hands were shaking. What should he do? He looked ahead at the darkened door, his objective, then back at his freezing fingers hovering over the keys. The importance of the moment wrestled honesty to the ground. Pressing the microphone icon, he said, louder than he intended, "I've got a stomach upset. A terrible one." This caused the girls in front to turn around and grin and he smiled back enjoying the kudos that deceit had earned him. His smugness was short-lived however because there was an almost immediate phone alert back from the salon owner. Ben read the words, 'What? Where?!' 'You were here a minute ago,' was pointed out, and she had included angry, shocked and crazy emojis. Ben put his phone in his pocket so he wouldn't have to look at it.

"You too..." said Izzy, the girl on the right, having just muttered a fiction about a sore throat to her own boss.

"Yeah, there's no way I'd miss this."

"Us neither," said Sarah, the right-hand girl grinning at him.

"Look," said the other, lifting a strand of hair away from her mouth. "We didn't mean to be rude before. It's just that we've come to see her, you know, the author. We don't really care much about reading. By the way, I'm Izzy and this is Sarah. We're definitely going to find out if the rumours are a pile of crap or whatever."

"Yeah," said Sarah, her friend on the left, "We want to know whether it's true about her kind. You know the magic and stuff. We reckon it was just exaggerated... a bit of spin."

"And," said Izzy, "There's no evidence. All that rubbish about video footage fading. Still, there were the deaths," she admitted, "and the government stating those fairy people..."

"The Fei," Ben corrected.

"Yeah, the Fei, were real." She patted her sodden hair thoughtfully. "Because none of us was born at the time, how can we tell what's real and what's not?

"Perhaps that's the point of the book, to set the record straight," said Ben mildly.

"Yeah, the book," said the girl on the left, looking at her friend, who raised an eyebrow. She asked Ben, "What are you here for then? I always think it's a bit weird when blokes are into fairies and all."

"Not really," said Ben. "Anyway, technically the Fei are an entirely separate species. It's us who make them out to be ridiculous, all tiny, with wands and tutus. It's a bit like putting an outfit on a dog."

"I put an outfit on my dog," said Izzy, glaring at him.

Ben nearly said, 'Exactly,' but just stopped himself in time.

"Well, why are you here then if you don't believe in it all?" Sarah took the lead.

"I'm going to film it for my social media account – you can find me on @sarahsstories. I expose fakers and stuff like that. There are a lot of con merchants out there."

"Yeah," echoed Izzy, but with gravity as if the weight of the world had suddenly hit her full in the stomach. "It'd be great if it was real though."

Gloom became a sodden blanket, wrapped around the two companions, standing stupidly in the rain, and a long pause followed until Sarah reverted to her aggressive tone.

"Anyway, what's the appeal of it for you?" Ben was intuitive enough to know that hostility tended to mask feelings of inadequacy. Excusing her, he decided unwisely to disclose a fascination he had with a real person who had lived and would surely feature in the book he was about to purchase. "Well," he said in deliberately casual tones, "I want to find out more about that changeling man...you know, the one who died, or disappeared, or whatever." Immediately he regretted what he'd said when Izzy rounded on him with, "Oh my good grief, you're one those grave lurkers. Do you put flowers and candles on his grave and all?"

"Izzy, film him; let's get him to do an interview with you. Do you mind?" she asked, noting Ben's expression.

"Yes, yes, I do... and no, I won't," he added, feeling his face becoming hot. "Turn it off," he said as Sarah pointed her camera at him.

"Alright, no need to get touchy. We just wanted to know what you actually do when you're there. I mean, do you chant or anything?" They both sniggered.

"It's just a fan base, that's all," Ben muttered to the floor.

"Yes, but he's dead, supposedly, and it's a memorial," was the cutting response.

Ben didn't know what to say. How could they possibly know what it meant to have a role model with the capacity to be all things? A series of ideas processed through his mind: the Changeling as a swashbuckling hero, a British army officer... a Fei prince. An everyman for someone like him, who felt so… so what, he wondered? But he knew the answer… so stuck. The Changeling's disappearance from this world was almost an irrelevance; where he had vanished, his thirty-year legend had taken over. It was as if he had never really gone. Keeping his memory alive was very important to Ben. The girls wouldn't understand. They had no doubt already formed an opinion of him as being more than slightly weird, but then he made matters worse by trying to explain.

"It doesn't matter that he's not actually there. You know, there are too few role models for men who are..." he paused.

"Are what?"

"Different." The word was exhaled and breathed into his navel.

"What do you mean different?" asked Sarah curiously, but without waiting for a response she continued with, "We're *all* a bit different aren't we?" She shared a furtive look with Izzy. "If *that's* what you mean?" Ben said nothing.

"Well, there's no point in being shy about it, is there?" said Izzy dismissively, somehow hitting the nail on the head.

"He's a gay icon isn't he," interrupted Sarah and it wasn't even a question.

"Yes. Sort of," Ben admitted.

Ben recalled the young men, whose faces he now knew well, who did indeed place candles in the old market square, now a backwater to the newer urban centre, though, there was nothing so ridiculous as chanting or rituals. People would usually stop briefly, place a token, nod and then walk off in a business-like kind of way. The event was like the man himself, who was known to have been quite unassuming. Even Ben's uncle, who was an antagonistic kind of person had thought him approachable. They'd met a few times because he used to work at the army fuelling depot where the Changeling had been stationed. "Nice bloke," he'd said when Ben questioned him about it. There was no way on earth that Ben's Uncle Andy would ever understand the legacy of the Changeling for the younger generation. "You're kidding, right?" he would have said and Ben knew the girls in front of him would have a similar perspective. Ben back-peddled, a knot of anxiety in his chest.

"He was just a regular guy who did great things," he said, but the girls had lost interest in him and were back on their phones.

"Apparently...," said Sarah without even bothering to look up.

"Hey, something's happening," said Izzy suddenly, alerting them to the low murmur coming from the queue trailing around the corner.

"Oh, my word, what? What is it?" whispered Sarah, half terrified out of her wits. She didn't even realise she was digging her nails into Ben's arm. His wide grin, on the other hand, was the outward mark of a man who felt finally justified.

"I knew it...I knew it was true," he said, watching a truly extraordinary woman rounding the corner dressed in a long, brown velvet cloak.

She was anything but dull even in the mud-coloured robes that dragged behind her, collecting leaves and winter debris as she swept past. In fact, it was difficult at first to sustain looking at her because she was so vivid it hurt the eyes. She was also moving incredibly fast.

Despite her speed, as she passed him Ben felt he'd been noticed, but he couldn't have said why. Then he was overwhelmed by the smell of earthiness combined with something else that could only be described as 'ancient'. It was the musty stench of time, preserved in antique chests, old buildings, and materials produced so long ago that the tailors were dust themselves. Naturalness in her seemed to overcome the man-made, and she wore a live garland of ivy woven into the crown of her curly head as if it had grown there. It was so difficult to sustain a further opinion about her beyond the obvious features of the headgear and cloak. One minute, she appeared relatively ordinary and humanoid in shape; the next, she gave the impression of being gigantic, and her skin had the ragged, uneven texture of a tree bole. Some of the crowd, eager to report back to friends were frustrated because one impression of her was erased by another in a matter of seconds. Others didn't have this particular issue, and perceiving her as regular in size didn't make space as she passed and found themselves suddenly and forcibly pressed against railings. Sarah told Izzy to get off her as both were now on the floor, but Ben was upright, having merely stood aside. Ben continued to watch the titanic woman accelerating towards the front of the bookshop, his absorption complete, his shoulders up near his ears. If anything, she was gathering speed; surely, she would smash into the front of the building. There was a collective gasp from many as the woman suddenly reduced in the blink of an eye and entered the darkened interior of the bookstore. The queue surged forward with hands reaching for wallets and phones to pay for the entrance fee, which was the book.

The interior of the shop had a very distinctive odour. "It smells in here," Sarah had announced making Ben feel uncomfortable at her rudeness. He rather liked it. "Leaf litter?" he'd suggested as they entered, and in fact that did fit in with the decor. Someone, the proprietor probably, had made a great effort in decorating the shop in a naturalistic way and there were strings of ivy and leaf garlands draped around the circular stairwell interspersed with green fairy lights. The shelves and bookcases also carried an abundance of leaves, conkers and twigs. These also spilt onto the floor. The depth of the leaves meant that the groups of people, let in four at a time, were having to literally wade their way through the shop. "Looks rather authentic, doesn't it?" said the silver-haired old man in their group. "They're going to have a heck of a job clearing this lot up though."

"Eww," said Izzy, recoiling with disgust and flicking her fingers, "Bugs."

The woman, who was no longer a giantess now sat in a still pool of calm behind the desk placed at the far end of the room against the wood panelling. A candle in an old-fashioned holder with a curved handle beside a pile of books did little to dispel the darkness that seemed particularly concentrated in that area as though a child had coloured around the figure and the candle over and over with a wax crayon. The darkness both contained and adored her, seeming to cling to her outline in a homage of formlessness and chaos against fixed form. Occasionally, the darkness became presumptive, erasing portions of her momentarily, yet when she re-emerged, it was with a more concentrated outline that was deeply satisfying. The stimulus to perception meant viewing her gave a sense of being slightly drugged. This new stillness of the author was intense, but Ben was glad to be able to finally see her properly; he could appreciate the remarkable beauty of her face, two perfect lips with a slight, barely amused smile that didn't disturb the cupid's bow above nor influence her long-lashed eyes. Ben was reminded a little of the inscrutable face of a Grecian mask, closed but indifferent, too. This was power, he knew it, and even the candle flame failed to flicker as if it, too, were painted in oils on a canvas.

In contrast, a man was energetically levering books onto a sack truck by a service door as if he inhabited a different sphere altogether. He looked up to take stock of the four rooted in the centre of the room and said, "You can go forward now," in a rather absent way before realising that there was a person in the group he knew.

"Hello, Ben," he said. "Why don't you hold back here with me for a bit?" Ben switched his gaze between the shop owner, whom he knew as Petey, and the author, who he suddenly realised was craning forward with interest. She held the candle close to her face as if her vision were poor, and the movement had caused her long sleeve to slip back over her wrist, revealing an appalling merging of three digits from ring to little finger into one mass. This combined limb extended at least double the length of the whole hand into a singular finger with a bony whorl on the end like a shell. The elderly gentleman in the group, who had seemed so conventional moments before, said faintly, "The wand," and took a step backwards. He clutched his right hand in his left and stroked along its length with an expression of deep sadness as if experiencing a phantom limb. Izzy meanwhile tapped her watch and sighed. The woman author was suddenly stood beside Petey, with her back to them all, though he hadn't seen her move there. Ben blinked and wondered how that had happened. Sarah, frowning, had momentarily seemed to track something across the room, but she shrugged and joined Izzy, who was sliding books impatiently off a nearby shelf.

An odd conversation developed between Petey and the woman as Ben heard her ask in a stage whisper, "Does he think he's one of ours?" Meanwhile, her arm, like a peripheral entity, continued to sweep away the advancing shadows with the candle in its holder in a gentle rhythm.

"No," said Petey, recoiling slightly from the proximity of the woman's face a mere inch away from his, "Just a young friend. Or that's how I know him now."

This was true. Ben knew that long ago before Petey had bought the bookshop, he had been a youth worker and still had very good relationships with the local kids whom he allowed to hang out in the backyard behind the shop. Some of the older people in the town said he'd been married to the Changeling, but no one really believed that. Petey must be about eighty now, at least twenty years older than the Changeling would have been.

"Is it definitely him?" Petey asked. Both heads turned around to stare at Ben then making him hot and self-conscious.

"Certain," she stated, "though, of course, it's hard to remember him being this young."

"We were all that way once." Petey pretended a world-weariness, but his voice was rich in memory. Ben realised the woman was grinning at him and suddenly she seemed less frightening, less...he searched for the word, wooden, that was it. Flicking her long, black curly hair away from her face, she sauntered back to the table in glacial and deliberate slowness, more or less as if she were on a catwalk, demonstrating a performance of control and arrogance. Ben suddenly felt exhausted by the shifting impressions of her, and Petey shot him a sympathetic look. "Hey, help me with the books," he said, handing his own Stanley knife to Ben, who was grateful to have something to do and commenced scoring the parcel tape on the many cardboard boxes.

"I'm going to have to get a move on," the woman said, seated back behind the desk. "I'm barely containing this space. Oona, the cow, has only granted me this moment with a few incremental shifts, though I don't know what it's got to do with her these days." She sighed. "Still, the decision was made and the worlds turned back to the way they were before."

"Who's Oona?" Ben whispered, "And what's she done?"

"Queen Oona to you, Ben, though, to be exact, she's no longer strictly the Queen, more like a gatekeeper between their world and ours. However, between you and I, she still acts as if she were Queen, and in charge. She's what you would call... dominant." Petey shuddered ever so slightly.

Ben and Petey had become oblivious to the other three in the shop, during their conversation, and Izzy, in particular, was not tolerating this well.

"They said, 'Go forward'," barked Izzy, an enraged ball of fury in the middle of the room, "and we've been kept here for ages."

"Don't worry dear, I'll re-set us," said the author lazily, commencing a kind of backstroke as if she were swimming on dry land. "I can only do it for a few moments though."

"What's she on about?" asked Sarah puzzled.

"Who?" asked Izzy, still deep within her anger.

"The writer," said the old gentleman on her right, who reached up on tiptoes to consolingly pat her on the shoulder. "She said she's going to get things moving for us now." He indicated in front of him to Ben, "I've kept your place," he said, but Ben shook his head, "I'll wait here with my friend." He glanced at Petey, who nodded his agreement but was immediately distracted by the jangling of the doorbell; then, he witnessed the impossible creeping into his life like a cold thief. Shock ascended from his sodden shoes right up to his head, and the ringing he heard was no longer the brass bell on the hook; it was in his ears. Through the door stepped Sarah, Izzy and the old man as if they were doing it for the first time.

"How'd you get in before us?" asked Sarah grumpily to Ben. "Bloody queue jumper."

Ben ignored her and lifted a pile of books out of a box. He didn't dare look at the author behind the desk, who was busily signing books. Ben was convinced there would be a sly smile on those lips. The ringing he heard became a roaring, the floor started to pitch, and he tried desperately to reconcile himself to the unthinkable idea that time had just been somehow re-arranged, but this only made him feel more light-headed. As reason battled against the improbable in his mind, a slight argument developed when Izzy finally managed to perceive the author behind the desk and challenged her about the admission price. Izzy suggested cheekily that they should only purchase one book as they were 'together', but Sarah became suddenly frightened and convinced Izzy to 'drop it' when she spotted something on the desk, something odd about a hand that she couldn't explain clearly. The door tinged as the girls exited, and he heard Izzy mentioning as she left that the so-called Fei woman seemed ordinary after all, if a bit musty and dirty. She, herself, was writing it off as a complete waste of time and money. Sarah didn't say anything in response. Meanwhile, the old man was shaking hands with the author as if he would never stop. The two seemed to know each other and the woman leant forward to whisper something in his ear, a very delicate ear like spun glass that didn't seem to go with the rest of his head. The man left, and many others followed until finally, Petey turned the sign to close on the door and they all fell back exhausted in separate chairs.

"Now it's your turn," said the Fei woman to Ben in a way that seemed to communicate affection and amusement at the same time. "I think Petey would like me to carve out a little more time for you."

"Like you did before, with that thing at the door?"

"No, just the usual way," she said, "Petey mentioned you had a great interest in our world and had a lot of unanswered questions."

"That old man that was just here," enquired Ben. "Is he, like, a Fei person?"

"Partially," she admitted. "It is quite rare for a human person to have congenital similarities to the Fei race, but not unheard of. Usually, it is just an affinity for the natural world and a sort of incessant fascination with supernature. That's why I asked Petey if you *believe* you are, 'one of ours'."

"Well, I'm not Fei."

"Okay," said the woman casually, grinning at him."

"But I do like supernatural stuff, you know, mysticism and suchlike. I've got an open mind."

"Hmm, that's not quite what I meant, but it does show itself in lots of different ways." Ben jumped; what exactly was she saying about him?

"I do know mortals are attracted to that kind of fakery, for entertainment and suchlike," she continued. "And actually, my good friend used to run a new age shop which was very popular, in this exact town." For a fleeting moment, she looked indescribably sad. "That was a long time ago, though – she does, different, things now." She fiddled with the cord of her cloak for a while, suddenly exposing a dramatic dress of crimson edged with gold. She seemed to be in a reverie and spoke rhetorically without making eye contact, "We miss people as they once were, with all their mistakes and imperfections..." she trailed off, still caught in a memory that didn't include him. Ben broke the spell.

"I wouldn't miss the person I am now," Ben said, firmly. "I mean, it's good to move on, isn't it?"

"Not really, no. I think that's a bit of a myth and part of all that lifestyle self-improvement rubbish. We are always the same, but in different scenes, we may act slightly differently; sometimes we are just better at being ourselves." She reached out and stroked then prodded his hand encouragingly, seeming to sense distressing impermanence about him. Ben withdrew it and noticed a bead of blood on his hand, like a minute ruby. He felt rather exposed and wondered if she was psychic like they said her family was.

"You're one of the Knight family, aren't you?" he asked, looking at her statement red robes and drawing on what insight he had into the Fei.

"Yes, and to answer your next question, yes, our strain is psychic."

"No, don't worry, I'm not doing it now," she said, noting his expression. "Perhaps," she added and laughed. Ben quite bravely held her look for a moment but then stared at the floor because he caught something quite unrepentant in her eyes. She then did a rather odd thing by craning around him to stare precisely into a low, fixed point in the corner of the room. Her face registered a barely suppressed excitement.

"I have to go soon," she said, bringing the sole remaining book towards her. Ben decided to bite the bullet before it was too late.

"I wanted to know about the Changeling," he said, abruptly making her flinch. "The human man…the statue in the town."

"Is that what you call him?" she asked with genuine curiosity. "The Changeling?"

"Well, you see, we don't know his Fei name."

"I suppose you wouldn't, and anyway, names are so problematic," she sighed. "Us Fei are particularly cagey about volunteering names - to us, names explain a person in process, not static or fixed. We don't like to be held accountable you see."

She gave him a cryptic look that he couldn't read. "Anyway, it's not straightforward with him because he had a couple of names in his lifetime, neither exactly conventional nor even fitting. Perhaps 'Changeling' does describe his life experiences, but…" she muddled some promotional papers on the desk, "…that certainly doesn't sum him up."

"What was he actually like then?" Ben asked eagerly. She didn't hesitate.

"Lovely, just perfectly lovely in every way, from childhood to adulthood. He could have been so much more, too, if only…" Ben waited for more but she broke off until she muttered something about it not being the time for sadness. Ben became aware of Petey banging boxes around behind him in an erratic fashion. "His line diverged," she said mysteriously, "And that is why you must interact with this book, fully and carefully, because history is a tricky thing. It tends….," she instructed, "….to fold in on itself and present a condensed version of events. Things get lost. People go missing," she said cryptically. "You might have heard that before."

"Are you saying that time isn't linear?" asked Ben trying to sound philosophical, though he knew nothing about such things.

"Not always," she said. "You should try writing a book about it," she added, with feeling. "It nearly killed me."

Mentioning the book reminded her that she had a job to do, so she signed Ben's copy of the text quickly and got up to go, though her attention was now completely transfixed by whatever was in the corner of the room. Ben noticed her gaze was focused precisely on a dusty fern on a stand.

"Quickly," said Ben, feeling that she was about to exit, "Why did you write a fairy story? Why not an autobiography? Surely, it would give a truer picture of your world."

"It might be a bit unbelievable in parts," she conceded, "but I can guarantee that it will do what all embroidered tales do – capture a bit of truth about the universe with no censorship.

Anyway, fairy tales are easy to remember, always a bonus for our kind in particular, who have the attention spans of gnats. The Fei learn life lessons from them as your kind do too. Do 'you' write, Ben?" she asked in a slightly accusing tone.

"Not really. I just keep a journal."

"Good, good." Ben noticed her dark eyes twinkling with a sudden fire; her evident pleasure seemed to him a bit over the top. "Always so useful to have a steady viewpoint drawing it all together."

"Drawing what together?"

"Just the facts," she said, smiling. Ben had a strong impression that she was humouring him. Her tone became whimsical. "After all, we live in worlds where dangers abound, and creatures defy description, and little makes sense. So useful really to have a pragmatic overview of it all." The capricious switches of tone reminded Ben a little of his Gran who used to get very descriptive, even in the most mundane of settings, such as when cleaning out the outside drains. The author, as if irritated with her words taking such a fanciful direction, shoved the book towards him. She refused to take the damp bundle of notes he offered her and served the present with a glib "Enjoy" as if she were passing over an ice cream sundae. She peered around him. Whatever was in or around the pot plant had now saturated all of her attention. He felt she was no longer there at all.

"It was nice to meet you, Ben," she smiled, her tone sincere. "Remember to pack your bags selectively when you leave next month."

"I'm not going anywhere," he said, confused.

"Oh, I think you may be," she answered. "Remember to be yourself too, dear, that is crucial." She hesitated on her way towards the corner of the room. "And actually," she clarified, "it is entirely enough." She smiled again. "Your 'Changeling,'" said that once you know. Turns out its sound advice." She stood up to leave.

"Wait," said Petey, charging across the room towards her. They embraced, the woman in the shabby brown cloak disguising her opulent interior and the old man with the single earring and well-polished gold ring on his left hand proving he was once 'Someone's'. They pulled apart as the shadows in the corner circled the fern just like a dense shoal of fish. They all watched as these merged into one, forming a flap that slid down into a repulsive gloop, revealing an off-white hole within that had a gossamer texture. Ben was reminded of his granny's net curtains before she became too ill to wash them, just before she died. He realised then that he didn't know who the author was and there was no name on the book cover.

"What's your name?" he blurted as she stepped up and into the void, her brown cloak ruched up behind her. A shower of dirt rained on the wooden floor of the shop.

"Look for me….," she said, her voice became rapidly swallowed up, and only her upper back and head were visible now, "Not just The Changeling." Her final words came from far away, "Understand...look, for us all...," and then she was gone. There was a wet-sounding slap, and the gap sealed itself, though a faint line remained for a couple of minutes. Petey and Ben didn't move for a couple of long minutes until Petey remarked, "It always gets me, every time," painting a very different complexion of *his* character. Ben felt suddenly as if the world were a very alien place indeed. Strangely, this thought was rather comforting.

"Well, sunshine," said Petey with forced jolliness, "It's off home for you now."

"Back to work, I suppose," Ben answered, "I'll have to face the music."

"I doubt there'll be anyone there now," Petey responded raising an eyebrow as Ben realised it was pitch-black outside. "What time is it?" he blurted, in a panic.

"Late," said Petey, pushing Ben and his book towards the door.

Something about Petey's face made him realise that he wasn't welcome any longer, but it was Petey not him that had reached his limits. He observed Petey's hand trembling as he turned the door handle. Therefore, Ben didn't take it personally when he found himself on the street with the bolts on the other side of the door being pulled firmly across behind him. Yet, he was left with a sense of anti-climax so acute that investigating the book, he thought, might alleviate that a little. Ben decided to go back to work after all as he had a duplicate key and it was warmer than his studio flat. This was how thirty minutes later he was sat comfortably in the staff kitchen with his feet up and a cup of coffee next to him. All four bars of the heater were on, and the book, being both heavy and a hardcover, was balanced on his lap.

***

The book was very unusual, having neither a title as well as no author's name. The cover was dark red and had a damp, organic feel to it, as if it had been exposed to the elements, though Ben had carried it under his jacket the entire way to the salon. Opening it, he was momentarily blinded by the gold margin that seemed to pulsate and shift in waves. His eyes quickly adjusted to this, and he noted the intricate depictions contained within the border, of mythical creatures: strange, hybrid mixes that weren't entirely tree or humanoid in form. There were conventional-looking Fei persons, too, with their pointed ears. These seemed to be generally misbehaving; stealing or beating each other up, though there were gentler images too of gift exchanging and warm embraces. Some animals looked directly at him: rabbits and toads that were neither cute nor ordinary. Ben felt that their stares demonstrated humanlike awareness. All the scenes and figures were strange and intense, black outlines on an emerald green or deep red background and it was just like being at the opticians undergoing a duochrome test. It was impossible to miss the tiniest detail, the red, green and black plunging him into a three-dimensional space. It was too much – he partially shut the book and leaned back, remembering what someone, a man called Hippy Phil, who ran the health store, had told him once; that red was the colour of the royal Knight earth-bound family and green the Aquarelle Sea strain. He had also mentioned that the Knights were slightly safer than the green kind, but then changed his mind and said that, actually, neither kind was reliable.

"I wouldn't trust them as far as I could throw them," he'd said, "though the current monarch keeps them all in check these days. Of course, the Fei 'can' be kind - 'if' you handle them right." After this disclosure in the pub, there had been the usual hiatus as he lost his thread. Phil tended to lurk in a certain dark area of The Crown, and anyone stupid enough to forget this and wander into his domain had it coming. He would physically grip people as he talked so that escape was near impossible. Despite this, Ben considered that he often had interesting information to impart, but only if the captive had time to spare to sift out the credible bits of the conversation. Even Phil had to admit that truth and fantasy with him were often the same, and he knew that from experience.

Ben rubbed his hand on the underside of the book as if soothing it, and it became much warmer to his touch. He was glad. Petey must have got the copies damp when he was loading them into the shop. After a while, he opened the book again and was surprised to find that he had missed a cameo of a very beautiful girl at the centre of the frontispiece. The girl had long, dark hair, wore a very minimal tiara with a ruby in its centre and a very sad but somehow welcoming expression, almost as if she were saying to him, 'Read on.' It was quite a strong impression; he felt he had he actually heard those words. Certainly, he was intrigued to know who she was.

As he was thinking, he noticed the gilt edges of the page looked dull and tarnished. Something must have gone wrong with the production process if this was what happened when the book was exposed to the air. Before he knew it, the images on the pages he'd looked at started to vanish. The girl's crown was no longer there and then nor was she. Finally, he was faced with a completely blank page. He realised he had to read on quickly. Hopefully it was only the top pages that were affected.

The next page was very strange, the only content being in bold ink as a footer. *Tempus omnia revelat* was printed in a minuscule font. Ben reached for his phone to translate the words, but before he could even begin to tap anything onto the screen, they started to whisper themselves to him. A woman in green with long, blond hair and slanted eyes materialised on the page and it was she who was speaking. Being sideways on, her lips occasionally revealed a row of serrated, dangerous-looking teeth. Her strange words had commenced with a sigh as if her particular role was simply too tedious to bother with.

"Tempus omnia revelat," she repeated over and again like an earworm, disregarding his presence, contained in her own world.

In contrast to the previous woman this one clearly disavowed communication. Ben wondered if the choice of Latin words was a deliberate ploy to hold the reader at bay. The impression of maintaining distance was emphasised by her appearance too. Unlike the previous woman's modest crown, this one wore an enormous crown encrusted with emeralds, taking up the greater part of the page.

"Tempus omnia revelat," she continued until there was no break in the words.

He felt it would never stop, it was unendurable and the repetition started to make him feel sick. Pulling the dustbin towards him with his foot he retched into it, suddenly understanding what the author woman meant by the book nearly killing her. It must have taken a lot to harness unruly magic (if that was what it was) into one place. What if it did something to him though – injured him or made him demented? He assumed that the woman was Queen Oona. Her manner certainly seemed to fit in with what he had heard about her. When a spot of light, like a drop of mercury slid down the green eye, Ben became aware of the book's special effect that suggested she was literally watching him - in real-time. The effect was the stuff of nightmares, and Ben was momentarily grateful for the fact that she was only a printed image in a book. That was just before her head and shoulders lurched out of the book to bark the words, "Time reveals all," as if she were at the end of her tether and he was the greatest ignoramus on Earth. Ben fell off his chair and dropped the book on the floor. Perhaps not the best person to promote a book, Ben thought once his heart had stopped racing. Not the right kind of gimmick either. Most definitely. It was odd that within a few hours Ben's fear had unaccountably vanished like early morning fog and he was only left with a compulsion to know more about the strange other world he had encountered. This change of heart would prove to be life-changing in a way that he could never have predicted.

Chapter 2 Sticky Issues

"I'm beginning to think you're not all there," Terri had laughed when Ben was late for work for the third time in a row. "You're going to get yourself sacked. I had to tell her that your stomach was playing up again." Terri was a stylist at the same salon Ben worked at. "Problem is, she didn't believe you the first time around," she said. "What's going on with you? You never used to be like this." Ben briefly considered how close Terri had come to the truth. Recently he hadn't exactly been here, there or anywhere he intended to go. In fact, he kept getting an overwhelming urge to literally fly off elsewhere. At that present moment he had wedged his toes under the rail around the reception area to stop himself from charging off out the front door or conversely catapulting over the counter in a forward roll. There were two opposing forces working on him: one that felt gravitational, that tugged and pulled on every part of his body to drag him forward into an empty space beyond him. The other was his own will to escape whatever that urge was. Ben theorised to himself that he had lost his stickiness, as if he were a plaster being slowly prised away from firm flesh. It was terrifying to feel out of control and his only response was to get away from the sensation at all costs. He made every excuse possible to leave through the premises safe spot, which was the back door. He volunteered to pick up products or lunch orders until Sandra, his boss, made the sarcastic comment that he was tending to spend more time out of the building than in. Some spaces felt far more volatile than others. For instance, there was the space he had to negotiate around at the front of the shop by the reception and another by the cricket ground to the north of the town. Of course, he could avoid that one by taking a different route home, but, unfortunately, there was another one in the doorway of The Meadows, the block of flats where he lived. Currently, he was clawing his way into the building daily, hand over hand from mailbox to security code panel, fighting the immense force that attempted to pluck him off the wall. Even his clothing was dragged behind him, choking him around the throat and crushing his heels painfully against the cup of his shoes. He dared not let go, because he had no idea where he could potentially end up. Only the day before, he had successfully engineered his way in, only to be rained on by a random cloud that suddenly appeared in the seconds between turning the handle and lunging onto the floor of the communal hallway. "Are you alright?" asked Mrs Strickland, appearing in the doorway of her ground-floor flat, and Ben, panting and sodden had to admit that he really wasn't. Leaving a pool of water in the lobby, he clambered up the stairs with the dreary knowledge that he'd forgotten to get milk and would have to go through the whole process again later. That night, he took his tea black and tried once again to read the book that had undoubtedly started all this trouble in the first place.

The story proper, which didn't have a chapter heading, began in a local setting which Ben quickly realised he knew as there was a very distinctive description of a tumulus on the margins of a seaside town. Ben had been there often as a child before a conservation trust had fenced it off citing ideas about erosion. In fact, his granny had often taken him there as she said it reminded her of happier days, which was a bit odd. Ben suspected she was referring to his mum when she was young. The barrow was massive and there was a dolmen integrated into it, forming an east-facing stone entranceway. The capstone projecting out of the mound like a colossal lip seemed to suggest the imparting of information but as the passageway stopped short after a few feet, the interior chamber kept its secrets. It was unpromising as a place to play, or hide in, too. The information board was as cryptic in the same way that the entranceway went nowhere and just disappointed– 'possibly middle neolithic,' it said unhelpfully.

Some generic information about long barrows followed. Ben had tried repeatedly to scale the fence with his friends from school after it had first been erected, but they soon gave up; choosing to drink and smoke elsewhere. That was the time just before the changes of puberty had broken the easy bonds between himself and the kids he had grown up with, and they all headed their different ways. The unspoken agreement not to talk about 'it' might have been taught them by the close-lipped monolith they had once played around. The 'it' event related to early autumn when Ben was fourteen, he had initiated a clumsy pass at a boy with flaxen hair, which had caused a significant pause and a look of contempt before the conversation resumed as if nothing had occurred. After that, there was no going back to the time before, and the slight adjustment to the mannerisms of the other boys told him that if they hadn't talked about it, they now sensed Ben's difference. What started as an adolescent miscalculation – a blunder – started to shape the group. There again, it might have been Ben's own self-consciousness that drove them away, and they were just reacting to Ben's own unease with himself, which he waved like a flag in front of every social interaction from thereon. Trying to recapture the magic of the previous summer, he became overzealous in his friendships, pandering to every opinion and every plan until they got fed up with him. "Ben? He's okay," one said, "… but goes on a bit nowadays." In reality, he was returning again and again to a flippantly made rejection as if it were the sum of all his worth. Likewise, his reading of the book stagnated, never progressing into the story beyond the first line, which began with the words, 'Around a long barrow, in a field…' and he immediately saw in his mind a woman huffing her way around the margins. Anticipating that her identity would then be revealed, Ben was perplexed to read the same sentence over again, but this time with the received image being just of the clover-covered mound in high summer. There was no indication of who or what was around the barrow. The woman had completely vanished, or at least he had no expectation of ever reading about her again because he seemed to have developed a mental block. Somehow the book had edited his expectations. Over the next two days, he tried again and again, but it was no use... the story would not reveal itself. There is only so long that you can read the same sentence before feeling so tired it is impossible to keep your eyes open any longer. The ephemeral woman seemed doomed to continue her endless navigation around the prohibited landmark for all time…it seemed the book wouldn't support that image that it had planted in his head, which was a bit misleading really.

Things got worse. Reality, a stable reality where the world behaved itself, began to slip through his fingers. One night, Ben had a perplexing dream where he was involved in a ferocious argument with a man promising to set his dog on him if he dared use his garden as a hotel again. Ben pointed out that he had done no such thing, but the sense of wrongdoing and shame he felt overspilled into the waking day, making the dream seem very real. Every night, as soon as he fell asleep, he was back in the same front garden surrounded by a wicket fence, and the homeowner was beyond frustrated, jumping from one foot to another with rage. From the ground, where he lay, Ben noticed that the man wore multi-coloured handmade shoes, like an archetypical hippie but his face was another matter being sharp of feature and slimy like a toadstool. In fact, drops of the odd substance dripped onto Ben's face due to the agitated movements of the man.

"Youse gone and done me little spore beauties in," he said, incomprehensibly, pointing at the ground.

Ben woke perplexed, thinking…. 'Spores?' to himself. Drifting off once more, he found that he was standing alongside the same man who reached no higher than his midriff and whose head, he realised, was freakishly shaped into a whisp, just like whipped cream.

"Back again?" the man asked in a tone of resignation.

"Uh...," said Ben feeling very much the trespasser. The man pointed to the outline in the snow, which was perfectly matched to his frame but in a foetal position. There were excavated and crushed toadstools within and around it. Ben woke up chilled and was perturbed to notice that there was a scattering of snow over the mantlepiece, the coffee table and his own bedclothes. Looking down at his hand, he realised that he was clutching a vivid purple mushroom with a metallic sheen.

"Not normal at all," he said aloud, and then a residual memory came back to him of his clutching the ground, for dear life, screaming, whilst it bucked and shifted around him. All the while, a tiny foot kicked him repeatedly in the butt... Ben sat bolt upright in the devastation of his covers; his thoughts as frozen as his transformed flat.

For inspiration and to quell his rising panic, Ben visited the Changeling's memorial late one night, when he knew no-one else would be there. This was really just a statue in the position where the old poultry cross used to be. The visitations from those paying homage had changed it from an aesthetic representation into a memorial, but in actual fact, it was completely unclear what had happened to the Changeling as he had vanished many years ago with no explanation. It was less a grave than a question mark, beautifully carved in bronze and protected from the elements by a disproportionally small gothic folly that looked more like the afterthought of the sculptor once they had realised the bronze would not weather well outdoors. Its plain, regular lines made it seem a little like an old-fashioned photo booth as if the Changeling with his sword and armour were just popping out on a mundane task to get passport photos. Or perhaps it was a doorway, Ben thought, from which he would never return, willingly or otherwise. Who knew? He certainly didn't and didn't trust anyone else's speculations on the matter either. Knowing a fair bit about fashion, though, and how a popular trend or idea can be forgotten in an instant was a useful lesson in remembering that society and all its convictions were deeply untrustworthy.

Ben decided to re-appraise the statue with objective eyes as if he had never seen it before. The golden choice of the material for the figure was appropriate and something about his profile from the side defined him as a mixed-race man, with a perfectly balanced symmetry of facial features as if the gestational forces had smiled on him. Tall of stature, and wearing segmented leg armour, a breast plate over a desert jacket but also D Ms, he was a curious combination of the modern and the archaic. The sheen of the crown on his head cemented the final interpretation of him as a heroic figure. Ben was often reminded of the Happy Prince from Oscar Wilde's eponymous story in the way that his gaze was set slightly down and to the right as if listening to the advice of a tiny principled bird to sacrifice his lifeblood for the greater good. Stupid romanticism, Ben thought, it always screwed up his factual relationships, though his gran had always had other ideas. She believed firmly in self-sacrifice, deepest love, and all the benefits it could do to the psyche.

**

Ben's gran had been the guiding force in his life ever since she had rescued him from an unspeakable situation in his mum's home. Finding him aged three, starving and in urine-stained clothes with his love-challenged mum drugged up and flat out on the sofa she had said, "The fairy bit of her 'as tangled 'er mind, but she'll come around in time." Neither thing was true, and Ben's mum, Alison, neither quit her habits nor came to see him in the following seventeen years. As soon as he was gathered up in the arms of cosy, sweet-smelling Gran, he ceased to exist to her. It was Gran's fictions that sustained him when his difficult past came back to haunt him from time to time.

"Oh, they is just the natural darkness that lurks around the borders," she said, quite literally chasing the shadows with her hoe from around the immaculate grass verges of her perfect garden. Was it Ben's imagination or did the garden take on a lighter shade as she said, "Off with you," to his fears, making him laugh as she also flailed the hoe dangerously around his head? "Watch them little ones whivver around, Ben – can you see them go?" Most of Gran's views were strange and extremely liberated from the norm. One day, when he was seventeen, he intercepted her going up a stepladder to the nook of a tree with a plate of home-made biscuits in her hand.

"Are you okay up there, Gran?"

"Perfectly," she said. A passing guest will like these, though if I see that loblolly, Roger De Clancy up there again, I'll drag him down by his laggens. These," she said, waving the plate erratically around, "are for they little folk that never gets much anyways." Wedging the plate within a nest of twigs, her back stiffened. "What is it, Ben?" quite suddenly, making Ben wonder how his hovering could have communicated so much.

"Gran, it's, uh, relationships and stuff."

"Oh, yes?" she asked with a note of falseness as if she already knew what he was about to say.

"Well, they never seem to last, and, uh, you know, I sort of would like a boyfriend…a proper one. That commits," he added, talking to his feet. Gran reversed her way carefully back down the rungs. She turned to face him. "Ben Sopher," she said, with feigned severity, "are you telling me you've been up to all sorts?"

"Yes," said Ben, staring at his feet.

"Well, thank goodness for that. It were about time."

"Eh? But...?" said Ben completely confused.

"Don't you think for a minute that I hold with this world's views on normal, healthy activities? Puritans!" she bellowed, to no one in the near vicinity. Laughing she picked up the cupcakes intended for the windowsill. "I thought you knew better, my boy."

"Yeah, well, I don't want to be a user," he said firmly. Ben thought. "Or used for that matter."

"Who's using who?" Gran asked, puzzled.

"I'm just talking generally," he said. "I don't want to feel like I'm wasting my time."

"Ah," Gran experienced a moderate eureka moment. "My dear," she said plucking a bright orange dandelion from the grass. "I think you're confusing common garden varieties with exotics. All very good in their own way, but you need both – I mean a good bit of everyday variety sex and precious love if it comes. Don't worry about picking the daisies if that's all you've got in your garden." She thought hard. "Consider '*it*'… 'sex', as you would brushing your teeth in the morning. You'd hardly call that a waste of time."

"Well, what about love?"

"What about it?"

"Well don't you think it's a good goal to have?"

"Of course, but you can't force it. True love is fated," she said dreamily and rather unhelpfully. "Look, I've been 'ere in my garden for years, hundreds of them," she added, smiling, "for someone to come and have me for all time. Happenstance it were not for me," she said, regretfully, "however, I've had some saucy times with 'em sassy ones that were hereright," and her strange, violet eyes twinkled and sparked with fire in their heavy-lidded almond frames.

"I don't think this is helping me much," he said rather dismissively. Gran always gave Ben the confidence to speak openly, a gift he didn't seem to carry over into his day-to-day life. "I just 'want' someone in the world," he said very simply.

"Of course you do. You is a bit fuddled at the present, that's all. Remember though, if you follow your true course, love will come…. some kind of it," she added under her breath. "Life is tricky," she admitted. "Things allus changes, just like them pesky Boggen!" she shouted, becoming distracted… "That pretends to be wooden posts, then stamps all over my borders when I'm not looking. Yes, I'm talking to you," she shouted, at an innocuous pile of timber in a shady corner of the garden. Gran tended to break off and talk to inanimate objects from time to time and this occasion was no different from the usual.

"You gave up a lot to look after me, didn't you, Gran?" Ben continued as if nothing had happened.

"I gave up nothing," she said, enclosing him in her arms. "I just followed my own dreams and found you instead," she emphasised, pinching his cheek between her thumb and forefinger. "You is just a nipper yet, Ben." Her gaze was loaded with love, but Ben, being a teenager didn't want to live in the beam of her mothering any longer, and he dug his foot back and forth in the soft soil as if he were already running away. "Anyways," she continued, a bit more casually, "Who else was going to look after a one such as you are?" Seeing his look, she qualified it with, "I was perfectly matched to you as you was to me, Ben. Mismatched gloves oftentimes makes a good pairing." They both looked at her hands which indeed had odd gardening gloves on. An urgent thought in the back of Ben's mind suddenly started shouting something about never having seen Gran without gloves on, even in bed. The oddness of it suddenly struck him, whereas it hadn't before. Gran sensed that his mind was elsewhere and suddenly resumed home grown wisdoms. "My advice to you, dear, is to follow your desires too and see where they takes you, and in the meantime, try not to worry. Love will come," she said faintly, drifting off with her trug, her plates and a trowel. She seemed to merge perfectly with the late summer sun, the hums of bees, and the cooing of wood pigeons. Nine months later, she was dead, and Ben was evicted from the property by the council, who said he could no longer stay. He packed everything that reminded him of Gran, which was a lot, into a dozen carrier bags and the rest of his belongings into a massive rucksack. Even his Uncle Andy didn't seem to want to know but Gran had always said that he lived in a different world entirely from the gentler folk. She said he was the very 'daps' of his father, whoever that was.

"Sorry mate," Uncle Andy had said, leaning against the lychgate of his substantial house, "Full house here."

Having no option but to sofa surf for nearly a year, each time Ben moved he would shift the troublesome load from place to place: until one day, he had saved a sufficient deposit for a studio. The bags he had so dutifully carried with him rested against a skirting board, unpacked, redundant because he now wore his grief around his heart. At night, he lay in bed staring at Gran's pendant that he wore around his neck, as she had worn it in life. This was a strange, crimson glass globe containing thin, vaporous skeins, and his constant handling of it, kept it warm against his skin. He loved the smoothness and the integrity of its unchanging patterns, as if the fiery glass blowing process had been compelled by the natural forces of a different universe to be obedient forever. When he was small, he used to sit on Gran's knee and rub it between his finger and thumb like a soother.

"It's older'n me, Ben, and I'm three hundred and ninety years old. That's not much to all accounts compared with they pure breed uns. I reckon' I won't make more'n half of their span. We will have to dig a big hole for us, in time, where the wild garlic grows."

"You won't die will you Granny?" he'd asked, suddenly panicked.

"Not right now and perhaps never in a ways. They didn't name me Ursula for nothin'. My name means bear garlic and my ashes will feed the family plot. Remember to have them bury me in the woods, Ben, in the place where I was originally so young and green as a girl and whatnot. Such a pity that the poor bears are no longer in the woods hereabouts, for it's them what I was intended to be for. I miss their whiffling in me ears."

"You're very funny, Gran," he had said, but she had only

looked sad as if he had missed the point.

In the strained pattern of his life, between work, sleep, and ruminating on the past, Ben found another outlet for his emotions that barely sufficed. At weekends he saw a much older man in the next nearest town, but, far from finding love, he had never felt so alone in his life. The man, Jim, was initially complimentary about his subtle style and his 'amazing', violet eyes. "Amazing," said Jim, who was a bit short on adjectives. "It's like swimming in the sea – ugh, drowning in the sea," he amended, pulling away suddenly. "All eye and *so* little pupil," he muttered, turning away. They never went back to his place, tending to meet in hotels or the houses of Jim's friends. Ben suspected he had someone else somewhere and deep down, felt the whole affair was a bit seedy. This was why he came back time and time again to the statue, where there was perfection, glamour, and mystery. Somehow, Ben knew that he would never settle for anything else.

Chapter 3 A Past Chapter Revisited

It was nearly midnight, and the pedestrianised areas around the statue were completely emptied. The night being cold, he touched the hand resting lightly on the hilt of the sword, expecting it to radiate a greater, freezing burn, but was intrigued to note that it seemed warm. Suddenly it was more than that; it was muscular. Appalled, Ben pulled away and fell back instantly into the hole he had been avoiding for weeks.

The first thing that Ben noticed was the fact that it was now daylight, an odd sort of daylight, as if he were looking through a reddish glass. The second thing was that the tiny crab-like creatures clustered around his hands in the unpleasantly warm pool he was crouched in seemed more inquisitive than startled by his splashed entrance into their world. They skittered around him like demented clockwork toys, occasionally making undeliberate contact before darting off again. Ben rocked back on his knees and took a look around him. The town was definitely gone. In its place were ferns – lots of them, both tall and mid-height clustered around the pools that were brackish judging by the salt drying on Ben's lips in the heat. It was very warm, and there was the stench of rotting vegetation. An odd thought popped into Ben's mind as he thought of cabbage being cooked in the school canteen. He laughed aloud because wherever he was, it was a long way from home. Still resting on his knees, this thought was reinforced when he made eye contact with a huge glaucous eyed fish on the opposite bank. It stared neutrally at him before turning and walking off on four feet towards a nearby pool, which it half fell, and half plunged into in a clumsy fashion. The creature looked like a mistake, a poor design, a first try. With his thoughts

stacking up like bread on a conveyor belt, he had just decided
to stand when he noticed, far off in the distance a slim figure
with its head down, stomping moodily in and out of the shallow
waters. The person was far away, and dark, like a sunspot through
a lens, but Ben wondered if he could get his attention. "Hey,"
he shouted, getting to his feet, "can you help?" Immediately as
he said this: whatever was holding him in that place lost its grip
on him and he only had time to see the person lift its head with
surprise towards him as he was propelled backwards. It was then,
back in the market square, flung against a concrete bollard, that
he realised whatever fear had been haunting him for months had
also been released. There was a place beyond the vortex that
was tangible and real, not as he secretly feared a dense black
hole waiting to crush him into atoms. It was interesting how the
thought of another 'place' did not undermine him. He wanted
to know more, but he appraised the statue in front of him with
new eyes; its face was as beautiful as ever, but for the first time
he found its detachment quite creepy really, as if art was being
used to conceal something. Ben knew that his relationship to the
Changeling had subtly changed and, empowered but frozen, he
made his way home.

***

Over the next week, Ben made calculated decisions, the most
important being making himself extremely unpopular with
everyone who knew him. He spent an evening baiting Jim and
demanding commitment until Jim stormed out of the motel he
had once again booked for the night.

"Goodbye then," said Ben, without regret to his ex-lover's
rear window swinging round in a spat of gravel in the car park.
At work, he wandered in a dream from client to client and was
non-committal to the point of being unhelpful about their style
decisions.

"Do what you want," he said to one particularly difficult woman who was getting on his nerves. Then his boss swiftly intercepted leaving him standing behind her with a pair of scissors.

"What are you up to, Ben?" she asked later. "This isn't like you. You've really changed."

"Well, that's the point," he replied. "I think it's completely like me…. I just didn't know it before," and he wandered away from her absently. Sandra followed him.

"We're here to help," Sandra said puzzled, "With whatever's going on." However, she became less sympathetic when Ben didn't turn up for work the following day, and she moaned to Terri that she'd rather have a plank of wood standing behind reception rather than a complete no-show. When Terri told Ben this later on, he had smiled strangely and as if his exchange for a block of timber were somehow amusing to him. Terri was very worried, though, because Ben had always cared so much about doing the right thing and his uncharacteristic nonchalance was a red flag that made her heart skip. On the first day he bunked off, she'd texted him throughout the day, but he didn't bother to respond until the evening when he said he was fine. Terri tried not to be irked at his unawareness of the impact his behaviour was having on his friends. If she'd known how deliberate his actions were, she would not have been the true friend she continued to be.

Ben's carried on cutting ties, and this included his taking all of his grandmother's clothes to a charity shop along with most of her possessions, but the 'broken' barometer that always showed different weather to the current one he took to Hippy Phil in his shop 'Wholegrains'. Ben had a new theory about this item. Without comment he slid it over the counter and watched as Phil retreated away from it smoothly.

"What's that? What's your game?" he asked, panicked, from behind his shaggy mane of grey hair.

"A gift."

"I don't want it – take it away."

Ben changed tack. "I'm in trouble, and I need your advice," he said in a pleading tone and this softened something in Phil who said, "Come out back then." Phil lifted up the hatch to let Ben through but pushed his arm firmly down as Ben attempted to bring the barometer with him.

"Leave that there," he said firmly. Ben looked at Phil's face and realised whatever he was, he certainly wasn't mad as everyone said. This was clarified when Phil made him a cup of hemp tea that he had already refused twice and Ben realised that Phil was genuinely shaken and his mild eyes held onto a deep concern. The mug wavered towards him with drops spilling onto the chair arm, but Phil steadied it himself so that Ben had to reach out and intercept it. Phil initiated the conversation with a somewhat random observation.

"Do you know," he said, nodding towards the barometer in his line of vision, "Ever after, I always tend to see a greenish halo around anything that comes from the 'Other' place."

"After?" Ben was intrigued.

"After the Great Synchronisation, when the two worlds merged, so things could cross over. I use the term 'things' broadly," he said. "Glamour, they call it – once something's been there, it leaves a residue; on people or things, doesn't matter, everything's tinged by it. Not me, though; I never went there to the other world. Didn't have to; they came here as allies. Well, sort of… Not that I'm saying they're all bad- far from it. In some ways, they are more us than we are ourselves. They don't hide anything you see." Phil seemed so eager to offload, that his thoughts and feelings tumbled over themselves like soft puppies. Ben instinctively liked Phil.

"Phil, I'm leaving. I mean, I'm going there." Phil's eyes opened wide at this.

"Why the hell would you go and do a thing like that?"

"I never felt I belonged here."

"Well, everyone feels that." Phil thought for a moment. "Do you mean about....?" He stopped. "Sorry," he apologised, "It's is a small town, after all, and everybody knows the ins and outs of everything. Sometimes I think we just don't evolve." Ben nodded, sensing a kindred spirit.

"No, it's not just that. It's a compulsion to go." Phil looked around him uneasily. He leaned forward.

"Is there someone here? Is someone making you?" Phil's eyes were suddenly bright and restless, belying his age. Ben could see why people might think Phil was a bit mad. He felt sorry for him.

"No, it's not that. It's more like an urgent feeling."

"Oh, I don't know what to say, really." Phil picked up an incense burner, spilling ash everywhere which he emptied in a dustbin unnecessarily as most of it by now was all over the table. "In my day," he said, "There were a lot of songs about hittin' the road and finding yourself, but I don't think that's what you mean."

"It isn't," Ben confirmed, "I'm literally being dragged there." Phil looked distressed at this, and, in sympathy, clutched the two arms of his own easy chair, just in case he, too was just about to be towed away, but then something occurred to him and he studied Ben perceptively as if seeing him for the first time.

"You want to go, don't you?"

"Yes," said Ben, feeling relieved at saying it out loud. "I want to go. I'm here because I need some advice, about what I'll find and what I should do – anything will help, really." Phil paused for a moment.

"Well, my first thought is that you need to 'keep your head'." Phil sounded like he was quoting, which he was, from a song with a similar line from a group called Jefferson Airplane. He hummed a musical phrase from it, immediately after, and this gave him inspiration. He said, "Couldn't you keep a journal, like Robinson Crusoe?"

"How weird, that's exactly what I was thinking of doing."

"Yeah, those fairies will screw with your mind. Mightily," he added. "Bit of reflection never did anyone any harm at all. It might help you know how to proceed…if you have problems," he said, leaning forward. The quietness of Phil's tone made Ben think that having 'problems' was a given.

"Is there anyone you think I could seek out that would be useful to know."

"Not really, most of them you're best off avoiding. That reminds me if you see a tall woman with long, blonde hair, and green eyes….," his fingers made the closing shape of two almonds, "Run like hell." Phil slumped in his chair. "Lots of them I knew once are gone now anyway."

"Well, you see, I don't think they have."

"What do you mean?" Phil asked suspiciously.

"I mean, I think I can go back – and see them."

"Go back?"

"To the past, the way it was."

"No, no, that's not right. What's done is done and can never be undone." Phil's frame moved back and forth like an agitated wind vane as he spoke, contradicting his theory and proving he, himself, was re-visiting the past at that exact moment. "Even they can't do that," he emphasised, "with all their, um, *abilities*." It was perfectly clear that Phil was skirting around the word 'magic'. In the grip of another powerful memory, he paused for a considerable time and started fiddling with a string of worry beads that he took out of his pocket and wrapped and unwrapped around his fingers in a continuous ritual. "People who are gone are slowly erased from their own timelines from the moment of their death. That's natural, and fairies are nothing if not natural. There's no corporeal resurrection – it's all just smoke and mirrors. All you will see is an unreal, ultra-vivid representation where the people used to be, like watching a movie in the wrong format."

"So, you *can* travel back?" Ben pounced on this nugget of information. In response Phil squirmed in his chair, feeling uncomfortable with the revelation. He studied the corners of the room as if he were being watched again and continued with a regretful tone.

"They've always been able to time hop, with the authority of the ruling monarch…whilst being monitored; but I wouldn't advise it," he added. "You might get lost, or injured."

For the first time, Ben felt that he had emptied the reserves of Phil's knowledge and that Phil was talking through the funnel of past traumas.

"You've been very helpful," said Ben, jumping up.

"No, wait," said Phil, "There's something else. They have their own definition of law and it's harsh and immediate. Do yourself a favour and study their customs early on."

"I fully intend to," said Ben ducking under the hatch. "Shall I take this with me?" he asked, picking up the barometer which explained that it was a day of high pressure and sunshine, though the wind and rain battened against the shop door.

"No, actually, leave it. I kind of want to keep a contact with you, even if it is only through the weather. By the way, you can eat the food. Some of it's copied off us; high-status fairies have a pseudo-interest in our ways, but in the main, it's greens. The high-protein moss is compatible with our digestive systems and has quite remarkable qualities. I wish I could get some. I wish I could."

A note of desperation crept into Phil's voice, and it wouldn't have surprised Ben if Phil had said, 'I wish' for a third time. Phil threw the worry beads over his fingers, clutched them tight in his fist, and licked his lips.

"Of course," he qualified, "It's organic too. They don't go in for much technology…probably because they don't need to." He looked around his shop with the huge tubs of produce and sieves for customers to fill up their own containers. "Some people would call that lack of progress." He sighed and looked up, but Ben had already left the shop. "I should have told him not to give them sugar," he said to himself.

Chapter 4 The Other Place

On the day he left, he only took a half-filled rucksack with him. The words of the Fei woman in the bookshop came back to him.

"Pack selectively, Ben," she had said, and he wondered for the umpteenth time what exactly she knew about his current predicament and if, in fact, she had somehow caused it. However, the notion of being forced onto a certain path didn't resonate with him. Ben had never felt more cheerful as he packed his bag. Of course, some of this could have been youthful bravado, a kind of psychological two fingers up to a small town where he believed he could only ever show a tamed version of himself. Other than his startling violet eyes that made people jump and seem uneasy, but he couldn't help that anyway. Ben wadded the lined pads of paper along the back of the rucksack against his socks, underwear, windcheater, hairbrush, soap bag, and spare jeans. He debated whether or not to put his best cream linen jacket in, but later on took it back out of the wardrobe. He believed he looked very suave in it and sometimes you need a disguise; also, it was thin and could be folded compactly. At first, he had put in basic foodstuffs but remembered what Phil had said and exchanged these for bars of chocolate, not for eating, but for possible trading and he also had a box of his gran's costume jewellery for the same reason. Somehow, he had the feeling that the Fei would be enamoured of sparkly stuff. In the front pouch were fifteen biros because he was holding tight to the idea that forming an objective detachment of whatever happened to him through writing it down, was crucial. He was determined to have the scrupulous honesty of a scientist and would document a classified account of all he learnt about the Fei as an entry into their world and as a potential means of survival. Knowledge would be his sword. Putting his phone in his back pocket and the money he had emptied out of his account the previous day into the rucksack, he looked around his studio for the final time. He said aloud, "It was never a home," and closed the door quietly, his departure imitating the life he had led.

***

It took two hours to get to Bourne because it was a market day, and he had to change buses twice. He was headed for the long barrow because he reasoned that it would take a tremendous power to get him to the 'Other' place and hold him there for longer than a few minutes. He couldn't have said why this particular location seemed a good bet; he just had an instinct for it. Also, the location of the barrow was promising, having always been populated, since neolithic times, due to its intermediary position between a brackish estuary and the open sea. Something ancient, dusty but alive haunted that area – he'd always known it. Why else would the ancients have buried their dead there if it were not in the barely formed hope that it was a doorway to somewhere else. Ben had a suspicion that the shallow entrance to the barrow was a misnomer and that if there was a way in it wasn't through a conventional door. He remembered the Fei woman's departure and how softly organic that was. Noticing how low the golden sun of winter was made him hasten over the stile and taking wire cutters out of his bag, he proceeded to cut his way through the fence. This doorway, at least, was easy to negotiate - with the right tools anyway. A teenaged boy bumped along the track on his bike, stopped, and watched him with interest, but Ben ignored him, and finally, he had made a hole wide enough. Throwing his bag through the gap first, he wriggled after it, but now it was almost dark, and he had no idea what to do. The barrow was a great tumorous lump in front of him, densely cutting out the night sky. He decided to walk around it, as he had seen the old woman do. Almost immediately as he thought this, he became confused and wondered why he was thinking randomly about an old woman. What old woman? He looked around, but there was no one there. Clearly, she didn't exist. He turned to walk clockwise but immediately tripped over something round and soft that squealed and ran away. He was convinced that the squeal was one of laughter and not pain, and the shapeless, baggy mass was now blundering around in the gorse at the base of the hill. Determined to avoid that direction at all costs, he turned and started walking anti-clockwise each step, gathering warmth and an odd feeling of contentment.

"Well, that's better," he said aloud, slurring slightly, and he started giggling. It became quite difficult to stay on the chalky path, and once or twice Ben fell over. This did not bother him at all, and he would have quite happily stayed there till morning, only he had a compulsion to keep the nice feeling going and this intensified with each step forward.

"Yup, this is the best way – the nicest way of all," he said aloud, wishing there was actually someone there to share the intriguing information of how wonderful it was to go round a mound in the dark in the correct way. Once the warmth reached chest level, Ben was no longer thinking at all, though moments before, when his belly button sparkled with fire, he had definitely thought, 'I'm being enchanted'. Soon enough he didn't care, but that was until his ears started to hum, gently at first, but then unbearably. He clutched both ears, but the sound was in his head and he couldn't escape it, and beyond the hum, there was a song.

If a song could retreat and recover in an army of sound, then this song was doing exactly that. There was also whiteness and an odd feeling on his face as if the word 'sparkle' could be a physical phenomenon. The effect was tantalising, only slightly marred by an unpleasant dragging over all areas of his body, so much so that he swiped at his sides to cut through cobwebby invisible threads. The intensity of the song diminished as he took a step forward and then, abruptly, it stopped, as did a woman who miraculously appeared on the path before him as if from nowhere.

"Get out of my way," she said, with no preamble whatsoever, but Ben was rooted there, disorientated by the blinding sun that was already making him sweat inside his sherpa jacket. Somehow, it was now daytime.

"Did you hear what I said? Shift, will you?" The woman was not only rude and aggressive, but she was also very odd. For a start, she was wearing clothes that were dramatically out of date from at least sixty years previous. She wore nylon trousers that practically crackled with electricity and a sweaty-looking yellow blouse. 'Crimplene' Ben thought, 'yuk, not a look to ever reprise'. Her oddness was carried over, but not in a good way, to her behaviour. She barged onwards with the intention of pushing him off the path, but was too weak to budge him. He stepped aside and she started muttering a string of words that sounded like a hybrid between Latin and regular speech. Ben caught the words 'find', 'absconditum', 'pueri', 'Regina', and finally... 'bitch' with a flourish, before she wound down like a toy. Wringing her hands in agony, she accused Ben of interrupting her and "ruining the whole bloody thing, and...," she said, "I've been nine times round this hill just like they said."

"Who said?" asked Ben, intrigued despite himself.

"Oh, this couple in Glastonbury. I gave them half my pension, and they gave me a ritual for finding a missing person, and it's all no good, and I don't know what to do now. I've come to the end of the road, after all these years." Her tone oscillated between anger and borderline tears, but settled on the red-hot part of the scale. She stared at Ben as if it were all his fault, and a sly look crept like a shadow across her face as she noticed he was dressed for winter and not summer.

"Who are you?" she demanded.

"Me? Just Ben," he admitted, taking a step back as she crept forward poking an interrogating finger hard into his chest.

"You're not one of...?"

"No," Ben confessed, quickly, not wanting to be in the firing line of her distress. The woman was quite scary, really with her hair cut in a severe, steely fringe across her forehead.

She dropped her hand after looking hard at the nervous face of the boy but then rallied, perhaps thinking that having a captive audience of one was better than nothing.

"They stole him," she screeched at him, in an alarming way like a mad bird, whilst looking down at her two hands and, after glancing at Ben as if he could literally see what she was seeing. "Snatched him, right out of my hands without a by your leave. It was this lot," she said, stamping her foot on the ground as if she could wake the dead. "That live in the hill." Ben took another step away from her. "Give it up," they said, those doctors…..." the woman became breathless.... "Psychotic they said. Can you believe it?" Clearly, no answer was expected and a silence followed as the woman paused to get her breath. Ben was unsure who exactly the woman was talking to: herself, him or some invisible accusers in her head. He soon realised it was him because when she could speak, she explained in a simpler, voice, marked by a brittle shock, "They stole my baby."

"When?" asked Ben, equally shocked, but thinking at the same time, 'You're a bit old to have a baby.'

"It was a while back," she said, on the defensive again after noting his expression. "Not that that makes any difference. I'm Frances, by the way," she said, having decided Ben was no longer one of the enemy. Ben was a little taken aback by this sea change, but taking the offered hand, he saw again a much younger, gentler version of Frances that haunted an exterior that had somehow gone wrong.

"I'm Ben Sopher," he said.

"Oh!" she replied, delighted; "I've got lots of Jewish neighbours. I'm from London you know." Ben wondered how this information related to him. He had never been told anything about his ancestry other than his gran having said their family had, "… Moved around a fair bit." His Gran had also mentioned living in Dorset for the past two hundred years, an odd way to put it, now he thought about it. He was intrigued to know what else Frances knew and if her insights could be useful to him.

"Do you think you've got a good chance of tracking your baby down, or even, getting into that world?"

"So, you do believe in it then?" Frances said, her former suspicion re-emerging.

"Well, yes, there are lots of young people who are interested in the Fei and their world since the troubles!" he replied coldly.

"Troubles?" asked Frances, her confusion, disarming her.

"Well, yes, it's not just you that's had losses. This part of the world really suffered. Some of them were never even found afterwards." Frances looked around her in alarm as if expecting an invisible army to come over the mound. When nothing happened, she said, "I'm sorry, I never thought there might be others like me in the same predicament, with... *losses*. I always hated this place," she admitted, curling her lip, "from the moment I got here. You feel much safer in the city."

"So, do you think you'll get in then?" Ben asked, trying to get her back on track.

"I have no idea, but I'll never give my baby up, never."

"Wouldn't he/she..."

"He."

"…be grown up now? I mean, what if you can't recognise each other."

"I don't think it works like that. Everything I've read says that time is different there… time has no dominion," she said grandly. "Read it in a book. Anyway," she sniffed, "it can't be a coincidence that it says the same thing…in every fairy story, everywhere. 'Time moves at a different pace.' That's good," she added bleakly, "because, I just don't want it to have happened. I want things to go back the way they were," and her words, descending into a whisper, cradling their unbearable burden.

"I'm really, really sorry," he said, but then recklessly added, "But I don't think the past can be undone."

"I never said that. Did I say that?" Frances asked the air, exasperated. "I said, I wanted to go back to that moment in time and rescue him... so we go on as normal."

"Oh." Ben didn't dare say that he thought it would be unlikely she could do that either. Recalling Phil's advice on the wild nature of the Fei, Ben thought that any child living in that realm would be changed beyond all recognition after all this time, even if it were cocooned in a time warp.

"I've no intention of changing things; I just want to put things right – the way they should be." Frances was like a dog with a bone and had no intention of letting this new injury pass. Ben, therefore, decided it was time to make a move. Whether Frances was mentally ill or a victim of a terrible crime, was immaterial to him in the exhausting wake of her mood shifts. He felt mean, but he just wanted to get away from her. By now, sweat had pooled in his boots to the extent that his toes were sloshing in them.

"Oy, where are you going?" she demanded as he moved away.

"I'm sorry," he said again, feeling irritated that he kept having to placate her. "I have to go this way." He pointed vaguely to a sparse clump of bushes.

"What's there?" she asked, suspicion twisting her expression, but he ignored her and continued his anti-clockwise navigation but on a lower level. He felt disproportionally cross at the interruption to his adventure, never realising that sometimes the obstacle is the necessary push forward. He could hear Frances on the level above him, her laboured breathing disclosing that she was attempting to keep pace with him. Great... now she was following him. Looking at her from the corner of his eye, she looked exactly as she had in the first reading of the book, with her handbag crossways over the lurid yellow shirt and her stiff walking gait. He jumped with shock realising that he hadn't even reconciled Frances to the person in the book at all until then, but it was clear, she was precisely the same person, and he remembered her exactly. He didn't have much time to wonder at this new insight before something went wrong with the air around him; dense and pressurised, it formed a seal around him as if he were barely aligned to the world around him so that the world clung to him desperately. He pressed his arms against the force of the thick air but this did little good because it just kept crowding back on him. He wondered if he should tear whatever it was with his nails but had the strong sense that he might irreparably rip the surrounding reality, and then where would he be? Anywhere presumably, so he pressed onwards until, exhausted, he stopped in front of a suspicious-looking holly bush at the side of the track.

Holly bushes don't normally look malevolent, but this one did because as he stared at it, the outermost branches formed a pointed head, and there seemed to be a face buried deep within the dense thicket. To make matters worse, it was singing in a harsh voice the exact same song Ben had heard before meeting Frances in daylight.

"Stop it!" he commanded the bush, making Frances on the track above jump. "You'll set them all off," he added not having a clue what he meant but feeling instinctively that this was the right thing to say. Unfortunately, his shouted words were a signal that inspired the clover on the grass, the wild campion in the verges and even the Italian rye grass started to join in singing in their distinctive voices, though the smaller plants had a more pleasant silvery tone than the rasping one of the holly.

Ben looked up at Frances who was watching him clutching his hands to his head.

"What's happening?" she yelled down at him. Ben ignored her whilst lurching towards the only thing he felt could stop the torment. In fact, as he moved closer towards the holly, the song separated into different voices in the way that a gradually tuned-in radio makes sense of discordance.

"That's right, perhaps a little more to the left," said the campion sweetly, acting as traffic control. As he put one foot on the tap root of the holly bush, much to the disgust of the bush who scowled at him, he had the momentary satisfaction of knowing that he had been right all along – the barrow was not the way in; it was always going to be a less grand entrance, something natural, something that had always been part of the organic fabric of the world. He thought all this before he vanished in the blink of an eye.

Finding herself suddenly alone on the hill, Frances howled in despair, "Sodding, bloody fairies!" she yelled, knowing she had missed her chance. For a moment, faintness threatened to overwhelm her but she was made of sterner stuff than that. "If he can do it, I can too," she said to the hill. Having no other contingency plan, she put one shaky foot in front of the other and marched grimly on, counting her rotations and spouting random words that meant everything in one way but nothing at all in a practical sense.

Chapter 5 Pomp and Peril

On an ordinary day, Queen Oona of the Fei, Queen, because in those days she was still the reigning monarch, might have felt the shockwave caused by an individual moving illegally from the human sphere to hers. However, she had bigger problems to contend with and was only a little distracted by the giant hole that had just opened up in the early evening highway. One of her courtiers plummeted to his death, still seated on his startled horse, before she could do anything about it. Oona quite literally moved on. Over the quickly re-sealed ground, her retinue paced, but those nearest to her turned their heads away respectfully. The Monarch's face had looked troubled, prior to this happening, though it was unclear why. They were all gathered for a happy occasion, notwithstanding holes in the road.

For the second time in as many months, Ben slipped unnoticed into a crowd that lined the road, finally seeing the advantage of being able to blend in. He wedged himself between a woman who seemed to have sticks for a head and an intense man in Jacobean clothing who deliberately blocked his view until the passing royal party adjusted their height helpfully above the crowd. Ben had unfortunately arrived too late to see the odd horses leading the procession that shone like beaten metal. Oona turned her own, sleek head framed by waist- length blonde hair back towards the secret source of her anxiety, which was her daughter, and not just the world that had been throwing holes and items at her in a very unorthodox way. The girl needed watching; even now, she had gathered up her skirts to charge ahead in an unseemly manner to the front of the Rade in order to have 'conversations' with an underling. Why couldn't she follow the correct protocol? Hadn't Oona done everything she could to raise her as a formidable Monarch? Oona loved rules…her own rules in the main, though she was rather partial to a little recklessness in the right place at the right time, that being the Fei way. In the case of a monarch though, there had to be carefully observed limits. She thought again, as she had so many times of the excesses of the House of Knight that she was linked to by marriage, and a look of such distaste travelled across her face that the watchful Chamberlain was struck with terror in case it was himself that had done something wrong. Her daughter, ahead of her, wore the robes and colours of her father as she was in no way like Oona's family, the Aquarelle Clan. Oona had deliberately given her daughter, Ensley, the red dress, to make a point. Her turbulent feelings on the matter came to the fore, and immediately a carpet of hot coals manifested at the front of the procession so that all came to a swift halt. For a moment, Ensley teetered over a dismal pit that singed her eyelashes until a dark, glamorous personage to the side of her on a mounted horse reached down and pulled her back by her hair. Smoothly, Oona caught up with her daughter, avoiding the train of the dress that seemed to have a mind of its own and which thrashed from side to side like an agitated snake. "Shall we?" she asked, linking her arm with Ensley, who looked appalled. The procession re-started alongside the hurdy gurdy music, that marked the day as one of celebration because the young princess was about to be crowned queen at last.

Ben moved his feet away from the dress that had deposited a hot, puddle of steaming red on the ground, inches away from where he stood. The man in the ruff collar and tights also sensibly lurched back but, in doing so, caught Ben's shoulder, sending him off-balance. In turn, Ben fell against the tree woman, crushing her branches and making her cry.

"I'm so sorry," he said, picking up the broken twigs and offering them to her. "It was an accident. Perhaps glue?" he suggested, making the Jacobean man snort and observe,

"The mistress is without consolation. There is no help that will stem her tears." Being in such a strange situation seemed to free Ben from his usual reserve and he spontaneously rose to the challenge.

"Well, you could at least say sorry – it was your fault, too," but the man turned his back on them both to survey the road where the dress was still processing by. He seemed very interested in retaining sight of the severe Monarch with the long, blonde hair for as long as he could. He didn't turn again even as the sobs of the tree woman grew louder, but Ben did hear him say the words, "... on her own tears made drunk," in a very condemning way, just as if she were being self-indulgent. Ben stroked the branch closest to the main bole of the woman and this seemed to soothe her a bit; in fact, after a little while, she became rather excited and asked if he could press harder. He did so obligingly, then he focused back on the procession, overwhelmed by the myriad of odd and confusing impressions that were impacting on his senses.

Ben's eyes also tracked the figures in the distance, but he was more interested in the young woman being virtually dragged along by the stern Monarch. From a distance, she was a perfect pool of red damask, and with the crown and the long, black hair, she was anyone's idea of a fairytale princess. She certainly had a kinder expression than the cruel woman who had almost certainly tried to trip her onto a carpet of coals. Looking closely at the passing train, Ben recoiled in shock from the passing dress, not just to avoid being burned. What had seemed so picturesque, if a bit scalding previously, became a run of images. Flowing in a viscous manner, like magma, its shifting patterns revealed story book characters in knee-high boots striking out, maps and occasionally tormented faces caught mid-sentence that reared out of the fabric before retreating, subdued to the captivity of the unnatural fibres. It was presumably a collation of the many dramas and dangers of the Fei world he found himself in. Despite himself, Ben leaned closer to read the enticing and often scandalous information, as if the dress were the equivalent of a human tabloid, luring him in. Ben looked again at the unsuspecting wearer who was dragging salacious content behind her so unknowingly. 'Poor kid,' he thought, before realising an odd thing was occurring two metres back. An artificial horizon had descended upon the highway, and the dress simply juddered into nothingness as far as the spectators could see. This was a deliberate set up by Oona, who had realised that not only was it inadvisable to melt the road completely and potentially set the distant unmonitored onlookers on fire, but she wanted everyone to see the exercise of her considerable powers. The dress itself was travelling beyond the horizon to different time zones right to the point of its inception in Damascus, an eternity away where single threads were linked to wet, bobbing cocoons in a big, wooden vat. The fact that no-one could actually see this magical feat was entirely beside the point. As far as Oona was concerned, the power was inferred and would highlight the Fei Monarchy's total dominion over time and space. What Oona couldn't control, though, was her husband, King Finnian whose story had somehow been incorporated into the narrative of the dress without her knowing. It was there by way of an apology for his absence, but as it showed a rather grand man posing on a mountain, it seemed to be more about him rather than his daughter's big day. As the dress hissed and sizzled past, it seemed to tell Ben why he should feel ever so sorry for this poor man in his determined solitude. Ben thought he looked a bit like Zeus with his long, slightly greying, curly hair; if, of course, Zeus wore a trilby and a pair of Wayfarer sunglasses. The kingly profile looked away towards the misty mountain tops and Ben just knew that the image was intended to capture his, 'best side'.

Ensley's father, King Finnian, had been resolutely 'disappointed' with life for two hundred years. The root of his problems was plain and simple jealousy of the human experience of life. He had been struck by gloom on realising that though he could imitate a mortal's touching enthusiasm for relatively mundane new experiences, he couldn't actually *be* like them. It was his extended lifespan that was to blame. As he would often say, "Been there, done it", and of course, he had, in every place in every point in their history. "I'm bored rigid," he would moan. "What's the point of it all?" More than anything, he longed to experience the intensity of an accelerated love interest, made exquisite by the ever-nearing creep of death. He loathed languor, craved stimulation and wondered whether he could awaken his senses vicariously. He didn't listen to Oona's suggestion that he could take his pleasure where, when, and with whom he wanted and didn't need to overthink it all. Yet, Finnian had spent far too much time in the mortal realm and had been deeply affected by the complicated manner in which humans found excitement through the gratuitous following of persons of status. He wanted to be part of this transactional arrangement and a perverse plan formed in his mind. He would 'watch' other people and conjoin with them in their moment of joy. Being psychic, this was entirely possible, though more than a bit suspect.

Taking his retinue to Armenia in the mortal realm, he watched re-runs of reality shows, romcoms, and selections from the classier end of the soft porn market, at the top of a mountain, until his own heart froze with longing for a keenly felt heartache... or any ache, anywhere. In the end, it hadn't worked as he was so many stages removed from the moment itself and, unknown to himself, the actors, too, were so many stages removed from any kind of feeling. Eventually, Finnian had become morose and indistinguishable from the glacier. Apart from the occasional movement of a fogged, blue eye and a subterranean growling, that equally could have been the slow movement of the glacier, his camouflage was complete to the human eye. Every so often a small, shivering elf would scrabble up through a yard of snow to check the Wi-Fi connection, and then miserably descend again to inhabit the King's breast pocket. It *was* a depressing scene, but as his wife, Queen Oona, remarked to anyone who would listen, "He brings it all on himself, and anyway, it's utterly disgusting." Though Oona had known what she was getting into when she'd married into the royal Knight family, who are earth creatures, she resented the cooled, lump of metamorphic rock she'd been landed with. She often thought back to that moment when she had emerged hopefully from the foaming surf of Donegal Bay to find her parents standing on the sand and the middle-aged Finnian wading in the shallows towards her with an appraising look. Oona meanwhile stood on a large, hovering scallop shell, radiating waves of power from her chest, causing the air surrounding her to waver and distort the sky and the headland to her right. A glow like a nimbus formed around her head, and she would have looked like an illumined angel if it were not for the slitted, lime eyes with their unrelenting focus on Finnian's. He handed her a freshly-mined ruby; she broke the rope of pearls around her neck, handed him one, and the deal had been done. On this big day, however, Oona was very glad that her husband was absent from the coronation. He got on her nerves.

The excitement of the crowd was undiminished, even though the procession had filtered away into the strange, rounded edifice called the Throne Room. All seemed content to sit down exactly where they were, though they seemed on high alert as if something were about to happen. "What are we doing now?" Ben asked the tree woman.

"We wait for the transducement." Noticing his confusion, she qualified this with, "When the young Queen comes into her power, all will be enthused and invigorated."

"Oh, wow, that's interesting. So, she's psychic, then?"

"I do not know what your meaning is," said the tree woman. "You are a foreigner?" she asked slyly, pinching his arm. "You like that?" she added, widening her eyes.

"No," said Ben, "it hurts. Shall we sit down then?"

"I have grace to be close. From there, we see the proceedings." She hustled him forward, and they wove their way around the clustered, seated people, most of which looked somewhat homespun and whom had flagons of drink and bowls of green mush that they shared and ate with their fingers. They all looked very happy and healthy with rounded bellies (those that had them). Ben thought of Phil and his look of joy when he talked about what was probably the same foodstuff. After a while, Ben noticed that the man in the ruff and tights was following them. This did not make him happy at all.

Chapter 6 Time Troubles

The royal party entered the earthy depths of the Throne Room antechamber leaving a prehistoric sunset behind them, though Ben had no inkling this was why the sky was red. They walked down the foot-worn central aisles where the clayey walls were concealed behind undulating hangings of green and red filigree and silks. The roughly hewn stone mushrooms that propped up the outer edges of the pavilions contrasted jarringly with the refined throne in the centre of the hall which was a drama of jade and coral. The rock benches and the central water rill were all visual evidence of the union between Oona an Aquarelle of the sea and King Finnian Knight, man of earth.

Occasionally, the throne, the staging, and the rostrum would jump sideways, and Queen Oona had to steady her gaze and level it back in position. She knew she was holding onto time by a thread. The Fei had occupied a fixed point in time for as long as anyone knew, but now time had become twitchy; it was threatening to charge forward, taking them all with it! As if to illustrate this point, a small but pleasing 'pop' sound marked the departure of a footstool from their world to human sphere 1990, where it tripped up a man in the Paris Metro. "Pop!" said Oona, looking around her ferociously for the cause.

"Pop?" asked the Lord Chamberlain politely, as if he hadn't heard it.

"Yes, 'pop' fool. What was it?"

"A footstool, Ma'am," said the Lord Chamberlain.

"Oh," said Oona with great weariness. "Is that all?" and she moved on.

Existing in a sealed vacuum of time had always brought many advantages to the Fei, not least being out of the reach of nasty historical catastrophes when they occurred although, these can be viewed in the human sphere for entertainment or leisure via bridges, commonly known as *burrows*. Fei youth consider these excursions great fun. Some humans are also aware of these entry points and call them *thin places*. The forced discrepancy in time between the two spheres means that landing points in time and space can be a little arbitrary and each burrow leads to a different era. Some destinations are quite famous, such as Trafalgar Square 1945; others, less so. Of course, no one particularly fancies going too far back as methane is so hard to breathe and there is no nice food there. Going forward is a bit dodgy, too, as all history tends towards entropy, and that is potentially a rougher ride than anyone wants. The freedom to move at will through time and space had always been considered a luxury worth defending, but it also guaranteed a way of life that was very important to the wellbeing of the whole species, generally, because it gave the younglings opportunities to work off excess energy in a rite of passage named 'Encountering'.

Oona took her responsibilities very seriously but was not really cut out for having continual challenges to her authority in the form of footstools or any other furniture. After all, the whole point of inhabiting a bubble in time was to avoid outward pressures and random historical events. The Fei's reluctance to engage in anything other than the pleasurable life of the senses was tantamount to slapping up a 'do not disturb' sign across the world for all eternity. They were children of Kairos living in a breathy dream of transitory thrills. Kronos could get lost for all they cared if they had ever heard of him, which many hadn't.

The system of the royal family artificially stilling time was another example of the phenomenal powers devolved upon the Fei from the beginning of creation. They were so chock full of energy that the Monarch's prime job was to siphon it off and be a living conduit for the often wild and uncontrollable capacities of the humblest of their subjects.

The reason for the uneven dispensing of these inherent

qualities to the Fei, as compared to the humans was a subject lost in the mists of time. In truth, the Fei spent all their time enjoying themselves and didn't concern themselves with ideas about their origins. The humans on the other hand seemed to have a bit of a hang-up about it and were always digging in the dirt like dogs, trying to find out whether they had always been so awfully dim.

Living life in a hedonistic blur, the Fei had rarely bothered about the parallel sister Earth past the age of 'Encountering,' but now the presence of the other sphere, was making itself known increasingly. There seemed to be an odd drive towards synchronicity that could not entirely be explained by the Queen's incompetent lassoing of time against the relentless momentum of linear history. Now, everyone had seen the invisible gravitational forces melding the two worlds together in arbitrary moments. There was a frightening sense that the objects appearing and disappearing regularly in gardens, fields and buildings were demarcating moments into capsules of time, like the human days: ready-made beds arrived early evening, toasting forks flew in like arrows in the morning. Who or what had created this historicising process, it was impossible to say. The population would have liked to blame the Queen, but were too frightened to do so, and instead just moaned about it; particularly when the shifting landscape caused them to get lost, or they were hit by missiles. Oona was aware of the murmurings; it made her difficult to live with. There were rumours of her pinning courtiers up against the wall for petty blunders, and this seemed to have a basis in fact, judging by the broken teeth in the smiles of the nobles. Even now, her erratic mood swings and fluctuating powers were mirrored by wavering objects appearing randomly, sometimes solidly, in her peripheral vision. She kicked a pair of straw-stuffed trousers and a floppy hat out of her path, and when a corn cob kept reappearing, she threw it, enraged, at the Lord Chamberlain. The fact that she threw it, missed, and didn't use her powers to shift it was a testament to her weakened state.

Oona, much to her disgust, was now middle-aged at three hundred years and therein lay her problem, because a Monarch must be in their energetic prime in order to constrain the world. Fairies themselves are not technically immortal and deteriorate over time as even the rarefied air of the home world cannot prevent ageing. It was whispered that Oona's long overdue abdication in favour of her daughter had been due to Ensley's unsuitability. Occasionally shrill words such as 'Imbecile' had been heard within the royal chambers. As she walked down the endless aisle towards the throne, it was clear to every observer that the Monarch was actually in pain and performing beyond her capabilities. With her shoulders set, she kept her eyes on the throne in the distance, muttering foul words with each footfall. Her daughter, Ensley, seemed to have no awareness of the urgency and was nodding, smiling and linking her hand to other's hands, paws, or claws, depending on the creature approached.

"Will you please hurry up!" Oona hissed between her teeth.

"Oh, but our subjects deserve the personal touch," Ensley said, reaching out to another odd creature with a hammer head. It leaned forward, sniffed her hand, and then the lips retracted showing a dual layer of serrated fangs. Ensley hastily withdrew her hand.

"You are wasting time," Oona emphasised, groaning slightly as a fearful spasm gripped her stomach. "It's taking all my concentration to hold our world together. Besides, they have no idea what you are doing."

"I disagree," Ensley said quietly as she glimpsed sideways at her mother. Queen Oona was often a tall woman of two metres in height, and her almond-shaped jade green eyes tended to be a little daunting. "We must set them a humane example," she said. Her mother jumped slightly at her daughter's odd notion but then lapsed into disinterested cynicism.

"I wish you good luck with that," she snapped, fixing her gaze on Ensley's discrete extraction of water weed from her little finger, left from the handshake with a water sprite. Sadly, it wouldn't disengage entirely. Ensley's eyes broke away from her mother's and she focused on the earthen floor, blushing furiously.

***

An explosive bang ricocheted around the hall, startling the populace who were already unnerved. No subject would dare to excuse themselves from such an important occasion as a coronation, but it was a dangerous undertaking. Those who had received an invitation in the form of a crown brand burnt onto their palms in village squares arrived with hands in pockets and a nonchalance that fooled no-one. These 'guests' were soon accosted by officials who demanded, "Show us your paws you lying little scoundrels," and they were shortly hustled into the hall. Everyone knew it was far safer to be outside where incoming missiles could be viewed more easily. Inside the palace, many had been forced to team up to keep a vigilant look out for shifting columns, furniture or other heavy objects that manifested suddenly, threatening to crush them. In the last hour, there had been a few misses but nothing worse than minor cuts through flying projectiles. Now, a shipping container had suddenly appeared from the mortal world, encasing a group of Gabron Dwarves originally from the Black Country. They stayed very quiet inside this, as calling attention to the Queen's weakening powers was a treasonable offence. Besides, the metal box was so lovely and cool as a contrast to the tropical environment of the Devonian epoch that Oona favoured due to it having many of her long-toothed relatives there.

There had previously been all too many 'officially unrecognised' instances of time and space anomalies. Once, during a state banquet, the queen's right slipper had disintegrated into a maggoty mess. Nobody, including Oona herself, mentioned this, and she spent the evening walking around with one bare foot. On another occasion, an ancient, mortal gentleman materialised who insisted on reading her long, tedious poetry until she had forbidden him from coming within a few yards of her on pain of death. That self-same man was currently hiding behind a pillar next to a tree woman who was digging her feet into loose soil on the outer margins of the throne room. Next to both was a young man in the process of jotting down the marvels he was witnessing on a pad of A4 file paper.

It was when Oona had to raise her wand finger like an anti-aircraft gun to track a flow of potatoes bouncing off the roof that she decided enough was enough, and, therefore, placed the crown on Ensley's shining head with unseemly haste. Ensley thought, 'Ow', but was too intimidated to say so. Everyone craned forward to hear the first words of their new Monarch and the Mer people swam down the salt wedge estuary purposely built so that Oona's people The Aquarelles, could attend. Ensley said,

"Brilliant...thanks ever so…very grateful," rounding her faltering words off with "Cheers!" There was polite clapping and the slapping of wet digits as Oona raised her eyes to the ceiling. It was no matter as the momentous occasion more than made up for the understandably flustered young queen.

Ben's hand could barely keep up with the flow of impressions that he was keen to capture. The throne was not terribly far from where they stood. Clearly, the tree woman was a most favoured creature to gain such close access. He tried to concentrate on the ritualistic proceedings which involved a great deal of incense and muttering in strange tongues, but he was distracted by the surroundings, some of which were so vivid he felt he were in a world of computer-generated imagery. He wrote,

'at first, I thought I was looking at a sea of jewels.' Practically every surface and every garment was encrusted with gems, but it was all an illusion.'

Ben recoiled in disgust after poking at some rubies when he realised, they were really ladybirds scrabbling in a futile attempt to escape their fixed form, only too conscious of a thwarted timeline. Much later on, as an old man, he would amend his writings to add, *'no-one could have failed to have been impressed with the opulence of the moment at Queen Ensley Knight's Coronation'*, though in the later days, he accepted magic as a matter of course.

Ben moved his shoulder away from the mud-coated pillar that was alive with clumps of tiny organisms. It was so repellent, he thought it best to just focus on reporting, in order to tolerate it better. Once he adopted this mind-set, he found his eyes orientated naturally to picking out the minutiae of detail in his surroundings. Having acutely sensitive eyes had always been such a pain at home, but here it was an advantage. His deliberate detachment soon brought the hoped-for peace, and then he began to see beauty; everywhere. Oona had her back to them, and he realised the crystalline sparkles of Oona's cloak were continuously descending drops of dew. He watched them in a trance, falling to the hemline, before osmotically blundering their way back up the hairy fibres of her corset. An aroma of summer lawns travelled even to where he stood, overwhelming him. His hand stopped; he felt slightly drugged, and looking up again, he gasped. There was a person standing to the right of the new young queen who had just been rather strangely named as 'Queen Ensley of the Fei and All The world to the Margins of What we Choose to See.' This young man, richly dressed in green satins, velvets, and soft leather was no other than the same person he had stared at so many times in the town square. "The Changeling," he gasped aloud, and dropped his pen.

Chapter 7 True Friends and Traitors

B. Sopher, the boy who eventually became the great fairy ethnologist, traced the word 'Changeling' to the human sphere, where it has bad connotations. The name is based on the true fact that in the distant mists of time, fairies stole babies replacing the missing infant with something else (The 'something' being any kind of magical creature depending on ancestry). The habit went out of fashion as the Fei finally realised that human babies need copious amounts of care compared to Fei children, and this is a great nuisance. Besides, it is a source of some outrage that the exchange is often documented in fairy tales as a poor bargain.

"I left my own dear little greenling with a dim-witted woman," bemoaned one Fei parent, "and all she did was hit it with a shovel and try to throw it on the fire!" Luckily, the said sprite was more resilient than a human child, and diving down a burrow outside of the farmhouse, it made its way home, dragging a knitted blanket behind it, filled to bursting with the contents of its former foster home. Sopher explained in his famous essay, *'Fairies and What's Wrong with Them'*, that the Fei are quick to get upset with humans whom, in a strange reversal, they consider immoral compared to themselves.

The problem is,' wrote Sopher, '*though the Fei seem carefree, they have an awful lot of hang-ups, and the historical misrepresentation of the Fei race in tales is keenly felt. As they are constitutionally impulsive and have a poor sense of chronology, the redressing of justice is somewhat arbitrary, and they'll pick on the nearest human regardless of whether they were involved in the slight at the time or not. Unfortunately, this does nothing to dispel the notion that fairies are capricious and dangerous; in fact, their reputation gets ever worse however hard they try to be 'good.' On the other hand, they have so little self-control that they are perfectly incapable of withholding sudden acts of great kindness and will arbitrarily choose anyone in the vicinity to share the love with; shortly after, they will return to form and the benefactor reverts to tormentor once again. Some Fei are more predisposed to being nice than others, and Ensley Knight is a perfect example of this archetype. Her constant need to please drove everyone mad by the time she was approximately ten. If she hadn't been royal, she would no doubt have been constrained within a non-sentient tree long before puberty.'*

The person Ben knew as The Changeling had not been part of an exchange. He was an acquisition. Oona, had once spent a little time with a mortal financial consultant in order to pick up some tips about ensuring a stable future. The man had talked in riddles, and she realised after a short while that she was probably not in the right place. However, she had a great love of oration, and before she made the businessman teensy tiny and locked him in his own filing cabinet, as a punishment for confusing her, she memorised some of the lingo he had spouted. Shortly afterwards, she presented a new-born human to the Court with the explanation that he had been *acquired* as an *investment*. Unbeknown to everyone, Oona, under her smooth exterior, was a nervous wreck and, surveying her rather in-bred and frankly strange relations, realised that it was crucial she inject new blood into a rather dismal royal gene pool before matters got worse. Often, when talking to her extended family, Oona didn't know which side was up any more.

"Strands and meat," she would mutter to herself in desperation at Court, looking at her clothed entourage, "meat and material," were her perplexed words as she tried to make sense of the visual conundrums in front of her. She would eventually take a stab at it and have a conversation with what looked like a mouth but may well have been a different orifice.

The baby itself had been most carefully sourced and everyone had to admit he was a beauty, and all looked forward to when he reached maturity and could start to breed. Prior to taking the child, Oona needed guarantees that she was on the right path in her decision-making and, in the absence of King Finnian, who had left her in the lurch, felt she had no option but to consult the most powerful oracle the world knew. This was known simply as The Mirror, and Oona knew that she could rest easy in any predictive assurances it would give.

The Mirror though cryptic in its foretelling, was pretty easy to decipher, with the help of experience, and Oona had lots of that. The use of it, though, by a person of such an advanced age as she hers was a reckless action, and Oona shouldn't have done it. It had only ever been used as part of a rite of passage for Fei children on the occasion of puberty, in order to gain self-assurance in all their future endeavours. At that age, all Fei children, regardless of their strain, need hubris to survive in the ego-driven Fei sphere. What they see is their essence extracted in a pictorial form, so that a dancer will be the greatest dancer, twirling in an endless sequence of pirouettes, and a silversmith will be surrounded by her beautiful endeavours on wrist, table, and shelf, whilst a tree sylph grows and extends its roots lasciviously, its canopy dominating others in the skyline. The mirror shows end results so powerfully appealing that the young person becomes immediately proactive in their own destinies. In keeping with the Fei nature, the mirror encourages megalomania. The key words, 'who is the fairest of them all,' uttered by a vulnerable teen, literally embeds in the Fei psyche a will to only live a selfish and pleasing existence. In this way, the mirror does not really effect magic outcomes - it just produces self-fulfilled prophecies.

No-one knows where the mirror came from originally, but as it is old and very dirty and the silver is coming off the back, it may have been around since the beginning of time. It also burns the hands horribly if anyone tries to move it away from its usual position in the broom cupboard of a palace in Fei Lisbon 1485, where it undoubtedly prefers to be. The Great Creator clearly made the mirror as a patent for how the Fei race must be: uncompromising, stubborn and with a tendency to do what they want to the detriment of everyone else. These attributes have never been questioned, and it undoubtedly works towards the success of the Fei species.

Oona's repetition of the words, "Mirror, mirror," in a humble way, pretending to be just like a little youngling, had activated the mirror whose frame spored individual fairy lights of many colours at her words. "So far, so good," said Oona, and she waited, perhaps a little impatiently for the predicted outcome of what she thought of as her 'noble transgression'. "Ah," she said as the emerald crown of the Aquarelle emerged alongside the heliotrope one of Knight. Below these two hands were interlaced. 'How perfect,' thought Oona, we will have friendship between the houses at last. She was also most relieved to see that the Knight hand enclosing the other had a wand finger rather than permanent-looking tentacles, and she turned away believing that the future of the monarchy was assured.

However, she couldn't shake the feeling of uneasiness deep within her. The images had a prophetic rather than empowering feel to them. She turned back, noting the mirror hadn't finished its work. The final presentation was of a young woman who was undoubtedly her Ensley but graver than Oona had ever know her, sitting solidly on a singular throne of granite grey. The emerald crown on her long, black hair was the only colour to detract from the darkness of the representation, and she had a most severe expression on her face. 'I do wonder why she's wearing an emerald crown, though,' thought Oona. Doesn't match that Knight-style throne she's chosen. The child always does get it wrong, but never mind.' She then went off for a lie-down, more shaken than she would admit to herself by the dynamic nature of the visions. She didn't exactly feel assured as was usual after viewing the mirror, but logic overcame her nerves. Ensley Knight, would somehow, one day, be a fitting Queen after all.

***

The stolen baby, that was now a man, was following protocol to the letter at the coronation. He presented a conundrum to the Fei as no one had ever known what to name him. Though he was undoubtedly an element more valuable than any of the riches in the countries of the globe, he was human and, therefore, secretly despised. Eventually, an abstract noun had to suffice and he became known by default as 'Incomer.' At Ensley Knight's coronation, he was a spectacle that drew the eye in a pleasing way. Today, Incomer wore a doublet of forest green attached by fluttering silk moths that occasionally twanged the strings of the lyre across his chest. An emerald-encrusted crown of gold with pointed filaments rested on his head. The audience hoped he wouldn't sing as the beauty of his voice was known to cause excessive joy or melancholy. Once, a goblin had deliberately drowned himself in a barrel of cider as he knew he would never hear the like again. Incomer stood back in a melancholy dream, momentarily detached from the ongoing proceedings. He thought about a composition that might reflect his increasing sense of dislocation and abandonment. The goblins from an upper balcony watched him intently for any suspiciously morbid hums. Then he started to play, and his voice soared to the rafters as he sang of desire, desolation and the deepest bonds of love broken forever by a wicked woman. Each verse accreted meaning and depth, and the melody of the chorus, so simple but memorable, was taken up by the crowd. Oona swung her foot in time to the rhythm, smiling and nodding at her courtiers.

"See, see," she said, "The result of our most careful nurturing." However, her grin faded when Incomer, bending to the salt wedge, grew a rose in the hand through simple magical means and presented it to a male head that bobbed up. The sprite realised he was being observed at the same time as Incomer, who faltered and lost his momentum. The head descended, Incomer returned to the rostrum bowed, clicked his heels and said "Mother" politely before taking his place to the right of Ensley's throne. He resumed a prolonged stare at the populace, who stared back at him and at the new queen, Ensley, who had forgotten where she was and had started to scratch her nose. Up on the balcony, two visiting Austrian goblins were holding onto the legs of a third who was trying to pitch himself over, saying, "He's gone and done it again...made me all verwirrt."

"Beruhige dich, Frederik," said his friend, grunting with the effort of simultaneously talking and pulling. "Think happy thoughts." He finally succeeded in dragging melancholy Frederik back with the help of two others and all three disappeared with a thump behind the walled railing. Everyone's eyes were on this spectacle.

"Hmm, well done, my dear," said Oona doubtfully to Incomer, trying hard to ignore the strangeness of the moment. There was then a pause, whilst all waited for the new queen to take the initiative and say something spontaneous and grand, but nothing occurred. Incomer felt desperately sorry for his friend but could do little to help. She was no good in the gaps between protocol, though he had rehearsed with her the proceedings of the day over and over. The two had been friends from babies and were both sixteen years old, though they didn't themselves even know their ages. Raised in a court full of individuals whose appearance often owed more to the natural world than the humanoid one, they had gravitated towards each other, attracted by similarity in form if not in status or even character. In truth, both were friendless and alone, though the world itself wasn't alien to either. It is true to say that both were unperturbed at pupil-less eyes, (or eye), fangs, wings or pointed ears, as this was the norm. They had no fear of pigs' trotter feet or arms of twig but were daunted by one and one only; she that undermined their every move…and they weren't even allowed to talk about it. In the past, they had sought out unfrequented places and had managed an existence based on the bare scraps of freedom. Ensley and Incomer had played in abandoned, twilight courtyards where they had dunked each other's heads in fountains of deconstructed gold that had reformulated in bubbles contrasting beautifully with his caramel skin and lacing her long, black hair with reflective highlights. They had prodded the statues until they squealed and woke to make them scrape the stubborn gold off.

During their excursions Incomer sometimes managed to dispel the despair that wracked his frame and she had a solid loyalty to him that would cause her to flare with anger if she ever saw him mistreated. They lived for moments when they could be alone in their close and symbiotic relationship like two halves of a walnut. Their laughter echoed through the caverns and palaces of the court, and sometimes they were heard by someone. From time-to-time Ensley had given in to the instinct of cruelty towards others that was characteristic of her race, but gradually, as their friendship deepened, Incomer had guided her away from these tendencies. It wasn't a hard task as Ensley had both her father's, reserved but still affectionate nature and her mother's single-minded sense of duty. In Ensley, both combined to produce a determinedly kind character. From where he stood on the day of her coronation, Ben Sopher was seeing neither of these qualities. All he saw was a self-conscious girl slouched uncomfortably on a throne with her crown skewiff and the glorious Changeling who was moving slowly closer to her, alert to the fact that something was wrong.

It was odd how Incomer displayed the mannerisms of a mortal adolescent as if the ghost of genetic memory had literally taught him lessons from early childhood on how to speak and think. His empathetic idiosyncrasies were plain to all and revealed clearly why he did not belong in Fairyland. This was proved when he rushed forward to his frantic best friend, signalling him over, her eyes wide with panic. Incomer realised simultaneously that the sceptre was slipping out of Ensley's grip and also that he must do something about it. On bended knee, he stabilised the sceptre and offered direction,

"Stop grinning; you look like a fool," he said helpfully. Ensley slightly moved her sceptre that sadly hit him on the head and muttered back,

"Stay…don't leave afterwards…don't leave me with her." Oona caught Ensley's last words and frowned into the mid-distance.

"I'll never leave …you … don't worry, *My Queen*," he added with a flourish and a bow, just in case the crowd suspected that the interchange was anything less than formal.

"Don't say a word," he whispered. "Go and eat some food so you can't talk."

Ensley grinned at him so that Incomer had to pinch her leg to make her stop. Sadly, Ensley didn't take this advice, and thinking she had to do something positive, touched one shoulder then another gently with her finger in a ritual that puzzled everyone excepting Ben, the Jacobean man and Ensley's rebellious cousin Hedera who always spent an unfashionable amount of time in the human sphere. In short, she decided to knight Incomer.

"You are our most honoured and trusted of servants, and now a knight of the realm", she yelled in an attempt to sound dominant, but sadly, this comment pleased no one as Incomer generally had a low ranking. Members of the Knight family were particularly put out, and these glared at her wondering why she was allowing Incomer to usurp their name. The Mer people gave up trying to look impressed, flipped backwards and vanished. Only the water sprites stayed, for Incomer, whom they loved dearly. Incomer deflected the next round of disasters by half dragging Ensley, her orb and sceptre, towards the banqueting hall.

As words had never been Ensley's friends, Incomer had become practised at deflecting attention away from her and also at priming her on what to say and what definitely not to say. Most of the Court ignored what she said publicly and in conversation politely referred to her as, 'well-meaning.' Another oddity in her behaviour was that she had inherited her father's strange obsession with collecting relics and customs from the human world. The tat and treasures of a thousand years entranced her. She could sense the fingerprints on an Athenian tile decorated with thrushes. She could smell the residue from long-dead lips on a Georgian clay pipe. Viewing them over and again in a soothing ritual, she often said, "These are the dreams and loves of a multitude." She knew that if she were observed, she would be ridiculed for breaking the fairy rules of continuous acquisition and disposal. Most fairy bowers are a literal scrapyard of damaged or dirty items. "Once seen, fully forgotten," is a common saying, that strangely applies only to human artefacts; showing the extent of Fei snobbery. Incomer would hide her antiques under rocks, then bushes (who shouted out what he was doing), then in underground caves (which flooded), and in so many other locations, that, to Ensley's distress, he himself soon forgot where they were. In the end, he'd placed a claim on a cast iron safe from the 1920s that had suddenly materialised one day in a meadow. He hid her treasures in there as they seemed to be so very important to her.

***

During the Coronation, Oona had split her attention between keeping a careful eye on Ensley and watching the wall nearest to her for signs of wavering. It was clear that both seemed stable, and it was an opportune time to lever Ensley into the next stage of the proceedings. The royal party being seated behind a huge banqueting table was a cue to an ancient ritual whereupon the new Monarch consolidated their magical control over the population, in between the first and second courses. The table itself was laden with exotic foods from the mortal world and included plenty of white bread, trifles made from packets, store-bought cupcakes, crisps, iced biscuits and many other delicacies. Sugar acts as a powerful narcotic over the Fei constitution, and even now, Oona was slapping hands away from plates and dishes before things descended into chaos too soon. Oona noticed that Ensley already had a finger roll but had only taken a small bite.

"There, daughter," said a very relieved Oona, handing over yet another, smaller sceptre, which Ensley put uncertainly by her pudding spoon, "Now you are queen, you must invoke the first of three wishes upon the kingdom so that your wrath is established." Rising to her feet, she yelled, "Bond us to your will!" dramatically, making everyone jump. Behind her, the lit brands in their sconces flared dangerously like blow torches at her words. Ben Sopher, seated on a nearby bench, threw his arms around his twiggy friend instinctively, but the Jacobean man, who they couldn't seem to shake off, was entranced by the spectacle.

He said admiringly, "She doth make the torches burn bright, dispelling our gloom, exiling night." Ben was suddenly overtaken by a memory of himself sitting in a Year Ten class bored out of his mind, hearing words distinctly familiar to those. "Oh, shut up," he said to the man who had stood up pompously to bow at Oona. "Anyway, it's not night."

"Tis a figurative analogy," the man snorted back at him, never for one minute taking his eyes off Oona.

"You just fancy her, that's all," said Ben, and the man scowled back at him and said, "A villein, a cur – it speaks poorly and is base."

"Shall I scratch him?" asked the tree woman, sliding her remaining twigs across the table, towards his eyes.

"No, leave him, he's just a twit, I think…" Ben said uncertainly, wondering if the man was truly who he seemed to be.

"Anyway, he's very conceited."

"I have consensus," said the woman in her faltering way. "Now we must watch." She directed Ben's attention back to some frenzied activity that was occurring on the high table in front of them, where Ensley was being shaken and pounded on the back by her mother. It was because she understood the importance of the three wishes in establishing governance that Ensley had choked on her roll. She had been reliably informed by an Oaken Elf that the wish took on aspects of the Monarch and had the power to carry over and influence the character of the world too for better or worse. It was a terrible responsibility, the problem being that, Ensley hadn't the faintest notion of who she was. She did tend to fluctuate a bit depending on who she was with. What if she were a very evil person deep down? She didn't fancy living in a world guided solely by the principles of meanness. The bread piece eventually plopped onto the table, and staring at the mush, and not wanting to create a claggy mess with words, she took it as a sign that words wouldn't do. She rashly decided to rely on the seam of psychic ability that ran through her family instead to institute the wish, although she hadn't rehearsed it. She concentrated - her thoughts becoming a restless wave, lapping over the many heads in tortured stages. She felt she was definitely linking at one point, though she should have felt a continuous surge of power instead of the bubbling sensation she had in fits and starts. Quite a few people started to burp in the immediate vicinity.

She tried to grasp onto a train of thought, but it slipped away from her like an eel in the hand. Another eel of thought cheekily appeared and just as swiftly wriggled away. Oona, meanwhile folded her arms whilst Ensley scanned the audience of thousands in front of her. She needed more time – she always needed more time to think. Magically, the smirking, black lipsticked face of her cousin, Hedera, appeared seated opposite. She hadn't noticed her earlier, but as Heds tended to live as an itinerant wanderer between the two spheres she may only have just arrived. For a desperate Ensley, Hedera was a welcome sight, because she was the kind of person that twisted protocol to suit herself. Frankly, Hedera didn't care much for it and was never daunted by what people thought about her, unlike herself. Ensley noticed that she seemed to have acquired more piercings in her eyebrows since she'd seen her last and could now easily pass for one of the humans that she admired so much.

Hedera was a true child of Knight and could have told her what to do psychically if Ensley had not been so panicked. Knowing Ensley so well, she, fortunately, resorted to more mechanical means in this moment of crisis. Her mouth formed shapes, she flicked her head towards Oona, and she mimed something with her lips that looked like, "Show her." Ensley, nearly said, "What?" aloud but just stopped herself. Hedera's breathy whispers found her in the end.

"Go on," she said, nodding again towards Oona who scowled back at her, and then Ensley clicked. Together, they had talked many times about the superiority of the human sphere as compared to the Fei, where the youth could do and say just what they wanted, apparently. To prove Hedera's argument, they visited human France in 1792, at the height of the revolution, to find some perfect examples of freedom. Hedera had translated the dramatically expressed concepts of liberty bellowed out by a man standing on a wooden stage. Ensley had grasped onto the essence of these words with enthusiasm as they sounded lovely, though she had become very distressed at witnessing the separation of head from body from the body of a noblewoman moments later.

"Is that equality?" asked the traumatised Ensley.

"Yes," said Hedera, laughing inappropriately, "Equally divided between shoulder and skull. Don't worry, the theory balances it all out in the end," Hedera had said, guiding her away from the Place de Greve whilst surreptitiously evicting the blood stains from her shoes with her wand hand.

Standing in front of a population that she had no intention of chopping up, Ensley felt a great affection for their wellbeing and realised that she was no doubt experiencing 'fraternity'. Her feet tingled, but she disregarded the phenomena of interconnectedness that already existed between the trusting people and herself. A series of flashbacks processed through her mind: her mother yelling at her, the courtiers sneering and the many mistakes in protocol that she made every waking moment. Her dear cousin Hedera understood only too well what life was like for her, and she trusted her implicitly. That decided it. She would establish a constitutional Monarchy based on free will. Carried forward on a wave of memory and emotion, she forgot to think and spoke instead.

"I wish," said Ensley with gravitas, "that this day forward will mark a new era of freedom for all time. Here, in this place, liberty is granted for each and every citizen." There was a shocking quiet, broken only by the rustling of bugs escaping enchantment. A bulbous spider, once a black sapphire, descended from her sceptre and ran across her hand. Ensley looked up to meet the eyes of her cousin, but she had mysteriously vanished. This was unhelpful as her mother proceeded to go berserk.

"Idiot, fool," screamed Oona, clawing her way towards her daughter by hanging onto the disintegrating table. Judging by the way that great hall fluctuated and rippled in waves, it seemed the whole world was losing cohesion. Oona had to reconstruct the ground, the table and various courtiers' unravelling clothes as she manhandled her way towards Ensley hiding behind a chair which itself was in the process of re-constituting itself as the rosewood tree it once was. "Look what you've done! You've dispersed your power and condemned us to a time of material instability in the palace."

"*If* it is just the palace." Ensley noticed that eight water fairies had simultaneously realised they had the liberty to lose cohesion. As this was rather unexpected, they had unwittingly created a knee-deep flood, and the Lord Chamberlain, Gentleman and Women of the court were busy with jugs and bowls. The tree woman next to Ben sucked in her breath and proceeded to turn into a hydraulic monster, her face merging horribly with her trunk so that she was neither humanoid nor tree. Ben and two other people in lavish but wet clothes had to physically restrain her from sopping up the deconstructed water fairies.

"I'll kill her," said Oona still fighting desperately against her world. Losing control completely, a maelstrom of energy and light circled in her chest, burning off the front of her dress and exposing her underwear beneath. A high-ranking diplomat hag with her Bogle assistant were in the path of this terrifying vision. The hag looked pityingly at Ensley but decided it was an opportune moment for them both to vanish, and having the freedom to do so, they both did immediately.

The following catastrophe was perhaps a blessing insofar as it headed Oona off and distracted them all. Up above them, the roof of the mound was in the process of separating from the buttresses and, in between, a dirty white gap was revealed; at first, it was like a thin line of ribbon but extending moment by moment so that it was soon as thick as a pillar and then broader. Something was moving behind it, too, and the Jacobean man cowered in horror, giving dramatic life to the word "eyeball", for the very first time in history as he pointed at the gigantic round, fleshy object above. He was correct. A large, brown eye shifted in an agitated way from left to right, then found its object and focused directly on Incomer, who had been frozen on the spot since the chaos had begun. Sound roared down upon them, and the bellowed words were incomprehensible.

"Seretse, my baby!" were the words the voice said, repeating them again and again, the tenor of the sound being shrill with anguish and so sharp that there was an involuntary clutching of ears. What did it mean? People looked at each other in confusion as the voice wailed, "Seretse, Seretse," like a broken klaxon.

Oona, still in a crouching position as if she were about to ambush her daughter, stood up and took control.

"An earlier event has infiltrated the present. Quick, we must seal the tear in our world."

The backs of a hundred Fei separated into two sections and beat together so quickly that the air throbbed with their effort. They lifted on their wings in a dense swarm and made their way to the opening surrounding the giant eye. As they approached, a phlegmy mucus began to form on their wand hands, though the onlookers below were only aware of this when it started to drip down upon their faces. Ben, still with his back against the tree woman, wiped it off, looked at his hand and thought with disgust that it looked like someone had hawked up in it. The fairies above, like so many worker bees began to seal up the rip in time with the substance, and slowly, the eye started to be veiled. Being so distracted, no-one noticed that Incomer was no longer the person he formerly was.

***

When the person who belonged to the eye had started to yell, Incomer had felt very different from the people around him. What Incomer felt was a distinct attraction towards the call rather than a revulsion. He literally stood on his toes as if he could climb or fly in response to the voice, but of course, he couldn't fly or do anything as he wasn't Fei. Somewhere deep within his soul, the anguished cry resonated with him, and he felt warm inside but also terribly sad. Someone else knew that shrill voice, too, and that was Ben who watched like a guilty bystander as an old scene worked its way through. The woman was undoubtedly Frances, and Incomer or The Changeling, or Seretse or whoever the hell he was, was her missing child. Ben didn't think anything else could startle him in this fluctuating universe, but turning round, he was shocked to see quite how affected Incomer was at this strange reunion with his mother. In fact, he was literally moving towards her through time, meeting her midway at the point they had originally met, being now no more than eight years old. Ensley, still crouching behind her throne, was immured to most magical events but even she screamed as she witnessed her greatest friend continue to shrivel down to the size of a baby. The Fei, who had finished mending the roof, landed on their feet around the baby gurgling somewhere underneath a heap of material, but no one dared talk until a courtier bravely spoke. "We have achieved containment Majesty," he said, generally to the air, not knowing whether to address Ensley or Oona.

"Yes," said Oona, tersely, "Yes." The overlong pause suggested that she was either too exhausted or displeased to say more for a while, but then her undefeatable spirit rallied, and with an air of reluctance she waved her wand in a circular motion in front of her face. Almost immediately the entire world reduced in size, and, accordingly the volume of air within it. "The world will have to be small to sustain us," Oona said, speaking primarily about herself and her own energy levels. It seemed that Oona was once more in charge. She fixed her daughter in her gaze, and Ensley stayed stranded there, too frightened to move. "We will adjust forthwith," Oona informed them all, and mercifully the feeling of closeness and strangulation eased as the population became acclimatised to their new, straitened circumstances.

Another long silence followed, with no one knowing quite what to say, until an ominous shuffling and dragging could be heard coming from a dark corner strewn with fish heads and guts. A very stinky old woman emerged clothed in an array of woollens, canvas sheeting, and fisherman's nets. They were not so much worn as applied to her body and held on with nylon cording. There were fish hooks hanging from the cord that jingled as she made her way towards Incomer as a baby, saying, "Give him to me, give me my darling. Nurse will fixes him."

"A sail, a sail," said the Jacobean man aptly, confirming in

Ben's mind that somehow this could really 'only' be William Shakespeare, and his masterpieces were probably inspired by the memories of his lived experience... from another world. Later on, he would test this hypothesis by saying quietly, "Oy Shakespeare!" from the other side of a hall and watch as the man responded immediately with, "Aye?" Ben had no time in that present moment to wonder further how Shakespeare could be in Fairyland and, accordingly, how he would return to his own time before Oona intercepted the fishy woman who was reaching out a large, grey hand to scoop up Incomer.

"Stay where you are, Mab," she said and the old woman retracted her hand sluggishly inch by inch. "It will need more than your 'talents'," Oona said the word scathingly, "to fix this appalling mess. I will be his only guardian this time around." Oona picked up baby Incomer from the swamp of adult clothing and rounded on her daughter.

"As for you," she said, "Consider yourself deposed forthwith. You are a traitor to your kind and not fit for the noble title of Monarch." She strode towards the palace entrance, her footsteps softened by the compressed mud of the floor, but obviously another thought occurred to her and she turned around.

"You only have yourself to blame, you know. A queen rules with authority, absolute control, not impotence."

"You are wrong, Mother," Ensley said bravely, "We have to be free to be ourselves, to dream our own dreams and follow our own paths."

".... And look where it got you," was the pointed reply. "What a mess," she sneered, smiling maliciously, knowing somehow that Ensley would think both about a regurgitated bread roll as well as her disastrous actions. Ensley did, and blushed. Oona sighed, "You are dealing with a race whose inner drives are impulsive and dangerous. We are," she paused, "Complicated." Oona pondered on her own, volatile impulses whilst watching a small pixie stamping very hard on the fingers of another.

"Stop it," she snapped, and the surly creature slinked off. Oona continued. Utter freedom for the Fei subjects could only ever be an affliction, destructive to wellbeing, a curse and not a gift. How could you not know your own people?" she asked curiously.

"I, I don't know," Ensley stammered. "I thought all for the best. I've learnt about equality and..."

"Tosh." Oona interrupted and shifted the restless baby into the crook of her left arm. "It's worth the risk," she muttered to herself, clearly having come to a decision, and pointed her wand at him. Immediately he started to grow, so she placed him on the ground. He looked approximately eight years old for the second time that day, and Oona had to quickly clothe him before taking him by the hand. The boy looked up at her, not exactly with trust but certainly with courage. There were possibilities evident in his demeanour. Oona thought again about the mirror's prophesies. Perhaps she had misread the meanings. After all, a crown like the boy's emerald one featured in the image, as well as the depressed version of Ensley, who was no doubt upset to be supplanted in power by a better option. Surely, that is what it all meant. Oona smiled, showing her fangs and making the boy tearful. "You are a little prince, are you not?"

"Yes," cried the child, sobbing. "Ensley," he pleaded. "I want Ensley."

"You can't have her. She's going away," declared Oona drawing herself up to her full height of two metres. Her voice and bearing changed dramatically in accordance with her newly, assumed, role as Regent. "Ensley Knight of the Fei," she said formally, "you are forthwith exiled from the realm, to live your days in the Other Place without privilege or powers." She moved her wand arm away from her, and a blinding, magnesium light arced high over her head. The population collapsed to their feet en masse, retching and clutching at each other. The sickening effect of Oona's outburst affected them like a heavy dose of radiation. It gathered energy and then plummeted as a great worm-shaped entity directly into Ensley's stomach, the force punching her through layers of space and time. Ensley screamed and writhed in agony and despair because she couldn't escape the ferocity of the pain. 'Stuck like a butterfly on a pin,' Ben scrawled in horror on his notepad as he lay on the floor, dictating the moment before she vanished. He placed an asterisk above the comment and later added that exile seemed as much a deliberate means of punishment as magically exercised protocol. He wondered how Oona could justify acting this way, but she seemed to take her royal duties very seriously and was already coaching Incomer on how to address others as the royal personage she had now decided he was.

**

The tormented Ensley was forgotten and continued plummeting to an unknown twentieth century destination. (Oona was not cruel enough to deposit her in the Earth-time Dark Ages or similar.) At last, she burst right through the membrane of the other world, but her relief was quickly replaced by despair at the dullness of her new environment where the colours of the plants and grass around her were muted compared to the Fei home world. The sun, in contrast, was as blinding as it ever was. Why did the humans have to have it that way, she wondered, and shielded her eyes. Soon, her eyes started to adjust after a nictitating membrane slid across them, but then she wished they hadn't as everything turned greyish. She noted streets of boxy houses in the distance with their perpendicular lines and shuddered. The shuddering turned to shaking as she went into shock; her skin then proceeded to turn light green, and Ensley Knight began to ail. It was not that she had never visited the 'Other' place; Earth was an interesting place, but it had always been a relief to return to the rich exoticism of a world that fed the eye and the spirit. With its curved naturalistic habitats that blended so perfectly with the natural environment, it was often difficult to detect in Fei sphere where a building started and nature began. Surrounding vegetation glowed within its separate colours as if backlit, both night and day and this was entirely natural. This feature of the Fei sphere held true whichever epoch the Monarch said they should inhabit. It quickly dawned on Ensley that this secondary world was all she had now. Her knees buckled so that she ended up on all fours yelling and beating the faded grass. She realised then she was on the top of a mound in the centre of a fairy ring. Noting the slightly darker patches between the mushrooms, she punched these with her fists. She had learnt as a child through The Legends of Blyton, told as part of the oral tradition of the Fei, that these were potential entry ways into her world.

"It doesn't work, though," she said aloud, feeling the sting of yet another betrayal. Overwhelmed with homesickness, too ashamed to cry, she lay on the hill and became dull and granite-like, interrupted by streaks of mossy green as, after all, she was her father's daughter, and he was mostly rock. She was completely unaware of how close and connected she really still was to home.

The energetic beam Oona had thrown at Ensley, was partially sentient, and like an animal, it was voracious and imprecise. This amalgam of light and energy was intended to harvest every attribute attached to Ensley. Unfortunately, the tiny, black spider that was once a nugget of obsidian sewn into her sleeve had become very active once it had been freed from captivity. In fact, from the moment, it had become 'alive', it had been busy forming a gossamer-thin web between Ensley's arm and the throne back in the Great Hall. At the moment of Ensley's exile, the strand of web acted as a hook that dragged the whole of the miniaturised Fei world into the human one. In this way, one became the host to another, and the absolute separateness of the parallel worlds was lost with human Earth having primary influence on the Fei world subsumed within it. When this bizarre situation was later discovered, it was the cause of great debate. The smoothness of one event leading to another caused some to think it was part of a sequence of fated events; others just thought it was hazard; a disaster, plain and simple. Many got drunk, argued, and injured themselves over the whole matter on a regular basis. Either way, the Fei sphere had landed in an extraordinary location, caught like a bug within a web with all the vulnerabilities that the position accorded it. Oona was entirely unconscious of this as she was occupied with 'growing' Incomer and mentally plotting his part in her revised constitutional plan. By the time, she'd stopped lecturing the audience about the 'amendment' to the ancestral line Incomer had regained his former teenaged self. As soon as he was adult-sized, he walked to the charred area where his friend had stood and touched the flaking ground. Standing up, he turned to Oona and said, "Well, that is just wonderful, is it not?" Oona raised her eyebrows for the umpteenth time that day thinking, 'I'm going to have problems with this one as well. When will it end?' Scanning her unhappy population cowering before her, she noticed Ben then for the first time, being different, completely engrossed in writing in his book. He had just got to the part where Incomer had looked devastated and angrily rounded on the evil Queen and hadn't noticed the self-same person stalking him in an ominous manner like a green praying mantis. In no time, she was right beside him. "What are you?" she demanded, breathing in his ear." Ben jumped and thought very quickly. "I'm a Sopher," he said, confusing Oona deliberately who didn't know what that was.

"Human?" she asked dangerously.

"Sopher," Ben repeated firmly, adding, "Your Majesty." Oona grabbed him by the chin and stared into his eyes. The deep green, of hers, were two slivers of emerald; he was looking into a terrifying ancient pit with unknown things in it....and then, there was a palpable change as she reached a conclusion.

"Hmm," she said, at last, transferring her gaze to the splayed notebook on the ground and back to Ben. "You are a scribe."

"Kind of," said Ben, lapsing into vagueness. This didn't go down well and she grabbed the notebook from his hands, tapping her wand finger on the paper.

"Decipher your scrivening for the Court," she demanded. Ben didn't dare read out what he'd written and he'd already guessed that Oona couldn't read. He had an instinct that fairies wouldn't like having their antics contained within the shadow of a bias rather than having these exalted in oral ballads or tales. He decided to go back to definitions.

"I am a painter," he insisted. "I draw descriptions of..." he waved his arm around to include the palace walls... "all of this. It is pictures in words, only," he added.

"Ah, good... pictures," she said, glad to be back on known territory. "The Sopher draws pictures. In words," she emphasised to the people. "The Fei are artists," she explained, turning back to him. "We expand, we glorify, we are not … contained by little, black words. Like … like, flies in honey." She laughed and all joined in. When the room quietened, she said, "Sopher, you may write your pictures and entertain us with your performed 'descriptions.' The Monarch," she said in a sudden severe tone, "draws the days. Only the Monarch," she clarified, and her green eyes gleamed. She pulled her cloak apart to show the spine of a golden book peeking out of a purpose-built pouch on her belt. "The Almanac," she said with reverence.

Everyone in the crowd went "Ooh" reflexively. The Court rustled, then settled into stillness. Ben also joined in, bowed his head and said, after a suitable period,

"Yes Majesty, of course," all the while thinking, 'I'd love to see what visual interpretation she documented about today's fiasco.'

"The Sopher will stay at our pleasure," she said, and Ben, relieved, stood up.

Oona, Incomer, and a whole group of courtiers moved off and

the tree woman linked her branched arm through Ben's.

"You are most favoured," she said, pleased, nodding at the pen still clutched in his hand.

"Yes, but I must be careful, I think."

"Very careful," she agreed, having no idea what Ben did with his pen. She put it in her mouth; he removed it. "You will be mine," she said, happily... "This eve."

"Uh, I don't fancy girls."

"I am tree."

"Or girl trees." Ben removed the knotty hand that was fumbling at his waistband. "You mustn't touch," he cautioned her.

"Sweet little Sopher," she said, and an unexpected stem snaked around his torso to tap his back. Ben realised he would have to lay down some ground rules. "You can hold my upper branches and only ever when I say the word, 'Hold.' Is that clear?"

"No mating?" she asked, so stunned that she stopped dead in the procession moving slowly along, and the courtier behind smashed his head on her trunk.

"None. We will be 'friends." The tree woman pulled a face at him.

"What is friend?" she asked in a sulk.

"I will be there for you, and you will be there for me."

"Here?" she pointed to the ground in confusion.

The man behind rubbed his head and said, "Can you *please* move it along?" Ben wondered how on earth he could explain commitment to a person whose only knowledge of linear time came through the artistic interpretations of events by an absolute monarch. He sniffed the ancient air and noticing the rays of the sun forming plateaus of orange light through the earthy entranceway of the palace and that gave him an idea.

"I will be with you at the rising and setting of the sun," he said. "Every rising, every setting." Ben felt that the tree creature could be a good ally and interpreter. He had nothing to lose anyway. She, meanwhile, was taken completely off-guard by his words.

"Sopher," she said aghast, marvelling at the concept of constancy. She bowed her head over his and kissed it lightly before realising what she had done. She clutched her own head in her branched fingers, ashamed. "I stupid, stupid," but he held her hand and said, "You are young, just a sapling. You will learn."

"Yes, yes," she said enthusiastically and immediately placed herself three metres away from him.

"Closer," he said, pointing beside him and she shuffled sideways in increments, much too slowly for the man behind, who took the opportunity to dart around them both. When she was near enough, he asked her, "What is your name?"

"Hazel," she said abruptly, surprising him.

"Hazel?" he said wonderingly, thinking what a pedestrian kind of name it was for such an exotic creature.

"I not looking my best," she said pointing to the withered catkins hanging from her ears.

"Ah," said Ben as the penny dropped.

Outside, they were dismissed by Oona who marched off shadowed by the Incomer who looked as if he wanted to be anywhere else but with her. He slung the lyre brought back to him by a goblin across his chest, before following. "Where to now?" asked Ben cheerfully turning to Hazel.

"Home habitat," she said and led him away to a little grove by a creek where they eventually, in the run of days between nights, made a very satisfactory structure for him of wattle and daub, during the making of which they both experienced what it meant to be 'friends.' He sourced the mud, not going too close to the creek that contained some dangerous-looking amphibians. She meanwhile retrieved 'dead' sticks; apparently there was a difference between some fallen wood and other bits that were just *resting*. Ben was relieved to discover that though Hazel made a pretence of living inside their hut, she preferred to exist in a stand with others of her phyla. She was particularly attentive to some wilted-looking birch trees that clearly did not belong in a sub-tropical environment. Hazel told him that the Court *had* to go where they were stationed in time and space regardless of whether the environment was suitable for strain or species. Watching her spitting water gently over the birch branches, educated Ben on a new definition of what kindness could be and how this was completely different from mercy, particularly when he found her stomping on an unfortunate, struggling fish in order to mingle bonemeal into the slimy ooze of the Devonian bank for her roots. In his journal he began to write about the casual affiliations between the many different species of creatures in the Fei world and the contrasting unbreakable solidarities between those of the same kind. He considered whether these behaviours were inimical to the world he came from but then reconsidered as humans didn't behave quite in that way. Regardless, his impression of Hazel was of a particularly compassionate and highly-regarded individual in her own community.

Ben Sopher's early domestic observations of Hazel and her friends, were undoubtedly the trigger for a lifelong interest in fairy ethnology. Ben found adopting a scientific detachment helped him discover the purpose of a crucial characteristic that all Fei share: being the ability to move through the fourth dimension in a scary and unpredictable way. Witnessing this in the invariably successful hunting expeditions of the trees, he thought it probably stemmed from a survival mechanism. Whether it was an early evolution or not, it was hard to say.

One hot day blurred into another. Fortunately, Queen Oona had seemed to forget about him. In the beginning, he would hang around the boundaries of the palace where there always seemed to be great masses of picnickers, eating green mush, laughing, singing and playfighting on the ground. He wormed his way into a group who at first loved the novelty of sitting with a human, but soon got bored with him as he didn't seem to do anything fun.

One or two had initiated sexual overtures at first, but they were perplexed by his response of,

"What here... by the food?!"

"No, no," they would say, catering to his foibles. "Behind the bush."

"Those bushes move around," he observed in a wry tone.

"Yes, but they will stay fixed for us and look away," observed the very beautiful young man shifting towards him.

"It's a no" said Ben, firmly.

After that, they left him alone and carried on amongst themselves. Ben would eat, doze and, in-between, write pretty descriptions of sunrises or plants in case Oona ever called him up to entertain the crowd. She never did. Though he was tempted to seek out The Changeling, he dared not. Somehow, he seemed so grand and unapproachable. Also, he had heard that Oona was tutoring him into a royal role and never let him out of her sight.

Ben would occasionally splash along the watery highways, overspilled by the many creeks, in the opposite direction of the fields to interact with whatever creature he came across, but mostly he stayed close to home, overwhelmed by the enormous strangeness of his new world. There is a child's performance piece about these days entitled 'Sopher on the Shore.' A fairy performer sings about a solitary figure crouched over a book near to a group of trees that he will neither cuddle nor fight with. Eventually, poor old Sopher dies of loneliness, and the audience weeps, having been educated about the dangers of fixed friendships over normal interactions. The ending was not true of course because Ben lived a long life; it is even rumoured, he had many lives, though there is no material evidence of this controversial idea to date.

Ben was not actually lonely, certainly not in the way he had been in Dorchester, but his new interactions were not without their problems, too. He discovered almost immediately that all Fei have a debilitating short attention span that tends to mar interactions. Hazel, not being immune to this characteristic, occasionally forgot what she was doing, and her hands would wander everywhere, before Ben remined her once again not to touch him without the key word. She was always apologetic.

Chapter 8 Missing

Terri was in a terrible state because nobody would listen to her.
She had been persistent to the point of being told to actually leave
the local police station two weeks earlier. From thereon, she'd
haunted the phone lines until a narky woman had told her that she
had to follow 'due process' with cases like Ben Sopher's.

"What the hell does that mean?" she'd exploded.

"If you continue to be abusive, I'm going to put the phone
down on you," was the immediate response.

"I'm not being abusive; I just want to find my friend who's
gone missing. No-one's doing anything."

"Hold on one moment."

There was a prolonged pause on the line before the voice
triumphantly revealed that as Ben was 'low risk' on the file, she
would have to 'follow due course.'

"You're a fucking robot," Terri said and put the phone down
before the other woman did. "It's hopeless," she told Sandra,
slamming hairbrushes into a draw and kicking it shut with her
foot. "Because he's an overage, single male, they don't want to
know." Sandra agreed with her, thinking she wouldn't like to
get on the wrong side of Terri, even if she were her employee.
However, the desperation in Terri's approach must have triggered
someone deep within the rank and file because the next day, two
officers came to the salon, insisting that Terri accompany them
to Ben's flat. "We're going to search it," they said. "Also, you've
got a spare key." This was true and Terri had already searched the
flat from top to bottom, but she didn't want to tell them that and
stall the process that was finally grinding along. Sandra watched
Terri getting into the rear of a police vehicle, a female officer
putting her hand on top of Terri's red frizzy hair as if 'she' were
the culprit rather than an ally.

Ben's flat already had the unlived-in coldness and absence of smell as if he'd been gone longer than a month. It was a space of evictions. Terri gloomily picked up a paperweight on his desk wondering if there was any hope at all. An unwanted worm of doubt about Ben's mental state caused her to think that.

"Put that down," snapped the male police officer. "We'll have to take your fingerprints now."

"Well, won't you have to do that anyway? You know, considering I'm in here all the flippin' time, as I'm his friend." Terri realised she wasn't helping matters as the officer reverted to official speak.

"I'll have you know this is a potential crime scene, and we must follow the rules... I mean, the system."

"Well, your so-called rules haven't been very effective so far."

"We're doing our best," said the young officer. "Lots of people go missing and it's rarely suspicious anyway, if that's not a contradiction."

Terri raised her eyes to the ceiling, thought about keeping quiet and then decided against it.

"Don't you give me that, Dean Hurst. I know your mum and dad, and they wouldn't be very happy with you if you just let Ben just disappear off the face of the earth."

"We're doing everything we can," he repeated, his face taking on a lighter shade of puce under his peak.

"You've done nothing yet. I'm definitely telling your dad. You know how he promised Ursula before she died that they'd look out for Ben, living next door as they did."

"Alright, alright, shall we get started, and then we can talk about what happens next."

"Okay." Terri's spirits dropped even lower as she realised 'next' might mean police divers in the river Frome and also cordons near to where he was last seen. She knew this would also be at a historical spot in Bourne because she herself had traced his last, known journey on the bus, having been told about it by an old lady whose hair she did each month. She had seen him actually get on a bus the day he went missing. Following the sightings of Ben, Terri had questioned a group of teenagers on mountain bikes. Her heart had raced as one told her about Ben cutting his way into the long barrow enclosure. They had shown her the hole, but the trail went cold after that. She watched hopelessly as the police ransacked the flat. Finally, the woman officer, who had maintained a frigid silence since her partner had been so unprofessionally exposed by the victim's friend, put the paperweight with its imperfect bitty swirls into a plastic bag.

"What do you want that for?"

"DNA samples. There are obvious fingerprints on it. Probably *not* just yours," she said. Then she went to pick up a tee shirt neatly folded over the arm of a chair, but Terri intercepted her; it was just too much of an invasion. There was an un-prolonged tug of war until the policewoman realised that Terri's face was crumpling into a heap.

"We need this," the officer said a bit more gently, and Terri let go.

"I take it you haven't removed anything else from the flat?" Terri shook her head no.

"Are you sure about that?"

"Yes, sure," she gulped.

This was not strictly true because the big Moroccan red book that had been on his desk was currently in her own flat. It was the last thing that Ben had bought, and because of that, she felt a great connection with it. She hadn't read it because her concentration had been so shot recently.

The three of them surveyed the devastation of the flat where remaining bag of old lady memorabilia had been excavated from the wardrobe and unceremoniously upended everywhere, just in case it contained 'clues.' Dean carried on being an officer and demanded the spare flat keys from Terri. She didn't care. It didn't matter now as she wouldn't be coming back – there was no point.

Once home, she sat staring at the blank T.V. screen. She dared not switch it on as the officers had told her that the case would be reported on the evening news, and that was making it all a bit too real for her. Instead, she rubbed her hand back and forth over the top of the red book, thinking how pretty it was and how like Ben to purchase something with style and elegance. She opened the front page and a serious woman with long black hair stared back at her quizzically, a little as if to ask, 'Why are you reading someone's else's property?' Terri shuddered, instinctively not liking the intrusive feel the drawing gave her. Intrigued, she decided to start the story anyway, which was all about a young male protagonist who lived a sad and solitary life in a small market town. Hmm, she knew all about that living in the dump she did. The story developed in an interesting way because it was a fairy story that pretended to be like a fact book, and the boy hero communicated lots of weird stuff about the creatures who lived in this separate world called The Other Place. Terri didn't tend to read science fiction, but she did think that the choice of words was a bit lame. Couldn't they have called it Zog or Phantasmic or something? The story soon got quite dramatic, telling how a vicious bitch of a queen called Oona exiled her only daughter to Earth, even though she did nothing wrong really. Noting the description of the girl, she flipped back, realising the narrator was the woman in the picture. Terri wondered how she had failed to notice the grand title Ensley Knight of the Fei underneath the picture the first time around. She looked appraisingly at the woman's sleek hair, her hinted at cleavage and neck choker sparkling with emeralds that matched her subtle tiara. She was really fanciable in a fantasy art sort of way. Terri felt intensely motivated suddenly to continue the story. She didn't enjoy the bit about Shakespeare as it was a bit random, and anyway, literature had been pretty ruined for her in her GCSE years, so she didn't particularly want to read about that old tosser again. He also seemed to be a total creep in this version, hanging onto the blond queen's every word.

Terri had just gotten to the point where the boy who was only described as a 'Scribe' was building a house of mud in a hot climate. This was in a picture form and Terri suddenly felt exceedingly mellow. She didn't want to read about that dark haired girl queen anymore, she wanted to read more pictures. She stopped for a moment. Did people read pictures? That was a very odd thought. A few disorganised pictures followed that showed lakes, glaciers, and bulbous houses that looked like wattle-coated igloos. The almond shaped eyes of the inhabitants glinted from within these, in the darkness. She found she loved this other world and was thankful that the lovely Queen Oona had made everything so perfect for the reader. She enjoyed looking at the pictures of mud banks seething with organisms and the fern trees standing in warm shallow seas that smelt of cabbage. Terri giggled, and three times, she tried to turn the page with a hand that was floppy and useless. When she eventually did, she wished she hadn't and the shock cleared her foggy mind. There on the page was Ben. It could only be Ben, sitting on the bank of a stream, by some trees, in a raggedy pair of cut-off jeans, writing in a book. She turned the page and found a sequence of pictures in storyboard form. These ones were in a completely different style to the previous ones, as if there had been an artistic breakdown midway through the book. Ben's close-up face was mouthing something at her, his awesome blue eyes flash-lighting something very important.

"What? What?!" yelled Terri at the book, but it was no good; there were no words returned. He pointed at his own book. She put her face so close to his that it touched, trying to read the tiny squiggles, because that's all they were. It was pretend writing for effect. Why wasn't he allowed to use words to explain his situation? What the hell was the publisher thinking? The next picture showed him laughing helplessly and, the following, shrugging. He had closed his book in the final picture and was pointing to the cover in such an exaggerated prim pose, index finger erect, that, despite herself, Terri got the giggles, too. Finally, she got it and closed the huge book with a great whoomph. There, midway down the cover, where there had been nothing before, was written in Ben's own handwriting:

And Ben Sopher

…but nothing before it. Terri started rocking back and forth in her chair, traumatised. She knew with a terrible certainty, though it was technically impossible, that Ben was writing himself out of existence and into a completely new one.

"Ben, Ben," she said, completely out of her depth, "What have you done?" Only, when she looked at the next explanation, it just said in a journalistic, straightforward style that the only thing that Ben missed in the months following his disappearance was his friend Terri, and he felt awfully guilty at leaving without explanation. He genuinely hoped that she wouldn't worry too much and wished he could somehow let her know. Terri kissed her finger and planted it on his lonely form.

"Thanks, Bud," she said.

***

Just a short while before, Ensley Knight was missing home so acutely that she was determined to never move again, though she ended up having little time to carry out this plan. The grassy area she was sprawled on was a level above the emerging head and torso of a fierce-looking person clambering towards her up the chalky path. The woman had greyish hair and clothes and was breathing heavily. She stared at Ensley with frightening intensity, never shifting her gaze for a second. Trouble, thought Ensley wearily, as if she hadn't had enough already. She closed her eyes and waited.

Frances thought she'd seen Ensley explode backwards out of the top of the barrow in a terrifying manner, with clods of earth being flung high into the sky just moments before. She went with the impression and was not at all surprised to witness the reassembling of reality into a more believable form moments later when the earth, the rocks, and the girl descended, and the ground looked just like it had before. 'At last,' she thought, almost crying with relief, 'I'm in.' The girl, Frances noticed, had long black hair (rather dishevelled), a pantomime dress, and was pretending to be a stone. Even now the edges of her legs looked like rock strata, her face was turning green, and her features seemed to be fading. With the last of her energy, Frances charged up the mound, did a sprawling leap, and pinned Ensley's shoulders to the ground.

"Give me back my baby," Frances hollered.

"What baby? I haven't got him," said Ensley, slightly disingenuously, as she still had the impression of a small, dark baby in green velvet.

"Well, how do you know it's a boy then?"

"It might be a different one. He was my grown-up friend five minutes ago."

This confusing response did not faze Frances at all who had done a great deal of research about the ability of the Fei to alter natural processes, including ageing.

"Anyway," said Ensley, "I can't get back in, so I can't help you."

Frances came over all shaky.

'So close,' she thought, nearly falling. Ensley had to grasp her arm to lever her down.

'So old,' thought Ensley.

'So, I'll try again,' thought Frances.

The air was positively buzzing with invisible interjections. Frances flopped out on the ground, and they lay side by side on the top of the barrow sharing an almost tangible sense of loss. Frances could see the desperation in the foetal position of the girl beside her, and her anger ebbed away. She didn't know why the fairy was catapulted out of the hill, but she had a strange feeling that if she hadn't turned up at that exact moment, the girl would have just dissolved into nothingness. Frances eschewed ideas about destiny because she wanted to be in charge of her own fate and sort it out good and proper. She reconciled herself with the thought that it was just a lucky coincidence that she appeared when she did. Neither knew what to say, as the circumstances were hardly ordinary, but there was a fairly relaxed silence between the two, which was odd in itself. Frances stared down at her considerable tummy, like a minor barrow itself, and further on to her big walking boots. She found something to say that seemed relevant,

"I love those boots."

"They are powerful boots indeed," said the girl, looking over her shoulder.

"Well, I always say that if you have good footwear, you can't go wrong." As soon as she said this, Frances was hit with a familiar pang. By default, she seemed to spout motherly truisms, even though she didn't have a child to tell them to. She regretted opening her mouth then because she didn't want to feel bitter; really, she didn't want to feel at all.

"What's your story then?" she asked, curving around to face the girl, who was creating her own half-moon beside Frances. Ensley twiddled with the grass stems in embarrassment, thinking how odd it was that someone fancied hearing about stupid old her... but anyway, she would start at the beginning – her beginning. Ensley told Frances all about the misery of having an unfortunate personality and her joy at having a constant true friend, a human friend no less. Frances sat up at this and became very still. "What's his name?" she asked quietly and Ensley started to pick the heads off some daisies in an agitated way.

"We... I mean... they, call him Incomer because..." The daisies around Ensley were by now all decimated, "... Because he came in, you see, from your place."

"What?"

"He doesn't have an official name, precisely."

"Why not?"

"It's difficult."

"Not that difficult, surely." Frances looked quite dangerous again, and Ensley noticed her grinding her teeth a bit like some barely evolved creatures her father used to keep in a pen.

"So, are you telling me that my child, what was stolen from me, never warranted a name? Because, it is him, isn't it?" Ensley lowered her face, ashamed.

"Yes. The Fei are funny; they don't include people very well. Even me." She looked at Frances, who looked back at her in a different kind of way. "There are rules, you see." She thumped her heel repeatedly in the grass, and this made a satisfying groove. "Is your world like that?" Frances lay back on the grass; she had to admit it was to some extent.

"But is he – was he, happy?"

"Many times, we sneaked off and played. For long times," she added. "Then we were happy. We collected treasures and hid them." Frances felt like her heart was breaking. She thought fretfully of the limited opportunities for normal relationships her dearest child would have had growing up. Watching the girl sit up and rock back and forth on her backside, her arms clutched around her knees, she dismissed this thought. The girl was immature to say the least, odd; even she could see that. Yet, she was a pretty little thing and clearly loved him, so she moderated her feelings on the matter.

"Your friend's name would have been Seretse," she told her, expecting a different reaction to the one she got.

"Seretse?" The girl thought about it. "It doesn't suit him much." Frances was a little shocked at the girl's bluntness and her inability to maintain eye contact. She tried to remember some crucial information she'd read in the Sunday supplements about a specific mental condition, but it escaped her, just like the girl who was now up on her feet jigging from foot to foot, spouting a rhyme about springtime.

"Hey, ring a ding a ding," she sang, out of tune.

"Cut that out. Sit down," she said, grasping the girl by her hand.

"I won't, I'm Ensley Knight of the Fei and I can do what I want now." The freedom from the Court had completely gone to Ensley's head and she jumped faster and faster in a manic blur, still spouting nonsense.

"I'm free as a Hyter, Free, free free, hopping on the ground, like a happy Nuckelavee."

"Ensley, sit your bloody backside down!" Frances tended to command attention from most people, but Ensley couldn't seem to stop until Frances bellowed, "Park it!" and Ensley did, looking very relieved that someone had taken control. She sat there panting like a dog. "Put your tongue in," Frances instructed. "I'll tell you my story and that might settle you for a bit."

"Oh lovely," said Ensley, crossing her legs and putting her elbows on her knees. "Us Fei love stories."

"Well, you might not like mine. It's very sad."

"Marvellous," beamed Ensley inappropriately, which Frances ignored.

"People always thought the nineteen sixties was a good time," she began, "A time of liberation, but it wasn't for everyone." Ensley looked blank, so Frances decided to get to the action. "I was in love," she said. Ensley looked bored. She beat her foot to an invisible rhyme. "…With the wrong person." That did it, Ensley's face was suddenly a mere four inches away from her own. All she could see were huge, blue eyes like two moist planets. "Get off, get away," she commanded, pushing Ensley back.

"I wasn't even that close," was the moody response. "I don't even like getting close," Ensley whined rowing herself backwards with her legs.

"Anyway…" Frances was determined to proceed with the tale, whatever. "He was from Guyana, it was called British Guyana in those days, which I always thought was never quite right, it being such a long way away."

"I know the place," said Ensley, surprisingly, "from my sphere." Frances would have liked to continue this interesting thread but decided her own tale took priority.

"His father was a diplomat whose embassy was close to where I worked on the Bayswater Road as a secretary." More blank looks. "Like a scribe," she explained. "We spent my lunch hours in Kensington Gardens at the tea garden by the Peter Pan statue. I don't suppose you've heard of it?"

"Have, he was horrible – glad he's dead…." Catching Frances's look, the words dried up.

"I'll go on," she said, trying to be patient because having a mad listener was better than nothing. Frances explained that she was struck by two bolts in one week; the first was discovering she was pregnant, and the other that the father and son were being relocated to Botswana. The latter was a terrible blow coming just after the horrendous scene with all the shouting when she'd taken Ayrton, her boyfriend, back home to her mum and dad. This was especially disappointing because the day before, both parents had been sympathetic, making plans to buy her baby equipment because, as her mum said, "Anyone can be caught out, and we shouldn't judge." Frances had come back in tears from her final meeting, when Ayrton had spent the longest time looking at the carpet, and his dad said that she would always be welcome to trace them later on. At the moment, though, it was important she build bridges with her parents and it was best if they broke contact, for the time being at least. When she got home, Frances noticed that her dad was wearing his Sunday best suit, and she had a suspicion that he had gone to meet Ayrton's dad. She accused him of 'ruining her life', and he said that she,'had done that herself'.

In no time at all, it was arranged that Frances should have her baby in a mother and baby 'home' on the south coast and return later with some concocted story about a failed marriage. Frances was naïve and agreed to this plan, but her mother did not kiss her goodbye.

"Terrible, terrible," Ensley said thinking about her own mother, whilst the sickly green patches on her right cheek re-emerged to form one large island. Suddenly, she threw herself upon Frances and kissed her on the cheek long and hard. This was fairly pleasant to Ensley as close-up Frances smelt of mould and toast, both of which things Ensley liked very much.

"What's up? Get off," said Frances untangling her. "I haven't got to the worst bit yet." Little did she know that far from being captivated by the story so far, Ensley had understood very little of it. She had no idea why a commoner couldn't reproduce if they so chose. Her subjects did it all the time. The part about the cold and heartless mother sending her dearest daughter away was the only bit she understood.

"What's up with your face?" asked Frances, who was more than a little peeved at being interrupted mid-flow once again. Ensley touched her face self-consciously.

"I ail," she said, cupping her hand over the area.

"Well, I'm sorry, that was rude of me." Frances prised Ensley's hand away to give it a quick pat, and mysteriously, the patch vanished as quickly as it had appeared. Frances sighed and continued her tale. The home was horrible, she explained to Ensley, just like a prison, and it was most fortunate that a kind nurse named Mab with apple cheeks and green eyes befriended her. "She was a friend to me when I didn't have anyone. I thought I could trust her, you see, but that comes later. In the beginning, the only odd thing I could see about her … well, that's not exactly true, there were a couple of weird things about her..."

"Did you say Mab?"

"Yes."

"Oh dear," said Ensley.

"As I was saying, she had a most unfortunate nose."

"Uh." Ensley was holding up her finger as if she were in a school room, trying to say something very important, but Frances ignored her.

"Yes, it was most odd, flattish, and squashed down on her face." Frances ruminated, "From the side she looked a little bit like, well, like a cuttlefish really. I found a dead one on the beach at Southend when I was a child, so I know. The other thing was, she was very pongy, and quite unlike a nurse in that way. Very unhygienic." Ensley was talking quietly to herself about the smell of seaweed at low tide, so Frances reckoned she'd got the picture. "In the beginning, though, we were friends. I can see now that she lulled me into trusting her."

"Yes, she would do that."

"How would you know?"

"Believe me, dear Frances, I know." Frances liked being called 'dear' but the inside knowledge about Mab unnerved her a little.

"Well, I'm not sure if it's the same person, but *this* 'person,' if I can call her that, used to sneak me out at night to the beach. I thought this was a kind thing to do as we were watched all the time. The staff could be very unkind, and they made all the girls feel like soiled goods, so it was a relief to get away from all that. Mab treated me as if I were the most precious girl on the planet. We would sit side by side on the jetty with our legs in the water and she would hold my hand tightly. Too tightly, truth be told, whilst I confided all my plans for the future. I was fully intending to follow my Ayrton to Botswana, taking the baby with me, though I had no idea how I was going to do it. In those days, girls were kept in such ignorance; stepping on a plane then would've been like stepping on a rocket to the moon. I didn't sink into despair, though. I've always been quite unusual in being such a positive and determined person." Frances stared into the distance. "Stubborn, my mum used to say, and no wonder I couldn't ever settle and be like a normal girl. I do remember telling Mab that books are a good way to travel when you're feeling trapped. That was how, even in my darkest moments, I never despaired. Books have always been a great consolation to me because there is always somewhere else to go where things are better." Ensley perked up and looked at Frances with great interest.

"I can r…" she began but stopped. She bit her lip.

"I remember Mab saying she didn't read much, and I think she was quite illiterate because I heard other nurses complaining they couldn't understand what she'd written on patient notes. Made me wonder how she became a nurse in the first place. I didn't judge, though, because she was so good on a practical level." Ensley didn't say anything but continued to stare without blinking. She couldn't imagine how anyone could conceive of Mab being 'practical,' but she said nothing. Frances must be an extraordinarily kind person. "I never judge," said Frances, confirming this thought. "Everyone is good at something – even if it's not apparent." She gave Ensley an appraising look. "When I look back, it was her that kept me calm, rubbed my back when it ached, and encouraged me to open my heart because she said it would calm the baby. I overlooked her weirdness... at the time... apart from one that stands out."

"Which weirdness?"

"Well, it went like this, I told her, 'I'll call the baby Seretse after Seretse Khama. I read he's a prince from Botswana and a nice man, so it will be a good link to his new country.' Well, Mab got all excited at first and said,

'Yes, a prince, a prince, that's right!' but then quickly changed her tone saying, 'Don't name him yet! The clay that binds is difficult to undo.'"

"That's true," said Ensley. "Naming him tied him to you forever."

"Interesting, no wonder she panicked a bit and said, 'Un-name him quickly.' At the time she made an excuse saying it was bad luck to name a baby before the birth. 'No', I said, 'I'm set on that name and it will give me hope.'"

"What did she do then?" asked Ensley curiously.

"Well, she got a bit flustered and said I'd get her in terrible trouble with the authorities. She used a bit of emotional blackmail and said she thought we were true friends and if I cared for her, I'd say the specific words, 'Child un-named'."

"Did you?"

"No, I said I wouldn't take it back. I would write it down for her benefit if she needed it officially, but she got sulky and said that wouldn't wash with her employer or words to that effect. I wouldn't budge, and then she did an odd thing and scratched me, deliberately, in a whip-like way. Impossible to believe, but I don't think it was with her fingers." Another person would have jumped at this information, but Ensley just nodded. "That's what this scar is on my cheek; she just missed my mouth. Nothing stops me from talking, however. I'm fated to blab." She managed a smile. "It's got me into all sorts of trouble, believe me."

Ensley did. "Continue," she said.

"Well, I didn't see her in the building for a full month, though once, I swear, I saw her spying on me. I looked out my window, and she was standing knee-deep in marram grass by the sand dunes looking up, but why would anyone do that? I forgot about it because that night, I went into labour, and as is the way with first pregnancies, the birth wasn't easy. Forty-eight hours later, in a haze of pain and exhaustion, I realised she was stood by my bed saying, 'Sign this. I've got it approved.'

Well, I'm no fool. I said, 'Sign what?'

'My dear,' she said, 'The baby is struggling. Sign this paper just in case we need to intervene with drugs. Or something...'" Frances clenched her fist in despair. "I'm afraid when you're in terrible pain, you just want it over, and I'd challenge anyone in that position to think otherwise. Of course, I cared about the baby too, but you tend to listen to anyone in a uniform in an hour of desperation, trusting they have your best interests at heart."

"You signed?"

"Not exactly. I could barely see the paper, let alone sign it. I'd had drugs, you see. I remember the paper flopping down on my face, so I was more or less kissing it rather than writing on it."

"Even worse," said Ensley. "Gestures are contractual."

From thereon, Frances seemed to be speaking in a daze; her voice grew distant and the energy seemed to have gone out of her body. Her arms flopped to her side, empty and useless.

"How would I know that two days later she'd return. I'd just been feeding the baby and he was sleeping. I couldn't stop staring at his little button nose, his tiny fingers, so perfectly curled over the shawl and those deep, brown eyes. It was like a miracle, and I couldn't believe that people had gone through this and not raved about the magic of the whole thing. Then she appeared at the end of the bed and the spell was broken. 'Give me the child,' she said, without a by your leave, and all her kindness fell away from her as she leaned forward. 'Give him to me,' she said, this terrible old hag with hands like shovels and her in rags, stinking of goodness knows what."

"Fish," said Ensley faintly.

"Fish," Frances confirmed, "and the shock of it and that terrible face made of a hard shell paralysed me, because by then I saw her for what she really was. By the time I came to, she was out the door, and I was running and screaming after her. People saw me go, but no-one stopped her. We ran and ran along a sandy track until we reached a hill. I thought it was a hill, but I know now it was a barrow, and at the edge, the ground was opening up like two lips talking. She ran through, but it started to close straight away. I lay on my side, and that was the last time I saw him, my Seretse, but this time lying in soft, green velvet on the floor, a long way down below. 'Seretse, Seretse, my baby,' I screamed until I was facing just brown earth, and I knew, just knew, I'd betrayed him with a kiss."

"It wasn't your fault," said Ensley, greatly moved. "It was a planned event."

"Yes, but that doesn't help. I was still his only protector, and I feel I let him down."

"Didn't the other people, the nurses, ask where the baby went?"

"Well, that's the odd thing; they just carried on as if it was normal, saying I'd done an unselfish thing giving him the chance of a good home. They actually said it was the whole point of the place, for mothers to have their children adopted. 'I'd agreed to no such thing', I said, but I got nowhere, and then the real problems started. I told them no one in their right minds would let a fairy monster steal their baby. What on earth were they thinking? I got some funny looks then; I can tell you."

"What did you do?"

"Being me, I wouldn't let it rest, and then they found me with a shovel at the barrow in my nightie, yelling obscenities down a rabbit hole. Sometimes I got a glimpse of a queen with green eyes." Frances paused. "Sometimes I still do – here and there, from place to place. I think she's in charge."

"Correct, that's my mother, Oona. She's definitely in charge." With this information, Frances's face changed, sealed into one position, the lips becoming thinner. Ensley felt that she had been talking to the echoed voice of a different Frances from long ago, but now that Frances had switched back to the angry one that had pinned her to the floor.

"Well, I was eventually dragged off and put in an ambulance. Postpartum psychosis, they said. The next few years were a blur of drugs and talking therapy, but I never, apparently, 'got better'…" Frances made quote signs with her fingers... "Because I wouldn't give up my version of events. I've even got a counsellor to this day, 'Mabel Turnkey', and she says that by revisiting the past, I will never move on." Ensley jumped when Frances named the counsellor and looked at Frances quizzically, but Frances seemed spent now and emptied out, so she didn't notice. She sat there, an old woman with her fists clenched on her knees against so many invisible foes. Ensley was very affected because she'd never seen love like it, so dauntless, so pure, so endless, even. She reached over and touched Frances's hand, but this new Frances rebuffed it, though she specifically noticed the tears in Ensley's eye that were threatening to overspill.

"I don't know why you're so upset." Frances watched in a detached way as the pools in the lower lid became runnels. "It's alright for you' you're privileged."

"…And yet... here I am," was the simple response. After that, neither spoke, and together they watched the sun become a tangle of tatty golden streamers behind Bourne's distant piers. The ending of the day affected Frances considerably; she shivered, got to her feet, and frantically started checking the bag across her chest in case she'd dropped something. Ensley meanwhile enjoyed watching the looming darkness of night that would soon overthrow the skies. Twilight, the bewitching time, or at least the only time fairies could see properly in this ridiculous world

"Got to go. My train leaves at ten." Frances was already a good distance down the chalk path.

"Where do you live?" asked Ensley, marooned in uncertainty on the top of a hill.

"London, Lambeth, the '*Big Smoke*'."

"Can I come?"

"No. I've got my own problems, thank you very much. I don't need any more."

"Wait. I think we will suit each other well. Consider…" Ensley slipped and skated down the hill on her bottom. It was quite painful, and she forgot what she was saying.

"Frances," she yelled, to the retreating back, "I must tell you, your beloved son did have a true name and it's 'Kosmo'. That's what I, his friend, knew him as. You need to know he wasn't just a no-person." The name clearly registered ahead of her through

Frances's sudden stillness, but she didn't turn, continued on, and was soon just a grey dot on an equally grey road. Having reached a cul-de-sac, she stepped neatly onto a bright yellow bus, and the doors hissed shut. Ensley looked up again at the comforting blanket of night. Lambeth – a mysterious place shrouded in smoke. A place of magic, Ensley thought, where anything could happen. She knew that this was her path. "I wish I lived in Lambeth," she said aloud, with a sudden surge of power, making her realise that she still had the wishes, at least, despite Oona's decree. She vanished, leaving behind a dead space. Deep within the barrow, the sleepers finally exhaled – and were released into the aromatic wild grasses and the nodding flower heads, eventually dispersing far above the land. The closing past was heralded by the clang of a distant gate and a dog barking. Ensley, meanwhile, was far away putting her shiny new key in a red door because she had used her second wish and was now a London resident of SW2.

Chapter 9 Rough Magic

It started with a ripple over the creek, though there was no wind that day. This was followed by ever increasing-waves until they smacked up against the large rock Ben was sprawled on. Most of his days were spent this way with his head emptied in the heat like a sun-dazed lizard. He later reflected that it was just as well that something happened when it did, as he might have wasted his entire life. He certainly didn't think this on the day the ground suddenly tilted in a terrifying manner at least four degrees and he plummeted back towards a cliff face. His life might have ended with him dashed to pieces if he hadn't recalled the key words that he'd given Hazel to memorise and use in a different scenario altogether.

"Hazel, hold, hold," he screamed, and she did, wrapping branches and hands around him, with her own kind behind bolstering her, because they had instinctively clustered together for security into a dense grove the moment the world moved. The ground then pitched forward, not quite regaining its original axis. Ben was pelted with the pebbles, aquatic creatures, water weed and debris that had sloshed out moments before. Though Hazel wrapped herself around his head, he sustained a severe gash on his arm and was very shaken up. He wasn't the only one. Hazel kept repeating over and over, "Ben... what is? What is, Ben?" After he told her and the rest of the copse multiple times that they had all experienced an earthquake, it dawned on him that the term hadn't registered with them at all. Clearly, this was a new phenomenon in this world.

"The ground is in pieces, under the soil and it smashes together sometimes," he said trying to explain tectonic processes. The trees' response was immediate. They roared back at him. "No, no shaking. Stupid human. Ground safe," They all shared a rustling kind of hysteria. "What is? What is" they demanded, grabbing Ben with their spiky hands, but they overwhelmed him every time he tried to speak.

"One at a time," he yelled, his nerves frayed.

"Ben," said Hazel, acting as the spokesperson. "We know our friend, the ground. It is…" She ran out of words and made a fist with her hand. "It is... tight. With us," she added. She lifted a minor root out of the soil and waved it at him. In response, Ben extended his arm one hundred and eighty degrees to encompass the scene of devastation before them with plants uprooted, and half-emptied pools. "I think you have loose soil now," he said shortly, "Not tight, and it's called an earthquake or earth-shake."

"An earthquake, an earthquake," they whispered to each other in despair, and the rumour spread from tree to tree until it reached Oona who said, "Send the Sopher to me – immediately."

Oona had been lying in bed feeling bored when the earthquake hit the palace, which unfortunately had been constructed out of the same clayey material as the Great Hall. She had descended three stories in a hail of grey debris, calling for her retainers all the while. They re-emerged painfully from under furniture and rubble once they had stopped falling. Some stayed where they were and blinked at each other in the darkness, spying on Oona shaking the dust out of her long, now greyish and yellow hair. It might be circumspect to wait until the Monarch had settled into her mood. Luckily, she was distracted by an ill-favoured human beating on a rock wedged in the entranceway.

"Lady, lady art thou well?" enquired William Shakespeare.

"Do not let him near, on pain of death," she said, pointing at the Chamberlain, who stupidly magicked up another boulder in front of the previous, sealing them in even more. Oona collapsed back on her pillows, and a dust cloud puffed into the air. She coughed and flicked through The Almanac, hoping it would tell her what on Fei Earth was going on. "Why am I having to read paperwork like a mortal bureaucrat?" she raged aloud.

"We grow more like them every day." Oona shook her fist at an uncomprehending pixie making vain attempts to clear the masonry with a broom, but then a birch tree whispered a human term outside of the broken window. "What did you say?" asked Oona, and the tree said it again.

***

It was the Changeling who was sent to fetch Ben. "Hop on" he said, from atop a huge horse, glorious in the midst of catastrophe in whitish tights and a jewelled jerkin. He had to literally drag Ben up to the saddle. "You sound just like a human," said Ben, clinging on for dear life as they galloped off down the littered highway, scattering Fei creatures left and right. Ben had never been on a horse before, but it wasn't how he imagined it would be. He was jolted and bounced so high that his teeth smashed back together forcefully chipping a front tooth. It was impossible to have a conversation when they were moving so fast, but eventually, the Changeling answered him.

"I am human, of course, but I take your meaning regarding casual speech. Our Royal Highness Queen Ensley kept close contact with the mortal sphere and brought me up to speed with human ways. Good of her, really." Ben had a suspicion that Incomer's blasé words concealed the fact the Changeling was trapped and couldn't go anywhere himself. He tried to be kind but bungled it.

"I bet you miss her; you being such close friends, Incomer?" Immediately, the back he clutched stiffened and Ben knew he'd somehow crossed an invisible line.

"We're here. Get off," the Changeling said abruptly

Ben looked down at the ground, wondering how he was going to dismount from such a high horse and then he knew when Incomer did something with the horse that skipped sideways and he slid off onto the floor.

"You did that on purpose!" he exclaimed, but the boy just grinned at him and moved away on the silvery horse as if they were joined together into one unit. Ben then had to wait for a very long time outside a strange edifice that looked like many upturned earthen bowls, even more so as most seemed to have collapsed one on top of another like a pile of pancakes. Clearly, the earthquake had wrought more damage near to the palace. There was then a prolonged wait as the whole of the entranceway had liquefied into a knee-deep grainy slip. Four Fei of the humanoid type were engineering granite rocks into a temporary causeway on top of it. These boulders were processing down the highway he had just travelled along in mid-air and, once they arrived, were pointed into position by the wand hands of one of the four. The activity was laborious, and it seemed that even the talents of the Fei had difficulty remedying this very natural contingency. Suddenly, a head emerged from a window above them and a nobleman remarked, "Rough magic indeed!" before retreating and forming a beautiful glazed window sparkling with icy swirls behind him. Eventually, Ben entered the palace and found that the inside looked nothing like the exterior, even in its collapsed state.

As with the Great Hall, the interior was opulent, but instead of there being an abundance of creatures that mimicked objects and furniture, the palace looked like a holding ground for a pilfered stash of antiques. This was actually the case, and each piece of furniture, stolen mainly from the seventeen fifties, reflected Oona's taste for gold gilt. It was a little blinding, and the retainers, who had very sensitive eyes, looked down constantly. It was impressive how they had learnt to negotiate around the heavy furniture, mostly broken now, and each other without ever looking directly at anything. He noticed for the second time the peculiar fact, that as with the Great Hall, there were no doors in each entranceway.

Ben drifted out of the antechamber towards an overstuffed,

domed hallway where every surface, every table or chair leg incorporated, animal paws, and bouquets of flowers into their design. It was tiring to take it all in. Chubby cherubs abounded on the ceilings as if rounded up and fenced in as part of a sinister baby-snatching enterprise. 'Figures,' thought Ben ascending the staircase, presuming he had to follow the hunched form of a pixie that had the unusual method of leaping wildly from far right to left on each step to get up the staircase. Eventually, the bouncing creature reached a half-obstructed gothic entranceway with a large green eye painted on its apex. The pixie finally raised its head as the iris within the eye shifted to look at him, and squealing it ran off back the way it came. Ben wished he could too but he took courage, politely knocked on the boulder in front of him, and squeezed around it.

Oona had both tidied herself up and was sat on a love seat with scallop shell shaped backrests in the centre of the room. Ben found the implications of being close to Oona quite unpleasant but sat down alongside her as indicated by the silent, uplift and direction of her head. Oddly, Oona seemed to have no clue about the inappropriateness of her being so closely seated next to a commoner in this instance. So far, Ben had only ever seen her subjects grovelling in front of her from a distance. Little did he know, that thinking in a purely utilitarian way was Oona's strength; that intimacy with Oona could only ever be a trap. Caught meanwhile in Oona's unintended pun, *Sopher* sat uncomfortably on the '*sofa*' and tried not to let his leg touch hers. She wasted no time getting straight down to business.

"Sopher, I have ascertained you have extraordinary knowledge regarding the 'quakes' to our land; she said the unfamiliar word carefully. You and I will investigate the causes of this dilemma and find a solution. I believe the instability was instigated through the unfortunate, but necessary, removal of the prior Monarch." Ben noticed Oona didn't say Ensley's name or take account of her own part in the situation. "I have searched and searched," she said, a little wildly, pointing to The Almanac balanced on her knee, "and there is only one instance where exile has gone wrong." Ben noticed one, thick strand of her hair had caught on the corner of her mouth

"It has happened before?" Ben asked, and Oona threw him a calculating look.

"Correct," she said in a tight, angry voice. "But an unstable Monarch has no place in the Fei realm. It will cause..." she sought for a word..." Permutations." Ben sensed the cold determination in her posture and decided to gain immunity for himself.

"How unfortunate," he said sympathetically, "I take it then that there have been similar catastrophes brought on by an absent Monarch's poor control of power?"

"Yes," said Oona very relieved that she was being both understood and respected. She smiled at the Sopher thing, and the Sopher thing made a wobbly smile back. "Look," she said, "I will show you." Shifting The Almanac towards him, she pointed to a strange illustrated tale that was easy to decipher because it involved line-drawn figures moving like stop-frame animation in a summary of a prior event. She closed it slightly. "Be warned," she said, "entries into The Almanac are always true; prepare yourself." Ben took a deep breath in preparation and held it for the longest time. He deciphered the images quickly and a slight squeak escaped from the side of his mouth. He put his head down, his breath working its way into a hum, tailing off into a slightly hysterical upward ascent.

"It's so shameful," said Oona captivated by the images. An absent hand wandered to her lip. Ben's shoulders shook slightly and Oona nodded her approval. She liked this Sopher, who was so affected by their traumatic Fei history that his body shuddered as the ground, too, had recently done. Ben harnessed as much self-control as he could, looked at the book again, but promptly exploded.

"Are you laughing?" asked the Monarch, bewildered.

"Yes, yes, I am so sorry, your Majesty." The danger of the situation made Ben even worse and he clutched his stomach, caught in a run of open guffaws. "My outrage," he wheezed, lying … "Affected me … sorry… so sorry."

Oona then did a very surprising thing, she leaned close to Ben, sniffed him up and down from knee to collarbone and started speaking to herself.

"Hmm, perhaps he is... no, I think not. Hybrid?" she mused. Oona was used to her kind losing control and giggling inappropriately. After making a full olfactory investigation to determine his origins, it was still slightly unclear what kind of a creature Sopher was, but she decided to excuse him anyway.

"Sopher, you must control yourself; we have work to do."

"Yes," squeaked Ben and looked again at the portrayal of the old Mad King clothed in full Georgian regalia. In the story, a strange ancestor of Finnian's, born with translucent red eyes painted his entire face a matching berry colour with his wand hand. Not being happy with the result, he then smoothed his nose into his face and made his head spherical. A reign of terror fell on the Court as the King descended into further madness and coloured every nearby face red. The King's mother, an elderly woman with a face like a hatchet, tried through many devices and enchantments to exile the King; at one stage, she tied his bed to a bull elephant and made it charge off into a desert. Each time, the King returned crazier and more determined than ever. Eventually, he was sent to the mortal sphere where he ended up on a fruit farm in Kent. There, he lived in a caravan and seemed content amidst the summer produce, showing a reverence to the cartons of harvested fruit, which surprised the farmer. Unfortunately, his work exacerbated his mania and he was inspired to do more with fruit. He could make juice dribble out of mouths every time his Fei victims tried to speak and he did all this remotely from a world away. Oona explained, "He was clearly a King of considerable talents though as Finnian often said, 'All Florian ever wanted to be was a redcurrant' – it was a disorder, you see and he cannot be blamed for it. The poor man finally got his wish when his head exploded. Too much juice," Oona concluded, and Ben snorted again. "I'm glad he's not from my line," she snorted. "Ours would never descend to such depths." Ben thought it was time he said something sensible.

"Did the next monarch fare better?"

"It was the start of the matrilineal option," said Oona. "There being no other 'suitable' males – it was a fortunate by-product of the disaster, females being generally so much more, um, focused." Ben glanced at the book and saw the fruit King's old mother sat on a big throne, elbows on the armrests, clutching sceptres in each hand as if she were holding a giant knife and fork. "Queen Rona the Determined," said Oona.

"She would have to be," reasoned Ben.

Oona closed the book. "I take from this scandalous tale that until a monarch is formally deposed, they have thrall over the kingdom," said Oona. "This is the situation we find ourselves in."

"Can the queen be deposed?"

"Only between sunrise and sunset on the day of the coronation."

"I see." There was a pause.

"We have no wish to kill our daughter; the other option," she murmured.

"No."

"Speak." Oona had a sense that Ben had something important to ask.

"Why would the current Queen wish to harm the kingdom?" Ben's unfortunate choice of the word 'current' brought another fruit image into his mind, and he made a superhuman effort to control himself.

"I don't believe she would or even dare to. She is... complicated. I believe she would have no awareness of her actions." Ben felt that they were wandering into the dangerous territory of disorders again. It was on the tip of his tongue to say, 'If you knew she was like this, why didn't you guide her?' Oona immediately jumped up and glared at him.

"That girl has been a trial to me from the start. She has had the devoted attention of the whole of the Court from her birth." Ben withdrew into himself, thinking privately that that may have been the problem too but Oona seemed to have lost interest in him and she busied herself placing The Almanac on a marble-topped table. Then she waved her wand and a gelatinous rectangular box formed around it. "Now, Sopher," she said, turning, "you will see the other thing that I have discovered." Within a microsecond she was sat back besides Ben; there, she wrestled his head to face hers and smeared a handful of gunk into both eyes.

"No, ow, no, stop," said Ben, realising with a horrible clarity the purpose of the love seat. "I can't see. I can't see anything," he said, terrified.

"Wait," commanded Oona "… for it to take hold." They waited. "Can you see?"

"No." A few moments passed.

"And now…?"

"No." Ben whimpered.

"How very strange. I have used the best revelation ointment so that you can have Fei eyes and share in my recent discovery. I cannot understand why you, as a human..." she raised her finger to stop Ben from interrupting, but he couldn't see it anyway, "… And don't say you are not humanish because I can smell you... cannot see," she continued. "Now I cannot show you my exciting clue, Sopher. How very disappointing." Ben, writhing in agony, didn't care about Oona's discovery. He hated her and just wanted to see again.

"Make it stop," he said.

"I cannot. It may wear off."

"May?" squeaked Ben.

"Almost certainly," she said, grabbing his arm. "I have another idea."

"Please, God no," groaned Ben.

"Don't take our Creator's name in vain," was the surprising and prim response.

She indicated to a beetle-like retainer who had been chewing dirt off a picture rail. It flew down. "Take the Sopher to the Great Hall. Carefully, too." She pushed Ben to the floor and the servant covered him with his body, clutched him with all its legs from the thorax to rear, and beat its wings fast.

"What's happening?" asked Ben

"Have no fear," Oona said in her kindest voice. "I will be with you shortly." As Ben ascended into the air, he heard the sound of someone rummaging around and objects clunking. He felt the fresh air on his face and heard Oona's delighted voice behind him saying, "Ah, there they are," before a lid slammed shut.

***

Smelling incense and earth in equal parts, Ben knew he had arrived in the Great Hall. As soon as he was deposited, quite carefully, on the cold, earthen floor he burst into tears. He couldn't help it; it was all very good being a stoic adventurer, but he had just had a very traumatic experience. Even though he hadn't been able to see that he was up in the air, he could sense the vacuum below him and knew that with just a slip, he could fall into that nothingness. His eyelids were open, but there was just blackness, though, after a fair bit of time he experienced cruel mirages of colour as if his eyes were recovering, which they were not. The strangeness of his situation and the realisation that he was alone in a world as uncaring as the one he'd left behind hit like a flood. And then there was a hand cradling his head, and a voice said,

"Don't cry, Sopher. It will be okay." Ben knew it was the

Changeling. He felt an overwhelming need to connect with someone human and not weird.

"My name's Ben - Ben is my name," he said, and the words came out in rags like the one wiping his face.

"It's good to meet you," said the mellow voice. "This is Ensley's work," he continued, dabbing at his cheek with the hanky, to show him what he was talking about. "She's a very clever girl and sewed it herself, without any magic. My name's Kosmo, by the way, not Incomer." Ben tried to say, 'Pleased to meet you too, Kosmo,' but only managed to say, "Pleased." He carried on crying.

"Would you like me to sing to you?" was said politely.

"No, you're okay, mate," said Ben and he was relieved to hear the Changeling laugh. "Can you help me sit up, though?"

"Certainly." There was a disorientating shift upwards, scissored within the crook of a muscular arm, and Ben thought with regret that this was not exactly how he'd imagined the moment. "You do realise don't you that you have just joined the ranks of a secret triad that knows my name. Use it carefully, friend."

"Kosmo, is there anything that can be done with my eyes?"

"I'm afraid I don't have any power. We are in her hands - the Queen Regent." Ben found it hard to believe Kosmo had no power at all. After all, he had seen Kosmo making flowers bloom suddenly in the Hall, and another thing, how would someone talk with such confidence, without fear, if he hadn't gained some supernatural ability. Kosmo anticipated him.

"I have learnt petty tricks in order to get by. The world lends itself to minor magic. It suffices," he added, a bit glumly and squeezing Ben's arm, warned him, "Hark, she comes, maintain your calm and all will be well."

Oona's strides were cloaked in the rustling of a heavy gown and she immediately got to work. "Hold him," she ordered. Ben braced himself for the next assault but was confused to find

Kosmo's hands merely engineering a chunky pair of spectacles onto the bridge of his nose. He looked around and saw everything in the palace through a shade of orange. It took a moment to compute the fact that he was actually no longer blind. "Well?" asked Oona.

"I see... everything."

"Good. Now look there." Ben followed her gaze from an upturned throne, and then upwards to the roof of the palace. He experimentally lifted the glasses away from his face by the rims and became immediately blind. He put them down and was immersed again in sunset orange and clarity. "How can I see?" He demanded.

"I have considered it. You undoubtedly have Fei blood in you. Translating your eyes from human to Fei meant that I took your vision. I worked in the absence of your honesty, Sopher." She looked at him meaningfully. "Regardless, you are now restored."

"I'm not though, am I?"

"It wants everything!" Oona explained with disgust to a nearby noblewoman who followed the correct protocol and said nothing back.

"Sopher," said Kosmo, strategically reverting to the name Oona knew him by, "Tell her highness what you see, interpret it, and we will discuss your vision problems afterwards." He turned and nodded to Oona. "Thank you, Mother," he said. The wand hand that was being raised high above Ben's head was lowered.

Ben was directed towards an immense strand, like a pale vine, snaking to the roof. As he looked, he experienced distortions if he so much moved his head a little. He tried to ignore this but it was hard. When he reached the throne, he attempted to pick the vine up, but the weight of it was incredible. Measuring the width of it, he found it was greater than the span of both hands. The party behind him craned forward with interest at these experiments. "A knife," Ben called back, and Kosmo took a small, jewelled dagger from his waist. Ben felt Oona's breath on his ear but ignored her as he dug into the fibrous texture, noting all the while the awful, sticky residue that was sticking his hands to the vine. He had to keep removing his holding hand, which came away with a prolonged rasp, just to avoid getting stuck. Also, he had to keep the pressure on Kosmo's knife, still prising the gash open, otherwise the edges just retracted back. "Help me," he said to a servant, and another knife was levered in alongside the former and together they widened the gap. He peered closer, closed his eyes, opened them again, and was presented with a close-up view of the structure of the strange material. Ben had always been able to see microscopically at will, and it was a total pain. Nobody wanted to be in conversation with a person and then suddenly be drawn to see deep within that person's pores. It was very off-putting. Shortly, Ben found himself on a visual journey, drifting onwards into amorphous material that occasionally formed into strange, block-type shapes, some of which were crystalline. The strands between each had a tension to them so that they pulled back and forth like coiled springs. Ben stood back saying, "Ah," as if a revelation had occurred, and a slight murmur rustled behind him. "I know what it is." He turned to Oona. "It's keratin based, it's hair, or, just like hair. I know this because I am a hairdresser." A series of impressions formed and fled across Oona's face as she tried to make sense of what he was saying. She found the mysterious word 'keratin' hard to link with the word, hair, and all understanding was demolished by the word 'hairdresser'. Wasn't the Sopher a scribe? Why would one dress hair, and into what? Ben could see he was in trouble again.

"It's a hobby, I like to do hair when I'm not writing pretty descriptions. Sometimes I write descriptions of hair too..." he blethered on.

"I think the Sopher means it is an invasion of a hair creature," Kosmo translated helpfully.

"Not quite. It is the product of a giant creature... actually, it's the protein-based spider silk from an enormous spider. That's why it's so sticky."

Oona grasped this but laboured with the thought of such a giant arachnid, until she had a brainwave.

"I know what this event all means now," she gasped, sopping up the credit for everything that had just been discovered. "At the time of the exile, small creatures had become set loose. The spider was not large at all at the moment of exile. Being caught in the vortex of the banishment, it travelled with the exiled Monarch, leaving behind a thread of its original size. We, being so small, are tethered by this enormous restraint, to her wheresoever she is. We are being bounced around like a bauble on the neck of a madwoman," she said with disgust, stamping the ground. "Sopher, you will find ways to disengage us from this silken thread, and you will have all our means at your disposal."

"But, but how…" Ben began but was silenced by a low clicking coming from Oona's throat. Oona's gills flared open and shut with her quick breaths. He noticed Kosmo engineering his way around her in a deft move, who then said in a staged whisper,

"Well done, Sopher, your talents will save us all. Let us discuss the ways forward." He took Ben by the arm and led him firmly away from the gathering towards his giant, stamping horse tethered outside. 'Oh no,' thought Ben for the umpteenth time and he took off his glasses and put them safely away in his trusty rucksack because he didn't want to see what was coming next.

Chapter 10 A Lambeth Fairy

"I think you've been sent to torment me," were the first words Frances said to her new neighbour. She had been appalled to get home from Bourne, only to find Ensley installed in 14B Kenyngton Row when she lived in flat 14A. As Frances later said,

"I felt in my water that things was going to go badly."

To say Ensley Knight was very high maintenance was an understatement, and even worse, all the residents seemed to think they had a close association and had turned on Frances too. The mutterings in the ground floor entranceway soon evolved into people shouting angrily into her letterbox. In the end Frances had called the lot of them out and given them what for. She also mentioned that as the young girl had 'probable' special needs, they should be ashamed of themselves for being so unsympathetic. Eventually, the angry hordes dispersed, looking both embarrassed and puzzled.

"I told them you're bonkers," she told Ensley that night.

"Everyone's being nice to me now," said Ensley happily.

"Well, I wouldn't push your luck; it's like a tinderbox round here. One false move and you're a gonner," she exaggerated. Ensley looked very confused.

"You'll be like a moth to the flame."

"They'll burn me?" Ensley looked terrified, and Frances thought it would be just as well to leave her thinking that if it stopped her being a pest.

"Right, now," she said, changing the subject, "We've got to sort this lot out..." Frances pointed to the enormous pile of miscellaneous items on the floor of Ensley's lounge. "You're a bloody kleptomaniac," she said.

"Ooh, we have maniacs back home too."

"I'll bet," said Frances with feeling. "Pity you can't be more of a discerning thief though." Frances picked up a blackened banana skin, and holding it at a distance, she instructed Ensley. "Watch me, this banana skin is worthless; we put it in the bin, because it's crap. This antique carriage clock isn't, and we put it '*back*' in Mrs Brown's living room. No," she said, as Ensley got up to go, "I'll do it. You've spent far too much time aggravating that poor woman already." Frances continued to work her way through the pile, and it took ages because Ensley hadn't seemed to make the distinction between what she called 'treasures' and other people called garbage. "A good rule of thumb is," said Frances, "If it smells, bin it, or don't touch it in the first place." Ensley dropped the bottle of Chanel Number 5 she was holding and took a step away from it as if it were plutonium.

"Well, that's just plain, downright silly. Look," she said spraying it in the air. "Doesn't that smell nice?"

"Foul," said Ensley, retreating to the back wall. "Sickness and death."

"Oh, well, I expect your nose is far more sensitive than ours, you being mystical and all. It may take you a while to adjust to our ways," she said with as much tolerance as she could muster.

"I love you so much, Frances Turner."

"Well, that's as may be, but you can't go around being so open with people, and you definitely can't go around nicking other people's stuff. It has to stop, and you have to buy your own from now on."

"How will I do that, dearest Frances?"

"You'll have to get a job, I suppose. That's what other girls do. You could be a secretary, like I was, and go and work in an office." She looked at Ensley's thunderstruck face. "We'll take it in stages. First, though, I'm teaching you about private and public; sit down and listen carefully." Ensley drew up a footstool very close to Frances, who pushed it back a little way with her foot. "Your flat is private, and it belongs to you. No-one goes in there unless you say." A smile appeared on Ensley's face. "However, you," she said pointing at Ensley and then at the balcony outside, "do not own either the balcony or other people's flats, so you must never hover outside nor wander in and out without being invited." This last instruction provoked an unexpected response.

"Communal, Frances, you said it was communal." Ensley did have a tendency to shift to anger in seconds. She jumped up and stamped her foot, just like her mother.

"Now you listen to me, madam, I said that we all share the entranceway in order to get in," Frances had learnt to be very specific, "But I said no such thing about you occupying the recliner chair in 14F for two nights, did I now? That's what we have doors for – to stop people coming in."

"Not in my world," Ensley muttered. Frances heard this but ignored it. She had seen how thin and weary Ensley had become in the last two weeks. The girl was like a stick; it must've been a terrible shock to move from one whole world to another when it wasn't expected. Ensley suddenly brightened.

"I've had an idea."

"Yes?"

"Now I know why the neighbours put up barricades, just like in the French Revolution. It was to stop me going in, wasn't it?" Frances jumped slightly.

"Yes, that's right, dear," she conceded. "Now, as you seem to have grasped it, why don't you go down to the chippie and get us a fish dinner. Remember to stay this side of the counter and hand over your money before you get the bag…and don't grab."

"Frances! The fishes and chip shop!" Ensley was beyond ecstatic… "But, can I get saveloy and chips please, because I don't like eating my aquatic relatives too well?"

"As you please, but come straight home and don't go nowhere near strange men."

"Of course. You're the best," said Ensley who had been

collecting colloquialisms as well as private property. Frances watched her from the balcony scuttling down the road in the faded to pink princess dress she had refused to either take off or wash. Sighing, she wheeled her shopping trolley laden with Ensley's thievings to the nearest door and knocked on it.

Nobody was prouder than Frances when Ensley started her first day at work, though even she had to admit that she was still a work in progress. Frances had been gratified to learn that Ensley could read, which was apparently quite unusual for a Fei person. Not only that, but she had taught Kosmo to read, too, so somewhere her son was a literate person, almost ready for the mortal world. "If only he could be here," Frances said over and again until one day she noticed the expression on Ensley's face and stopped.

Frances took Ensley first of all to the Jobcentre, where she pointed at Ensley as if she were a specimen on a platter. "This girl," she said, "is a friend's daughter from Albania, who is now dead." On hearing the word Albania, Ensley started to say, "My Papa …" quite convincingly, but Frances didn't want Ensley to say anything else, particularly about fairies in Eastern Europe, so she kicked her in the shins and said, "Shut up" under her breath. "She needs to learn skills, and I thought computer," Frances said, turning to admire the pristine rows of screens where people were busy typing away. A woman then helped them to fill in a form, which Frances said was like a, "Bloody Book," but then they hit problems when it turned out that Ensley was only sixteen or thereabouts and she had no identification papers.

"You are an illegal alien," said the case officer.

"No, I'm not. All my family are Fei from Fei England because we like the temperate climate. Well, we did until my mother made it all Jurassic and hot. Also," Ensley moved closer and took on a confidential tone, "My auntie is a tree in Dorchester and we can't uproot her. She's so established, you see."

"What is Fei?" asked the woman, perplexed.

"Fei, fairy. I'm a fairy queen." Frances covered her eyes with her hand and groaned.

"Is she okay?" whispered the woman.

"Not really, no," replied Frances with feeling. Ensley felt she was losing ground somehow.

"I might not look like a fairy to you because I haven't got any wings. I know you mortals all think we have to have wings to be authentic, but I'm too young. Some Fei don't even reach maturity until two hundred years. Then Kapow!"

"What? What's she talking about?"

"Ensley, you need to stop talking," Frances said quietly.

"No, I won't," Ensley said, infuriated. "It's the truth, and this stupid woman needs to '*listen and learn*!' So there!" Frances recognised her own phrase being re-cycled and also that Ensley was having some kind of meltdown.

"Go and run round the block, and we'll finish off. Now!" she added when Ensley stayed glaring at them both whilst rocking back and forth in her chair. Eventually she skulked to the door, and then they saw her charging past the plate glass windows in the direction of Streatham Common.

"Well, Mrs Turner, I think your first port of call is the doctor's surgery and, thereafter, the courts. She needs to be made a ward of court unless, of course, you are prepared to sponsor her?"

"I suppose so, but I'm going to have to get a private assessment at Harley Street. If she goes to a regular GP, they'll lock her up. Trust me, I know. Thank you very much for your *help*," said Frances in a less than sincere voice. She got wearily to her feet.

"What a pair," said the case officer to a passing colleague as Frances ambled out with her trolley. "I almost hope that neither of them comes back again." She cleared her desk by dumping the entire form in the waste paper basket. "Next," she yelled at a very old man in a cloth cap.

"I want to be a bus conductor," said the man in clipped English

"They don't even have them anymore."

"Damnation," said the man, taking his stick and striding out.

"I think I'm going mad," the case officer said to no one.

It turned out that Ensley was sane, according to Mr Ramchandani consultant psychiatrist. The verdict was the result of Ensley learning by rote a convincingly tragic tale of her life as an orphaned Roma individual. She even spoke a few phrases of Romani, rehearsed day and night. Luckily, oration is a Fei skill learnt from babyhood, so Ensley made a good performance of it. However, Ensley's distractibility and bluntness didn't escape the sage notice of the doctor, who said there were anomalies in her presentation.

"What does that mean when it's at home?" asked Frances, thinking to herself, we're doomed.

"I believe she's autistic; in fact, I'm convinced of it. You will need to become her guardian and help socialise her." He gave Ensley information all about it and she read it afterwards in a café.

"What is the point of it?" Ensley asked, in confusion.

"It means you've got a disorder."

"I don't think I have," Ensley explained. "All Fei are like this anyway." She wagged the leaflet at Frances cheerfully.

"So, I've just paid two hundred and fifty pounds to be told what you know and I guessed?"

"Apparently," said Ensley, who was sounding more and more like a regular teenager.

However, the visit was an investment that paid off. Ensley was ascribed a social worker, and the Home Office fast-tracked Ensley's application for permanent residency on the basis that Frances became her legal guardian, which was a lot more than just being a guarantor.

"So, I've ended up with a daughter that I didn't particularly want," Frances sniffed outside the Court on the great day she at last became a recognised parent.

"I know you don't mean that," Ensley said, snuggling into Frances's raincoated arms.

Frances had to admit that she was 'getting used' to Ensley and marvelled at the way her foster daughter quickly learnt to type at great speed and do remarkable things on the computer. In fact, Ensley had taught her how to use one, too, and she now had her own office in the spare room.

"You look very nice," said Frances when Ensley came round one day in a grey business suit complete with a blinding white shirt. "Don't fret about your red dress," she said, to placate and also orient her to the world of work, "You can always wear it next weekend."

"Ooh, can we go there now for a moment?"

"Where?" asked Frances, confused.

"Next weekend."

"No." Frances took a breath. "I don't think it would be possible for you and me to travel in that way like you used to. You have to go to work now, remember? To make a living?" Ensley smiled at her,

"Yes, yes, of course."

"Now mind you don't mention any of that fairy business to no one and keep your head down. No – not literally down, lift it back up now, there's a good girl. I mean, just talk about your work and going out to the pub or something."

"Righto," said Ensley, using one of her Papa's old phrases, and, together, they walked down to the bus stop. Frances saw her find a seat at the back and Ensley waved wildly at her as the bus moved off.

"You've done very well with her Mrs Turner," said Mrs Levy who was waiting for the next bus. "She's changed a lot."

"Thank you, yes she has," agreed Frances who walked away quite suddenly, really because she had to.

Sadly, things weren't all plain sailing. Ensley worked at a prestigious auction house inputting data, and this she did well.

Often, she would revert to using the one Fei travel ability she had left, which was to move through the fourth dimension in order to distribute documents at super speed. Irma in reprographics didn't like her much,

"She gets on my nerves – always appearing and disappearing right next to you when you don't expect her."

Everyone in the open plan office generally assumed she was foreign and, therefore a little unusual in her habits. Ensley sensibly said nothing to contradict this; so that for a while, she was generally tolerated and even liked for her 'quirky' ways. The problems stemmed from the staff Christmas party two months later. This was a big event in Ensley's mind because she felt it would be an opportunity to make friends. Every time she'd tried to join the clique by the coffee machine or in the canteen, she'd just ended up standing there like a spare part because the other people would ignore her or walk off. At the Christmas party, she discovered, they would all be seated around a table behind little place cards; this meant the others couldn't get away. Sadly, it didn't work.

"I warned you," said Frances when Ensley came home crying at midnight like a wrong version of Cinderella. "I told you not to wear that bloody pink dress, and definitely not a tiara too."

"But it's who I am Frances, undeniably who I am."

"Yes, well, you doesn't want no-one to know that do you?" Frances became hyper- cockney when she was upset and it did distress her seeing Ensley in such a state.

"Come on then, out with it. What did you do?"

"Frances," Ensley lifted her puffy face towards her, "I think you must be psychic like our family."

"Quite possibly," was the wry response.

"At first, they stared at the bottom of my dress, particularly at the raggedy ends where you cut the train off."

"To stop you falling down the outside steps again."

"Yes." Ensley tucked the asymmetrical bits underneath her

knees. "But, this nice boy from the framing department asked me if I'd like to dance anyway."

"Oh yes," said Frances knowingly.

"No, it's okay, he didn't say, 'Let's have sex'."

"Well, that's all right then."

"It wasn't a slow dance; it was a very fast dance, and I danced even faster than most. I suppose I was showing off a bit. I was a veritable blur, Frances."

"Oh, my giddy aunt."

"Yes, I was very giddy like your aunt, and then I became very thirsty, so I sat down in my seat next to Irma."

"Who's she?"

"The most popular girl in reprographics. I asked her for a pen and made her hunt for one in her handbag in the dark, even though she wasn't too keen. I encouraged her because it was so important to me. Then I explained very carefully what I was doing."

"What was you doing?"

"Why, changing my name card because it was wrong. It just said Ensley Knight, so I corrected it to Ensley Knight Queen of the Fei. I ran out of space on the front so I wrote.... and All the World to the Margins of What We Choose to See,' on the back."

Frances moaned softly to herself.

"They passed the card down the table and I tried to snatch it back, but they held it away from me and laughed. In consequence, I spilt stuff on them all."

"Spilt?"

"Well, threw actually, and poor Irma is now covered in meringue and cream."

"From what you've told me Irma had it coming, but two wrongs don't make a right. You'll have to apologise."

"It's worse than that. I have to go and see Mrs Bennet, the office manager, for a reprimand. She is a witch-like creature and it's after the holiday and I don't think I can bear to think about it all that endless time." Frances grabbed both of Ensley's hands.

"Now, you listen to me. I know you don't like lying, but just this once you're going to have to if you want to keep your job. You were drunk, on vodka, and that made you lose your temper when the others teased you." For once, Ensley didn't contradict Frances. "You didn't drink at the party, but at home just before. You did it to make yourself popular – Mrs Bennet will understand that."

"Yes," said Ensley quietly. "The problem is though, it didn't work?"

"What didn't?" asked Frances, confused once more.

"The invisible drinking. I'm still not popular." Frances couldn't think what to say, so she just patted her on the shoulder and they watched the fire die down together in silence.

Ensley would have preferred being laughed at to what came next, which was being ostracised. She didn't care about the formal warning on her blue file, which also had the wrong name on it, because she'd learnt her lesson about that and also about the crime of throwing food. It was the fact that the others couldn't see the kindness in her gestures. It was there: in the chocolates left on workstations, flowers put in the staff kitchen and healing potions left in pots next to snot-nosed people. Any common fairy, with their ability to see into things, would have got it right away... but in the office, nobody understood. In the end, the good impulses within Ensley got lost inside her, circled around in a maelstrom and started to attack her like a demented immune response. She also scowled a lot.

"I am not the person I think I am," she blurted out over tea one day.

"Course you are," said Frances moodily who was experiencing a return of her PTSD symptoms. Frances had booked another train ticket to Bourne without telling Ensley, to resume her search for her baby, though Ensley had seen a phone alert so she knew all about it anyway. "You just need to find yourself a direction.

Look at me."

"Isn't that called an obsession?" asked Ensley, who had been reading Frances's psychological therapy leaflets.

"Same thing, though some might call it a hobby."

Ensley stirred her tea round and round and round.

"I don't think trying to find Kosmo in a burial chamber is a hobby." Frances flushed in embarrassment, and for the first time ever, she shouted at Ensley.

"I've told you time and again, I don't know him by that name. To me he's Seretse and small, with tiny feet."

"But Frances, he isn't... he isn't that at all."

There was a brief moment when the two contemplated everything that people were not, and then silently, Ensley picked up her shoulder bag and left. After that, the two avoided each other on the outside landing for a few weeks.

Chapter 11 Two Worlds Collide

Ensley spent most evenings alone, though, for a time, she would go to a club where people danced, which she dared not do in case she made a fool of herself again. Instead, she sat in a darkened corner with a soft drink. Once a young man tried to pick her up, but she had lost her confidence in speaking to anyone. She managed to say, "Hello," before bolting for the door. The man, who had small features but pointed ears that were an inheritance from his father's line, thought it was an awful pity that she had gone. He could see that she was so sweet, so kind, but perhaps It just wasn't the right place for her. He went back to the club a few times, but he never saw her again.

In her lonely flat that night, Ensley listened to the melancholy clunk of the skateboards below. She attempted to write a poem about how the objects of the city related to the feelings within her, but she couldn't seem to marry them up in clever ways. Looking out the window she saw a dead shopping cart on its side and thought about rhyming trolly with brolley, but it wasn't raining; she tried again with 'paper bag' and the word 'sad' but then gave up. "It's crap," she said, imitating what she'd been taught, "We put it in the bin," which she did before brushing her long, black hair ferociously one hundred times in preparation for bed.

Unbeknown to Ensley, the Fei Kingdom that had been wrapped around her wrist with spider silk transferred temporarily to a lock of hair, but was then caught back up in the tines of the brush head. Ensley finished up by pushing her hair behind her ears and it was then that the silk wound around the butterfly clasp of her earring, and the world rested there for a time. This position was less precarious than previously because Ensley was very expressive with her hands when she talked. Now, the Fei people the world over enjoyed a static, aromatic existence that stemmed from Ensley's use of a posh conditioner. For a time, it seemed that the combined efforts of Sopher and Incomer had succeeded in achieving stability, though it took a while to get used to the distant stranded shadows that criss-crossed the exosphere. "Just like getting used to windmill generators in the sea, really," said a relieved Ben. "Once you get used to them, you don't even know they're there."

"I have no idea what you are talking about," said the cousin of Finnian, who didn't like the smell of Glosswell Shampoo and walked around with a lace hanky glued to his nose to prove a point.

Ensley had thought deeply about the direction her life was taking and also about Frances's advice, which she still respected, despite their falling out. She wondered if she could practise being the person she was by taking up a hobby and funnelling her efforts into that. "I am going to become an antiquarian," she told Mrs Levy who was walking her pug on the communal green.

"Well, my son has got an aquarium for sale if you're interested. He won't want much."

"Oh, no, thank you, I will be collecting old relics," said Ensley a little impatiently.

"Oh, oh, I see. Well, don't snap me up dear," she laughed. "I'm a bit of a relic myself."

"Don't worry, I won't. You'd be far too troublesome in my flat."

Mrs Levy thought she'd better have a word with Frances Turner. "She's getting worse again," she told her son Jay that night. "I hope she's not going to flood us all out now with tanks of water."

As it turned out, it wasn't the residents of Kenyngton Row who were troubled with floods, but Oona's Court and its surrounding areas. After a particularly difficult day at work, Ensley shed a few tears. It was extremely fortunate that she had become emotionally stagnated and didn't cry overlong; otherwise, the Fei world and everyone in it would have been fully submerged. Ensley had wiped her face and then nervously twiddled with the back of her earring, little realising that hot, salty water fell on her subjects in colossal splash just as if someone had upturned a cosmically giant bucket on them. The flood was mostly concentrated on the area where the spider thread originated, which was also a blessing, though Oona, who was yelling at everyone to, "Save the furniture," would have argued against that. The following sequence of events became known generally as 'The Wrath of the Queen,' and Ensley is unfortunately portrayed in The Almanac as a crazed looking alchemist, with greasy hair, clutching fluid-filled vials and beakers of smoke, ready to tip onto an unsuspecting world.

The populace had been filled in via carefully managed rumours regarding Ensley's hold on the Fei world, but most were originally sympathetic to her. "It wasn't her fault, it was an unforeseen occurrence," many said. "She's just a clutz anyway, poor dear... no disrespect intended." Their view of her didn't take account of the absolute determination and belief in hard work that was a feature of her mother's personality. Like Oona, Ensley liked to see things through in a systematic way. This positive quality could have consequences both good and bad, depending on the caprices of fate. In this instance, it was very bad. Ensley initially made a list of objectives that she had to follow in order to become a self-supporting antique dealer. She made a cup of coffee, stuck her pencil behind her ear and thought awhile; then, pulling the pencil and its suddenly adhered passenger world out, she unknowingly flicked the Fei world across the kitchen. Landing undamaged on its side, the white-tiled windowsill became the firmament, but the axis had altered, leaving half the world in blinding sunlight and plunging the rest into extended evenings. Great migrations occurred depending on the proclivities of creatures for nocturnal or diurnal lifestyles.

Eventually, the world did settle back into its former position in space-time, and gravitational forces resumed their hold. Oona shooed the strange, reptilian creatures basking on grass rafts in the palace grounds, back to where they came from. Though minutes had passed in Ensley's kitchen, the specifically-named, 'Trial of Excessive Water' had lasted some months, and many boats of fanciful construction, including gondolas and yachts, had been made to support the people.

Worse was to come. The pleasing return to moderate-length days and nights was enhanced by the sunny days, as human London was enjoying an unprecedented spell of high pressure. This was particularly nice as it was still only May. People were going about in tee-shirts and shorts saying, "Isn't it lovely? Isn't it weird?" and it was weird but it became most unpleasant for the Fei. At first, the intense sunshine deflected on the world through the kitchen window was most pleasing, though many had their hats go rigid with salt and sun combined. Oona was in her element and spent much time drifting down the principal highways on her back in the sun until the tributaries eventually dried out. The excess boats that littered the place were soon requisitioned and converted into covered verandas in this new cataclysm, documented later on as, 'The Torment of Blinding Skies.'

The ensuing drought was merciless and caused the populace to scream in shifts to get Ensley's attention, but to no avail, as she couldn't hear them. In the end, an expedition of three, sunburnt gnomes charged through a very ancient thin place in Southwark and, holding on to each other's tails, caravanned through the mayhem of traffic and pedestrians, all the way to Lambeth. Their entry into the human sphere was acknowledged by Oona who, feeling them go, assisted their journey on the other side through the use of runes, chants and the use of some of her remaining reserves of power.

The gnomes intended to plead with Ensley not to punish them

all if that was what she was doing. After all, she was known as a benevolent person, and they felt sure she would listen to their petition. Their hopes were dashed, however, when they got to her abode.

"What is it?" asked Fritz, who, at one hundred years was inexperienced.

"It's one of those door things." Steffi was the best travelled of the three.

"I don't like it," Fritz said, backing away.

"Well, none of us do," said Steffi, pushing him forward, "but we must be brave."

"We'll never get in," said Frederik, who was a gloomy kind of character.

"Why did you let him come? He's no help at all," whispered Fritz.

"I couldn't shake him off. He kept moaning that he wanted to see the person in charge, and that's that."

"Are you talking about me?' Frederik asked.

The two said, "Yes" and "No simultaneously. They then tried many strategies to get in the door without touching it. All Fei are conditioned to never touch one, so the first and most obvious idea was to get themselves invited in. According to legend, that is the only way that common Fei can get into a human door (though high ranking are an exception and even they prefer to crash through a window, the imprinted fear of doors being so great). Thinking hard, they attempted to make psychic contact with Ensley, whom they ascertained was actually within but with her mind elsewhere. This was true as Ensley was writing down her helpful cleaning objectives on her list. Once this strategy failed, they got sticks and beat on the lower part of the door, making sure they did not touch it with their hands. Finally, they formed a human pyramid with Frederik and Steffi, their tails linked over each other's shoulders for reinforcement, leaping up and down beneath, so that Fritz could reach and look through the wire reinforced glass of the upper portion. He mouthed his requests, threw caution to the wind, and beat frantically with his tiny fists before the pyramid collapsed beneath him. Disheartened and with their plans in ruins, they couldn't bear to make the exhausting journey back to Southwark or return to the horror of the home world. Instead, they went AWOL and charged westward, jumping between gutter, pavement, traffic island pedestrian area and shop awning until they found the grass of Wimbledon Common that they had sniffed from afar. They remain there to this day and their amazing journey has been captured into a ballad with a very jaunty rhythm because as Ben Sopher has written, "Nothing is bouncier than an Austrian gnome. Nothing."

Sadly, the efforts of the gnomes could not prevent the sad fate of fourteen Asrai water nymphs, delicate as minnows, who dried out in the drought, nor the two Gabron dwarves, caught in open country, who turned to stone.

"Perhaps she is oblivious? Or perhaps she is upset we let her down," were some opinions expressed between courtiers.

However, the tide of opinion really turned against her in the next disaster. Ensley's first objective was called 'Collecting and Placing'. She would need to prepare her flat for the arrival of her precious antiquities just until she found a shop to rent. Ensley had already made a good start on her stock and she knew the difference between Art Deco, Nouveaux, Baroque, Pop Art and many other trends. The second objective would be 'food disposal' so that the mould could not infest wooden furniture. The flat was very cluttered and grubby because she had neglected it in her depression. Objective three was called 'Sparkly Clean,' so once she had dragged furniture hither and thither, disposed the rotten food in bin bags and after putting small things into shoeboxes, she unwrapped some brand new cloths. Unfortunately, she botched the final stage. Being unfamiliar with basic rules of hygiene she mopped a spill of sour milk, then proceeded to wipe all the counter tops down with it before rinsing. Inevitably, the world of the Fei was caught up in the most appalling miasma from which there was no escape. Fairies have different constitutions to humans and cannot vomit, but they can retch... and retch they did. With wan faces, they would meet each other in the street, gain eye contact, gag, and then shamefacedly retreat behind closed doors.

Only Ben and Kosmo were out and about in the silent lanes and avenues. Kosmo made a ginger pomade for Ben to sniff, so that sorted him out. Kosmo, being human, could actually be sick and feel much better afterwards. In the meantime, Ensley, in Lambeth, was satisfied that she had made a good job of her spring cleaning. She had ignored the knock on the door heard earlier because she hadn't wanted to lose momentum. Whoever it was, would come again. Giving a final wipe to the dressing table ensured the Fei world stuck to the side of a pearl necklace. Exhausted, she sat on her doorstep with a fresh cup of tea and her hair tied in a duster as she had seen it done in old movies.

"You've been busy," said Frances going past.

"I certainly have," said Ensley, proudly. A minute later, Frances was back with a duster and polish.

"You've missed your door glass," she said, giving it a spray. "It's filthy!"

"Oh yeah. Thanks."

Frances rubbed away the tiny little hand prints patterned all over the glass.

***

Ben Sopher had never, even at the start, found it difficult to assimilate the notion of two parallel worlds containing vastly different life forms, because he was so open-minded. Generally, people sceptical of magical phenomena, say if it were true, then there would be evidence littered everywhere. Of course, there is, much in the same way that apparently extinct species are sometimes found going about their business outside of a Burger King or in the parking lot of Walmart; these are usually found by some random person or child who have been tricked into going shopping and are convinced there are more intriguing things in life than shelves of stuff you don't need. It's all a matter of keeping cheerful and on the lookout for something better. Ben, being optimistic and obsessive about detail ('picky' a good friend once called it), decided when he was thirty-five years old that he felt a need to understand the science between the two sphere realities of Fei and human Earth. The older he got, the less inclined he was to tolerate anyone saying things like, 'It's just the way it is,' and he baulked at the idea of settling into dumb acceptance like many older people do, (Fei included).

Using his old trick of blending in with the crowd, Ben followed a group of students into a physics lecture in 1985 and sat at the back, fully prepared to use his own brain to link theoretical knowledge with his practical experience. He would have to do this because no one in both worlds seemed to have the faintest clue how two inhabited worlds could have always simultaneously co-existed in time and space with so few people producing material about it. Ben suspected the explanation involved supernatural as well as scientific answers, but as the Fei hated science and the humans sneered at magic, it was clear that he was on his own in figuring it out. The blanket objection humans have to supernature was very unfortunate because Ben had actually travelled to Oxford, to this particular lecture, through magical means. He felt it was also a pity that he couldn't have attended a more up-to-date source of information, but there were no other time portals to relativity lectures. He shook off the clumped soil from his jacket, because the burrow had been a rather small one in Christchurch Meadows and promised himself that he wouldn't stay too long. The human sphere tended to get on his nerves after a while, and it was always a shock to have to return to dealing with people passing comment on everything, including himself, in a very intrusive way. He even wore a badge on his lapel that said, "Do I look like I give a shit?" It didn't work, though, because his face told everyone he did. Feeling suddenly very homesick, he reclined on the oak backrest and read aloud to the ceiling what he had written on his notepad; "I won't be long, don't worry." He wasn't sure if the message would carry forward, but it was important to at least try for the sake of the one he loved so far away (or so close, depending on how you looked at it). A girl next to him gave him a very funny look and said something to her neighbour. Ben noticed her dated batwing jumper and stonewashed jeans and smiled to himself. This also didn't go down too well with her.

A bearded man started a slide show, and the lecture began. At first it was very interesting because the man raised the theoretical idea of multiverses existing, growing exponentially like bubbles, but straightaway, he vetoed the idea of these places hosting life. He explained that the composition of these universes bore no relation to the known Earth.

"You don't know it very well then," said Ben a little more loudly than he intended.

"Did you say something?" the youngish lecturer asked, standing puzzled, pointer in hand.

"I said, how do you know there's no one in these worlds?"

"Hypothetically, we have to assume there isn't. Even according to the postulates of string theory that supports the view that there are other dimensions, there is no connectivity between these and us, so we can hardly check it out."

"Well, just because you can't get there, you can't just assume they're empty worlds."

"I certainly can, that's good science. If it's not demonstrable, it doesn't exist."

"I've never heard such unimaginative narrow-mindedness in my entire life."

"My dear young man, you can imagine as much as you like

that you have an intergalactic spaceship to travel to other regions, but," he suggested, "My personal feeling is you should be across the way in the arts faculty instead," At this, everybody started laughing, and Ben felt very exposed up there in the air, on the top row of the auditorium. The lecturer continued, "However, if you somehow manage it and bring a life form back, feel free to let us all know. May I?" he gestured back at the screen and turned his back.

Ben had a sudden wild urge to drag a few Fei with odd-shaped bodies into the burrow he'd just travelled through, but he had a feeling that this science crowd would somehow see it as a stunt and wouldn't believe the evidence of their eyes. 'You're all just sheep,' he thought, 'trapped in a mindset – bound to the past and too scared to think beyond the moment'; and then he felt sad at suddenly seeing all the young people looking so much alike from shoes to shirts to hairbands; their wet look hair gel capturing them in the dimming amber light of the times. 'When would they all learn?' he wondered and this prompted him to reflect that he wasn't exactly doing any learning himself.

The lecture continued with a whistlestop tour around black hole theories. It was very unfortunate that it was a warm early spring day, the estate staff had not turned off the heating and the lecturer's voice was fairly monosyllabic. When he eventually woke up, the lecturer had taken a detour from black holes to white matter. Ben found he had flopped, dribbling, onto a boy on his left.

"You were snoring," the student said, shouldering him away. Trying to tune back into the lecture, Ben's heart quickened hearing the exciting idea that white matter was like a barricade through which nothing could enter from our universe. 'I know this,' he thought, his brain recalling the dirty white entrances into but not *out of* the Fei world. He knew the other way was black and dense, hence the word, 'burrows.' The droning lecturer expounded on how energy matter could actually escape from a white hole. 'Yes, yes,' he thought, thinking about the energy-volatile Fei and their transformative powers. He could suddenly see them as bundles of matter, collapsing like the spine of a rat as they squeezed through space time into the human universe. He had that ability himself. He thought too about Kosmo as a baby being wrapped in the white, energetic power of the Fei to enable his passage to the Fei home world. Beginning to hum in his excitement, he suddenly realised the whole lecture was once more on pause because of him.

"If you don't stop, I'm going to have to ask you to leave."

"Sorry, so sorry," he said, meaning it because the man was such a good explainer even if his voice sounded as boring as hell.

"Please," he said, raising his hand like a kid. "Could I just ask? Can anything actually get in, I mean, into a white hole from our universe?"

"Actually, that's a very good question. This answer is no. Nothing can get in or affect the interior. Therefore, time within the white hole withstands our own universe's past. It is entirely separate – almost as if the laws of nature supplied a barricade, or, you could say, a door." Ben thought about how Oona stilled time many years ago, intent on creating he own version of history that resisted Earth history. The Fei world was naturally time resilient – it just needed a little magical poke to alter its linear progression.

"This is so freakin' interesting," Ben said, and all the students started to laugh again.

"I'm so glad you're getting something out of it," said Dr Lowenstein, who was shortly to become Professor Lowenstein, the laws of physics accelerating him to a time where sturdy probabilities could be fulfilled; though, he was in the dark about this at that moment. A very dark, dark, was his future, like a black hole from which there was no escape. Ben felt sad. He suddenly recognised Lowenstein and knew they would meet again, in very tragic circumstances thirty years from that moment. He shut his mind so that it wouldn't exist anymore in the present.

"Anyway," said Lowenstein, "the thing about any white hole is that it may have once been a black hole that became ever so small, to the point that it fails to behave on common sense principles and becomes quite arbitrary." For some reason, the idea of Oona crept irresistibly into Ben's mind. He saw her as a hail of whiteness as bolts of light extended from her fingertips; she was so like the universe she inhabited!

The lecture eventually concluded with Dr Lowenstein expounding on how white holes cannot exist for too long as they are presumed to be the final death throes of a black hole.

"... and remember," he said, "The important rule of thumb is: that a black hole cannot influence matter outside it, and a white hole is uninfluenceable from our side." This was an eureka moment for Ben as he pictured the Fei buckling the laws of nature. The ability of the Fei to travel to the human world and back was accountable to the universe being held in stasis, exactly at the moment of transformation between there being a black or white hole between the two spheres. Managing time was crucial in keeping this gateway between Fei and human Earth open. He did actually tell Oona about this on his return, but her reply was laconic rather than excited. "How tedious you are," she said, "Where's my doughnut?"

Ben felt satisfied with what he'd learnt, but as he slung his rucksack on, he glanced again at the last slide Dr Lowenstein had shown the class: a picture of two universes linked through a wormhole, as if one had spawned another. It was an arresting sight. Dr. Lowenstein was waiting for him though at the bottom of the steps. He shook his hand and said, "I'm sorry if I was a bit short with you. You're clearly not a student."

"No, just an interested layperson." Dr Lowenstein nodded. "You know, I'd love to see another universe, wouldn't you?" said Ben provokingly.

"Oh yes, of course, but sadly, we never will. The light trapping surface of the event horizon means that we, on the parent universe could never see the other world." Ben said nothing but just smiled, his eyes like a night-time cat. They parted, and Abe Lowenstein watched Ben and his shabby rucksack disappearing through the swing door in a daze. He shook himself thinking, what a strange person the interloper was, and what weird eyes he had. They reminded him of something... he'd seen once... but when and where he couldn't tell.

Ben found the student canteen and was perturbed to find that chai lattes and cheese and rosemary focaccias had not yet arrived in the U.K., so in the end he went straight home, back through the burrow. Shortly after, he realised he'd forgotten Oona's doughnut.

Chapter 12 The Ways Back Home

In Dorchester, Sarah Frayne put the remaining energy she had into knocking on the door where she recently attended a strange book launch, but once again it had a closed sign on it. She'd been back four times already, and the bookshop was always shut. It had to be open, it just had to be. She couldn't sleep properly, eat or concentrate on anything anymore, and she had to get answers. A tension headache tracked its way from the back of her left eye around her skull like a tight-fitting cap. Creating a visor with her hand, she peered through the window and caught a sudden movement in the back room of the shop; a light was switched off, and that door was shut, too. For a split second, she felt like giving up, but that wasn't the kind of person she was, and then suddenly she was hammering on the door with both fists.

"Open up, open the bloody door," she yelled and then started kicking it too.

"Can you hear me? I know you're there. You've done weird stuff to me - messed me up, with that book you sold me, and I'm not," she kicked the door, "Not, having it. D'you hear? I'll expose you. I'll tell everyone." She was so lost in her feelings; she nearly missed the subtle pat on her back.

"Would you like to come round?" asked Petey, his voice gentle.

"Yes. Yes, please," she said, immediately tamed, and followed mutely behind.

Inside the shop, Sarah, for a change, didn't know what to say. She had always had a tendency to pre-rehearse meetings in her mind, but she felt pretty drained. Petey told her to sit down, and she was a little startled to see a black coffee and two Hobnobs on a plate opposite a full mug of tea.

"Just like..." she gulped and stopped.

"Yes," said Petey, "Just what you normally have at eleven."

An ornate clock on the wall confirmed the hour. Eleven o'clock. They both looked at it as it chimed, but Petey waited until it stopped before talking. Sarah picked up her coffee, which wasn't too cold; she hated it lukewarm. She tried not to think about everything seeming very 'planned'.

"I tend not to worry too much about time these days," Petey said, apropos to nothing, "which is a privilege of being old and not having a work schedule. You realise that time has got a lot to do with perception when you're unaware of what day it is and forget to open up shop. This place is more of a..." Petey waved his hand to encompass the sink units and door, "... well, a place, really, more than a business." He took an absent bite out of one of Sarah's biscuits, ".... these days at least. Not like you, having to work day and night in order to get by." Sarah took the opportunity to speak about something that bothered her a lot at this point.

"Yes, that's what I want to talk about. It's the nights that are so bad..."

Petey cut her off. "Of course, no-one can escape time forever, but that's just ageing; even the long-living Fei can't get around that one. We're all slaves to it, mortals and Fei alike, and even I'll soon be dead and buried in that old churchyard outside of town. Do you know it?" Petey asked this quite cheerfully as if he were going somewhere a lot nicer than a damp and neglected graveyard where most of the ground had subsided. Sarah nodded. She did know it surprisingly, and wished she didn't. This was because her acquaintance with the little churchyard and its ancient lych gate was through her having *dreamt* about reading it at a later stage in the book. She was two stages away from the reality of ever having been there - and it was so vivid! Even worse, the dream was accreting detail every night. She recalled walking up the cracked paving stones to the main entrance, taking a key she knew that was there behind the notice board outside the ancient, wooden door, and turning it in a very precise way to engage the locks. It occurred to her the previous night how much the wood had warped on the old, studded door. She still felt the twisted brass ring handle that was brightly discordant against the dull iron struts running down the door. She hadn't turned that handle yet, but she knew, eventually, that she would. She felt herself drifting away, lost in a memory of something she hadn't even done in real life, and Petey was still banging on and on about time as she reflected. He leaned forward then and spoke confidentially,

"The thing is," he said, as Sarah ignored him and bent down to her bag on the floor to lift up something heavy, "Our perception is flawed. There is no such thing as time, and we can't put up with flux like the Fei can. I mean, they draw pretty pictures to remember what they did, and they're happy with that. We have to demarcate the days with absolute precision to feel comfortable, and if we can't keep up with the schedule, it's treated as a disability. Being out of time is tantamount to being slightly mad." He sat up straight and took on a perky tone. "Just out of interest, how old do you feel in this present moment, and more importantly, how do you *feel* about it?"

"A hundred and ten," said Sarah, slamming a large red book on the table, making the mugs jump, "... and I'm completely pissed off, so, you either start talking sense or I'm going." Petey looked at her steadily.

"But where are you going to go?" he asked. Sarah thought about this and leaned back.

"Not got the faintest," and then she laughed hysterically, smashing the tension into bits. "I'm afraid, I've only got two reactions in my repertoire these days: storming in and storming out." She smiled disarmingly. Petey liked her very much, as he knew he would. There was so much more to her than the angry face she had been hiding behind.

"Why don't you open the book?" he suggested.

"I hardly dare. She exhaled and messed around with her biscuit. "It was a terrible shock recognising myself in it when I started to read... and that boy's in it too, isn't he? The one from the queue."

"Ben, yes, he's an important character."

"How can you call him a character? He's a real person, isn't he? You make him sound like he's nothing."

"The thing is, Sarah... sorry, do you mind me calling you Sarah?"

"As you seem on easy terms with my name, I suppose not." She adopted a posture she hadn't used for a while and stared at Petey with considerable intensity. Despite himself he wriggled his feet in his shoes. She was definitely someone to reckon with; an uncompromising equal.

"Ben's very much a someone, but he's caught in an alternate reality. If he doesn't assume responsibility for his own role in that, the contingent time line he's in doesn't come to fruition."

"How horrible. So, he's trapped in to being an actor in someone else's story!"

"Well, let's just say he's working his way through a particular plotline." Sarah raised her eyebrows.

"Ben could have chosen to not go down that initial burrow - but he did, freely. I suppose you could say he's both living history and making it at the same time."

"What history? That's not how history is made. I think that's bollocks. What would have happened to those other people in the plotline, who are also apparently real, if he hadn't turned up to kick start the story? What about Frances and Ensley in Lambeth? Are we all making it up as we're going along?"

Petey said, almost to himself, "Not at all, we're dealing with truths here. We are raising up stories that are always there but, sometimes, they aren't told." He swivelled the book round to face Sarah and thumbed along until he found the page that he was in, sat opposite a girl with mid-length curly hair, her evicted bag collapsed against her chair leg. The tap in the sink had a suspended drop of water underneath it. Sarah went to turn the page, but Petey stilled her hand.

"Wait, until we finish the conversation. There's a reason why you avoided reading on at home, isn't there?"

"Yes," she sighed. "I was curious but worried too because I felt different when I was dreaming about the church. I didn't want to break the spell. It's been a long time since I felt okay. When I was there, I felt so happy like I used to. I didn't even want to wake up every morning, and when I did, I felt knackered as if..."

"As if you were actually living your *real* life in your night dreams," he added.

"Yes. That's pretty much it."

"I'm already caught in the book, aren't I?" Sarah realised she was shaking.

Petey shovelled some sugar into her coffee, and then he made her drink it.

"You can walk away from here right now, and your character trajectory will end. It's okay."

"And the book will have dead ends. It will be a rubbish book," Sarah's tone suggested that she cared very deeply about that.

"Well, it won't win any awards, but we don't care. That's not what it's about. Our story will remain intact."

"We?"

"Myself and him." Petey took a formal photograph of two men in dress suits off a shelf. He pointed to a young man with a flower in his buttonhole. "His name was Kosmo, and he was stolen by fairies." He laughed. "He was also my husband - I loved him very much." His index finger briefly stroked the young man's face. Sarah put on her glasses and peered closer. "Yes," said Petey voicing her hidden reaction, "he was much younger than me. Shoulda known it wouldn't have worked out." Sarah was unclear whether Petey was referring to the age or fairy thing. She wondered if she would ever read about them both in the plotline. She watched him put the frame carefully back on the shelf and made a snap decision.

"I think, perhaps I would like to be in the story after all."

"Good. Now I can tell you what you're here for. I want you to write my will and be my executor." This request had a strange effect on Sarah. Her face tightened perceptibly and she stuffed the book back in her bag.

"I can't do that. I'm not a lawyer. What made you think...?" She headed to the back door.

"Yes, you are. You mustn't tell lies. It's a small town; people know who you are and it's not that image of yourself you perpetuate on social media." Petey's voice was very calm but took on a firmness as he spoke. "It wasn't your fault what happened with that asylum seeker. The odds were stacked against him."

"How did you know? How can you know?" she spluttered. "You had no idea what that did to me. I had to escort him to the plane, otherwise, they would have done it. He said it wasn't my fault."

"It wasn't."

"He had special needs; he was excited about going on a plane." She dropped her bag and started sobbing. "I wanted to help people - I only ever wanted to help people."

"And that's why," said Petey guiding her back to the chair, "You gave free legal assistance and spent hours doing paperwork at the asylum seekers charity after you'd finished work. You wanted to influence people who were blind and uncaring, and eventually after you had a breakdown, you took on a role as a social media influencer and commentator so that you could fail to influence an audience about things that didn't matter anyway. You set yourself up to fail, in a no-win situation; to prove to yourself that you had no power at all, over and over again."

"If you put this in that bloody book," she said, "I'll have you. I'll sue you."

"At last," said Petey, "Spoken like a lawyer."

Sarah left two hours later and returned the following week with a ream of documents for Petey to sign. They had many discussions about the power of the book to influence destiny, but Petey always refuted this.

"After all," he said on one occasion, "the odds of you and I meeting in a small, market town were incredibly high. I needed a lawyer whom I could trust and that had the same kind of values that I did. Also," he said, his tone becoming slightly more mysterious, "Your story would have been there regardless of it being mentioned in the book. Really, the book just, sort of, raised it up and made it public."

"But that's exactly my point." Sarah's voice was a mixture of repressed excitement and awe. "The fact that it's mentioned does change the course of history. Once people know things, and its shared, a kind of collective consciousness develops. People remember information that they thought was irrelevant and they tend to take on a new power, or significance; a key opens in an unknown door." Sarah said this with a great sense of irony.

"Perhaps... perhaps not." Petey was noncommittal. "I suppose it depends on how what's mentioned in the book grabs the reader in the first place. Some people can be remarkably unaffected by even quite extreme stuff." He sniffed. "Just think about how we react to global disasters on the news. Also, as I said, we probably would have met anyway, and what difference does it make, us being described as having a cup of tea or making estate decisions? Or," he added, his pace slowing, "hearing your backstory. I mean, we're small players, aren't we? How can *we* make a difference?" He smiled at her, a luxurious cat's smile. Sarah looked out onto the dusty road, seeing a light lasering between the buildings, making landfall onto a discarded crisp packet.

"......All the difference in the world," she murmured.... "To me, at least."

Sarah's visits to the shop became a regular thing, and Sarah attributed her healing and new sense of purpose to their friendship. No-one was sorrier than she was when he later died at the age of eighty-five. Petey left her the shop in his will as he'd promised, and she followed his burial wishes to the letter. This seemingly trivial subplot turned on private significances, held away from the readers' eyes, until the appropriate moment, which of course is an author's prerogative and is very respectful of the fictional characters' wishes. Frayne's bookstore, meanwhile, became a very successful landmark in the high street and was extended four times over, growing like an unnatural plant that engulfed the two adjacent coffee shops. Sarah often laughed that her particular purpose in the book was really as a mechanism to explain the effects of trauma - how it could literally extract you out of time and the here and now, but also how it was possible to re-invent yourself and in this way, grab time and bend it to your will. The fairies had been doing this for thousands of years... very effectively. Her later transition into a being a shopkeeper was a seamless evolution. She often said, "I'm quite content taking a backstage role - big dramas are just not for me." She herself had gained personal equilibrium and a steady income from her interactions with the weird book, so that was okay. She deliberately failed to question the supernatural nature of her new start and put it all down to being a bit more imaginative about her situation.

Meanwhile, others also gained a psychological stability from visiting the bookstore that was so profound that visitors wondered if there was magic at play on the premises. In time, the three buildings on the row were linked into and modelled on Shakespeare and Company in Paris. They provided both resting places and inspiration to the inquisitive and weary in a busy world. Shortly after it first opened a middle-aged woman in the throes of menopause lay in a heap underneath a bookcase in the children's section, explaining that was all she could cope with at present. She didn't actually read the books but slept and sweated under the ones she had loved as a child. Sarah asked her if she wouldn't prefer to lie on the chaise lounge in the self-help section, but the woman snapped that the whole point was to saturate herself in positivity and *not* assimilate the notion that there was anything fundamentally wrong with her. She shifted herself a little so that she was immediately under E Nesbit and closed her eyes. It was then that Sarah realised that the woman believed she was engaging with the texts in her dreams and so she put a cushion under her head. A passing person thoughtfully threw a cellular blanket over her. After a while, the woman moved on to poetry, which coated her in a veneer of restlessness as she slept, just as if she'd been plugged into the mains.

"How's it going?" asked Sarah, when she awoke her one evening, handing over a plate of food.

"Thanks, I needed the stimulus," the woman said, spooning up a large mouthful of curry into her mouth. "I'm confronting a few demons... it's tricky, but useful. Goodness knows where I'll go next, though," she said, a little uncertainly, glancing round the section."

"How about modern fiction?"

"No, not at present, it's a bit too gritty for me. I need answers, I don't need to re-live stuff," and she unbuttoned a very well-worn crocheted cardigan and fanned her face.

Strangely enough, her final destination, after a few weeks in Science Fiction and Fantasy, which she felt was "Freeing," was in the history section. She explained to a man who was leaning over her trying to get to volume two of Gibbon's Decline and Fall of the Roman Empire, that she understood a little about her own supposed breakdown now. "It's a natural process," she said. "Like the collapse of the Roman Empire. Disintegration is a mere sloughing off of peripheral areas of your life that are no longer useful to the concept of yourself. My own life was the same as the overblown Empire - it was too big, too exhausting to maintain. It's not us that fail or have breakdowns; it's the stuff we carry that doesn't make sense anymore. I don't know why I got so anxious about things not adding up." The man nodded,

"I get that," he said. "Sometimes we just need to let it all go."

"Yes, exactly," she said. "Um, I hope you're not going to drop that bloody great tome on me."

"Getting out of the way would help," he said under his breath - and that's exactly what she did. Sarah was saddened when she couldn't find her anywhere the next day, but that's what Frayne's is like - very transitory, and people can stay or go as they please. If they buy books, that's a real bonus.

"I wonder what her name was?" Sarah said to a co-worker. "I didn't even think of asking."

"Does it matter?" asked Jen flippantly.

"I think I should at least have asked. Perhaps I'll call her after a mythical figure... Ariadne, say, because she worked her way through a maze."

"Hey, let's all do it," said Jen. "Call me Scarlett O'Hara," she said switching on the desk fan and flicking her hair backwards.

"Suits you, you spoilt little bitch."

Jen picked up the abandoned cushion, whacked it around Sarah's head and chased her round the shop jumping over bean bags and soft furnishings. A few kids took the opportunity to join in, and they all ended up collapsed on the floor in the cafe section. That's exactly what Frayne's' bookshop is like - very unpredictable. Some die-hard Fei, who maintain an affection for Fei Earth love it and use a local burrow to travel there. They don't read, because they can't, they just stroke the books, hog the best chairs and wait until the chaos breaks out. Somebody recently gave a one-star review on a website because it apparently caters in the main to the freaks and oddbods of the town. The person didn't like the atmosphere of anything goes.

People in Fancy Dress! was the exasperated subject heading of the review.

***

Across town, Terri threw Ben's red book into her bag and ran full pelt down the road, pushing pedestrians out of her way. When she got to the bookstore it was still called Dayes, was decrepit, and also shut. Clearly, that part of the story she'd read was pure fiction. She felt a great sense of disappointment as she was quite getting into this magical stuff; it was such a blast. As it was her day off and she'd already traipsed across town, she thought she might as well go into the coffee bar next door to the bookshop. At the counter a young woman was arguing with the barista.

"It was three pounds for a latte last week and four this." The man shrugged.

"Cost of living? I don't know, I only work here. Things change."

The woman begrudgingly paid the price and sat in a window seat, where she talked loudly and in a complaining voice to someone on her phone. Unfortunately, the cafe was full, so Terri ended up seated opposite, and when the call ended, she found herself being apprised next. The eyes opposite lingered for a while on her own; the Cleopatra eye liner drawn to a point and metallic green eyeshadow. A barely hidden distasteful expression emerged but a conversation was initiated. Clearly, Terri would have to do.

"They changed the price."

"Things do change."

"That's what he said." She pointed to the busy barista who realised he was being talked about and scowled at her.

"Well, they do, don't they? I've learnt to expect the unexpected."

The woman across from her didn't want this extra information.

"Yeah, right," she said and was going to ghost Terri, but Terri was already occupied pulling the red book out of her bag.

Opening it, she was delighted to see that the book had altered and the she, Terri, was in a stuffy cafe, doubting the plausibility of the book being able to parallel reality. She realised she would just have to wait to see if the bookshop changed over time, and as she ruminated, her actual thoughts were depicted in the form of thought bubbles on the page. The section ended with her being very rude to the girl who sat opposite her, who, she apparently and thankfully, never saw again.

"You're another mug who bought that stupid book, then?" Terri shut the book and lifted her eyes.

"Actually, I'm quite enjoying it."

"Well, I've read it right through, and it's just mostly pictures. Horrible ones of things with teeth and labelled with close-up illustrations, for information, just as if they were real. It gave me the creeps."

"Oh, that's weird. I haven't seen many pictures, it's mostly just a story about a boy in another world."

"Trust me to get a dud. There aren't even any page numbers; I couldn't keep track." As she spoke her face crinkled into frustrated lines. "I feel like going back to get a refund from that stupid old man." Terri felt protective of Petey, even in his presentation as a fictional character, though she'd never met him personally. She did know in reality he was part of the very small gay community in the town and that was enough to make her snap,

"They don't take returns."

"How do you know that?"

"Says so on the door," Terri lied. "Anyway, terms and conditions don't take account of someone being too dense and narrow-minded to understand a text."

"How dare you!" said the girl, named Izzy. She jumped up, her squarish shoulders blocking out the light that was refracting right into Terri's eyes through the plate glass window.

"Oh, I dare," said Terri picking up her bag. "You paid your money; you had your chance, and you blew it."

"What the fuck are you on about?"

"Oh, I think you know. You're not exactly Ms Popularity at the moment, are you? It's your own fault, too. Open your eyes," was the parting shot. Terri put the book in her bag and swanned out of the door leaving Izzy to reflect that the aggressive girl sounded like Sarah these days who she wasn't getting on too well with; her always banging on about being broad-minded and spending all her time hanging out with that old man. Suddenly her thoughts paused, she had an idea... of course! Perhaps Sarah could get her a refund. She'd probably call her after she'd finished drinking her very expensive latte. Then she had to busy herself with a serviette around the eyes. She wondered how that woman knew she had a problem with reading. But it wasn't her fault the whole world was geared to reading stuff. She could just about manage with her phone and the rest of the time she pretended. Eventually people did find out though, and then they acted all shocked. A tiny bit of coffee spilt on her own copy, and as she wiped it the book fell open on a page where it explained in big bold words that the Fei couldn't read either. Suddenly Izzy felt much more cheerful and she was even happier when she realised that she'd just read and made sense of the words on the page. Because of that, she never did return the book.

A mile away, in Wholegrains, Phil was filling waist-high containers whilst the weak spring sunshine flooded into the shop. The warmth was intensified by the glass, and it felt good on his back, especially on the old wound that had never really healed despite the strange creams and unguents he'd been given to put on it. 'Still,' he thought. 'It could've been worse. I could be dead now.' He leant on the counter then and studied his big, red book, left open at a full-page picture where Ben was striding around a translucent globe superimposed within another one, rucksack on back. Phil had watched him march through ferocious snow storms. Later he would also see him struggling with drenching water and afterwards, relentless, blazing sun. He glanced across at the barometer on the shelf and saw that it tallied with the snow picture. 'They seem to be experiencing some pretty severe weather over there,' he thought to himself. 'Poor bloke.'

Chapter 13 The Freeze and the Thaw

Kosmo and Ben were in hysterics. Kosmo was flopped over a chair, gasping for breath. A short while before they had evicted a Weird Woman in black rags from the Great Hall. It had been a fairly prolonged struggle because the woman had taken a great shine to Ben from the moment they had recruited her to try and get rid of the giant spider's web, and she hadn't wanted to go.

"Lawks," you isn't going to shift me now, are you, when I've just got meself settled?" she had said, but as she had been crouched in one position for around three weeks muttering runes, it seemed unlikely that she would achieve anything at all. Even worse, neither of them had been convinced that the things she was saying were actually spells.

"Did she say 'large fleas'?" asked Ben, puzzled, making Kosmo explode.

"Shush. I think it was 'enlarge' and then the word 'please'." The woman muttered the same thing again. "My apologies," said Kosmo, "It is 'fleas', oh, yes, and 'enlarge' but that's no good, we don't want anything made bigger; that's the problem we already have. I think the 'fleas' bit is just an aside, though. Look, she's scratching now." Kosmo had been sceptical from the start at recruiting the woman named, 'Dian' from the woods where she sat by an old well giving prophesies.

"It won't work," Kosmo had said from the start. I don't think she's got the kind of power you're thinking about.

"Well, I think it's worth a try, after all she looks like a witch and she's even got green skin."

"Doesn't mean a thing. That's just the chlorophyll she's storing because the winter has been so extended." Ben found this an unlikely explanation, because the woman didn't look like a tree to him. He was also surprised that Kosmo used such a scientific word as 'chlorophyll', given that the Fei espouse a contempt for science anyway, but Kosmo was amused and wondered how else they could all talk about real things.

"Yeah, but they don't believe in science, just magic."

"True," but describing isn't the same as seeing the world scientifically. Anyway," said Kosmo, about Dian, "I asked her and she doesn't want to come."

"Couldn't it just be a sign that she doesn't want to use her powers unselfishly?" said Ben, stubbornly maintaining his point of view. "After all, witches are meant to be very self-centred." Kosmo gave him an appraising look. He didn't want to flatten Ben's initiatives when he had been having such a difficult time with his eyesight. It was nice to see him displaying confidence even though it was slightly embarrassing to Kosmo that Ben was stereotyping Dian as hag-like because she was old; after all, he could have shown him a real hag like Peg Powler who inhabited a river in the Northern territories, though it could have been dangerous and she could have drowned them both. Eventually, he decided to be a supportive friend and follow Ben's plan.

"I propose we grab her and wrap her in a blanket," Kosmo had suggested, and this they had done, afterwards throwing her in the back of a cart pulled by a helpful Kelpie friend. Ben had to lie across Dian to prevent her from escaping and the so-called 'witch' enjoyed this immensely. Of course, she could have punched the boy out with no difficulty at all, but it was boring at the well, and she hadn't had any company for days. She decided to play along,

"Help, oh help, I'm being borrowed by a naughty boy. Murder, assassins," she bawled. The blanket muffled her words a little so she screeched ever louder, alerting some heathcroppers along the way, who were stamping away snow with their hooves and plucking up the blades of grass with their hands. The whole herd ended up following the cart to see what was going on, and many others joined in so that there was a considerable crowd laughing at the antics in the end. That was quite a while ago, and Ben and Kosmo now had to get rid of her before Oona returned to survey their lack of progress. She had seen Dian, one whom she considered a very poor specimen, grovelling on the ground the last time she had visited unexpectedly. Oona had been clothed from head to foot in green velvet so that only her eyes were visible. On her head was a strange hat, coiled in soft folds like a snake. In fact, it was a snake, a green mamba from East Africa, that was having a horrible time. It emitted long, drawn-out hisses due to the fact it was trapped in a frozen moment in the freezing atmosphere of the Hall. Oona's non-wand hand occasionally reached up to tuck the desperate creature back in place when it managed to break through the charm. She glanced again at Dian muttering and swaying, and knew the old fool was talking random words about poor dinners and lonely days. She raised one eyebrow at Kosmo, who looked shifty, explaining,

"It might be worth a try."

"You young men had better resolve this situation before I return and evict this creature," she had growled, but she also seemed to find the situation amusing. Kosmo wondered if that were a snigger escaping the velvet muffler covering her mouth. In reality, Oona was not at all concerned about the web tether anymore. The momentum of the world had resumed its usual spin; she had enjoyed a nice hibernation recently, and she felt immensely powerful. Clearly, her daughter had limited powers still, as nothing further had occurred and she felt nicely secure in her position as Regent. In the meantime, she found tormenting the boys by setting them an impossible task most amusing. She had spied on them many times and had nearly been impaled by flying shards of marble when they had employed a phalanx of workmen to blast the edge of the throne with their wand hands. Now, half of the back of the chair was missing, making it even more imbalanced. It was all very entertaining. Feeling an agitated twist by her temple, she realised that if she didn't move to a warmer room soon, her costume accessory would undoubtedly expire. She stroked its head to reassure it and promised it that she would create an orb of fire above its cage to reanimate it. Before she left, she adjusted the wool coat on Kosmo, plonked a felt hat on Ben as if he were a doll, and patted him on the bottom very inappropriately. "The Sopher's eyes have improved?" she asked, knowing full well they had as Ben tended to peer over the glasses occasionally, caught between the vision being imprecise but adequate with them on and also with them off.

"Yes, Mother, he improves greatly," affirmed Kosmo. "Soon, we may dispense with the eyeglasses altogether." Oona lost interest then and vanished, because she suddenly felt very chilled and this was exacerbated because she was a cold-blooded woman anyway. At the time of decision-making, it had seemed a sensible idea to move the world to a colder epoch, because the heat of the Devonian time had exacerbated the terrible sour smell caused by her daughter's cruel manipulations of the world. The coldness had curtailed the smells somewhat and even prompted a great fashion where her subjects walked around with triangular lengths of linen, like bunting, tied around their faces to avoid the lingering odour. All excepting the Knight Clan, who had weird olfactory tastes and tolerated odd smells. Oona, standing invisible for moments before she lurched through the fourth dimension, heard Kosmo calling Fabian, Finnian's cousin, 'Peculiar' as he passed the entranceway, breathing the air into his lungs.

"'Tis wondrous to have such a rare, breathable air," he said.

"That's a matter of opinion," said Ben, tying his sensible bandana closer around his nose. He wasn't one for flags on faces.

"We Knights are known for having delicate constitutions and fine sensibilities," the man said. "The frozen air is invigorating."

"... Still stinks," said Ben.

"Come, you must admit that the previous odour, though fierce,

184

was most absorbing."

"Not really." Fabian glared at Ben, whom he considered an upstart. The boy deserved to be killed for even daring to speak to him.

"Minion," he spat, balling his fists to his chest and turning greyish in colour all over. As a man of rock, he unleashed himself through the seven-foot snow drift blocking the exit of the hall in the form of a seven-foot circumference boulder. Fabian left a circular tunnel behind him that held momentarily before collapsing behind him.

"He is very lucky to be a Knight really, in this situation," Kosmo mused. "For one, Knights are earthy creatures constitutionally enamoured of decomposing smells, which is why that idiot is walking around thinking he is in a fragrant meadow. The other is that his transformation can take account of the strange climatic conditions we find ourselves in."

"That's very interesting," said Ben, still rather stunned at Fabian's dramatic shape- shifting, "But remember to use contractions when you speak. Don't say, 'he is.' We have to keep you speaking like a modern man." Kosmo nodded.

"I will, I mean, I'll try and remember."

Ben mused aloud, "I still don't get why Oona's brought us to this time; we're no better off."

"Hush," said Kosmo, "I think it was a mistake."

It was very unfortunate that Oona had tried to lessen the trials of her subjects by choosing the exact moment in history,1881 when both worlds were experiencing a little ice age. In fact, in Fei sphere, conditions were even worse in the Fei northern hemisphere because the axial tilt was still slightly off, following Ensley's seismic disruptions. No-one was getting enough sun and food was being rationed out.

"Going back to the smell problem," said Kosmo, "Ensley takes after her father's line. I mean, she had a nose like a Barghest, for goodness' sake. I can't tell you how many times I found her face down in rough grassland, sniffing the earth."

Ben found this comment extremely strange, but he let it pass because, in those early days, it was unusual for Kosmo to talk about Ensley, a fact that intrigued him greatly.

"Ben, we're drifting off-topic," said Kosmo proudly showing off his new, human-style colloquialism. "We have to get rid of the Weird Woman."

How they eventually got Dian out was through trickery. "You must be very hungry, dear Dian?" Kosmo sympathised, touching her shoulder briefly.

"No, luvvie, I has everythings I needs. I have my mash, and I licks the drops coming off them stalactites for me thirst." She gave Kosmo a smirk. She didn't like him too much, creepy little incomer sort, and she wasn't falling for it. As she grinned, Ben noticed the green mush that had caught on her grinding molars that rounded the front of her mouth like a post and rail fence.

"Dian...," commenced Ben.

"Yes, my dear heart. I loves you so, come closer to us and I will embrace you in these twidddick arms, forever if you likes."

"I would *like* to make you a gift," said Ben, maintaining his distance from her."

"A gift, oh you is kind. Dian was wildly excited. She'd never had a present before. What is it?" She tried to stumble up but her legs had gone dead.

"I have got for you, some chocolate and a shiny bracelet."

"Oh, oh, chocolate," she said, ignoring the mention of jewellery. "I only ever 'ad it once, and it made me head buzz remarkably. Oona won't let us have it no more. Where is it? Give it to me," she said, reaching forward.

"It's in my backpack, you must come with me."

"But your backpack is on your back, dear heart."

"I have another one by the hazel stands."

"Oh!"

Dian wasn't too bright and tended to work her way through

one thought at a time. For starters, she knew that Ben had made a home for himself by the little creek, which had then become a gothic folly once they all landed in the present day. It made perfect sense to follow him to this destination. When she got there, she would have chocolate. Afterwards, she would lure Ben back to her well through trickery (or force), and after that, she would put on him the embroidered gown she had stored in a chest for many a day. Ben would go abroad and draw people back to her so she could have chats, and even if no one came, she would never be lonely again, because she would always have one person to be with: her dear heart, Ben.

"I'm coming," she said, falling sideways and Ben gallantly dragged her towards the drift where Kosmo was waiting with three dwarves and five shovels. Later, she would lament that she munched and munched on the chocolate, her mind seeing rainbows and sparkles, and when she came to, her little mannikin was long gone, and she was back at the well again. Alone. She cried many bitter tears over the embroidered gown until one day, she woke up to find someone had placed a small, soft doll in a tiny gold embroidered gown next to her. She clutched it to her chest, ripping its arm ever so slightly. The little creature had a felt hat on and a pair of glasses. Dian called it her 'Dear Heart'.

It was very unusual for this anonymous craft item to be gifted because they are normally retained by their maker. Craft making is a sacred activity in the Fei world and all fairies and magical creatures have mastery over at least one skill. Volume Two of Ben Sopher's study of Fei culture is devoted entirely to Fei occupations and is simply entitled 'Working'. The word in Fei sphere has two meanings but is always used as a verb linked to creativity. In other words, it can mean sewing, landscape gardening, weaving, pot making and a myriad of other things. "I'm off to work," a person might say, picking up a paint brush and looking vague.

The second definition relates to the pursuit of a deep

psychological state that artistry stimulates. When a fairy is 'working' (a human could compare the verb to meditating, to understand that it is an active pursuit), they are literally deep in a comatose state whilst their hands and other limbs are fully occupied in the creative task, despite themselves. Fei can choose to get this way, too, when performing magic. Though they are extremely talented they don't create for public approval but for their own, private satisfaction. The remarkable tapestry that Queen Oona has created, for instance, spans the height of the palace drawing room. In human terms it is ten metres high and five across. This details two women lying side by side in a wildflower meadow. They are caught in a moment of laughing and smiling, and the one that looks a little like the queen is clutching her middle helplessly. The women are dressed in the style of nineteen-thirties humans, and the homely-looking one with brown hair is wearing an exotic gown known as a, 'nylon overall'. Oona tends to stare at her creation just prior to taking a long and satisfying sleep. Others extract similar pleasure by jingle jangling necklaces, bracelets or weapons they have created and they immediately go into a soporific trance. "Making stuff is so sexy, and I love Working," said a teenage fairy recently and her friends all agreed and promptly dispersed to be creative, alone.

It is also important to note, these artistic products are never used for monetary gain. This is because there is no money in the 'Other' place and only a very spasmodic barter system for items that persons might want to exchange when they get bored. Other than that, if people want something rare or out of the ordinary, they tend to steal, which is explained as 'borrowing' though no one ever has any intention of giving something back. Missing art works are merely replaced by doing more work. Oona's tapestry is an exception, and she gets very twitchy about it.

***

The world had thawed, and Hazel realised she had been Ben's companion and carer for ages; she liked it that way. She had looked after his most intimate needs, but her involvement had affected her. Sometimes, her feelings for him distracted her, and it had taken a great effort of will to pay attention to what she was doing: bathing, leading him back and forth to the hall, sourcing him food, washing his clothes and rocking him in her boughs at night. Though she preferred humanoid form, she was prepared to shift to tree when asked, in order to accommodate him. This played havoc with her sugar levels but she didn't care.

When he was totally blind, Ben couldn't tolerate the glasses for too long; they made his head ache as if it were in a vice, and after prolonged use, he saw piercing rainbows scissoring into his eyeballs. In the end, he chose to see for only for a third of the day, and the rest of the time he removed the spectacles and was in darkness. His mood was as volatile as hers and he could be taken over by random bursts of anger. He felt violated and despaired that he would ever be the same as he was again. "I can't believe it's happened," he would repeat.

"Shush, she did not mean to afflict you," Hazel would say logically, but this didn't help. After a while, she gained insight and realised, that it was unhealthy for him to focus on the perpetrator. Instead, she encouraged him to share his story.

"It happened this way, Sopher, it happened," she would murmur, repeating his own words and swinging him back and forth, in a constant rhythm.

"Yes, it did," he would answer the lovely tree, "that's how it all happened," and her affirmation of the crime meant he didn't have to keep replaying it in his head anymore.

Kosmo had also decided to play a part in Ben's rehabilitation. The project in The Hall was a secondary consideration, even though Oona had been a pain at the start and kept threatening to kill them both. She herself had now lost interest and was "practising being ladylike," she said. She was spending many days sitting at a white-painted wrought iron table in a field, eating scones that she said tasted like the dung of a Nuckelavee. The despairing cook had to hide from her.

As the snows had retreated, the trees shook droplets off their branches, and the few remaining Devonian fish that had been caught in the crossover, died in the creek. Instead, brown trout flitted in the sunlight-spotted waters that were finally safe for Ben to paddle in and he liked this sensory experience. Kosmo watched him using his toes to feel his way across the pebbled shallows with ever-increasing confidence, and this gave him an idea. He disappeared for a few days, and when he returned, he had a shimmering horse, led in hand, wearing a newly-stitched saddle.

"I'm sorry it's taken me so long," he explained, dismounting. "The saddler kept going into a trance, so I had to take over. I don't think I made a bad job of it really, but I wouldn't hold too hard onto the pommel, just in case it gives way. I did that bit," he said with a wry grin.

"What do you mean?" Ben said, wriggling back into his tunic and hose. "I'm not going on that thing."

"It will be fine," Kosmo assured him. "He's a very helpful horse and his name is Fenrir."

"Doesn't that mean wolf?"

"Yes, relates to his tawny and gold colour, like a Eurasian wolf."

"I can hear it stamping from here. I'm not getting on."

"He's so well-balanced," Kosmo said, ignoring him and running a hand over his shoulder. "Fantastic confirmation."

"Sounds unbalanced to me with all that snorting."

Kosmo convinced him not to put on his glasses.

"But why?" asked Ben, "I won't be able to see much."

"No, that's the point. I think you will use your senses to connect with him and develop a better seat. Seeing will actually inhibit you."

Strangely enough, this proved true, and Ben learnt to feel every micro movement of his mount and adjust his centre of gravity accordingly. Soon the two were cantering out over the fields with Kosmo shouting directions. On one perfect day, Ben realised that he could see distant landmarks like the mill, the earth dwellings that formed a town across a grassy plain and his good friend riding alongside him. Sadly, that was the only problem that marred the day because Kosmo was determined to just be a friend and nothing more. When they reigned in, and Ben told the good news about his eyes, Kosmo leaned across and kissed Ben lightly on the mouth, making his heart race. He also stroked his head much in the same way, Ben noticed, he touched a horse.

"That's wonderful, Ben. You're restored. I'll be able to devote a little more time to Dillon now, whom I've sadly neglected."

"Who's Dillon?" asked Ben quite sullenly.

"My lover. He is a water sprite. We have been involved since I came of age. He lives by a river, west of the palace," he rambled on, noting Ben's face.

"Ben," he said, touching his hand. "Look at me. No, look at me" he insisted. "You're my best friend. I enjoy every moment with you, but that's it."

"Is he important to you?"

"We enjoy ourselves." He shrugged. "It is what it is. We have happy days and long nights. With you, though, it's different; you compensate for an important absence, a loss."

"For 'her,' 'Ensley'," he nearly spat it out.

"Yes," Kosmo affirmed.

"So pleased that I can fill in."

"Your tone's strange, Ben." Kosmo was puzzled.

"I'm sorry, it's called sarcasm. It's just that I don't understand. What is it with her?"

Kosmo gestured in front of him, and they pressed the horses into a walk.

"Do you remember how angry I was when you mentioned Ensley, that day you rode pillion with me?"

"My back does."

"Well, I was in a terrible state when she was sent off. It had always been us two, from the moment I was born practically. We complemented each other because we both had talents that could overcome each other's problems. I am invariably calm and socially confident; this was useful to her. She, in return, included me in everything she did. In fact, she elevated me beyond my given status by celebrating my social skills as exceptional talents. This was good of her; I'm just an ordinary chap."

Ben studied the proud, suddenly serious features staring into the mid-distance; he couldn't really see how anyone could consider Kosmo ordinary. It was also difficult to see Kosmo as a sixteen-year-old - he just seemed to escape time. Ben was reminded how rare it was to see Kosmo being truly serious when normally he was in the centre of drama and laughter, covered in jewels, wearing rich, golden robes, a sprite on each arm. Kosmo called his glum face, his 'Court Face'. "Putting in on now," he would smirk, before marching stiffly towards the Palace. Kosmo caught Ben looking at him, and a barely emerged smile travelled to his eyes. Confused, Ben asked,

"So, you weren't just her minder then?"

"Certainly not; Ensley Knight is immensely powerful. I think one day she will surpass her mother and her father, but not yet. As a Fei, she has barely started her life journey." He sighed, "I wanted to be there as she blossomed. We had vowed to be a complementary team. I made that promise to her. I know it sounds stupid, but....".

"What?"

"Well, I believe it was our destiny to meet. I can't explain my life course in any other way. It's too bizarre."

"Perhaps just hazard?"

"Not on your life. The events themselves are unlikely; I mean,

Oona conceiving of such a plan, the kidnapping of me when she already had her own daughter. Doesn't make sense..., but it's more than that. It's a feeling that I've always had, that I was meant to be with her and she me. When she was exiled, it felt unnatural and wrong. I was very shaken."

"I think I get it," said Ben, who didn't. He was remembering the commonly known plan of Oona to use Kosmo as a human stud. He knew that was the reason for his being there, but he felt raising this subject was a bit insensitive. Kosmo and Ensley forging a friendship in solidarity against a despotic queen was another matter entirely. Fate or cosmic destiny had nothing to do with it. Kosmo grabbed hold of Fenrir's bridle, preventing Ben from moving away. "Try, please, to understand. I am an outsider here, and an outsider needs allies above anything else. Ensley, could have tired of me but she didn't. That was good fortune but it's the same principle. You and I could get physical, but it might not last. I know sex, Ben, believe me."

"Not that I'm likely to find out," was the smart response.

"That's exactly what I mean, Ben. You make me laugh. You're fun and interesting. We have an intellectual compatibility but it's more than that, I know that you will always defend me and always have my back, and that's rare. I won't sacrifice a potentially lifelong friendship for a romp in the fields which could easily ruin it all."

Suddenly, Ben knew that Kosmo was right. He was blinded by beauty and caught in an infatuation that had started even before he knew the actual man. He had never told Kosmo about the statue - he hadn't wanted to expose his hero worship to ridicule.

"I shall just admire you from afar." Ben barely succeeded in keeping the irony from his voice, which Kosmo, unfortunately, translated as bitterness.

"Look at others Ben, you'll get over it soon enough."

"Yeah, yeah, I've heard it all before, plenty more fish in the sea."

"Fish?"

"A metaphor."

"I've really taken to figurative language," Kosmo said cheerily, "it really sums things up."

"Well, here's another kind for you – oxymorons. Love is rough, hate is gentle..." He rambled on, thinking how he wouldn't mind a bit of roughness. "A kiss is a blow, passion is dull and... and..." He ran out of contrasts at the same time as he wondered where he was going with it all. "I don't know what I'm thinking," he said, looking disorientated, "I've heard it all before, somewhere... I think." Kosmo just looked at him with a grave concern.

"Ben, stop, there is someone for you, I know that person and..." Ben kicked the horse into a gallop. He didn't want to hear about any pitiful substitute that Kosmo had in mind. Suddenly, Kosmo swung round, in the blink of an eye, drawing his sword out of its scabbard. He'd heard a rustling in the bushes and knew it was a person. He leapt from his horse.

"You are a creeping little insect," he said, clutching a neck ruff and levelling the point of his sword against Shakespeare's throat.

"Desist, I intend no harm," he said raising his hands, palms outwards in surrender. Shakespeare had been looking particularly sorry for himself of late. He looked like a kicked dog, his beard looked like an overgrown coir doormat and he smelt very pungent.

"Your friend hath many torments," he said, lowering his hands and rubbing them together. "Tell me more," he said.

"Certainly not. That..." he flicked his sword, making a neat cut just below the Adam's apple, "... was a private conversation."

"Argh," said Shakespeare, clutching his throat and glaring at Kosmo.

"Thou art a wretch, a churl. Proud, insensitive. I will revenge myself on yon youth, as you treasure him."

"You will not. I'll gut you first." Kosmo laughed and lowered his sword. "Where has this come from? Are you jealous? Is the Queen bored of your poetry again?"

"She honours me daily with her presence."

"You mean you sneak into the hall and get going?" Kosmo laughed again. "No, seriously, your poetry is terrific, but she's just not the literary type; she hates pretty words that go on too long. Short descriptions and little songs interest her. For your own safety, I recommend avoiding her. You really mustn't enrage her." Kosmo sheathed his sword and Shakespeare stood there with his mouth open, trying to figure out whether he was being complemented, warned or insulted. The poor man stumbled over his boots that had rotted badly in the thaw as he retreated into the bushes. He was thinking too hard about little songs and poems to watch where he was going. Ben's words, 'loving hate,' whirled around his mind all that day, plaguing him, until he wrote them down.

Chapter 14 Exit - Stage Right

Mab dislodged a bit of kelp out of her tooth with a finger spine. She chewed on it and tried to think. This only caused the genesis of a tiny headache just above her wavy eye. Mab had been in a dank place, semi-conscious, for a full human month. She had lay, where the sluice gates fed into the harbour, because she believed that feeding there with her mouth open would stop her fearful thoughts. Sleep was known to be a great healer; even that odd Jacobean man, whom she secretly despised, said that it "unravelled the day's cares." Anyway, it had been worth the try and she had to admit, the respite from the terrifying vision of Oona looking for someone to blame for her constitutional woes had been very nice. Unfortunately, a person has to wake up in the end and now she was obliged to attend a compulsory entertainment night in the Great Hall. The air was frigid, though the weather had improved and when Mab's guts started a nervous rumble, even though she wasn't hungry, she had to finally admit that her dormancy plan had failed. The thing was, Mab was haunted by her past mistakes and they were living and breathing around her. There was no escape, and if Oona found out, she was done for. She flicked her specially-elongated spiny tail over her head nervously.

The source of her anxiety was posturing in an effete way directly in front of the throne, because Shakespeare had infiltrated once again to bore everyone rigid with his relentless oration. No one knew what had possessed him to start singing his sonnets this time, but it was a terrible error; even more so because the fool was tone-deaf.

"What is it? What is he doing?" Oona asked as the man concluded his performance with a wavering finale and the proffering of a bunch of limp daffodils. When no-one moved or said anything, a nearby kelpie started munching on the flowers. He promptly collapsed, as they are poisonous to horses, and had to be dragged away by his costume bridle. His neighs of pain echoed back to them. The silence hung in shards until Oona finally spoke generally to everyone,

"Whosoever bought this elf-skin to my door," she said, pointing at Shakespeare, "I will personally skin alive." Oona was nothing if not succinct. Unsurprisingly, Mab made the instant decision not to own up, that it was her. However, she did bring attention to herself by nervously fiddling with the hooks around her waist. Oona gave her a long look, noticing the agitated movements of Mab's stinger tail. She also always had a habit of picking seaweed out of her earhole when she was nervous.

Sixteen years ago, Mab had been given one job to do, which was to acquire a child, but somehow, she had also recovered an older show-off kind of person, that Shakespeare fellow. It had all gone wrong during the kidnapping of Incomer. In her haste to shake off the determined and athletically inclined mother, Frances, she had entered the barrow at the wrong point, resulting in the baby and herself inadvertently ending up in 1586. Poking her nose out of the hole, a startled voice had said,

"Yet, what is this tiny creature, like to a mote of dust?"

Retreating backwards, Mab attempted to escape, whilst the blundering man with extended finger fell forwards. Touching her nurse's uniform, he seemed enveloped in a blinding white gauzy film. The rest of the world seemed black around him and then he decreased in size. Close up and noting the baby, so obviously new-born, his face had creased like a tanned hide, "Ah delightful…" he commenced, before realising in a panic that the entrance to the tunnel behind him had closed and his quarry was charging off into the shadowy burrow. Mr Shakespeare ran with all his might after them, the fear of claustrophobia being worse than the fear of ripping his only good hose. He was fairly exhilarated by the experience of zooming up to a normal size once he reached the other realm and by the exoticism of everything and every creature he found around him. Now, he was in the Fei world driving everyone mad, but it wasn't so much his poems that were the problem but his attitude of superiority and the fact that he took no account of the Fei constitution and short attention span. He rained words on them in a deluge where a short spring shower would have sufficed. He talked of manners and motives that were incomprehensible to them, and all this in a flowery form. He was an Elizabethan, rooted in his times, utterly oblivious to the fact that he was no longer there, which was a bit odd anyway, as the Fei world was in no way like home. Being obsessed with rank and outward appearances, he took a poor view of Mab's true form, spitting on the ground, calling her 'monstrous' and 'unnatural'. He also directly blamed her for bringing him away from his beloved wife, Ann, but Mab was not fooled by his specious words. She reminded him how he spent all of his days sucking up to Oona;

"'Tis very ill-advised," she said, grinning under her beak and mimicking his speech forms.

"Do not mock me, thou monster of the deep," he responded.

"Suit yourself," said Mab. "But do not say I didn't warn you."

Actually, she hadn't... properly anyway; fairies are cryptic, and she didn't specifically tell him what not to do. This was deliberate. Mab waited hopefully for the moment when Shakespeare forgot boundaries altogether and did the unthinkable... which would solve some of her problems and hopefully get rid of him for good. Then Mab's longed-for moment happened. Shakespeare, seeing that his audience was rooted to the spot, thought that they were transfixed by his talents. He forgot again where he was, bent and kissed the Oona's hand on what he assumed was a ring but was in actual fact, the bony part of her wand finger. This was an extremely intimate thing to do and, accordingly, the gathered crowd roared their dismay whilst the Monarch withdrew her hand as if she'd been stung.

"How dare you! How... How... dare..." Oona's words started on a shrill platform but descended into a guttering growl. She did growl. She looked at her wand and held it away from her as if it had been defiled. She made it glow white hot, pointed it at cowering William and said simply, "Be gone." The blast blew him off his feet and swept him against the side of the hall. Off he went through the membrane that separates the spheres, then back and back again on a trajectory of unthinkable pain and confusion. Every part of him was on fire, and something was happening to Shakespeare's brain, too. "Bad," he tried to say over and again in a whimper. "Bad," his head felt like it was about to explode. His mind became a dragnet as he travelled through the ages. In the microseconds of his journey, he saw flashes of scenes he barely had time to comprehend: fire, war, liberation, debate, freedom and death.

Something went wrong, and he was caught in a space-time ripple that threw him massively forward in time, only for him to be taken back again by a slower rip tide that linked him to his original course. He spent what felt like ages in different places. Residues of thought, images of inventions and memories of historical events that he should never have seen, remained this time and embedded themselves into his executive functions. He found it hard to move when a man poked him with a bayonet and demanded, "Wer bist du?"

Then he was in a teashop, and a woman in a large hat explained firmly that windows could be broken, as she was inciting the whole meeting to rebellion. Someone else, in another time said, "Chill man,' in a dark basement room with swirling walls and handed him a small, lighted brand. There was no frame of reference there for what he saw and he started to become someone else. A cerebral renaissance commenced within his consciousness like the clashing opening bars of an orchestra as he witnessed great birds roaring alongside him, filled with scores of people like dark insects, swarming as insects would within a fruit. Somehow, sky was exchanged for sea, and he clung to a titanic boat of iron, not sailing on the surface but descending into the freezing depths as the waters rose. He joined the laments, tied the useless, white lifejacket around his waist, as the rest did, before leaping into the pitch-black waters. "All lost, all is lost," was heard, and he gasped as the needles of ice pierced his flesh. Shakespeare fainted.

Grabbed again by a tide or perhaps the unrelenting hand of Oona, he was flung like a puppet onto a dense carpet of pine needles... He wanted to tear his mind out to get rid of the images within. Everything, everything; the existence of two worlds, not the one globe, and the recent torments, he would have gladly clawed out with bloody hands. He wanted to forget, but he knew he would not, because deep down he always believed that there were more things to heaven and earth than met the eye.

Eventually, the neurons stopped their dance and settled into a reliable pattern. Some of Shakespeare's motor faculties were temporarily damaged, and recognisable speech would elude him for some time; that was until his mind realised that it wasn't still on the move through the epochs. It would later take considerable practice to link the brain to the mouth and make sensible shapes. His own children would laugh at him.

Shakespeare staggered through a dense wood in darkness, bow and arrow in hand. He dropped them and tried to say, "Damn the poaching," but it came out as "Bamama peh." Seeing a candle-lit cottage in the distance, he realised he was home, fell to his knees on the soggy ground once more, and wept. It was a dramatic moment for him and he felt intensely sorry for himself. As the heavens didn't seem to recognise his noble despair, and the night was cold, he clambered painfully to his feet, took a piss against a tree, and completed his journey on wobbly legs.

***

Back in the Great Hall, Oona looked at her hand and screamed because the end of her wand had come off. A faint line of smoke drifted upwards and away from it. Mab thought to herself, 'Will it never end?' She wasn't the only one of the Aquarelles blowing bubbles of anxiety out of the side of her mouth. One man with a mussel head had withdrawn and shut himself up completely. Two retainers who were used to handling Oona marched towards her with a huge tapestry held between them to conceal her shame, and they all trooped off down the aisle without comment. In silence, the rest of the nobles dispersed.

What had actually occurred was that Oona had overstretched herself. She had already torn through time with Ensley's exile. Doing this twice was a grave mistake and her impulsivity had quite literally damaged her. Normally, time travel occurred via the established and mysterious burrows that were literally self-contained pockets in spacetime. The original establishment of the burrows was a mystery bound in creation myths and also referred to in The Almanac which unhelpfully just provided an illustration of them from long ago. Everyone accepted that they were just a facet of the world that had always been there, part of the firmament, like a mountain or an ocean. Although, as everyone knew, even the supposedly fixed aspects of the world could change in a moment, whether by an individual's magical manipulation or not. All Fei accepted that the world was in constant flux, and that was what made life so exciting. You only had to travel through a burrow once to realise the swirling patterns looked very volatile as they spiralled into a never-ending vortex. It was best not to touch the walls.

Mab looked across at Incomer, who had placed a steadying hand on Sopher's shoulder; he put his finger to his lips, prompting him to remain respectfully silent. That was the problem with Incomer; he was over-proud and had formed many liaisons, one of which was with the half-breed who had recently

come across from the Other Place. He was also avoiding his
principal task, procreation, even though the young women had
practically thrown themselves at him. She remembered how
she had trawled the prophesies for any indication that he was
unsuitable as a breeding choice but had found nothing untoward
in his composition. Prior to the kidnapping, she had consulted
the stars in the final trimester and they had clearly foretold the
boy would have the strength of a Serengeti lion, the luminosity
of a peacock, and the wit of an unknown mortal named Wilde.
True, she had not consulted his prospective lineage, but with
so many positives in his favour, a trawl through the prophesies
seemed a waste of time and incense. Mab was a very lazy sea
being, she tended to do half a job before just giving up, and in
truth, didn't have the brain to follow Oona's specific commands.
She still believed a rutting beast of the field would have been a
preferable choice, for at least it would have gotten the job done;
but the nobility had already messed up their lineage and were
getting a bit choosy about who they did it with. Mab looked
across at a maidservant who was trying to pick up the remains of
the feast with cloven hooves and she did wonder for a moment
if they had a point. Still, as the nobles never did tend to do
much work, surely it wouldn't have been an issue for them? She
drew her thoughts back to the matter in hand, and her w-shaped
eyes took in the entire area of the hall that looked shabby and
lacking in glamour. The smell of burnt finger lingered in the air.
The kingdom had suffered many disasters, Ensley had gone,
and the boy was a bad choice. She had done nothing to help the
situation; quite the contrary, she had a foreboding sense that her
own life was hanging in the balance. She took another look at the
remaining scandalised, whispering courtiers. It was probable that
she would be sliced and diced, and her sepia used to document
her disastrous role in it all within The Almanac. Her eyes took on
the aspect of deep sadness and wisdom, but actually, there was
nothing in them. She was just a cuttlefish.

Ben had been very disturbed by the events in the Great Hall. His recent involvement with Oona had changed his view of her to some extent. It was not that she was trustworthy or even nice, but he had witnessed patches of calm within the storminess of her rule. He had even written a few descriptive pieces that he read after dinner, celebrating the opulence of the Court, for her benefit. This was a kind but dishonest undertaking as everything was a total mess, but Oona appreciated his efforts, and a small, crocheted cushion was delivered the next day to his home. He had a feeling that she had created this as a lot of gold thread had been incorporated into the design, which made it very itchy to lie on. Twelve more of these followed, and Ben got a passing wizard to magically seal them onto the wall in a pattern as he didn't know what else to do with them, and he didn't just like to store them away. Oona's excessive reaction over a week to one, small act of kindness, was not atypical of the Fei, but Ben still wondered if there was something else wrong with her beyond, her recent injury. He sensed a deep-seated hurt somewhere. He also remembered how he found it hard not to do or say something helpful as he watched her howl and scream with pain at the time her hand had been damaged but Kosmo had somehow anticipated this and he held him back very firmly.

"Don't," he'd said quietly, "I'll explain later."

At sunset, he sat with Kosmo on a bald patch midway up a mountain because Kosmo had warned they needed to be wary of spies.

"What on Fei Earth is it?" asked Ben, picking burrs out of his leggings.

"It's about what happened..." Kosmo looked around him. "She's really taken to you," he sniffed. "I've never been so fortunate, or unfortunate, depending on how you look at it." Ben though Kosmo was grinning in the gloaming, but it was unclear as the mountain in front had totally blocked the descending sun. "Your current position in the Court could be very useful to us both as I'm falling even more out of favour, but I've got to explain about this thing with wands, just in case you land yourself in it."

"Is she actually maimed?" Ben thought back to the moment when he saw blood and the incomplete tip being held aloft. He still felt deeply affected by this memory.

"She will be able to perform magic," said Kosmo. "Nothing would or could stop that, but it's more to do with identity and religion."

"What?! What religion?"

"I don't know exactly. I've been brought up to accept that there is a primal force in the universe that has both created and still manages every aspect of the world, beyond the immense powers of the Fei. There is no literature about it, of course and no pictures. The entire world bows to the Great Creator - even the Monarch, especially the Monarch," he emphasised.

"Yes, yes I've seen that." Ben had been bemused to see Oona periodically prostrate herself on the floor when the mood took her and the population would creep respectfully around her. She was also fairly accommodating if the same impulse took any one of her subjects, though she would raise her eyebrows and sigh if it was in the middle of dinner and the person was serving her food.

"So, what has this religious impulse got to do with Oona's finger?"

"Wand," corrected Kosmo. "It's a wand, remember, and every Fei person has one, regardless of strain, even the beasts, who have special horn variations. It is what separates the Fei from common humanity and it is considered a blessing. From a human perspective, they are freakish, because of their form, but from their perspective, they are blessed with the beauty and power of nature, and the wand is a working symbol of that. The Creator set them apart for some reason." Ben fiddled with his hair.

"Got it."

"Yes, you have. I read your face as Oona's wand exploded.

Tell me what you experienced."

"Disturbed," Ben admitted. "I felt like it was happening to me. I felt her pain and despair."

"Exactly. Everyone felt it except me because I'm not Fei. You are... what's the word? Hardwired?"

"Yes, hardwired."

"... You're hardwired to feel what is sacred in this world. You belong. I don't., because I'm not Fei."

"There's a lot of truth in that, Kosmo. Even after everything that's happened and the total weirdness of this place, and everyone in it, I feel happy. It's a very deep thing." They sat in darkness, one boy disturbed and the other somehow consoled. They'd switched positions, and Kosmo knew he had to look out for himself from thereon. Ben's path and his must surely diverge.

"Kosmo, why are the Fei so lucky, having magic and long life and the humans aren't?"

"Are you joking? They aren't lucky at all from my point of view. Think about it, they are held in thrall to a Monarch that has to tether them in. Without this willing slavery, if that's not a contradiction, they would destroy themselves. Imagine having so much power that you are constantly at risk through your own behaviour. In a volatile moment a Fei creature can destroy all and everything that is dear to them. It takes the self-control of the Monarch and the populace as an entire organism to prevent this, and sometimes it still doesn't work. Just thank your lucky stars that you are mixed race and your Fei energies are diluted." Kosmo seemed to smile in the darkness again. "It's really not that bad." He touched Ben's hand. "There are one or two advantages to not being too tied to any particular world. I think so anyway..."

"What will happen to Oona?"

"Oh, she will go off and sulk for a bit and then re-appear in a grand form, probably with a bit of finger decoration to disguise the broken tip."

"Oh, like yours?" asked Ben, lifting up the heavily coated

silver and jade finger sheath that Kosmo always wore on his right index finger.

"No, mine is like a prosthetic device and it doesn't do much. She won't need all that." He pointed his finger at a bush, and jasmine interwove among the branches. "Pretty, but not practical," he said cheerily, "The mark of my shame, my bondage."

"Well, I can't do anything at all."

"I'm not so sure about that." Kosmo leant closer. "After all, you haven't even tried yet."

"Nope," said Ben. "I'm not even going there. Anyway, my fingers are normal."

"So far," muttered his friend.

"Well, I don't care anyway, my magic will be in words and study - that's my direction."

"Oh!" said Kosmo, disappointment clinging to that small exclamation. "I was hoping that you could help me out."

"With what?"

"It doesn't matter. I'll tell you another time." They clambered back down the hill and afterwards went their separate ways. This was Ben's choice, as he said he wanted to be alone to think things over. Kosmo made a lonely figure on the highway back into the city; he hadn't brought his horse with him as he didn't wanted to be spotted. This was a futile gesture as Kosmo wasn't the kind of person that anyone could miss. The road ahead seemed to go on forever and the people he passed sensed that the Incomer seemed uncharacteristically uneasy. Kosmo was thinking about allies and a prospective meeting with Oona. He had never missed Ensley more than he did that evening. He felt a gentle touch as he passed a tall wood elf. She hoped he would feel the sympathetic smile still on her lips, even though she hadn't turned around.

Chapter 15 Excavations

Being summoned to the Palace was serious; you couldn't just say I will be along very shortly or question the message bearer about time and place. Mostly, this had to do with the fact that time doesn't exist in the Fei world, but primarily it meant that you were in serious trouble with the Monarch, and your best option would be to run, gallop, or fly there, depending on which limbs you had. Also, everyone knew there was one and only one place to meet up and that was in the place which Oona mysteriously called the Debriefing Room. This terminology probably came from the time she spent as a broker in New York City in the 1980s. At the time she caused havoc by throwing digital money around wildly, upsetting the markets and causing her grey-suited colleagues to go weak and limp. It is a fascinating point of reference that her ignorant meddling made an awful lot of people rich, including herself and there are piles of money for her to collect in real estate commodities, green belt reclamation for the leisure industries, and orange juice shares. She has never done so, as money means absolutely nothing to her.

When Kosmo heard he had to go, he galloped up to the gates and charged around the building, where an opening between two Doric columns led to a huge room, with a ceiling so distant that it was an entirely different, very moist climate up there even in midsummer. Skeins of wet cloud wafted down to the lower levels invariably soaking whoever was unfortunate enough to be requisitioned to that dreadful place. The room itself was made entirely of stone and was filled with mausoleums. Kosmo heard a faint tapping coming from one and a quiet, sad voice enquired,

"Hello? Hello, is there anybody out there?"

He shuddered, thinking it might well be himself within one of those if he put a foot wrong. Oona, like most Fei, would react instantly and repent bitterly later. It was only Ensley's presence, he believed that had stilled her wand before. Oona was dressed all in purple to suit the depressing occasion.

"Do you, ooh, ooh, know why you're here, ere, ere, ere?"

"No, oh, oh," echoed his voice back to her.

"Oh, for goodness sake," she said, lifting her wand and making an adjustment to the wave frequency of the room to stop the echo.

"Well, I will tell you why you're here," she said, creeping around a stone plinth like a spiky, green mantis. "Dereliction of duty, inability to do the *one* thing," that has been asked of you."

"I'm very sorry Mother." Kosmo knelt on one knee and lowered his gaze immediately softening Oona's mood. She chucked him under the chin; really, he was very lovely. Look at all the pretty sparkles in his curly hair and himself so lean and strong of thigh in those leggings and chaps. Thinking about Kosmo's physical attributes brought her back to the matter at hand.

"You are not mating with the noble girls," she pointed a finger at him. "What's wrong with you?"

"Wrong with me, Mother? Why nothing." He looked at her with liquid brown eyes and she noticed he had magicked permanent kohl around them as was the fashion with the water sprites. Oona knew he was telling the truth, but that didn't help Kosmo's situation because if he was functional in the loin area, then he was being disobedient, and that was one step away from treason. Oona felt that she, more than he, was on dangerous ground, that may give way at any moment, plunging herself into an action she didn't really want to commit. "Explain yourself; your inactivity," she said in a tight voice.

"Dearest Monarch, Mother of us all, I have found a friend. That is why I cannot..." he rambled. "Oh, are you well?"

This confession had had a surprising effect on Oona. At the mention of the word 'friend', her face had turned as pale as a pitcher of milk. She reeled back and gripped the surround of the stone plinth behind her. When her head cleared, she looked at Kosmo with great suspicion. Somehow, he had played a perfect card, and she knew it. Every one of Oona's inner circle had seen her compulsively surveying the giant tapestry of the woman in nylon, but all would only have comprehended it as an accomplished piece of craftwork. Oona, being well- travelled, knew then that Kosmo had perceived something else in both the tapestry and her behaviour. She didn't like it at all.

"Who is this so-called friend?" she spat, in an attempt to re-align her thoughts.

"Dillon, the water sprite."

Oona threw her head back and roared with laughter. "A sprite? What would a sprite know about friendship, and what, indeed, would you?" Kosmo stood up, pursed his lips and folded his arms. For the first time ever, he looked his age and, leaning on one hip, took the stance of a surly teenager. This actually helped his case enormously. Oona felt she simply couldn't take this youth seriously - he was young and mistaken; that was all. It was a great relief to her, but that was before Kosmo forgot himself entirely.

"You can't make me do anything I don't want to anyway," he said.

Oona was still leaning against the plinth, fiddling with the belt around her kirtle and dreaming about a person long ago whom she could safely say 'was' a friend. Kosmo's words broke through her reveries and fanned her like a flame.

"What did you say?" she asked in a dangerous tone.

"I said I can't do it?"

"Can't? Can't? What kind of human imbecile language is that?" Oona studied him, realising suddenly how apparent the changes were in him. In her mind, she didn't link these to the Sopher but to her old prejudices she had always held about him. She had waited for the human qualities in the Incomer to emerge, as a person would an inherited illness. "What you believe you can and can't do is irrelevant," she said, you have just informed me that there is no malady in you, therefore you will do it. You will reproduce and strengthen our line."

"No," her stepson said quietly. "Just no. I am a gay man."

"We are all gay... mostly. Oh! I see. You mean the human orientation towards one gender."

She leaned on an elbow. "... but why be so specific?" she asked, her tone mocking.

"Ben, I mean, Sopher is too, just like me, as well, anyway." Kosmo was scrabbling for a justification that would mean something to her, but he realised he just sounded petulant. "It's just not who I am," he confirmed.

"What, by the truth of my days, are you for then, if not this?" Exploded Oona

"Dunno."

Kosmo thought he heard her call him a 'gowl' under her breath. She started to stride up and down the room. Striding was a dangerous sign in Oona.

"I will tell you what will occur," she said. "I will watch you, very closely, every move, every word you speak, and..." she turned to face him, "And you will do as I command. I can tell you now, if at least one noblewoman is not with child by the summer solstice, I will not be responsible for my actions. Invest wisely," she said with a surprising flexibility of speech, cleverly reverting to broker speech. "Have you got this down?" she asked her beetle-like chamberlain who was furiously painting on an easel-hung parchment.

"Yes Ma'am," said the creature who was slopping paint here and there, trying to get in the effect of Kosmo's movements.

"Mother, Majesty, could you not recruit another individual with better credentials, and lineage, than mine." This threw Oona off for a moment. She had been so determinedly set on one course, that she hadn't thought of another.

"Hmm," she pondered, whilst a rhythmic tapping was heard coming from an ornately carved stone casket in the corner. "I can't think with all that tapping," she said. "What is it?"

"Hello? Hello?" said a timid voice from the casket. "Is there anyone there?"

"Yes, it's me, Durian." Oona, feeling distracted said, "I'm trying to administer commands. What do you want?"

"A petition, a petition, please Majesty." The voice was desperate.

"Well, I am doing something else. Say it speedily."

"Please, please let me go. There is no light in here. I cannot stand it."

"Well, why do you not go back to your dormancy stage if you do not like it?" Oona's voice was sulky; she didn't like seeming to be nasty.

"I did. I could, but I *so* want to be free."

"I understand," Oona's voice was smooth and impervious. She stopped pacing. "Yes, why on this earth not?" An exclamation of joy was heard coming from within the stone, until Oona suddenly interrupted.

"However, there is a condition, and that is you never, never chase after the noble ladies again. I do not want any more anomalies birthed in my court; do you hear? And do you know, I have a niece with a head like a pin cushion who stinks of waste matter?"

An explosive laugh erupted from the casket, which Durian hurriedly smothered.

"I am certainly not taking that as assent," said Oona. "Your petition is denied." A wail arose from the corner of the room. "You only have yourself to blame. Shut up or I will place a bonfire under your casket and roast you." The sounds within the casket ceased, and Oona turned her attention back to Kosmo. Her voice resumed a languid, poisonous tone.

"Do you see the problem that I have?"

"Yes, Mother, I will follow your command." Kosmo beat a hasty retreat backwards and galloped off on his horse.

The Chamberlain, who shared many of Oona's confidences asked her, "Will he comply?"

"It is difficult to say, Tomalin. We may now have his compliance, but my threat could well undo his vigour." The two leered at each other briefly as they shared a base image. Tomalin noticed a sea change in the Monarch who became aware of what she was doing and touched her crown nervously. Oona admitted, "The idea he raised in recruiting others instead of him, could well be the only option."

"Perhaps," Tomalin admitted, drawing the two of them pondering on his second sheet, "but then the forced growth of a human child to adulthood from the start can be disastrous too, and I presume you would like to begin the plan immediately?"

"Yes, if I see another weird hybrid in my Court that is impossible to countenance because of smell or its discourteous nature, I will shift myself to Albania and drag Finnian back by the scruff of his neck."

It was not a done thing for one Monarch to refer to the others' errant behaviour, but it was a measure of Oona's stressed state of mind that she did this. Tomalin tactfully edited that part of the unfolding scene and painted a beautiful Queen Regent bemoaning the absence of her consort in the Accursed Mountains. Her spiky hand reached towards him across the miles and space-time, and the motive was impossible to determine. He drew Finnan as a most unattractive, lumpy, greyish rock with eyes, because his fealty was with the Monarch in front of him and not the other one that had buggered off for unknown sundry reasons.. He plonked a few love hearts and doves around Oona and put his brush down.

"Perhaps we should merely anticipate Incomer being unable to perform?" mused Oona. "Long ago there was a gatherer of human children en masse with horns and a green jerkin. Was his name Pan?"

"Peter Pan," affirmed Tomalin.

"Yes, that's it, we could 'accrue'..." Oona looked at Tomalin so that he could acknowledge her clever business speak... "Many adolescent children en masse instead of a few dribs and drabs."

"Unfortunately, not, your Majesty. He is no longer available. In fact, he died," Tomalin admitted.

"Really? How so?"

"By popular opinion Ma'am. He ended generally torn and ripped, much as his clothes were, because he was a shabby fellow, actually by an incensed mob. You know how the population reacts if they feel they are poorly represented in the human sphere. It seems that over time, he became most disreputable with his aged, flabby legs pressed into those green tights and his addiction to fine wines. He would scurry between the worlds, compulsively collecting children who did not want to come."

"And how was this a problem?"

"It was the biting, Ma'am."

"He ate them?" Oona was a little stunned. "Barbarism!" she exclaimed.

"Not entirely. He tended to nibble and chew. The children complained."

"I heard nothing whatsoever about it."

"It was managed by her Royal Highness, the then Princess Ensley."

"How interesting - I did not think she did anything useful."

"The children found a compassionate ear with the princess." Tomalin cleared his throat. "It was due in part to her sympathetic connection with The Incomer. I do not think she intended for Pan to be deceased," he added, "but when she approached him, he was most rude to her, and the nearest population acted accordingly before they could be stopped."

"How dare he be rude to my daughter!"

"Exactly," said Tomalin. "None could brook it, and so they

didn't."

Oona took a moment to digest this interesting story, which also ended up in The Almanac as a flashback to a righteous moment in Fei history. 'Look how we deal with poor publicity,' it seemed to suggest.

"Well, I am very exhausted after all these revelations, and will rest," said Oona. "We will wait and see how Incomer's intentions will transpire for now, though waiting is tedious." Oona opened The Almanac, then waved her wand over Tomalin's paint-splattered offerings that were on casks and floor. The images lifted onto the page and were transformed by her quick hand into a standardised form on the pages of the official record. In one frame, the unhappy Durian slept soundly for what might be an eternity. Oona dismissed Tomalin and walked around the corner into the palace entrance, stopping briefly at the tapestry of her and Mary lying in the long grass, a flagon of cider besides them. "Friend indeed?" she snorted referring back to Incomer's misappropriation of the word. She did not, however, extract the import of Tomalin's tale and how clearly it portrayed what Incomer meant to her daughter, their friendship having inspired notions of compassion shown in the affinity to the human children who had been garnered by the erstwhile and malicious Pan of the Green. Oona learnt nothing at all from these revelations and slept soundly that day.

Chapter 16 Truths and Travel

Ben was finding Kosmo quite a challenge to be with; he was uncharacteristically moody and distractable. Her also kept making him put his hands into dangerous looking burrows to see if he was yanked away.

"I think you're abusing our friendship somewhat," Ben told him, withdrawing his arm from a swirling maelstrom of black that sucked his fingers like a lamb on a teat. "Now they're going to tingle all day," he said regretfully.

"Sorry, but actually, I'm in imminent danger of being shut forever in a tomb in a death-like sleep. Think about that?"

"I am, but on the other hand, I'm in imminent danger of being dragged off to goodness knows where just when I've found a place for the first time in my life where I'm really happy." This was true; Ben had settled into a calmness of mind that he had never experienced before, and he delighted in the odd diversity of the world he found himself in. A place where flowers talked (until they regained their humanoid form), rivers were full of sentient creatures, and all of nature was enhanced to a crescendo of beauty reflected in the luminescent plants, creatures, and landscape. The sky was always reddish in tone, from rose pink to evening crimson, like a perpetual sunset to allow comfort to the sensitive eyes of the Fei.

"It's a matter of priority," said Kosmo.

"Oh, what? Me sacrificed before you?"

"Well, if you don't want to help me...!"

"I do. You know I do." Ben squeezed his friend's arm. He had spent a great deal of time cajoling Kosmo into a better mood and trying to alleviate his distress. This hadn't gone unnoticed by Hazel, meanwhile, who shadowed the two on their explorations. She was often left standing helplessly at the side of the tracks on the days when they used horses. She felt a terrible wrenching inside her that wasn't entirely due to the dragging of her tap roots away from the grove practically every day.

"I really don't think Oona will do anything rash," Ben encouraged. "You know how she is; blows red hot and then forgets what she's doing."

"This is different." Kosmo curved his glamorous frame over into a ball of misery. "My entire life has led up to this - from Oona's point of view, anyway. I either perform, or I'm completely redundant. I'll have no purpose in this world. But you know, it won't end there. If I accept being slaved out by her, it will set a new benchmark for how she treats me. I'll be less than nothing, and that *is* dangerous."

Ben hadn't seen his friend so cowed before. He called Hazel over.

"Hazel, do you know anything about time travel?" he asked.

"To trees, burrows are taboo. We no travel, and we not grow near to them."

"Kosmo and I are going to try travelling." A thrill went through Hazel of fear and illumination.

"Sopher, do not travel from us. We will...the grove will miss you." She stood there perplexed.

"Thank you, Hazel, and I, you." Ben stared right into her eyes for a moment and felt as if he were becoming transfixed. He broke the gaze with difficulty. Hazel turned to Kosmo.

"The Incomer will be crushed." she said, "If alone. Perhaps Fei escort?" she suggested.

"Yes, of course, that is how he came into the world, and I suppose I will do it."

"No!" Hazel's response was swift. "Sopher is only little portion Fei, and great danger for his person." Her tone became sly. "Mab will take Incomer."

"Mab?!" was the simultaneous response.

"Mab knows places of intersection where Kosmo found as a

babe."

"Yes, but I don't want to go back there exactly, being grown."

"Time moves," said Hazel cryptically, "Like trees, like persons." She turned away, sensing that she had planted a seed of an idea. She didn't want to ruin it. Soon the Incomer would be gone and all would be well, though it wouldn't stop the discontented murmurings in the grove. The trees had all sensed a change in Hazel and had begun to ostracise her. The mycelium signals between them had sent excited impulses as a kind of speech, "The hazel tree says I, as a person," they accused as Hazel started to identify as being separate. "It denies wholeness with us...has become 'me' to itself." They withdrew their roots that used to intertwine with hers seamlessly, and the mycelium did a detour around her. One of Hazel's branches had rotted and fallen off with a loud crack two sunrises previously as a consequence. Time indeed was moving, showing itself in this instance as premature ageing; it was as though Hazel was growing up. The other trees were right and it was Hazel's adoption of pronouns that was literally killing off her old self.

"Ah, so it might be possible to find the moment where Kosmo would be seventeen, as if he had never left?" Hazel didn't respond, but she noticed the Incomer had become very excited.

"There might be hope, Ben." Kosmo hugged him and danced around. "Come on, I know Mab's, well, Mab-ish, but she got me into this mess, and she's got a responsibility to get me out."

"Um, I'm not sure that Mab exactly thinks that way," Ben cautioned Kosmo.

"Yeah, well, it's worth a try, and what else have we got? Also, it means you won't have to leave. Bonus!"

"Ha, you really are beginning to sound contemporary Kosmo. Perhaps it's a sign."

"Perhaps, let's go and find her." As Kosmo grabbed him once again, Ben took the opportunity to plant a kiss on his cheek. The trees in the grove turned and looked as one, and one individual in the group shuddered.

"Okay, let's do it," Ben said, somewhat relieved that he wouldn't have to be the litmus paper for any more burrow experiments, though he would miss Kosmo terribly. Strangely, he wasn't at all perturbed at the thought of confronting Mab. Like Kosmo he was evolving into a different person, but one who was confident in the realm of Fei and in dealing with its volatile inhabitants. In short, he had become naturalised. The personal changes weren't limited to the two men, though, behind them, an extraordinary event was occurring and Hazel was now powerless to stop the process. As they walked away, Hazel's entire physiology was now changing and it was all because she had made a choice to leave behind the community that she had been interconnected with all her life so that she could follow her desires and become authentic. She had long thought her life to be an act, and her heart was never in her actions, but the appearance of Sopher had brought her feelings to the fore. She just always felt the need to be separate and the others were quite aware of this idiosyncrasy. Regardless, in her community she was a very revered tree who had withstood many seasons, but she was prepared to sacrifice all that to become other' - a distinct self. Her freedom to disengage might involve sacrifice and exclusion, but she didn't care. She had plotted a simultaneous gender switch as a crucial part of her transformation, and this would bring her a happier future; her future time itself would be on her terms alone. The Queen Regent herself had always had the greatest admiration of her demonstrating her femaleness so abundantly in springtimes following harsh winters when she could have preserved something of herself instead of propagating seeds all around her. The other trees always thought her exuberance could be a little over the top, a bit fake, but never said anything as her behaviour garnered respect from the highest source. Hazel couldn't have cared less what her kind thought any more. She had become miserable and despairing as she was and didn't want to live her life fulfilling other's expectations. She recalled Oona's words that didn't mean anything to herself or, or in actual fact, any of her kind; but least of all Hazel.

"See, see," Oona had often said. "Here is a perfect example of someone putting duty before selfhood." As this made no sense to the trees who did not have individuality or a sense of self, no-one clapped the announcement at the time, though many specimens stood apart to let Hazel have the greatest share of canopy light in accordance with her observed status. Now, she would throw that all away willingly, moved by her love for a half-breed man named Sopher.

Hazel flicked the catkins along her arms vigorously, producing a cloud of male pollen that smothered the tiny red protuberances blended into her twigs and torso. She did this until every droopy flower was empty, but no pollen reached another tree. The tiny red buds, inundated with maleness, began to wither and die. Hazel harnessed every bit of magic she had in directing water and nutrients again and again to the catkins and away from the female parts of herself. She was so depleted by the process, that she bowed herself to the ground, creaked, and groaned, but the others took no account of her distress as they believed what Hazel was doing was tantamount to suicide. Many plants are monoecious, but keep the male and female parts of themselves separate. Hazel was deliberately favouring one gender, her already preferred one of maleness, in order to become a new creation. Recovering slightly after a while, this evolved creation took first, unsteady steps away from the region that had previously been 'home' and kept walking. Ben was later extremely upset to see her gone, but when he questioned the trees, they wouldn't answer him. He felt this was an ominous reaction and hunted high and low for her around the creek but couldn't find her anywhere. The trees in the grove, meanwhile, regressed in their sentience, because Hazel had been a galvanising and cultured force in their midst. Shortly, they forgot how to talk, too.

Chapter 17 A Wending Tale

Ben combined his task of 'searching for Hazel' with a greater exploration of the Fei world. Kosmo urged him to look for Mab too whilst he was at it, because, unfortunately, she too seemed to have disappeared off the face of the world. He agreed to this plan and concentrated his early searches along the coastline of Fei Britain. As always, he took his backpack but had ditched the last of his human clothing, which had pretty much fallen to bits. He now wore pseudo mediaeval garb, with a lined cloak and chaps made of an unknown flexible material on his legs whilst riding. Ben estimated he had been away for about a year now, had a substantial beard, and had lost the willowiness of adolescence. Though he scarcely admitted it to himself, he did occasionally perform primary magic using the outer edge of his right hand. The first time he did this had been by accident, when, after packing and leaving, he realised he had forgotten to put his flints for fire-making inside his rucksack. He waved a frustrated hand dismissively at the folly, now far behind him and then saw two dots appear in the distance. He realised they were coming closer and closer, and he dismounted in a panic as they gathered speed. He started to run off the highway, shoeing Fenrir the other way, and kept running, but the flints caught up with him and whanged deep into the backpack, coming to rest against his spare leggings. He observed there were two holes of four inches in length at the flints' entry point that he would need to sew up later, otherwise they would fall back out of the bag. However, he soon discovered that he didn't need the flints anyway, as immediately he thought about being cold, there was suddenly a crackling pile of wood just in front of him. He had begun to change into a magical creature despite himself, though from that time on, he avoided magic in the main, as he didn't have a clue what he was doing with it, and the flint incident could have ended with a fatal blow. Admittedly, he did forever after resort to making campfires through magical means, as he reasoned warmth was a fundamental need, and also to bring fruits on trees that were out of reach down to his level; both actions were useful when you were tired and hungry. There also came to be moments when it was necessary to raise stones to cross a ford, or to seal the threadbare backpack when you didn't have needle or thread, but these instances were hardly worth mentioning and he didn't write about it in his journal.

One day, Ben followed an overgrown, barely recognisable, trail in a wood through a dense layer of dog's mercury that reached to the top of Fenrir's hocks. Ben pulled on one rein,

"Not for you Fenrir - poisonous stuff."

Eventually, they found a recognisable ride bordered by young hazel bushes, making Ben think regretfully of his missing friend. He was beginning to think he would never find her again. Deep in thought, he let the horse take the branching fork to the right away from the sea that he could smell in the distance even though he couldn't see it through the trees. Shortly, they arrived at a cleared site with many gnomes on bended knees cutting fruiting fungi with tiny knives. Ben knew what this kind of place was; he had already written about a similar place in his journal. Ben had chanced on a mushroom production plant and knew the workers were completing a compulsory length of service as harvesters in the field. The time Fei spent farming was more a rite of passage than a burden, and every recruited Fei, (that had hands), looked back on time spent at the encampments with great affection. The food they harvested was a core ingredient in the green vegetable mush that most Fei subsisted on, and therefore, working to produce this was a great honour. There were great, talked-about opportunities to socialise in the evening, and Ben noticed the long trestle tables in a nearby courtyard and the barrels of beer and mead ready for that night's feasting. He knew that many took the opportunity to find life partners in the duration of their service at the farms; this was why they postponed their conscripted time to when they had reached a state of maturity and no longer wished to experiment sexually. Suddenly, one gnome looked up, and, spotting Ben gibbered something excitedly to his neighbour, who was a female with an odd head that ended in a swirled point. She grinned mawkishly at Ben before rubbing her soiled hands on her apron, and then she entered the fourth dimension and disappeared. This seemed ominous, and Ben wondered who she had gone to fetch. By now, the entire workforce was stood up laughing and pointing at Ben who was feeling confused about his reception. This was until he spotted the tiny cottage to the left of him, fronted by green lawns and surrounded by a white, picket fence. It was then he realised where he was: the scene of a previous nightmare. "Hell!" he yelled, thinking about the memory of himself as a trespasser, flailing around on the ground in a time before back in Dorchester, and immediately trotted Fenrir back the way he came. He heard a shout behind him but broke into a canter, knowing it was unlikely to be a positive call in view of the demolition job he had done in a dream, on a wintery night. He felt a subtle movement to his right and realised he was being overtaken. Sure enough, the angry fellow with the ice-cream whip head whom he had encountered before, was now stood on the track in front of him, hands on hips. A milky ooze descended down this person's chin. Ben reigned in and was concerned to see the man reach up and grab his reins. This was before he started gently stroking Fenrir's neck.

"It's good to see you again," he said, his tone as warm as his expression. "Shall we?" he pointed back towards the house and Ben mutely allowed the man to lead Fenrir.

"You caused us a fair bit of upset," the man commenced.

"I know, I'm so sorry."

"Don't ye fret. We was more concerned about your welfare."

"Were you?" Ben was completely lost.

"Yes, after you vanished like a bubble... the last time..." The man was busy unbuckling Fenrir's cheek strap as they walked. Ben instantly recalled waking up in his snow-speckled flat.

"Well, I thought you would have been glad to see the back of me," said Ben, surprised.

"Not so, Glenna was most disturbed at it, and wanted to find you, on account of you being so betwattled, but we didn't know where to start." He pointed to a tiny elf who had materialised on the other side of the horse. She nodded her agreement. "Poor thing," she said, stroking his boot in the stirrup as if he could appreciate it through the stiff material.

"Why was everyone laughing at me?"

"They were not," said the man, "They were overjoyed to see you. They are coming to the end of their duration here and had given up hope that they would one day see you again, and hopefully this time hale and hoddy."

"Oh, that's nice," said Ben trying to keep the bemusement out of his voice. There was a short hiatus. "Perhaps we could sit and go over it," he suggested, "Because I have no idea what you are talking about and I feel we need to fill each other in."

"That's certainly true, Sopher," said the elf, smiling. She had noticed Ben jumping at the mention of his name. "Your legends precede you, as you are so favoured now by the Queen Regent. You must tell all to Gideon here, and we will anticipate hearing your jolly tales this eve."

"Back to work," called the man to the crowd now gathered around them. Yes, Sopher will bide with us now for a while," he reassured them all.

"Good to see you Sopher." A gurning gnome with a face like a bag of potatoes shook his hand vigorously before opening up his pocket knife and kneeling back down again in front of a toadstool bed. Glenna, meanwhile, walked towards a stack of pallets and did something weird with her form, extending like purple smoke over them until her head was a flat sliver with her eyes at the outer edge like a sea skate. The pallets vanished, and she drew back like a bolt of cloth into her former shape. Then she turned to another stack, covering them entirely, and started to do the same thing - transporting them to some pre-planned place, Ben assumed.

"A lissum creature, she is mostly o' the element," said Gideon, pointing to the sky. "Though, 'tis odd," the man ruminated, turning Fenrir out into a field. Ben only nodded his agreement, unable to stop watching her unrolling and retracting. "Let us go over the memories, old friend," Gideon said, practically dragging Ben into the house.

"Why not?" Ben agreed, a little uncertainly, wondering exactly what kind of good memories were about to be uncovered. "Hey, I don't suppose you could make me a cup of human tea, could you?"

"Certainly," agreed Gideon, cheerfully, who immediately turned his cat into a teapot, much to its disgust.

Ben sipped tea, and a bowl of junket was produced, chock full of sugar, which was unusual, it being practically outlawed from Fei use. "I keep it for guests," Gideon confessed, looking particularly furtive. Ben looked around the homely cottage. There seemed to be crocheted doilies and runners on every surface. For the first time, he noticed that his host was wearing a crocheted waistcoat. This was more utilitarian than the pink and white examples on the furniture, as it was brown and made of twine. Clearly, Gideon's leisure time was expressed mostly in fibre. When two huge dogs with studded collars entered the room, Ben had an unfortunate flashback to these same creatures with their studded collars, barking at him furiously. He shrank back into his chair but Gideon merely patted them and said, "Look who's here – our friend!" To Ben's horror, one of the two made a gigantic leap and landed on him, but then it started to lick his face. The other came alongside and sniffed his hand before also licking him. Gideon pulled the dog off, laughing wildly and saying,

"Branwen 'as always been a dog of singular taste, Betty is far more refined. Off you goes." He patted them and magicked the spilled junket back into the bowl, which was now full of hairs. Ben put it down on a doily and asked whether all dogs had little wings like that.

"Yes, but they is like hen's wings, not best at flying. Thank the Creator! Otherwise, I would be always searchin' here and far for them." Ben noticed that the dogs lolloping and flying one or two paces past the window. Gideon noticed him observing and added, "I 'ave been told it is called pseudo-flying. I don't know why they don't just says unreal flying. Means the same." He sniffed.

"Talking about unreal," said Ben. "I don't think your memory and mine are in agreement. I mean, I remember those dogs trying to attack me."

"Never!" said Gideon, with horror. "They was trying to get at you to comfort you when the malady took your mind once more. I had to hold 'em back in case you kicked or punched them, though there was one time when I was so concerned, and the Betty was so desperate to offer you relief that I had cause to allow her to offer you assistance, but it were no good. You was beyond words and sense, you see." Ben had a sudden flashback and felt the weight of the female dog on his chest once again.

"So, you didn't say I was treating your garden like an hotel?"

"What's anotel?"

"Never mind. I'm really sorry I trashed your nice garden." The man bowed his head so that the tip of it was pointing at him like a petrified albino snake.

"You is forgiven, Sopher. Most of the damage was due to us trying to get a gobbet of our prime Spore Beauties into your throat We couldn't get them in, you were so wild. It is a medicament you see."

"Purple-ish?"

"Oh indeed, my very best. That would have sorted you out, or knocked you out; one or another leastways."

"I'm beginning to feel a bit mad."

"Oh dear." Gideon stood up, looking perplexed.

"Oh no, it's okay. I mean nothing adds up."

"...and why should it in pertikuler?"

"I wasn't raised here, Gideon. I'm not from Fei Earth. We tend to like our life stories to link together in a regular order with no hitches. I mean no alternative versions of the same event."

"Well, that may be why you is going mad as March hare then. Whoever heard of such a thing? To us, change is life. We is all caught on the cusp of a wave, but there are many accounts of how that wave shapes. Look yonder at that that there Muddy-want," he pointed through the window at a gnome slinking along the ground, cutting the smaller mushrooms in a blur of swipes as he went. "His view of this farm will happenstance vary greatly. On the dawning his elbows will ache and he will curse, but because he is enjoying hisself beyond measure, he will look back on this term fondly. Which version of his life and work here will he choose as his truth, the pain or the pleasure?" Gideon threw him an arch look and warmed to his theme. "Whilst that elder gnome in the store room is a different matter," Gideon pointed to an open barn door at a very knobbled creature that looked like a fungus himself, weighing and sorting endless piles of cut produce into pallets, "That one looks forward only to finishing his cheerless task for good and for ever; he conceals his satisfaction at being useful in his decrepitude from others and, more importantly, himself. He knows not what he is because he's too busy counting the days, and that is a tragedy. Time wants to capture us and tell us the way things are. It would swallow us up in misery like a bloodsucking wraith' disappear us altogether, our magic and strength – the whole lot. Look again at those two; he pointed with his wand. To one, I am a monstrous overlord, to the other I am a friend. We must resist time, resist its despotic hold on us!" Gideon pounded his chair, repeating the word 'resist' and with the call-to-action sparks snapped and bit around him. For a moment his face looked malevolent and pinched. "Where are you in your world Ben Sopher?" he asked, stopping abruptly.

"I, I don't know," Ben began, but then he said for the first time, "I am Fei, I am happy, and I'm here, aren't I?"

"Yes Sopher, you is finally here. And myself? What do you think of me?"

"I'm not sure about you at all..." he quipped. Gideon roared and clapped Ben on the back. "I know you does not mean that. I is thinking of all they nights when you and I had larks and danced on the benches singing your favourite song, The Journey to Armadillo."

"Amarillo. What? Did I do that?" Ben felt cold, confused and startled all at once.

"I recall you waving a dockery-stick and fallin' off. You 'ad to be stopped, eventually. Never mind, it were nice to see you raising a homany that were not all wailin' and lamenting." Ben reflected back to another version of the same event in the Crown in Dorchester when he was seventeen and felt very adrift. That time he had drunk five pints and had many shots, ending in him causing a real commotion, until he was kicked out of pub, weeping. He wondered why he had been so upset and leary in a similar way, in Gideon's place. A hand touched his then.

"My grandmother was a Knight, like your'n. Ursula, was a grand woman. Never did understand why she stopped where she did on human Earth." He exchanged a look with Ben. "We all felt her passing, though. It took me a while to settle after my kin went too - it's just natural to feel that way, but then we must forget." His blue-slitted eyes closed like a cat's for an instance and a gentle purring could be heard from the teapot. Ben felt immeasurably at peace. He heard the ticking of a clock, far, far away, or a timer sound, though there was no such device in the room.

"One thing I don't understand is..." Ben said lazily... "Is how I can have been here at the farm when the deep freeze occurred when I was also at the Court during that time period."

"Oh, I suppose you was just popping in from 'ome and tellin' us how you were at the time. You 'ad to tell someone. Caught in a little time fold no doubt. It does happen oftentimes. Events are otherwise forgotten; people go missing in the moment. Ave you heard that before?"

"I have - it seems so long ago now. A lady... There was a bookshop."

"Yes, yes," said Gideon getting suddenly evasive. "We must get on now and there's no time like the present and that's the only way I'll 'ave time in my hwome."

"I'm beginning to think there is no time at all in the usual way."

"I think you might be wrong there - sadly." He said almost to himself, "For good or worse, we is going forrard though there's others that will tell you otherwise." He shook himself. "Let us do the rounds of the farm and you can scribe it all down for posterity." Gideon urged him out of the door and away from dark thoughts. He only remembered to turn the cat back much later who complained all evening that he felt stewed and not at all himself.

Chapter 18 Mab's Machinations

Mab had been diving in and out of burrows like a merrow in a sea cave. She was determined to find Ensley Knight as she had a plan to dispose of the Incomer by depositing him on her doorstep. If Incomer were in contact with Ensley, his position would be made untenable through an association with an exile. There might also be grounds for treason if it could be proved that the two had conspired to be together all along, in which case he would be destroyed. Mab favoured the latter outcome, and the probability of this happening would rest on a written confession, which, of course, she would create herself. Incomer, being a mortal, would undoubtedly resort to such base practices as illegally documenting his actions. Apparently, Incomer could write - a Phooka goblin had spied him doing that on a scrap of Sopher's parchment. This same goblin was very interested in telling Oona all about Incomer's literacy practices to bring favour on herself. The goblin had been driven far from the Court and all others ever since she had eaten Oona's dog (cannibalism was very frowned upon in Fei sphere). Mab didn't stop to wonder at the logic of why an escaping subject would be carrying a note of confession on his person. All she was concerned about was hard evidence and her own rise to prominence in the Queen Regent's estimation once again.

Mab was delighted when she actually found Ensley, who was in a letting agent's, in London, listening to a man explaining that he had just let a very nice shop in Lower Marsh. It had always been difficult to hire commercial property in London, but to Ensley it seemed impossible. Her plans about being a shopkeeper were in ruins.

"I tried to call you umpteen times," the agent said, noting Ensley's disappointed face... "but it just said, unobtainable or no such number."

"I think there's something wrong with my phone," Ensley said a bit disingenuously as she didn't actually have one, knowing full well that if she tried, all she would hear was static and not voices. She put it down to being Fei somehow.

"Couldn't you have sent a courier to me, like we agreed? I don't mind paying," she reminded the agent, watching her put numerous calls on hold, as she spoke.

"Listen, love, they're practically beating down my door to get premises in The City. You're going to have to be a bit more proactive."

"Fast bidding," mused Ensley, thinking about her quick reaction times in the auctions she haunted."

"Exactly," he said.

Mab listened to all of this with interest, and though it had nothing to do with her plan, which she had momentarily forgotten, she decided to have a little bit of malicious fun for her own pleasure. From that moment on, every time Ensley went to a viewing, she was hit by unscalable odds. Sometimes she seemed to be lost in a maze of streets where she would wander for hours round and round in circles until she eventually realised that she had passed her destination continually and a 'let' sign was already outside the door. It didn't matter that she camped in dangerous situations overnight, outside estate agents in a borrowed tent, just in order to be there first, because she would always be inhibited by one obstacle or another. Once, a flock of sheep caused havoc in the street she was visiting, though sheep hadn't been driven over London Bridge into the city for hundreds of years, apart from for charity events. The police didn't seem to know where they'd come from either. Ensley tried to talk to one ewe who bleated in terror that as far as they were all aware, one minute they were nibbling grass in a lush field surrounded by mountains and then they were in a hard, noisy place with no grass at all, and, for that matter, where was the sheep dog?

"I think they belong in a place called Wales," Ensley told the police officer.

"You're right about that!" he replied. "I wish they'd go back there."

Ensley couldn't get the sheep to move. and the leaseholder, trapped on the other side of the flock said she didn't have the time to mess around and Ensley never heard from her again.

***

Human people who have read Ben Sopher's many volumes on Fei life and constitution have been puzzled as to why so little time is devoted to the compelling fact that fairies can talk to any kind of animal. This wondrous ability is underplayed precisely because it's not a big deal. Taking into consideration that all Fei have the ability to shapeshift into a designated form, according to their particular strain, they are really just talking to each other, and the fact that someone has temporarily got furry ears, tentacles, or a tail is irrelevant. "In that case," an argumentative human would respond, "... How about human animals who are just that - simply animals? Surely, it's a remarkable feat to be able to communicate?"

"So, we talk to impaired versions of our own creatures..." would be the reply, "Nothing clever in that, and you should try talking to a regular cow that *can* speak, it's not exactly a great experience!"

"What's it like, what's it like?" the over-wrought human, might insist."

"Grassy," would be the curt response, "And if you must know, endless. We wouldn't recommend striking up a conversation."

A more controversial skill is that of *transducement*, and a whole book is dedicated exactly to that magical skill because this is where a Fei individual can enter into the mind of another - co-habit it, so to speak. It's a very direct route to communication and a terrible invasion. Imagine someone sitting on your frontal cortex, pinning you down, and refusing to go away! This is why there are very strict rules regulating the consensual management of transducement and to breach these results in the death penalty. Unfortunately, the rules are so complex and difficult to interpret that Ben upset the balance of his own text by dedicating half the book to these rather than some exciting historical anecdotes which would make a livelier read. Unfortunately, neither he nor his readers were any the wiser after trying to ingest the second half, though many felt that they were 'getting it' at the time. Oona Knight sorted the whole matter out during her reign by suggesting one of her own verbal formulas as a governing directive.

"I just warn them with the words, 'don't you DARE!'" she explained. Oona's other favourite aphorism is, "Those who try - die." As no one would even consider that route, especially with her, she commented that she hasn't had to use it very often. In this way, breaches of transducement are pretty much unheard of in recent history, and anyway, most Fei have enough of their own minds to deal with, without taking on another Fei's problematic psyches. The inhabiting of a human mind is a different matter, because that's a whole lot of fun. In ancient times, when the Fei were much wilder, and basically out of control, this was a common practice. The Dark Ages in England were called precisely that because many humans walked around in a fug, not of their own making. Existing in darkness and confusion, they also took on the Fei impulsivity and tended to aggressively chop up other people for no particularly good reason. Similar historical epochs can be found the world over and can all be attributed to the transducement actions of mischievous sprites with their different names according to their country origin: 'Spiritello,' 'Nkisi', 'Kitsuni', 'Yaksha' etc. Nowadays, the practice of non-consensual transducement is frowned upon as it is a contemptible use of a very revered skill and brings the Fei race into disrepute.

Therefore, the urge to mess with a human mind, however much fun it promises, must be resisted at all costs.

Mab's own meddling came to a halt when she made a mistake. Ensley had been given a lead by someone in the Prince's Trust about a potential business premises. Ensley had a very constructive interview with a woman who ran a cooperative that helped young people to set up trading units within an ancient arcade. Emma, The Trust's leasehold manager, explained that there were two premises left and four potential clients were already on their way - she would have to be quick.

"Noted," said Ensley, grabbing her portfolio and vanishing instantly."

"Keen," said the startled woman, wondering how exactly Ms Knight had managed to get out of the door without her realising.

Travel through the fourth dimension took a minute rather than seconds as Ensley was very agitated. Despite this, something was wrong. She checked the address three times and ran up and down the road, but where the opening to the arcade should have been, she was confronted by a solid Portland stone wall. There simply wasn't an entrance. Then, a handwritten note, lifting and falling in the breeze grabbed her attention. Peering closer she read words that came from a very illiterate hand,

Get Stufd Ensley

which was a dead giveaway, notwithstanding the lime-green trail of ether floating around the note. One of her own kind had left a trace of themselves! This strand sensuously stroked her hand before becoming disengaged in the wind and floating off. Rather hurt, she wondered why the fairy population was continuing to punish her, but her mood changed to anger as she considered how hard she had worked to establish herself. No, even more than that, she had even changed herself, so that she would fit into the human world. She'd had enough and because she had one, final wish, at her disposal which was frankly wasted on the fairies, she used it to invoke a 'ceaseless solution' charm for her own benefit.

"I wish that I had a shop with an indefinite lease. Forever," she said to make it absolutely clear. Immediately, a kind man with John Lennon glasses welcomed her in through the revealed archway. She chose a pretty corner site with white wrought iron porticoes over the doorway.

"We're very into recycling, and you're just the ticket," he said, on hearing about Ensley's business.

Ensley walked into her new life made up of leaseholder's agreements, beautiful, salvaged artefacts, and self-employment. From thereon, she would be self-determining in all things and whilst she considered her future, a slight slimness affected the profile of her face, because in Fei terms she had jumped a developmental stage, one that probably should have occurred ages before. Having reached partial maturity, she comforted herself with the thought that everyone evolves in their own time.

"You're looking a bit mean around the chops," said Frances later that day.

"Charming way to talk about the new me," said Ensley, smiling anyway. "I'm just starting to get older, that's all."

"Comes to us all," said Frances with feeling, heading off to the loo for the fourth time that evening. "I'm going to have to stop drinking tea in the afternoon." She suddenly stopped and opened the window outward, dislodging an item that had been placed there by a seagull.

"Piss off!" she yelled.

"What was it?" asked Ensley startled.

"A squid, a bloody squid, dropped on the windowsill."

"How strange," said Ensley, frowning. "That's not right."

"You're telling me."

Mab didn't think it was exactly good either to be in a gutter covered in dirty water. She decided to get on with her former plan, and floating downstream, joined the London Sewerage system until it merged with the Thames overflow burrow. She regained her humanoid shape and briefly lamented the hole in her side made by the seagull's beak. Reaching the 'Other' place' she landed on the path directly in front of Sopher who exclaimed,

"I was just looking for you!" She was disgusted to notice that he had put on weight, had glowing skin and seemed to be thriving. The Sopher proceeded to communicate in his human 'talking about nothing' kind of way.

"I've been exploring the firmament and observed so many fascinating things about your world. It's a glorious place - so unspoilt. You must love living in the sea..."

Mab closed both eyes and kept them shut for a meaningful time. With less certainty, Ben blethered on, "I was also looking for Hazel. I don't suppose you've seen her?"

"No," was the sullen response, though from Ben's point of view it was hard to tell what her mood was as she just bubbled some kind of fluid at him. He continued on.

"Anyway, I don't suppose that you would consider helping Kosmo and me. We really do need to get him away from you-know-who."

"Yes, I will," said Mab, surprising Ben who was already constructing enticements for Mab towards the plan. He was also alarmed when she then sprang up behind him on his horse. "Let's go," she said, and he kicked Fenrir into a gallop, keeping his face averted from the intense smell of fish guts, rotten seaweed and something that resembled excrement, until they reached the creek where a moody crowd of trees told him that Hazel had still not returned.

For days, Ben and an eager Kosmo explored different burrows in the vicinity, little realising that Mab was duping them all along.

"Try that one," she would say, pointing to a funnel of blackness under a mossy rock.

"Are you perfectly sure?" Kosmo would ask, unconvinced. "Will it take me to where Ensley is?"

"Eventually," was Mab's response.

"... And I have to accompany Kosmo on his journey?" asked Ben.

"Yes, otherwise he will be crushed by the vortex, make yourselves ready."

Kosmo pulled the very tight finger shield encrusted with tiny emeralds off his finger, and Ben noticed the grooves it had made on his flesh from long use. He flung it into a nearby bush, and his lips met in a momentary smile as it caught on a branch and hung there, glinting in the sun. Kosmo didn't dispense of all Fei paraphernalia; he was wearing his armour as he said it gave him the sense of being protected. In a sack tied to his back, he had salvaged a few items of clothes, a silver art nouveaux bracelet Ensley had given him, and some green foods in a box to sustain him on his journey. He and Ben had already discussed what he should do for a living once he reached the human sphere, thought the discussion about money had caused some puzzlement.

"I don't mind working," Kosmo said, "... I'd do it for nothing, but are you telling me that if I didn't do a particular thing, I couldn't have sustenance?"

"Correct," said Ben, "you'd be on the cold streets."

"Oh." Suddenly, Kosmo had a misgiving about the place of his birth.

"Hurry up," said the dull voice of Mab, who was getting twitchy. For all she knew, Oona would sense the movement of the young men through the membrane and she would be caught at the scene. It was important that the witness to her machinations should be quickly dealt with too, because she had a separate plan for Ben. Kosmo noticed Mab casually putting a piece of parchment into his pocket. Immediately suspicious he asked,

"What's this?"

"A letter of introduction to the Queen of London."

"United Kingdom," Ben corrected. Mab merely sneered back at him. "Actually, that's not a bad idea; I mean, working for a queen, because you're used to queens and I think you'll find this one a little easier to serve, but you'll need to join the Blues and Royals; that's the army" he emphasised, "You can't go straight to her. No, it's okay, you can keep the letter as a reminder," he said as Kosmo was just about to throw the dirty thing on the ground. Kosmo replaced the letter in his pocket, and both he and Mab took deep breaths, but for different reasons. Kosmo suddenly felt excited to be experiencing the moment he had dreamt about for so long.

"I will tell you what to do, and you must do it direct," said Mab engineering them towards the lip of the hole that seemed to shiver as they approached. "Step in," she said and they both did, immediately feeling the drag on their legs. She told them to sit on the rim and remarked as if to herself,

"Nice and firm this one, I remember now. You was a fine little sprat you was Incomer - that other Shakespeare feller was the problem, and I was fair puffed after the chase." Mab closed her eyes and thought about how the man with the ruff was equally exhausted by the chase and sweated like a pig. She patted the side of the tunnel. "It is a good rule to always go back the ways you came. This burrow here is a travelling one going the other way, and it will take you fast. Now, Sopher, stand and wrap yourself around the Incomer, tight as you please, and don't let him loose whatever you does as you is the means of his passage." Mab seemed to find this instruction very funny indeed, and she chuckled and snorted, spraying regurgitated kelp around her head. Ben wrapped his arms as tightly as he could around Kosmo and also one leg around his calf. A strange, white miasma started to form around the both, clearly coming from Ben. The two looked briefly into each other's eyes but no message was passed as they were helpless in the situation. "Fair sad to see you go Sopher, you will be missed," Mab said, being unexpectedly sympathetic. "Think it through as you goes, to settle yourself, I mean," and she pushed gently on the two men's shoulders.

"Wait," said Ben, "I will be able to get back wont I?" but his urgent words were immediately lost in a strange power that overwhelmed and drained them away from him.

Slowly, they fell sideways and plummeted into nothing. After that, it was unclear whether they were falling up or down but the force tearing against their clothes and skin was immense. Ben's hair, which was now long, streamed behind him. Kosmo's scarf flew up against his face but he dared not release his grip on Ben to push it away. Time might have been endless or momentary, and Ben pondered on how he was losing the other sphere, a place he had come to love. Feeling loss as a pain in his chest, his fingers automatically started to prise off Kosmo's armoured jerkin. It was as if a person were doing it specifically. It was as if the thought had triggered a reactive process and his body wasn't linked with his thoughts. In a terror, he knew with certainty he couldn't follow the onwards journey with Kosmo. His will was pulling him the other way.

"Kosmo, Kosmo, I can't...." Ben exclaimed. Kosmo couldn't feel the release of Ben's hand through the armour and he only had time to say,

"What?" before he was flung like a doll far away, becoming increasingly small as he covered either an immense distance or a short one. Either way, blackness swallowed him... he vanished into the gloom, yelling something that Ben couldn't catch.

***

Time stopped and so did movement. Ben didn't realise he was doing this himself, actually slamming the brakes on his progress, only that he was hovering like Hermes in one place with nothingness around him: no person, thing, or destination. Even worse, no Kosmo. Panic chased through him. Had he killed Kosmo with his thoughts? Would he be crushed within the burrow? He had no idea, but even in his weightlessness, he felt a crushing sense that he had caused his friend's demise through his own selfish and self-indulgent thinking. 'I just didn't want to go in the first place,' he thought to himself, and that was foremost in my mind. 'I should have put him first.' As with much guilty thinking, Ben proceeded to berate himself for a situation that had been entirely out of his hands, caused by forces far beyond his own simple powers - caused by Mab, in fact.

He decided to go back, to find out what really happened and if he could do anything about it. This seemed a logical step, but it was not so easy going the other way. Finding that there was some kind of ground under his feet, though it flew up at him in flurry of flakes like a cloud of tiny bats, he mentally encouraged his feet to make contact with the insubstantial stuff. Then he walked for miles through the darkness, amorphous blackness shifting into different mounds and configurations on the wall-type structures that were also apparently there on his right and left; though he had to concentrate at first to make himself believe that. He remembered thinking how odd it was that black could have so many shades. Once, he touched whatever it was that he was travelling through and gasped as a fizzing shock rocketed through his hand. He knew he had been changed forever by the contact, and this later proved to be true with the initiation of a bony growth on the side of all his three fingers: index, middle, and ring, that would eventually cause a merging into one. In short, he would grow a wand. He clutched his now madly painful hand in the other and lurched onwards like a hunched medieval serf, giving more thought to the idea of blackness. He knew then why the thin places were called burrows; they were causeways made from the same substance that life came from and which initiated life itself. Earth was life but what he was walking on wasn't exactly ground earth - it was invested in something else: a will of some sort, a biological power that was unstoppable. He didn't know how, but the darkness was life too, and he could understand why the Fei dressed their new-born children in robes and shawls of black and gold. Children of the chilly stars, he thought lyrically - they have more of the darkness in them than humans. Humans are so, so... diluted, he thought, a little prejudicially. Ben intuited all these revelations with no evidence whatsoever, though later, he would need to substantiate his ideas a little more than just thinking about them; being half human after all meant facts were the secure cornerstones of his existence.

Progress through the tunnel involved strenuous effort. Sometimes, he felt he was going uphill and sometimes down, but at the same time the firmament still felt quite unsubstantial so that he was never too sure where his feet were. It was all quite exhausting mentally, and he lost the thrill of his earlier thoughts after a while. He wondered how on earth Mab had traipsed through with a newborn baby on her arm. By the time he emerged out of the burrow he was in a very poor mood and wasn't at least surprised to see Mab still there, squatting on the ground like a mollusc in her skirts. She prised open a wavy eye,

"A success?" she asked casually.

"You know dammed well it wasn't - primed me, didn't you?"

"I did no such thing. Take your hand off my throat," she choked.

"Where's Kosmo? I mean, is he still alive? I mean, he must be, mustn't he?" Ben was in a frantic state. "I seem to feel...."

Mab interrupted him, "Don't know. Don't care neither," said the wretched creature, ducking under his arm.

"But is you alright, my boy?"

"Never mind that, get me back right now."

"I will," she said, mustering up what she hoped was a sincere tone. It still didn't match the flatness of beak and the uninspired eyes, but he had no options. Whilst Mab clutched him by the hand and led him across a lane to an entirely different burrow, suspicion caused him to protest. "What's this?" he asked, trying to unclamp a tentacle that appeared from somewhere behind her.

"Oftentimes it is best to take a different way in. Look how nice and smooth is the patch of grass afore and the lead in."

"Wait a minute, I know that holly bush!" The holly scowled at him.

"It knows you too, Sopher," she said and pushed with all her might.

Ben found he was walking, in a field, around a long barrow. He thought about the words in his mind, 'in a field around a long barrow...', and his spirits sunk. "Oh hell!" he roared, knowing he'd been tricked, and threw his rucksack on the ground. He was so distraught, he didn't notice that behind him, something else emerged quite silently. This thing lingered momentarily by the entrance to the burrow before concealing itself in nearby undergrowth.

Chapter 19 Brave New World

Kosmo wasn't happy, and he wasn't dead either. He hadn't ended up right near to Ensley as Mab had planned; in fact, he had been flung towards a monarchical-sounding place as that had been uppermost in his mind before he and Ben separated. Apparently, he was at Victoria coach station, and it was pretty awful. Some desperate-looking people immediately bothered him for coins when he landed as he looked so kempt and shiny. However, when they saw his distress and confusion, they tagged him down as one of them and offered him a sip from a can of Special Brew. Kosmo declined.

He knew that the coaches reversing quietly in and out of the station were methods of transport because Ensley had been somewhat fascinated by cars, buses, trains, boats and planes. Seeing these, in reality, was a different thing though and a frisson of horror went right through him initially as he observed their size, power and the cacophony of noise they emitted. After a while, horror was translated into excitement, and he decided he rather fancied having an experience on one, after all. He knocked on a closed door of a silver coach where a man was eating food within and the door hissed open like a contented snake.

"Good day," said Kosmo, stepping onto the gently moulded floor. "May I have a go at controlling your fab vehicle?" Kosmo used a colloquialism that Ensley favoured for expressing admiration.

"You havin' a laugh?" asked the driver.

"No," said Kosmo, in confusion. "I just fancied having a drive? Rather than a laugh, I mean."

"Out!" said the driver, fiercely, pointing with the remains of his sandwich. Kosmo retreated immediately. "Bloody nutter," said the driver looking at his phone and he closed the doors with an efficient button.

Kosmo lingered on the street outside for a while. By looking at a map attached to a lamp post, he found out that he was in a town called London but had no idea that Ensley was even in the same country. Though she was actually only a twenty-minute drive away, she might as well have been on the moon. The scale of the map meant nothing to Kosmo. Quite used to feeling dislocated from his previous land and its people, he now realised he had never felt so alone in his life.

That first night for Kosmo was terrible. The depot was never quiet, and it seemed to be coated in some kind of dust. The air was leaden and poisonous to him, so he covered his head and face with his scarf and tied it at the back. This seemed to make people nervous, and a wide zone of exclusion materialised around him. Taking his breastplate off, which he put over his torso like a shield against the world, he lay down on a metal bench once night fell; then he settled himself into a foetal position. Sadly, sleep wasn't to be his friend, and when exhaustion did finally creep up on him, he soon woke with his limbs deadened. Every single position was painful after a few minutes, and finally, he gave up and sat up. He wrapped the scarf back around his neck, put his armour in the sack, and watched the dawn emerge in rose tints over the buildings opposite. The early morning sun threw lights across his face, and a kind person, seeing the beautiful youth sitting stranded and forlorn in the middle of chaos, took pity on him. This nameless person, who spoke a different tongue, bought him coffee and a croissant and touched him gently on the shoulder with immaculate fingernails.

"Bon courage l'ami," she said, and Kosmo knew she was his guardian spirit of the day so he took heart immediately, having such a positive nature, after all. Refreshed and with a sense of new beginnings, he set off down Buckingham Palace Road, fully intending to find out what destiny had in store for him. A few miles away, Ensley sat in her shop, drinking 'her' morning coffee, wondering at her selfishness in using the last of her wishes on herself, though, as she reasoned, a girl has to eat.

This was the same argument that a hungry Anne Shakespeare had, in a previous time, used to motivate her husband to poach on Sir Thomas Lucy's land just the once as "A good bit of venison will do us well." The result was calamitous, with her bedraggled husband returning some six hours later as a madman with twigs in his beard. Anne never knew that her husband had been away for far longer than she had presumed, years in fact, though the number six would haunt her for the rest of her life: six hours in the forest and six years to regulate her husband's behaviour sufficiently not to cause gossip in the town. Her husband couldn't speak at the start of the calamity - she didn't know why. Her relief when the unintelligible gibberish that initially came out of his mouth was formed into words, was short-lived, however. He would then relate all sorts of craziness about faeries, particularly a venomous one called Mab, with each telling getting faster and wilder. At times such as this, his wife, placing each hand on either side of his head in a vice-like grip, would stare him in the eyes and say, "Peace, peace husband, thou talkest of nothing, 'Tis but fantasy born of an idle brain." This seemed to calm him greatly, and he decided that productivity was the key to managing his affliction. Sitting at a rickety desk, his inspirational thoughts took on an organic life and formed a skin. A bulbous shape emerged from his right temple, which initially caused him distress as he sensed it grow, but this changed into relief once he felt it detach. It was a magnificent bubble that lowered onto the page and he felt unreasonably proud of it. Prodding it tentatively, the bubble burst, providing a scattering of words upon the page. Shakespeare traced over these quite happily. Then the next descended, but he left this whole and merely looked through it at the beautiful people and spirits roaming an island in the sphere's interior. "A brave new world," he muttered to himself, glancing up to see Anne frowning at him. She only saw his fixed attention to a ghostly nothing and she crossed herself. Within the bubble, there were also red bellowing monsters charging around, until they stopped and disgorged passengers; but he didn't know anything about buses, having only seen these briefly in the time vortex, so he ignored these and focused on the people who populated the bubbles. These people were often in disguise, never revealing who they truly were and what they were up to until much later when they changed clothing. He felt this was a clever conceit and used the idea of identity and confusion many times in his work. After all, he was as much confused as many of the characters he brought to life, or was inspired to bring to life through his travels in the other sphere. In the end, Shakespeare felt somewhat compensated for his traumatic and demeaning experiences in Faery. Occasionally, he wafted a few bubbles onward through the gap between the worlds, for he knew that the Fei liked to 'read' images and would appreciate the interesting, and sometimes bloodthirsty worlds he had constructed. He also knew they loved conspiracies and fighting. Ben Sopher agreed that in all Fei folk tales, it is a case of, "The more blood the better." Shakespeare's works have plenty of that.

Mortals tend not to see Shakespeare's' works in bubble form unless they are particularly weird themselves, though their shifting, prismatic nature does invariably manifest in the tangentially different interpretations of Shakespeare's works. This causes a great deal of dissension in keeping with fairy troublemakers and is a carry-over from Shakespeare's time in Fei which tainted him all his days. On one particular day in 1972 a student, did see the bubbles for what they really are and said, "Man, those colours!" but he was told off for coming to his English seminar stoned, which, in fact, he wasn't. He was forcibly evicted by a caretaker when he started chasing invisible bubbles around the room and climbing up the lecturer's bookcases. Again, contention plagues those who have any contact with the Fei.

Kosmo's progress across London was sedate compared with the general furore in the 'Other' place. Of course, Oona felt the movements of the Sopher and Incomer like a tidal bore plunging away from her world almost immediately after they had left. This was because Ben's power in holding and protecting the Incomer was distinct and new in him. He was effervescent with emergent power and she knew, finally, he was a force to be reckoned with - even if he had incomprehensibly suddenly departed from them, just when he was getting interesting. She was determined to find out why and was dragging Mab, whom she had captured gliding quietly out of Poule Harbour, by the neck, back through the burrow the two men had travelled through together.

"Ow, ow, ow," remarked Mab as she was grazed along the containment field of the burrow, sparks flying everywhere. "A confession note, a confession, Your Majesty," she burbled.

"I'm not listening to you, foul mollusc thing. If you were not my great aunt, I would squash you here and now. Regardless, we will get to the bottom of this without reference to your conniving, two-faced nature."

"I 'as one face Majesty, I can prove it," said Mab, proving the exact opposite by wavering between cuttlefish and humanoid and settling on neither in her distress." Oona didn't respond to her, and soon both were trailing after Kosmo, who was looking in a window of a shop where there were pictures of men and women in fine regalia, seated on horses. Oona paused. She noticed the Incomer's relaxed frame, his gentle smile, the red buses passing and his learnt obliviousness to the hustle and bustle of the town. She knew, finally, he belonged in that exact place. Oona's pause was overlong, then she abruptly addressed the cowering Mab who was beginning to stink in the sun.

"What did you want to say to me then?" she asked.

"A note, a note," Mab said, realising how stupid she sounded suddenly. Oona didn't care about writing at all. She was Fei; actions were everything. The ill-favoured goblin, her co-conspirator, had already broken her curfew and gibbered to her about her daughter's supposed treason. Of course, Oona had her destroyed on the spot before she even finished speaking. Oona raised her wand very deliberately, Mab winced and her shoulders concertinaed down into her chest, but the object of the pointing wand, a thin parchment, lifted from Kosmo's back pocket and sailed towards them.

"Open it then!" and Mab, in faltering words, read the contents,

Me and her, the erstwhile Majesty is betrayers
We always did have to be together
Sorree
Incomer.

Oona stood, transfixed onto the spot, lost. 'We always did have to be together,' caused a bit of a pang. She was reminded about something else to do with hand holding and the sad and lonely Monarch at the end of a mirror's vision. The nonsensical words on the paper struck a chord as printed words always did seem to do when they were read to Oona; she felt that was another good reason to avoid ever learning to read herself. She plucked the note out of Mab's hands and folded it over and over as if by the folding she could make it so small, that it would disappear. She knew it told a truth and was a ripple of something yet to come, though the note's genesis came from the hand of a liar. In a distant voice she said,

"Forget this pursuit," to Mab... "All of it. It's over," though she knew deep down that was far from the case. "He will stay here now..." Her tone was melancholic for a moment, but then she rounded on the sea creature who was blowing the remnants of sea water in and out of her gills. Apropos to nothing, she screamed, "... And you can avail yourself of the moment and get out of my sight." Mab did as she was told; picking up her skirts and wrappings, she fled, never to be seen or heard of again. By this time, Kosmo had opened the door of the shop, making Oona shudder, bringing her imprinted fear of them to the fore. This was a standard Fei response to doors, but the reaction was heightened in Monarchs. Her nightmares of being made to go out, or even worse, *to go* in at the discretion of another, had not left her from childhood. She stood awhile, watching people bustling up and down the pavement, going in and out of buildings and vehicles. Two individuals above her clambered up scaffolding. Her right hand wavered around, deliberately, as she took it all in, causing burrows everywhere in the entire world to seal shut, for now, until at her command. There had been quite enough comings and goings without her say-so, she believed. Oona watched the workers on the roof answering phones, opening coke cans, and hammering in nails. She mused that for some, this place would be a paradise, a relatable home, though she was struck at how anyone could ever conceive of such an idea. She thought it was perfectly horrible, so bitty, so abrasive with no synchronicity in thought or action. "Moronic" was her final, damming verdict as she stepped back into the only burrow that was still operative.

***

Ben made his dreary way back to Dorchester. He walked for miles because he had no money to get a taxi or a bus. From Poule town, he managed to hitch a ride to the junction between Dorchester and the west country, but he still had a way to go. It started to rain lightly as he approached the town, and a light mist partially concealed St Peter's tower, which always looked so much like battlements, rather than a church, to Ben, on the cusp of the hill ahead. The idea of hiddenness and duplicity, struck a very ironic chord with him and he thought regretfully of the sunshine and freshness of the world he had been tricked into leaving behind. Instantly, the warm rain stopped and a late summer sun appeared briefly before descending a bit hopelessly between the chimney pots as night fell. The warmth and the fact that a passer-by recognised him after a pause and said, "Hello," might have encouraged him a little, but it didn't.

"Where've you been? Can I book in with you tomorrow?" the woman asked and Ben, not knowing what else to say replied, "Okay," in a tight voice. "Ten-thirty?" she shouted after him. Plodding onwards he took a left hook down Durngate Street cradling his right hand, which was agonisingly painful, vowing to make a wormwood poultice as soon as possible to soothe it. As this thought drifted through his mind, it occurred to him that he was irrevocably changed by his adventures and would never be able to settle in the human sphere again. Coming to the end of the street, he suddenly realised he was headed back to a flat he no longer had, so did a detour towards Terri's place. Ben nearly groaned aloud when he thought of all the nights ahead on a sofa bed when he had had a four poster back at his Fei *home*, and with that, he felt ridiculously close to tears when he thought about the word, and what it meant to him. Home, that crazy, unpredictable place of exotic sounds, textures and tastes so that every day was a sensory feast and thinking, mundane thinking, took a back stage position. He had left a world lived by the senses for one where everything was shackled to a routine and there was little time for spontaneity. The rich texture of his existence was a world away now and he didn't know what to do. If he went back now (if he could go back), would it even be the same? He passed a man who interrupted his depression, saying,

"Oh, it's you - the wife will be pleased. I'll let her know."

The only certainties he had were in knowing Terri was sound and wouldn't turn him away and also that he would probably be booked solid in the salon all the next day. He walked on, his footsteps echoing down an extremely narrow road that terminated with an old Methodist chapel at the end. There was a footpath that bordered its margins, and he took this, knowing he was five minutes away from Terri's and rest. His strange eyes noticed the microbial life busily taking apart a half-eaten sandwich at the side of the road and a very large brown rat approaching the whole with great absorption.

"Hello you," he said to the rat, and was surprised when the rat answered back,

"Oh, hello, nice to see you again." 'Again?' thought Ben, but his mood was too flat to think about it further, and he just passed it by.

Chapter 20 The Dorchester Creative Arts Club

There was the usual dissension at the club with Izzy saying she had brought her paints and, in that case, why the hell were they doing reading.

"We're doing reading, *again*," she stressed.

"We're not 'doing reading'," Mr Sims corrected her. "We are reading."

"Yeah, whatever! I thought this was an art club and we're always doing it – reading, I mean."

Mr Sims sighed. As Isabel frequently reminded him, he was 'old' and therefore didn't exactly know much about art, apparently. He wondered how his grandson could have produced such a creature. Words failed him – frequently. In the meantime, he placated her with the suggestion that after the reading circle, they would still have plenty of time for individual work, and that could include lots of different creative projects, because that's what art was. For instance, he explained, Bettina Esterhazy had brought her knitting. Izzy prodded Bettina's tangled web of wool doubtfully and pulled a stupid face behind her back. James Sims was tempted to suggest that her own pictures looked like something an infant school child would do, but he didn't. His voice wavered on, talking about William Morris and his many accomplishments in the literary and physical arts, interior decoration, everything... until his words collapsed into a vaporous wisp. He really didn't have the energy for her and wished he'd never suggested she came in the first place, but it did give his grandson a much-needed break from Izzy's perpetual moaning. At ninety-three years old, James Sims was still running his very successful militaria business, but just online now. Even so,

Thursday nights with Izzy tipped the tenuous balance of his life the wrong way a little more than he cared to admit.

"Wot you talkin' about wallpaper for now."

"I didn't say that. I was giving Morris as an example of someone who could do lots of things – I wish you'd listen. Help me!" he appealed to Hippy Phil, who was stirring a cup of tea into a maelstrom which he kept having the urge to do after reading about burrows in the big, red book in the previous session.

"Shall we start?" Asked Sarah Frayne, sensing the tension in the air. A circle was formed, and they read together. Miles Johnson, an eighteen-year-old student shook his head once they'd finished Chapter seventeen.

"Nope, sorry," he said. "It doesn't make sense." This gave Izzy the opportunity to chip in,

"Nothing makes sense in that book, and I don't see..." She stabbed her finger on the page of the book she shared with Phil... "why we have to read each little bit at a time together and not on our own." Phil gave her an incredulous look and snapped the book shut. Izzy said, "Ow", though he hadn't actually caught her finger.

"Because it makes more sense to do that," said Miles coldly to Izzie. "We've already discussed how there's a supernatural element to this text and it throws up different versions sometimes for different people – just like you had a problem with only seeing strange creatures at one point and no text at all." Izzy blushed at this. "If we're to gain a consistent reading, we have to do it simultaneously, because there's such a.... a plasticity about the whole thing. We don't just want to read what's in our heads if that impression is dominant, and I'm sure that's what would be transposed on the page. Monsters!" he said again, as a challenge, and Izzy looked away, embarrassed. "To be honest, what I'm bothered about is the recent inconsistency of characterisation."

"In what way?" asked Bettina Esterhazy, her dark eyes

twinkling, her hands engrossed in finger-knitting some lurid purple yarn.

"Well, considering that Ben has just lost his closest friend in a dark tunnel, I think his reactions are a bit muted. He wouldn't just walk home in a bad mood. I mean, where's the description of him scrabbling at the burrow in despair?"

"Well, there wouldn't be any point, would there, dear?" said Bettina. "Oona put a block on travel and that's it. One just accepts these things." Mr Sims looked up at this point and stared hard at her.

"Anyway," she continued, "the Fei wouldn't react that way to a separation."

"Good point," said Faith, Sarah's friend. "Ben has become naturalised as a Fei person, so it follows that he would take a more brutal view of relationships. In the description, it seems he's more homesick than lovesick, and that makes sense when you compare how Ensley Knight was when she first came over to our world. The dislocation from her natural environment was devastating to her. I mean, she nearly died."

"Well, I want to say something," said Izzy. "For a start, I knew that boy, and I reckon he was wet. A right dork. He'd probably be blubbing all over the place by now."

"Knew?" asked Phil, making sure he gained eye contact.

"Yes, I knew him in the queue when we went to get my original book that went wrong."

"You – knew – him – in – a – queue..." Phil spelt the words out slowly and she blushed again. She hated the lot of them, including Great-Grandad who never took anything she said seriously.

"Izzy, said Sarah quietly, it doesn't matter that the other book went wrong, somehow or even that the characters are somewhat, well, different now. This version's okay. The way Ben is here, must be taken as a more honest overview of his character." She ignored Miles snorting at that. "Shall we finish the chapter? Ben has just arrived at the outskirts of Dorchester and he's obviously feeling depressed judging by the pathetic fallacy that the other co-author..."

"Whom we don't know...," said James Sims.

"Whom we don't know," echoed Sarah, "... has used to emphasise Ben's mood. For whatever reason, homesickness or love sickness, he feels just terrible." Sarah nodded at a girl called Millie who was sharing her book with Bettina. "Might be just as well to stop her knitting for a bit." Bettina was slumped to the side with her eyes closed and her mouth open, but her fingers miraculously still busy at work. Millie sprang into a well-rehearsed response, carefully untangling the skeins from around Esther's fingers, managing to retain the loops so that the work wouldn't be ruined. The random sunbeam that was darting through the window but around the furniture specifically to shine on Esther's left cheek switched off abruptly, and Miles said something about laser toys and kids, it being dark outside now, and all.

Faith read aloud then in a quiet, melodious tone, and Phil pointed to each word in turn for Izzy's benefit, but she preferred listening and was sitting, rapt, taking it all in before she suddenly yelled, making everyone jump.

"It's now, it's here!" she yelled. "Our lives are happening in the book - I threw that sandwich down before I came in, and it was egg and cress."

"Disgusting," said her great-grandad.

"I don't care. I got in the book, or, my sandwich did anyway. So, stuff the lot of you."

"I'll take a turn now," said an eager Millie, who strangely didn't contradict what Izzy had said. They had all got much more accepting of the book's strange hold on reality. Millie put on a very good cockney accent for the rat whose captured words now said, "Alright, mate?" rather than just 'Hello'," to Ben. Millie was a performance poet and went on to extend the rat's speech for effect and also dramatise him in an entertaining way by snuffling and squeaking in a jolly way. Clearly, though, the parameters of the book didn't allow for ad-libbing because when they all turned the next page it was blank. Flipping the page back, Bettina discovered that the rat had now vanished altogether but the sandwich was still there, rotting away. Mille said, "Oh, I'm really sorry, I erased him," and Ben was depicted as noting nothing more than a small, dark shape in the bushes that made an unconvincing squeak.

"You've gone and done it now," said Bettina, unconvinced. We're going to end up with flawed copies at this rate. We've lost a bit of perspective here."

"I don't agree," said Miles. "I think the rat was just an irrelevant detail anyway. It needed to be edited out."

"Poor rat," said Sarah. "I rather like him."

"Shush, shut up, all of you," said Izzy. "Listen!" They did, and sluggish footsteps could be heard passing by on the street below. On cue, everyone charged to the windows and hung out, yelling at Ben, who, in turn, looked up, and was startled to see a group of angry people shouting, "Oy, Stop right there! Don't move..." and things like that. Ben's heart lurched from a steady rhythm to a pulsing charge. He did the only sensible thing anyone would do; he ran away.

"Oh dear," said Bettina opening the nearest book on a chair, "We seem to have panicked him unnecessarily."

"Perhaps not," said Phil, reading the next page containing some worrying information. "It says here that unbeknown to Ben, the '*something*' that had slipped through the burrow after him, had actually been tracking him for miles. Occasionally, it dropped to the ground on all fours, grabbed earth to itself, and sniffed it as if it were a dog. It always kept just out of sight, barely concealed, but its hidden presence was helped by the fact that Ben was so distracted. I think that boy's troubles tend to follow him wherever he goes," Phil concluded.

"It's hard to believe that he wouldn't be aware of a dog thing following him over such a long distance, even so." Sarah, normally so trusting, was highly sceptical. For me, the plotline has lost credibility.

"I agree", said Faith, "Also, bear in mind that an acutely sensitive, self-conscious man like Ben, would never be unknowingly stalked. Miles is right about the character inconsistency."

"No, no, you're all wrong," said Bettina, strange, orange sparks flaring in her dark eyes, an illusion created by her position she was in, in front of the street light beyond the room, no doubt. "You is not taking account of his true nature. For goodness' sakes, he's Fei through and through, which means he would have a heightened sensibility, far betterer than any animal on your Earth firmament...." Bettina, normally, so reserved, became agitated, and her syntax collapsed accordingly. "... E'en so, he mightn't respond to what was following him, if..."

"What?" asked Sarah.

"He knew the thing following him so well that his radar was not on alert."

"I think that's even more worrying." Faith was genuinely troubled. "They say that crimes are committed mostly by people you know well." But Bettina was dismissive.

"You is talking about humans and their propensity to be sneaky and devious in their vengeance, not open like us... I mean, them. A Fei creature would kill you outright as soon as look at you. They don't hang about." She picked up her knitting and her fingers absently continued their work as she walked back to the window. "Look," she said and pointed to a figure lurking in the shadows of the terraced buildings in front of them. They all caught a glint of light-coloured hair (or fur), but only for a moment because it suddenly vanished.

"There it is again," said Izzy, who had raced across to the east side window. It had covered the distance in less than a second.

"Definitely Fei then," Bettina said.

"Do you think we should warn Ben about it?" asked Miles.

"Yes," said Phil, who was watching the strands of green that both the departing Fei, Ben and whatever had been tracking him, had left behind on the bushes below, "But there's no rush, I think we should listen to Bettina. If there's no imminent danger, it can wait until tomorrow at the earliest. We should let the poor bloke settle in for now."

"Do you want to do it?" asked Sarah.

"No, this is a young person's game. I've been there and done it."

"Have you?" asked Izzie, interested. Phil ignored her but he threw James a significant look. Izzy caught this look like a baton that passed like an invisible shudder between them.

"Grandad?" she asked, uncertainly. "What does he mean?"

"Nothing," James said with a finality that Izzie was programmed to respond to. Grandad was both strict and a pain, so she slumped back down into a chair moodily nearly tipping it backwards.

"It's alright Izzy," said Phil. "I think Miles will sort it out as he's very organised." Miles jumped.

"Oh, okay." He smiled, pleased to be nominated to do something. Miles always had the worrying suspicion that people found him a bit boring. He was becoming used to his words having little impact. In a way, that was what had led him to the Dorchester Creative Arts Club because it tended to follow a democratic process for speaking and people were surprisingly amenable to listening to him, even if he was talking crap; which he thought he had a tendency to do from time to time.

"I'll chase him down at the hair salon tomorrow, before it closes," he said.

"Good man," said Phil with undisguised relief. He felt in his pocket for his hip flask and turned away discretely after unscrewing it with fumbling arthritic hands.

"I'm going to bring this session to a close," said Sarah. "It's been fun." The rest of the group looked at her a bit dubiously, but Sarah just smiled. These days, she preferred challenges. She was way past subduing her perception with drink or drugs, or, the worst thing of all, plain avoidance. She wanted to bring the weirdness on, because it somehow matched a deep, shifting rhythm inside her. She did realise others weren't quite at her stage and the book's effects sometimes overloaded them. She watched Phil helping Bettina down the steep stairs, though it was unclear who was helping who as both looked in a near state of collapse, and Phil appeared to be slightly drunk. Izzy held back, left her chair once the others had filed out, and approached Sarah at an angle.

"I expect it's quite hard working in that bookshop?" she asked Sarah shyly. At one stage she and Sarah had been close friends. She hoped they could be again.

"It's not too bad, I only open in the morning. In the afternoons I visit Petey in the hospital, just to reassure him everything's ticking over in the way he wanted."

"I expect you've got big plans, for... I mean, for later on."

"I do, it's going to be great. Do you know about it? You weren't in the group when we read that bit – about the shop changing."

"Oh no, I mean, I do know." Izzy's face was beaming. "All those fairy people and the other ones, too, sleeping on couches and stuff."

"You read it!"

"Yes, I did." Izzy seemed to grow a bit as she admitted this. "I was in the cafe next to the bookstore one day, and this woman was really rude to me about being too dense to understand the book. I thought I'd prove her wrong. Also, I was stuck with the bloody book, because I couldn't get a refund." Sarah thought about Terri and sighed. Good old Terri but she could be a bit short-sighted about people sometimes. She wouldn't like Terri venting at her!

"I was in a mood at the time; you know how I get when I'm stressed."

"Yes."

"I had my money out ready when I went to buy a latte and they'd changed the price. The man told me to read the board if I didn't agree. It was in swirly chalk. I couldn't make it out, so I freaked. Terri, who was in the cafe, took his side when I was in a meltdown, so I wasn't exactly going to explain what was going on with me, especially when I felt like punching her head in."

"It's a shame. I'm sorry you were so upset but your reading must have come on if you read that whole chapter."

"Oh, it has, and you know, the weirdest thing is, the font seemed to get bigger and in green, which always helps somehow and slowly the pictures, which I read before, faded behind the words until they just weren't there anymore." Izzy paused, deep in thought. "I think it helped that there was something about me in the book too, even if it was nasty – I wanted to read about me. It felt good to be included you know, even if I was being a little bitch."

"You read about me too, didn't you? Earlier? When I met Petey in his shop."

"Yes."

"Thank you." Sarah's voice was so quiet, it was barely discernible. "I kept feeling, a while ago, that someone sympathetic had my back. I wonder if you reading that section actually firmed up my storyline."

"Dunno. Glad I did something good though."

At that point, if it were the old days, and Sarah and Izzy were still acting parts, the two might have hugged, but they didn't need to. "Anyway," concluded Izzy, "... who gives a shit why, you're a loser and I'm thick, but it doesn't matter because we're both stars in the book."

"Just like your famous sandwich."

"Too right, I'm gonna frame that thing."

"Not really!"

"Yeah, I am."

"You're a bit like Oona and her magic case." Sarah noted Izzy's incomprehension. "She kept her magic book, in it; it's in an earlier section."

"Well, I'm keeping mine in a clear box from Poundworld." Izzy grinned, her grounded nature charging back to the fore. The joking clicked the earlier sentimentality off just like the lights were, the next minute, and the two left. A sun spot remained like a gold coin on the floor for a moment next to Bettina's chair, but then that, too, blinked off.

Chapter 21 Sickness and Health

The start of Ensley's day went something like this: She would hop out of bed, take a quick shower, and then scroll through the auction sites for anything valuable that had somehow been undervalued. Ensley had a good eye for antiques and retro items that would soon become in vogue. Of course, it helped that she had moved both back and forward in time with cousin Hedera and didn't need to rely on guesswork as far as market trends went. At first, the auction houses didn't understand her motivations to buy any old thing that seemed worthless, but then they came to admire her canny insights, and dealers were told to watch the Knight woman to see what she was up to next. Ensley still didn't relate well to the concept of money. She had learnt, in part through Frances's interventions, that without money in contemporary society, you were pretty much doomed and would probably end up grubby, depressed and wailing for loose change in the subways. Ensley still gave money to these poor folk but not £20 notes, as she had at the very start, because Frances told her that was a bit excessive and she had to look after her own interests too. Also, a very large group of homeless people tended to be waiting for her every day when she tried to catch the tube.

"Excuse me, excuse me, dear friends," Ensley would eventually say, trying to weave her way through the mass of them. "I haven't got time to converse, but here are some sandwiches and crisps." She would dump the bag and run before anyone complained that the value of donations had decreased dramatically. Ensley felt embarrassed, but she knew now that she was better off paying directly to the night shelters. She had no idea that for four nights her dear friend Kosmo actually benefitted from her generosity and had slept on a little camp bed in central London. Eventually, the crowd that she had created on

Westminster Bridge Road depleted to one hopeful soul and then none at all, so she could slip through the station without delay. However, she still had to make time before leaving the flat to brief Frances about her day. Ensley would ask over and over, "Are you alright? Really? I mean, how do you feel? Have you got any plans for the day?" Frances would rumble something incoherent that sounded a bit like, "Leave me alone," but in a clearer voice, once she'd woken up properly, she would say,

"I'm okay, love, don't worry about me, I've got a ton of washing to do...." or something in a similar vein. Ensley knew that all this was perfectly untrue because Frances looked and probably felt terrible, and she definitely wouldn't be doing anything constructive, like washing. Though it seemed implausible, Frances had become even greyer in complexion than previously, and her actions had followed this decline so she operated like a faulty motor in its death throes. Her deterioration had manifested in slow and fast modalities, and normal movement was exiled. For instance, she would travel in glacial steps around the kitchen whilst making a cup of tea but would charge like a charioteer down the high street, dragging her trolley as if the hounds of hell were after her. Caught in a remembrance of a vanishing child, if she heard a baby's cry, or saw a bonneted head, this would trigger a flight back into the past. Her old legs would be galvanised just as if she were still on that sandy path years before, and it was clear, she couldn't stop. Though Frances insisted she was, "Okay, all things considered, insisting, look, I have everything I need," Ensley didn't believe her words. She knew Frances was talking about material things and not the intrinsic deep needs of her inner self. Ensley had intuited that Frances's 'self', had actual portions of it missing and far from having everything she needed, she had very little in terms of solace and comfort. Coming home from work, Ensley would sometimes find the abandoned shopping trolley in the gutter, fruit and veg spoiled and dinted tins rolling everywhere. Ensley would pick it all up and buy replacements, even though she was tired after her long day. Neither she nor Frances mentioned how Ensley micro-managed the onslaught of trauma in the present and how far things had gone. They both politely skirted around it all, but Ensley knew, deep down, that the trauma would eventually kill Frances, if she didn't kill herself deliberately once she became too exhausted to cope. Something had to be done, and soon, but how? Ensley had used her three wishes to support her own needs, and she believed she had insufficient power to restore Kosmo to Frances. Even if she did find him, would the prolonged separation destroy any hope of a positive reunion? Linear time was ever dictatorial in the way events played out. She learnt all about cause and effect when she met Descartes briefly - the old bore. Ensley sighed. It was because Frances was lamenting the loss of a baby, that she wondered whether an adult replacement fail to suffice? Perhaps the solution to the old hurt is never that clear because the hurt takes on a life of its own. Also, Ensley felt sorrowfully, there never is any going back to a previous place exactly as you were. She had often applied this concept to her own situation, believing that if she ever managed to return to the world of Fei, she would go back as a stranger, because so much had happened to her. Anyway, all of this was hypothetical because she wasn't going there, and Kosmo wasn't coming back, unless she really pulled something out of the bag. Ensley loved that colloquialism because she had once known someone with a magic bag who effectively pulled a small abode out of it and then lived in it happily for years. She wished she had a magic bag too, because if she did, she'd pull all sorts of fantastic stuff out of it, including Kosmo.

Later that day, Ensley studied her profile in the mirror above the sink in her shop as she washed up two mugs. The day had been good; she had made two very profitable sales; one being an arts and crafts pewter bowl with feathery ferns hammered into the rim. It had been difficult to let it go, and after a protracted battle over the price, she had encouraged the buyer to sit down with her and have tea and biscuits, so that she could say goodbye properly - not to the customer, but to the bowl. She was most surprised when the bowl kept creeping towards her and nuzzling her hand, though it pretended not to. Somehow, it had become invested with magic, though she couldn't explain for a minute how that had happened. To distract the attention of the customer, whose name was Edwin, she wrapped the item tightly in some iridescent paper that had been within the sheaves of standard tissue paper on the counter top. The paper was so lovely, she was reluctant to let that go, too, but was pleased to discover lots more interspersed within the other pieces. In fact, as she lifted the plain sheaves up, she seemed to find endless quantities of it. She made a note to contact the suppliers to ask them if she'd been charged for this 'extra' item.

"That's nice," said Edwin, talking about the paper, as she turned the bowl over and sellotaped it in... tightly.

"Isn't it just?" Said Ensley happily. "Do come again," she said to him as she led him to the door, "... but not you," she muttered to the bowl under his arm.

"What did you say?" asked Edwin confused.

"Nothing, just clearing my throat." She shut the door and leaned against it. This brought her to the moment by the sink. She lifted up her hand, peeled off the rubber mitt, (most gloves didn't fit her), and pointed it at the window intended to magic a little bit of stained glass, just as an experiment. Perhaps she still had all her functions. Her wand finger twitched as if a benign spasm were passing through it, but nothing happened; the glass in the window remained clear. She thought about the bowl and shrugged. "Just a fluke," she said to her reflection, and then grinned. "That's just like me - a silly old fluke." She moved away from the mirror and exited the shop, intending to buy a salad from over the way. Feeling happy and satisfied with her life, she skipped and twirled on the red, tiled floor of the arcade as she went.

"You're looking happy, Ens," said Sam in the sandwich shop, immediately destroying her mood. Kosmo always abbreviated her name. Missing him could cut into any situation, any mood, ending like a pain in her chest.

"I was going to have a salad, but I think I'll go for a baked potato. Stomach's not good," she explained.

"Good choice," said Sam. "All well over there?" he nodded at her shop front.

"Yes," she said, without thinking. "Well, mostly. Perhaps in my dreams," she amended misappropriating the human colloquialism, causing Sam to pause.

***

Fairy dreams are such literal places. They're not even called dreams; they are known as 'wanderings' because, technically the person travels to a place where reparation to the psyche can happen, usually at times of illness or confusion. It is important to distinguish this from worship, which is a state of deep reverence that happens in the waking day. During wanderings the subconscious travelling to meet with another Fei, in a different place, is only partly consensual. As everyone knows, Fei are principally ego-driven creatures who live in the moment and tend not to fret over what has gone before, and therefore 'wanderings' come from a very deep need that a person may not acknowledge even to themselves, but which emerges whether they like it or not. It is not culturally sound to just go up to and ask for help in the brazen light of day, either, as most Fei are selfish, and any demands are instantly turned down. This is why acquiring support can only ever take place under cover of darkness and veiled in sleep. If a ghostly figure, for instance, is found seated in a chair at the end of your bed, it is a poor soul that has no other option but to call on you, therefore, it is quite unacceptable to turn them away - all petitions must somehow be accommodated within the boundaries of the sleep period. Wranglings about someone's problems can take ages, and the chosen 'helper' must make sound decisions on the ill person's behalf, even if all they really want to do is get back to sleep. Everyone knows what someone is talking about if they look haggard and keep saying, "I've had a terrible night," but no Fei would ever ask why - it's completely confidential. Strangely, wanderings don't occur that often due to the fact that most fairies are utterly incapable of feeling sad; if they do, they die anyway. The instinct to wander is based on trying to figure out a very baffling situation, as a person would a puzzle. This is why a stranger can be accosted in a dream, if they look like a good bet or know a lot about a specific issue. As Ensley Knight had lived a very cloistered life, and she needed a helper well versed in magical lore, it made good sense for her to hijack her father's sleep.

"Oh, hello, fancy seeing you," he said in his lovely booming way as she drifted towards him in her Coronation red dress that had somehow, in the way of dreams, reconstituted itself. Ensley noted that Finnian's eyebrows were encrusted with rime and the tip of one ear, which was currently the consistency of slate against his olive skin, had crumbled a little. As he surveyed his daughter descending quietly onto a hunk of ice, his eyes, that had flared orange as he defrosted, settled to a fairly startling cobalt blue.

"How have you been, your Highness?" she asked politely.

"Oh, not bad, not bad," he said shucking loose snow off his cloak. "Can't complain.," he said, though he looked like he wanted to. Blinking against the glare of the snow, he positioned a pair of Wayfarers onto the bridge of his nose and pushed them towards his eyes.

Ensley smiled sweetly at him; she knew he couldn't moan or gripe about his own predicaments as by law, she had centre stage.

"How can I help?" he asked, fiddling with the cord on his red velvet robe.

"It's about power, you see," Ensley opened out her arms helplessly before retrieving her wand onto her lap.

"Oh, yes?" said Finnian, his attention suddenly arrested. "Anything about power, and I'm your man, he rumbled, striking his chest with his fist," and a minor landslide started on his left taking a surprised elf with it.

"The problem is Papa; I don't think I've got any anymore."

"Not got what?" he asked, confused.

"Power."

"Don't be ridiculous," was his curt response. "Remember who you are."

"No, really, it's absolutely true," I've used all of the Coronation wishes up."

"Ahhh," Finnian levered his head back and exhaled, causing the falling snow to turn immediately into diamond dust. "You're talking about the joke, I presume? The Three Wishes Joke."

"It's hardly a joke, Papa, I've made a right, royal mess of things, as they say in London."

"Ooh, I do like your colloquialisms dear. I can see that you've been spending time doing human research."

"Actually, Papa, I'm living with humans, not researching them; I've been residing in London, and I've even got a job."

"Oh, I say, I really am out of the loop, aren't I? Loop means not knowing everything that everyone familiar to you knows. Do you like it?"

"Yes, it's really lovely, but what about the three wishes? Can they change the course of history and re-do things?"

"Well, yes, I suppose they can in a way," Finnian started scratching his stomach, "but remember, we are all subject to the dictates of fate, linear or otherwise, I'm beginning to suspect, so the wishes are just used to impose a cultural flavour onto the populace. It's just gilding the lily. Look I've done another one," he said cheerfully. Noticing his daughter looking confused at this saying, he told her that it made the everyday, just a little bit more exotic. Ensley thought about the permutations caused by her own wish-making and felt that her dad's trivialising of the Three Wishes didn't sound quite right.

"I just don't get it," she said. "I thought I could change everything for the better, from the bottom upwards, and all I've really achieved is to make things better for myself." Finnian zoomed up to her face, rather angry that she had become so warped, distanced from her self-seeking Fei nature. Ensley was too sad to retreat away from him, and anyway, her face seemed to be made out of vapour in this dream place, so it was okay.

"What is the problem with yourself?" he accused. I can see that I have been away from home for too long."

"That's what Mother used to say too." Ensley looked thoughtfully at her father, "She doesn't say it anymore though." Finnian, who had moved back through the fourth dimension to stomp up and down the ledge he was standing on, turned at that.

"Really? For how long?"

"Ages, she gave up hope and said I was hopeless too."

"Oh," he said and looked at his boots. "Oh." After a pause, he looked at her a bit sheepishly. "What do you feel you want from me?" he asked.

"A fourth wish, Papa." She spoke quickly before he had a chance to interrupt. "I know it is not the way of things, but I need a fourth wish precisely because the things that have gone wrong, I feel here." Ensley touched her chest. "I don't think it's a very constructive emotion, it drags and it's not normal. People are suffering in my plain sight and frankly it's disturbing me. And for that matter, I also don't think the three wishes are a joke because they're cruel, promising something and then taking it away, and that's not funny."

"A fourth!" Finnian said, then said it again, fixating on the notion. "We never circumvent the eternal triad. Never! You know the younglings' rhyme, 'three in one makes us strong, or fun, or something. I can't remember precisely..."

"What does that mean exactly Papa?"

"Well, I think the Great Creator thought if you wish once and the result is unpleasing, then you can have another try, and if it all goes to hell with that one, you can put things back the way they were. I'll concede that they aren't exactly a joke, but can't they be considered a kind of tutorial? An easy first try at constitutional magic? Frankly, if three wishes aren't enough to make an impact with, then the practitioner is a bit foolish. Are you being foolish, dear? You know, corrupting the established order, can bring unforeseen consequences."

"That's exactly my point. Some things need to be resolved, finally, even if it is not clear how that will pan out. Perhaps that is the whole point of the Three Wishes tradition; it shows us how striving against the odds is invariably difficult, impossible even, but it's like a benchmark that sets us the challenge. You might revel in being thwarted, Papa, you might like sticking to the three wishes principle of catastrophe and revision, but lots of us don't."

"I certainly do not!" said Finnian aghast, wondering who this spiky person was, so different from the other Fei girls who normally liked to lark around, even the royal ones.

"Well, I want a fourth wish." Ensley resumed, because I want to see what happens when someone rights a wrong. I'm overturning this tradition as Monarch." Then she knew she had him, because he bowed before her.

"Very well, I will abdicate rights to my own unused wish back to you (your mother wouldn't let me use it before, and she said two was enough for her), but I will be most interested to see what you do with it - don't be surprised if it backfires though in an unexpected way. That is the nature of power," he rambled on in a boring way, not realising Ensley had already left. He was about to tell her something else, very important, about her own power and how she shouldn't just fixate on constitutional forces, which were entirely different. He was quite peeved to realise that he was talking to himself, but two dwarves clapped when he droned to a halt, which appeased him slightly. Back in her bed, Ensley turned over and smiled in a dreamless sleep. On her bureau was a parcel addressed to Armenia containing a 'recently evaluated' pearl necklace she had excavated from her jewellery box. This, she discovered, had something very precious stuck on it. She loved her dad very much and wanted the best for him; she reasoned that if she couldn't be a proper monarch, she could at least be a kind daughter and give him a nudge in the right direction. There was that unresolved business back at home as well as in Kenyngton Row where she lived which was top priority, but it was also time Finnian and Oona sorted their own problems out or gave it up for good.

Ensley's meddling knew no bounds, which was appropriate, her being Fei, after all. Having slept well for the rest of the night, she went to her shop and sat expectantly, in a nineteenth-century carver chair waiting for the best moment to commence her plan. The fact that it could all go wrong somehow, magic being so unpredictable, caused a frisson that excited more than scared her. Then, every organ and her guiding will even deeper within said, "Now." Her body and spirit sang in unison. She gripped the arms of the chair, and her normally quiet voice took on a thunderous accent, very similar to her father's, but not Oona's whose practising magic voice was like the scream of metal wheels halted against a rail. Darkness flocked to her, and a wish was born. Ensley sat in the chair all day, and when customers did enter, they exited pretty quickly, muttering that they would come back on a good day. They had no idea what they were talking about, but it all felt very wrong in the shop. The only person who did stay for longer than ten minutes was a tenacious tourist who was determined to buy what she said was a Ming vase. She flicked it over with her fingers to hear it chime, but the strange girl in the seat wouldn't get the person in charge even when she demanded it. Suddenly, the woman knew she had to get out. She tried to loosen the scarf around her neck and sweat poured down her back. Searching blindly for the door, she found the handle, and crashed out straight onto the tiles, her legs still sticking into the doorway. People from the shops around rushed to her aid, but Ensley didn't move. Normally, she would be the first one at a crisis, fussing around like a startled bird, but she did nothing but watch from her position at the back of the shop. Ensley was waiting for time to spit out a determining event, and this was not it.

"It was thick, cloying..." the semi-conscious woman on the ground muttered.

"Yes, it's very close today," said the sympathetic voice of Sam from opposite. "An ambulance will be here soon." He held her hand, but after she had been shovelled onto a gurney, Sam quietly made his way to Mystical Moves, and, making eye contact with the unnaturally still form of Ensley, just the once, he lowered his gaze and closed the door, which was still ajar.

Chapter 22 A Circle Closes

The doorway that Oona had seen Kosmo stepping into some time before, was an army recruiting shop. Sergeant Lowell had been a little stunned when Kosmo entered. For one thing he was bored out of his wits in his dull-looking office, and it was interesting to see anyone choosing to come in. For the other, it wasn't every day that an extremely tall young man dressed in velveteen breeches and a matching waistcoat insisted on taking him back out the door and pointing to the pictures in the window of the Blues and Royals on horseback.

"I think I'd like to do that?" the boy said making Sergeant Lowell feel a bit huffy as the recruiting bit had just been taken out of his hands.

"We'll see. Come inside and let's have a chat first."

"Certainly, but may I ask to use the latrines quite soon, please?"

"You come from a military background then?" Lowell said noting Kosmo's use of terminology.

"Oh, yes, all of my... um... family is... uh... military." Kosmo's eyes flitted to a leaflet on the desk which asked in a demanding font, "Do YOU have equestrian skills?" Thank goodness Ensley had taught him to read. "I have equestrian skills too," he said to promote himself, the words sounding strange in his mouth.

"Useful," said Sergeant Lowell, feeling ever-more hopeful, but there was still the problem about the odd clothes and the jingle of metal in the sack the boy had lugged in, which was now propped against the table leg. Surely that was chain mail spilling out?

"Been to a party mate?" He gestured to Kosmo's knee-high medieval boots of red leather. The sergeant's eyes and Kosmo's both lingered on the morning star attached to a short pike that caused the flimsy bag on the floor to collapse down again.

"Not exactly," said Kosmo, reprieved by fortune as he glanced across the road at a poster advertising medieval tournaments and banquets. "A fun day for all," said Kosmo perkily, reading straight off the advertisement.

"Oh, I see," said Sergeant Lowell, following his look. "In that case, come right this way, and then we'll see how we can help you. You don't want to be doing anything commercial - no future in that. The army can offer you a *real* career."

After Kosmo had been to the toilet, this is exactly what the army did, and he joined the Household Cavalry.

Within a relatively short period of induction, and six weeks learning how to drive a tank in Dorset, Kosmo was soon Trooping the Colour, though a captivating glamour set him apart from the other soldiers, so that all eyes were focused on him alone. This was particularly the case with Queen Elizabeth the Second, who seemed to see something else beyond the shining young man with perfect etiquette and a fluidity of movement that was seamless. "Hmm," she exclaimed mysteriously.

Living in barracks was okay, but Kosmo longed for a home to return to. He would often wander around London as if it were possible that he would fall into a place or a situation that could guarantee him a satisfying future and comfort in one go. One day, he went to Leadenhall Market on his day off as he seemed to have an irresistible urge to go there. An unorthodox fourth wish led him into the golden glow of a nineteenth-century glass atrium. Walking past the Corinthian pillars, he almost fancied himself back at the 'Other' place. The shops had the flavour, quite literally, of Fei sphere, too, and there was a scented fusion of artisanal soaps, unpasteurised cheeses, candles and wood. Kosmo stopped at the window of an eatery and adjusted his white tee shirt that had caught inside his waistband. He caught the eye of a cheerful man serving paninis across a glass counter top and reckoned he might just call in on his way back, but then he became very still. How could it be possible? He became aware of a person, one he knew as well as he knew himself, just behind him. She was there, Ensley Knight, he just knew it. The hairs stood up on his arms as he heard a chair being pushed suddenly across a boarded floor, and like the wind, she flew towards him at the moment he turned around, her long black hair streaming behind her. She jumped up and wrapped herself around him and placed her head against his, his sister and friend in the world. "Gotcha," she said, and he held her close.

Sam had been very busy, but when he had time to look up, there was an interesting event developing out on the central aisle. Ensley, having broken from her weird trance, and a stranger were just staring at each other, she balling the front of his tee-shirt in a grasp and he holding her right hand. They made a pretty dramatic spectacle, and, as he stared, Sam's eyes tricked him; for a moment he saw them clothed in long, strange robes that pooled around their feet. The light from the glass above formed crystalline halos around their heads as if they both wore golden crowns. He blinked and saw that they now seemed to be ordinary, if a bit more glamorous than the norm. The young man was casually following her back into her shop, clearly laughing at something she had said. He watched her make some tea and take out some antique cups and saucers. In the way the boy first of all lounged against a bookcase, grinning, then started picking up items and pointing to others, he got the sense that they weren't lovers; they had the ease of long-time friends. They talked and laughed but once he saw her lean nearer to him, touch his hand and her shoulders rounded in a confidential manner. A bit later on, he saw her lock up the shop early and practically drag him towards the main entrance, and then they disappeared around the corner. Whatever event was coming next, it was clearly a big one. They boy's face had changed from relaxed to apprehensive as she pulled him along. Sam had the strongest urge to follow them to find out what they were doing, but it had nothing to do with him.

"Hurry, hurry," said Ensley, dragging Kosmo off the tube and towards the stairwell.

"Why? Why?" he mocked, panting in her wake. "She isn't going anywhere after all this time."

"I can't get used to you speaking so contemporary," Ensley said. "Anyway, I'm so excited I could burst – we have to run."

"Oh, that's why?" he laughed chasing after her and by then they were nearly at Kenyngton Row and the enormity of the situation brought them both to a walk. It was mid-autumn, and leaves like golden coins provided a collage over the paving slabs bringing to mind fairy gold which is really golden fruits. 'How the Fei world does interfere with my thinking,' Kosmo mused. 'Well, of course it will,' thought Ensley back to him.

"Can you stop that?" Kosmo said.

"What?"

"Getting in my head."

"Oh, sorry, I didn't realise I was doing it. Strange - I didn't think I could do that with a m..." She stopped.

"A mortal," he finished. "A mere one." His look was wry, but his tone mocking.

"Yes. Not mere though... different."

She held out her hand and he took it. Understandings would have to change in this new world. The unspoken things of the past would have to be spoken aloud. Fei or human, they all fell into the same trap, believing that prejudices didn't exist if they didn't manifest in a dramatic way.

"We can do this," she said. "... And it will be okay. Me being here will be a new start for us all."

"Good intentions are often forgotten after the event that prompts them," Kosmo said wisely.

"I will *never*," she emphasised, "Never, forget what I've learnt...people like Frances....those raggedy ones on the street..." All those forgotten ones," she mused.

Kosmo realised that Ensley had an authority that she certainly didn't have before.

"I'm not like this all the time," she said. "Oh gosh, sorry, sorry," she spoke aloud, "I did it again."

"It's okay, it doesn't matter."

The two walked up the outside steps until they reached 14C, and Ensley knocked in a distinctive way on the door, one rap, followed by three and ending with one. An audible groan could be heard from within.

"I'm coming; hang on. Why are you back home early anyway... no bloody peace around here."

Kosmo heard a shuffling followed by the prolonged undoing of many bolts, chains and a heavy lock that Frances clearly had difficulty turning. Finally, the door opened and Frances was temporarily blinded by the vision of Ensley blocking the doorway, bathed in the glory of a late season sun like beaten gold.

"Ow, my sodding eyes," said Frances.

"Look who I've found," said Ensley, stepping aside.

The man in front of Frances filled the door, and she took an instinctive step back, blinking and off-guard. On one level, the ordinary, everyday conscious level, she failed to know him, but on another, she knew that this was her moment when the heaviness of old bones was replaced with a strange tingling from head to toe. Kosmo didn't say anything, but then their eyes met and she knew. The last time she had stared into those eyes, they had been two days old, but she would have recognised them anywhere; she had looked for them everywhere. 'I mustn't cry; I won't,' she thought to herself.

'No, do cry, thought Ensley, reading her clearly. Cry for everyone who has ever let you down. Cry for the betrayals of your family who should have protected you and your mixed-race son. Cry because of the false friends who made callous remarks in unguarded moments. Cry for a world that denies the unbreakable bond between mother and child and "*traipses*," like you said, all over it. Feel free - go ahead.'

'Sod that!' was the immediate rejoinder, and in her contrary way, Frances decided to fall down in a dead faint instead.

***

Frances often wondered how she could ever have thought a reunion with her grown son wouldn't work, but then, she was a very determined person and she often thanked her lucky stars that she was made that way. At first, she had pandered to Kosmo's every wish like a slave, but then she got fed up with that and started moaning at him when he left his socks and pants all over his bedroom floor. The wall of time that had held the two apart for so long began to collapse and in the psychological rubble it left behind Kosmo and Frances assumed the identities of the harassed Mother and early teen son. It was a good starting point because, in most families, teen years are the stage where all is flux and relationships need to be worked through. The two would, no doubt, begin a history all of their own.

Other, even stranger things were happening at 14B Kenyngton Row, though they didn't know it. Finnian had tracked his errant and confused daughter back there because her behaviour had puzzled him. What was she? He had reflected on her words, and it was clear that the child was stagnating and not growing. Though she was semi-awake, somehow, she was still asleep and had no idea that she could become an omnipotent force in her own world. He didn't think it was his place to bring her to a state of realisation and ruin her developmental trajectory, but he just wanted to investigate her current situation. Besides, he hadn't had much to do with her up to that point. The last time he'd seen her in the flesh, she was still playing with toys and performing rudimentary magic tricks.

Finnian had gained access to Ensley's flat by making himself small and crawling through the vent pipe of the flat roof. He sat awhile as a pebble in an indoor water feature, the water sploshing on his head, but he felt great embarrassment studying his daughter without her permission. In this case, he knew he was crossing a line. Besides, she didn't seem to do anything interesting; after arriving home at dusk, she would construct a meal herself (which was a bit demeaning), stare intently into a dry and deathly book with no pictures, and then go to bed. 'What a life!' Finnian thought to himself. At a loss of what to do next, Finnian decided to explore the other flats and did so by following a network of rodent holes, thus circumventing the terror of navigating doors - known in legend as objects of fatal entrapment. He shuddered as he thought about the ones he'd viewed outside: horrible red-painted monstrosities, in this case.

Emerging into a bedchamber that smelt of eggs and burnt bread, Finnian was astounded to discover Incomer installed in a bed whilst a ferocious hag intermittently appeared to yell at him. This was more like it. "Great viewing," Finnian whispered to himself. "Wow." A delicious shudder went through his miniscule body. The conversation ran like this:

"Get up," said Frances.

"Okay," responded the still deep asleep Kosmo.

"Are you awake?"

"Yes." The word ended with a sigh that linked to a gentle snore.

"So, you're up."

"Yees."

"I can't hear you in the bathroom."

(There was the sound of Kosmo turning over under his duvet).

"Your eggs are cold now."

"Okay."

"Are you coming or not?"

"Kill me," (said sotto voce.)

"What?"

"Nothing."

Eventually, Incomer staggered upright, washed in a poor, minimal stream within a blue-tiled room, returned and put on a strange uniform. He then kissed the hag, quite bravely, Finnian thought, who in turn made an offering of bread with thinly sliced animal remains in a small bag. Incomer tried to leave this behind an ornamental vase, on his way out, but was caught in the process. Then a door slammed, causing an adrenaline rush to surge from Finnian's miniature boots to his curly hair. "Wahhh," said Finnian, "Taboo-breaking stuff indeed doors, meat, hags and strange relations!" Thinking ahead, he took a camera out of his robe pocket, meanwhile coating himself from top to toe in a layer of quick-set cement in order to blend neatly into the skirting board. The camera featured in the centre of a raised section as a tiny, black dot, like a blackhead.

Over the course of the next couple of months, Finnian enjoyed and recorded a number of videos. This included many comic appearances of the Hag, who liked to mutter and groan to herself about pretty much everything, including the people who had annoyed her in shops and on transport. The rants were interspersed by exciting moments when she tried to force-feed Incomer food.

"Steak and kidney pie," she would reveal and there would be a steaming pile of animal corpses offset by a glutinous shield of cooked flour and fat. Kosmo would expertly deflect the torture by saying he had, "eaten at the barracks and then the disappointed hag would pound on the wall and yell as if inconsolable, "Ensley Knight, come and get it!" Immediately, his own daughter would charge through the taboo door, like a retracted spring, just as if it were nothing, and plunge herself into deep, brown broth and meat.

"What the hell's going on?" Finnian asked a house pixie, who shrugged noncommittedly. "This girl is like a flippin' stranger to me," he murmured, and then jumped, realising that he had become vocally contaminated by the hag. However, this worrying trend didn't stop him filming or cause him to question his position until one day Kosmo brought home a young man he had met in a city bar. The two men were sat, a little self-consciously on the bed when Finnian, quite excited by the developing relationship, panned in closer. Immediately, Kosmo heard the zoom and said, "Hang on, wait a minute." He then went to the bathroom and came out with a wet flannel. To his lover's consternation, Kosmo knelt and began addressing the skirting board. "My liege Lord," he said, "I knew you were there, but this is one step too far. The greenish aura gave it away weeks ago." Saying this, he made a great swipe from right to left, which removed Finnian and his camera. Cupping the wet mess and the Monarch, he carefully placed all on the balcony outside before going back in. Finnian then materialised to full size, wet, claggy with cement, and humiliated. He had come to his lowest point and he knew it. Inside, the young man on the bed said,

"What...?!! What happened?"

"It was nothing," said Kosmo, "A little mouse that lost its way."

"Ugh," said the man, looking around him.

"It's okay, it won't come back, I've shut the door, you see." Kosmo, putting his arm around the man, then tried to salvage the rest of the evening, which, to an extent, he did.

Finnian sat for a while dripping clayey drops on the communal balcony of Kenyngton Row. He stared at the plaque on the wall for a while wondering what it meant, until he psychically forced a passing girl to read it to him. Of course, he knew instantly what it meant, once he heard it - 'Place of the King.' "Indeed, I don't think so," he said looking at the yellowish bricks and the uniformity of the flats. Finnian was at heart a snob, and he was very clear about kings inhabiting palaces and suchlike, not little compartments. Still, it was a little odd that he landed up where he did and it was most embarrassing too. He held up to the light a small sphere of boundless energy between his index finger and thumb. This was his place, Fei home world, recently sent to him by his daughter. He didn't know why Fei Sphere was embedded into the inferior human world, that certainly wouldn't do either. He required an explanation as to why it was so tiny; he also wondered whether Oona might have been struggling. So many unanswered questions - but whilst he pondered, part of his thumb was already being attracted into the stratosphere of the minuscule world. He understood that it was because his concentrated and energetic life force was finding its way back to the dynamic world that suited it best. He was being drawn, just as Ben Sopher had been into Fei world, because he belonged there. It felt lovely, but his senses were still his own and he realised if he didn't act soon, he would be taken in and the world would still be captured within human Earth Sphere. He had to act. "We're going home," he said to his seneschal, who materialised on his command.

"Thank The Creator," the bedraggled, frostbitten man groaned, falling flat on his face. Finnian sighed. Leaning forward, he whispered back to him in clipped tones, "Hurry along the worship, if you can. We're rather late, I fancy." The prostrated form of his servant didn't answer; what did time mean to him apart from the enduring misery of serving his capricious lord?

Rolling the sphere into the centre of his hand, Finnian flung it overhead with immense force, his olive complexion taking on a thunderous hue as he exerted himself. He was pulled in the wake of its momentum as if the world were recently blown glass, soft and malleable, and he was the wispy stem stretched out and still connected. "It was a rough ride," as the Seneschal later reported. "And I'm glad that I was lying down with my eyes closed when it happened." It was also just as well that Kenyngton Row was in the position of a very thin place, exactly on the intersection of two ley lines; this is why the membrane between the two worlds simply gave way at the appropriate moment. Finnian, of course, anticipated this would happen. Once released, the Fei world regained its normal size like rehydrated matter meeting moisture, and a worldwide cheer went up with everyone realising how compressed they had all really felt despite being talked out of it by the authorities. The excitement continued as a group of noble travellers daintily stepped into the world from an open cast burrow. "Finnian returns, Finnian returns," was the rumour, like a wind, circulating the globe. This puffed Finnian up; he'd forgotten how nice the adulation thing was. His entourage around him blinked twice, stimulating the protective nictating membranes in their eyes to slide back as they wouldn't be needing them now. When they also removed their sunglasses, Finnian didn't. He made a footman hold up a mirror so that he could adjust his Wayfarers, and he tucked a golden, slightly greying curly lock behind his ear before he strode forward towards the palace.

Oona was reclining on a Louis the fifteenth chaise lounge, in teal, when he arrived. This had the unfortunate effect of clashing with her emerald-coloured eyes and chiffon dress of mint, khaki, olive and pine. 'Just like a clump of seaweed,' thought Finnian rather unkindly, but then she tilted her head, and her platinum hair fell in a cascade to the floor making him gasp. He had forgotten how dramatic his Queen could be. "Very sexy, dear," he said, bending to kiss her hand. Oona shrugged and said, "I suppose so." Her indifference shocked him, and he watched, mesmerised, as she picked a fruit from the platter on a side table, collapsing it whole with her side incisors. She rolled an apricot with her fingertips into her palm and moved languidly towards the doorway that had never contained a door, not taking her eyes off him for a minute. Once there, she took a contrapposto pose for a studied amount of time, juice dribbling down her chin, which she wiped with her newly sharpened wand, before turning abruptly and heading off towards the gardens. This was a new Oona in the same way that his daughter was different and it unnerved him; something was off. He realised then that something else was very off when his nostrils were assaulted by the stench of something acid and sour.

"Lactulose," he correctly identified to a nearby retainer who looked blank. "Bloody cow juice... gone bad," he added. "Why?" he roared, and then he noticed the decapitated heads and limbless torsos of the precious statues his mother had left him before she disintegrated into dry flakes at the grand old age of seven hundred and forty.

"What the hell's going on? It's all broken, and what's that terrible smell?" he shouted after the turned back of his wife.

"Disasters," Oona's distant voice carried back to him, "... the aftermath of Ensley's exile."

Oona's uninterested tone suggested exiling the new queen and her covering the broken world in sour milk were everyday events. Also, that she wanted no responsibility in the matter. Far away he could see her pruning a gone-over rose with her fingernails, her back towards him. There was a movement and he jumped. His nerves were definitely on edge but it was only one of two very intricately-made dolls that had fallen off the chaise-lounge onto its face. Two others were in the process of construction and he supposed his unexpected entrance had interrupted her work. Finnian became aware then of other activity in the room: of the stonemason feverishly carving the gothic arches in the room and a pixie servant wetting too dry cement on the wrecked stone floor with his spit. They were practically rebuilding the estate around him.

"Exile?" he said vaguely, thinking about Oona's throwaway words. His mind had already been working overtime, trying to fathom the idea of an incarcerated Fei world and the shock of finding his daughter living in a squalid situation. Because he didn't have a foothold in the situation, he decided to play up. He kicked the statue of an extinct woodland elf on the floor, amputating yet another arm, and then shouted, blowing out the newly glazed windows.

"I leave this place for five minutes; five sodding minutes and it all goes to hell!"

Oona stopped attending to her plants, her back went rigid and a flock of small fairies that had been circling her head, fled into the bushes, trembling.

"Fifteen... earth... years," she said, dragging the strangled words out of her mouth. She crushed a beautiful bloom in her hand. "Fifteen...years," she repeated. Then she was there, her nose an inch from his face and the wand arm was arched over his head.

"You wouldn't dare," he said, without thinking, realising too late that he was throwing down a gauntlet, but Oona was not stupid; she knew the limitations of power, and she was ever a servant to the needs of the constitution. Regardless, she did say,

"Try me."

And Finnan having been immersed in soap operas and reality shows for so long, knew she was talking his language. He appreciated her making a concession to his recent mindset, though he was sick to death now of humans and their fictional angers and false affiliations. At least when a fairy did something, they meant it. He wondered if she would have a slanging match with him and go off with his best friend (not that he had one). Oona, though, was too dignified to lose control and expose her feelings; she was Fei to the core. Accordingly, she hit him once on the head, and his legs buckled. She snarled, and her eyes elongated into slits through which peeped one iris as a malevolent stinger and the other as a watchful ambush predator. Finnian thought instantly of cameras as he fixated on the latter.

"Is it mating, dear? Is it? Is it?" He asked hopefully, trying to make sense of the new Oona.

"Don't be ridiculous." She looked him up and down in an appraising way, making him feel somehow ashamed. "I am condemning you to three solar rotations of discussion about the young people and everything that is tedious about them so that I may clear my head a little; that includes Ensley, Incomer and everyone else I can think of who has recently annoyed me. All will be from my point of view, and you will be the sleeping partner in this arrangement for the duration with no interruption. Do I make myself clear?"

"Yes, perfectly," he said, realising that something had gone wrong with his mouth and he was only thinking the words and not actually speaking them. Oona smiled and held out her arm. Finnian, without hesitation, took it.

Chapter 23 A Fairy Abroad

Ben had been surprised to find Terri waiting in an open doorway when he arrived at her doorstep out of breath. She grinned and said,

"I gather your lot don't like doors too much. I read it in the book."

"Eh?" Ben was a bit puzzled for a moment, but following her in he said that he wasn't affected by that phobia, not having been brought up in the Fei sphere.

"Anyway," she said, punching him in the arm. "I was going to ask how the hell are you, but I know anyway."

"I don't think you could know for one minute how I feel at this present moment."

"That's true," she agreed. "I just know how you got back," she said mysteriously. So..." she helped him off with his rucksack because he suddenly went limp with exhaustion, "How *do* you feel?"

"Awful," he said, "Just awful. I don't want to be here."

"Oh!" she was a little put out for a moment but Terri quickly took a moment to think how she would feel in his position. "I suppose you'll miss all your friends."

"Not just that, the world, the magic, the colours and even the danger. It's so, well, just so vibrant and alive."

"Can't you go back? I mean, would you?"

"I don't know. Kosmo is goodness knows where and I don't know if it would be the same somehow. I can't think... I'm just tired."

Terri thought privately to herself that perhaps a degree of separation between Ben and Kosmo might not be a bad thing. After all, unrequited love is a such a bummer. Ben sank onto the sofa next to her and rested his arms limply on his knees.

"Well, I can help you with the Kosmo thing, because I know where he is."

"What? How?"

"It's in the book, here." She handed it to him.

"He's in London then?" Ben looked as if he were about to spring up but Terri put a restraining hand on his arm. "Wait, read it first..." and he did. It didn't take Ben more than a few pages in to realise that Kosmo and Ensley were inhabiting a time period at least forty years previous to the present one. Of course... Frances would probably not even be alive in the present day unless she were over a hundred.

"It's a big decision," Terri said, "and I don't think it's one for tonight. You can stay as long as you like," she said, kindly, realising that Ben was barely listening. He had flicked forward in the book after reading about himself feeling depressed in Terri's flat, only to find that Ensley and Kosmo were happily sat in a fast-food outlet eating burgers.

"Did you get this far? Doesn't the resolution strike you as a bit of a lame one?"

"Well, it's a happy one."

"Not for me," he pointed out.

"Umm." Terri was beginning to feel slightly irritated at his determination to see things as hopeless. This was not the upbeat, fun Ben she knew from before, and what the hell was going on with the shaggy beard. He looked like a tramp. He was also covered in some kind of dirt stuff that was going all over the carpet. "To be honest," she said, "I think you should go to bed, get up for work tomorrow, which will take your mind off things, and then just go on from there." She shoved a glass of water into his hands, noticing one looked extremely weird, kind of distorted, and switched off the light before he could argue. Ben dragged his rucksack towards the spare room and was asleep before his head hit the pillow.

Over the next few weeks Ben worked very hard, and, as Terri

predicted, his mood did lift. Sharon was pleased to see him; he had come back as a more extroverted character, and good male stylists were hard to come by. She noticed his strange hand deformity that reminded her of something that she couldn't altogether remember, but as it didn't seem to affect his dexterity, she politely ignored it. Poor thing must have had some kind of accident. Perhaps that was why he had disappeared for a while. Still, it didn't seem to affect his skill prowess at all. In actual fact, Ben found that his manipulation of objects was vastly improved and he seemed to cut hair at a very rapid pace; so much so that one man complained that he'd only been sat down for five minutes and it hardly seemed worth the fee. Terri pretended not to watch when combs literally flew across the counter towards him or when he went into a trance whilst creating the greatest hair tints without seeming to put much in the basin. On the whole, he was cheerful and fun to be with during work time, but the evenings were a different matter. He became edgy and paranoid as soon as he left the salon. Miles, a local student, had visited Ben on his first day back at work. He had explained in a very ponderous way that the Dorchester Book Club, that he belonged to had cause to be concerned about his welfare. "Why?" was Ben's nervous response.

"Because we think that you are being followed." At this, everyone in the salon, clients included, looked around themselves.

"Really?"

"Yes," said Miles, "We're not altogether certain what it is..."

"What or who?" squeaked Terri wanting to be in on things. Miles ignored her.

"...But we've got a good description." Here he took out a piece of paper which didn't contain much. He looked to make sure he had everyone's attention.

"It is beige coloured and sniffs the ground. Whitish fur, we think." He folded up the bit of paper.

"Is that it?" asked Terri.

"Isn't that enough?" questioned Ben.

Miles left a little stiffly when no-one asked him anything further about his news. He said goodbye and left, disappointed that his message didn't have much more impact on the salon audience.

"What a strange guy," said a customer. Ben didn't say anything, but from thereon, a cloud of both gloom and worry would descend on him immediately after he locked up. At Terri's, he would comfort eat a huge pile of whatever staple he found in the freezer, but soon realised he didn't have much tolerance for human food anymore. He spent many dreary hours with his head down the toilet pan until he finally approached Phil at Wholegrains who advised him to stick to pulses and grains in small quantities and gradually increase from thereon.

"Glad to be back?" he asked.

"Not really."

"Oh dear," said Phil. "I think you've become a naturalised."

"A naturalised what?"

"You tell me," said Phil. "Why don't you come down the pub? That might cheer you up." Ben didn't think that spending time with an old codger, even a nice one would be conducive to a good mood. At first, he declined, and for a couple of months, he spent his leisure time typing up the copious number of hand-written notes crammed into his rucksack. Some of these were very dirty and torn, practically illegible, so that he had to remember the exact time, place and situation when each one was scribed down to fill in the gaps. It was interesting to note how some of these entries started to appear in the big, red book and some didn't as he typed. Still, it was useful to keep his own files, and perhaps the missing information would pop up at another, time, if it became significant. Making his final entry one night, he saved the entire file, switched off the computer, and thought, 'Oh shit! Now, what am I going to do?' He scratched his cleanly shaved chin and made his way to The Crown where he joined Phil in the dark well of the snug. It was quite depressing to see the pint, already pulled, waiting on the bar.

"I don't like the predictability of all this," Ben said to Phil.

"Me neither, mate, but it is what it is?"

"I've never really understood what that means."

"I think it means that the nature of reality is completely out of our hands." He followed this up with a loud and disgusting burp, like a plosive vowel. "Sorry," he rubbed his nose with a big, spotted handkerchief, "Actually, I don't really agree with that; I'm just making conversation. What I really believe is that reality is constantly in flux. Think about it. I mean, *we* know, don't we boy?" he explained as if they were both part of some elite but undesirable club. You know what I mean, because of our experiences? Want another?"

"No thank you. Phil? Do you think we're stuck in our situations?"

"I'm just living my life in a place I'm used to and I don't care whether I chose this life or it chose me. I quite like it here and, anyway, I'm old now. It '*is*' nice having someone to talk to who knows what I'm on about, though." He noticed Ben trying to repress the sadness in his face. "I think it's different for you though and in time, perhaps you'll make a different decision about your life." He emphasised the word 'different' and for a moment Ben was sure that Phil knew something about his future life that he didn't, but Phil didn't initiate that thread. Instead, he nodded towards Ben's wand hand resting on the bar. "I don't think you want to be talking to a boring old codger like me forever and a day, though," he said. "I don't take it personally." Ben squeezed Phil's arm realising Phil had probably read his prejudicial comments in the book a little while before.

"Come on, drink up," he said, contrite. "It's my shout."

***

It happened that shortly after that, Phil Whitaker had pneumonia and his long tenure in The Crown ended. A very boozy wake followed the service and Ben ended up with his head on the bar whilst the barman, who was a long-standing friend of Phil's sang an old rock song, called Wishing Well, a cappella, with the man who ran the dry cleaners' shop and also a mechanic from across the way. All the other local business people had cleared off by then, and Ben suspected that it was after hours, though, as he couldn't lift his head up to look at the clock, he couldn't be sure. He could hear it ticking, though. He always heard a ticking clock wherever he went. It was like a psychological problem he had since living on the Fei sphere.

"I have no idea why that clock's so loud," he said to the landlord.

"It is what it is," said the landlord, waving an ungoverned hand at it and nearly falling backwards.

"Heard that one before." Ben snorted with laughter, propped his chin on his upturned palm, nearly missed, and decided to sink his head in a pint glass to stabilise it. Reality, meanwhile, became impatient with him and decided to move things along a bit. No-one heard the gentle knock at the door or even the prolonged scrambling afterwards as something climbed through the open window on all fours. It had been left open because it was a hot evening and provided a ripe opportunity for something to gain access. Initially, on all fours, it then stood upright, and there was a careful readjustment of coverings. The thing that had been following Ben for weeks, waiting in the rain or sun outside his and Terri's flat, night after night, looking up at a certain window, had arrived. It stood, just watching, as the object of its hunt slowly fell off a bar stool. Temporarily oblivious of the new addition in the room and with glacial and precise actions, Ben clambered back up to his perch, thinking in desperation, 'I'm back.... (not meaning the stool), back where I started from, in a hideous life.' He felt he was practically oozing bitterness out of his pores. The drink was exacerbating depression rather than dulling it, but suddenly, a different instinct kicked in, from somewhere deep and subconscious, and he realised he was miraculously sober. His mind clear, he saw him, a boy, a perfect boy, in the middle of the room, in the moonlight flooding in through the open casement window. He had blonde hair flopping down across his face from an irregular parting, and he was tall but not skinny. In fact, there was a solidity to him that was strange. He had a sense that nothing, not even a tempest could knock over that young man.There was also something odd about the way this person held his head slightly on one side as if Ben had said something, though he hadn't spoken. Perhaps it was an invitation. The hands dangled by his sides as if he didn't quite know what to do with them. The words, 'too formal' crept into Ben's mind and then slipped out again as the stranger took steps towards him. For some reason, Ben felt nervous on the stranger's behalf, as if worried that he would make a mistake, rather than himself. He was most surprised when the boy, reaching him, drew the opposite stool so close that their knees were touching and then proceeded to riffle around in the pocket of his cream linen jacket without explanation.

"Ah," he said finally, dumping a bundle of twigs in Ben's open palm. It only took a moment for realisation to burst into Ben's consciousness like a new day.

"Hazel?" asked Ben, somewhat alarmed.

"Hugh," corrected the boy, touching a very bristly face, and he drew Ben's head towards his with long, thin fingers. The barman looked away, politely.

When they came up for air, Ben mentioned somewhat accusingly,

"Hey, is that my jacket?"

"It was left, dear Sopher. I wear jacket now," said this new creation who had travelled so far to find the one he could not live without. He clutched it around himself, claiming ownership and ripping the seam on the shoulder a little.

"Okay," said Ben. He flicked the hair out of Hugh's eyes.
"Only...."

"Yes, Sopher?"

"Please call me Ben."

"Yes, Sopher, I will."

And he did... eventually.

***

Ben later discovered that Hugh had coped amazingly well in a
new body and in a new life. The biological process initiated in
the Fei home world, transforming Hazel into the male genotype
of her species, had *not* been the cause of her exclusion from
the copse; it was the individuation that had set him apart and
which could never be supportable in a world where individual
trees were linked into a composite identity and acted as part of
a hive mentality. They could not tolerate him; it was jarring to
them to have someone outside of them, and so, they would have
chased him away in the end. It was never the case that Hugh had
ultimately caused his own exile through deliberate actions. He
had spent many miserable months haunting cold regions where
forests were sparse, but the hazel species could thrive in a more
solitary setting, but it was no good – he simply missed Ben so
much. To his horror, when he did eventually return it was to
discover that Ben was leaving Fei sphere with his nemesis, The
Incomer, and, even worse, both of them were foolishly taking his
advice and trusting the evil and duplicitous Mab. He regretted his
rash and jealous earlier words immediately he saw them both step
into the burrow, and he saw Mab give a push. Without missing a
beat, Hugh dragged the cackling creature away from the burrow
and fell into nothingness himself. This was not only a brave
thing to do, but an unselfish one too, because even if he could
keep track of Sopher, it was not at all certain, that Ben would

want Hugh's presence with him. After all, he had The Incomer with him... didn't he? When Incomer was separated from Sopher a short while later and spun off into the vortex, Hugh could have felt relieved, but he didn't. He felt the loss of such a noble individual and great sadness for Sopher, who was close to him. Hugh charged forward in terror, through the ripping membrane of his world. Was this love? This running into the black with no hope of a happy outcome?

Hugh was desperately happy to eventually see Ben far in the distance staggering out into daylight, but it was a colourless world, and Hugh finally understood Ben's account of the heavy spirits that drove him originally into their world. He ran for many leagues to catch Sopher, who was always too far away, though from time-to-time Hugh wondered if he, himself, was being deliberately slow, not knowing what he would say once he eventually caught up. What if Sopher were angry? He couldn't exactly say, "Good evening, Sopher, how strange to meet you in your own world!" A few times, Hugh lost sight of him completely, but then all he had to do was crouch down, bury his hands in the earth, and the mycelium sang to his fingertips, telling him exactly where to go, being so sensitive to impact and disturbance. Other below-ground voices hummed in a metallic voice: some slightly above the firmament carried people carriages in a blur of conductivity, and there were others that communicated pulses to dead-end places that he would come to know as 'screens' and 'computers'. He instinctively loathed these captive voices as they had no life beyond their trapped trajectory. They were rendered dumb and unknowable to themselves. Still, dear Sopher followed a parallel course to the wires and tracks until stopping at a township where he remained. Hugh didn't know what to do. Should he reveal himself and risk displeasure or bide his time until Sopher truly needed him? In the end, he chose the latter and gravitated to a garden nursery called 'Green Man Gardens' on the outskirts of Dorchester. This way he could be close to Sopher and in a place that suited his constitution.

***

Alan Ross, the owner of Green Man, had been surprised to see an early 'helper' sitting on the bench outside the nursery door with one hand resting in the soil of a stone trough filled with orange lilies. Thursday was the day that residents of a nearby sheltered accommodation were taught horticultural skills.

"You're keen," he said. "Best to use a pair of gloves when you're doing that, though. He physically removed Hugh's hand. What's your name, bud?" Hugh maintained a continuous stare, he was confused and also felt quite depleted from his recent activity. The dew plastered the lick of blonde hair across one eye, in a piratical way, adding to the mystery of him. Alan pointed to his chest with a thick digit,

"I'm Alan." He pointed at Hugh, "Who are you?" Hugh shifted slightly on the bench but said nothing. Alan tried again. "Who?" he said. "Repeat after me." He got a bit too close which he knew he shouldn't do with people with learning disabilities. The finger pointed again and nearly touched the crumpled linen jacket. "Who?" said Alan with a hint of desperation. He had a busy day ahead and needed to get on. Hugh helpfully made a lot of windy h sounds, repeating what the human had said, but he was also shivering, because the fixed humanoid form had some definite disadvantages. He sounded like a small gale blustering through a copse of beech trees in spring. He tried again, merging the 'h' with the 'who' for the nice man's benefit. A bit of spit gurgled the h bit out.

"Oh Hugh!" said Alan finally, very relieved. "Well, I'm glad we got that sorted out, come on in." Alan stopped suddenly, puzzled, turning to look at the trough full-on. "Well, I never! I thought them lilies were on the turn and they are positively flourishing. Never seen nothing like it." He held a very thick stem attached to a burnt orange bloom the size of his thick hand. "I thought they was white too! How weird." Hugh just smiled slyly and wiped his hand on his leggings.

It turned out that Hugh wasn't the person Alan thought he was. "He's a foreigner," Alan told his business partner Michael. "His English is terrible, very stilted, but I have never seen a worker like him. Chucked him a few quid and told him he could sleep in the shop at night. Couldn't take seeing him sitting there every night on the outside bench anyway." Michael observed the abundant stands of vegetables in the greenhouse that were still fruiting so late in the season and agreed that he was a rare find. Everything Hugh touched turned good and if he was a bit strange and liked to stand under the hose in between watering the seedlings, who was he to judge? They gave him a pair of overalls with the green man logo on and Hugh was very pleased, but he had a very strong attachment to the cream linen jacket he wore at night and wouldn't let Michael's wife Belinda anywhere near it.

"I'll wash it for you," she said, making rubbing motions with her hands.

"No, no, I like smell. Good memories." Hugh clutched it to his face and nose and fell into a reverie.

"I think it's some kind of trauma," Belinda insisted. "Perhaps he's in trouble."

"Nah, he's alright," said Alan. "Leave the poor bloke alone."

"Well, I think you're taking advantage a bit."

"So?"

"And you think that's okay?" Belinda sniffed, emanating disgust, and finished cashing up the till.

"He seems happy enough to me, likes his job, etcetera."

"But he sleeps on the floor!" Belinda pointed to the blankets under the counter. "I feel uncomfortable about it."

"Well, he doesn't, 'cos he sleeps nice and sound. Anyway, I know he's alright because he smiles a lot, alright? Alan didn't like anyone thinking of him as exploitative. You being picked up?" he asked, trying to change the subject. "The nights are starting to draw in."

"Yes," she said, "in about five."

Belinda watched Alan's burly figure disappearing in the gloom towards his car. 'Because he smiles,' Belinda wondered to herself, slamming the till shut. How can men be so oblivious? She was right in guessing that Alan was completely wrong, though; Hugh wasn't happy at all, he was absolutely ecstatic. His nights consisted of tracking Ben from a workplace that smelt of astringent chemicals that Sopher put on heads, to his home, occasionally to an alehouse, and on a regular rotation to a very hectic place with artificial lighting. This place was full of dead foodstuffs all in rows, for Sopher to collect and later ingest. At all times, Hugh maintained a great distance. Under his concerned gaze, Sopher could go about his days and nights free from harm, but his main intention, which was to gaze longingly at the one that had caused a deep stirring within him from the start. Hugh's new gender was immaterial to him; it was just a comfortable accent that married well with his new, singular status, and anyway, hazel trees are naturally a combination of male and female with fluctuations of emphasis.

To be fixed into a purely humanoid form was a different matter though and it took a lot of willpower to suppress his sylvan characteristics. Sometimes when he had viewed Sopher overlong, he manifested products despite himself.

"Who the hell keeps scattering hazelnuts around?" Alan at the growing place had said more than once. "I'll bloody kill myself one day." Hugh had to put the shower hose over what he called, 'his canopy head' on many occasions, to steady himself.

One day Hugh noticed that the ancient man Sopher ingested barley drink with at a public house had been placed in the earth. This seemed a very good thing to do, and Hugh was happy that the decomposers in the soil would now take the man, named Phil. He would have liked to have said,

"Be of good cheer, Sopher," your friend is now busy deep

below," but Sopher was struck with gloom. He neglected his appearance, and consumed copious amounts of the barley drink, making him clutch his head with pain on arising from his bed. Sopher was looking a bit withered, though he was young, and that is how Hugh knew it was time to reveal his presence, as Sopher needed him.

"I can't believe you're a gardener just down the road," said Ben, completely overlooking Hugh's accomplishments of moving through time and space and with a new identity."

"I very good at it," said Hugh proudly.

"Well, I think you're amazing," said Ben, and the next day he told a relieved Terri that he was moving, and, together, he and Hugh took on a small flat overlooking Trinity Street.

***

The two were very happy for over a year, but Ben was often preoccupied.

"Tell me what troubles Ben," insisted Hugh.

"What troubles '*you*, Ben'," corrected Ben.

"Yes, Ben, very troubled," said Hugh.

"Hmm." Ben smiled at Hugh's pronoun muddles despite himself, thought for a moment, and then pointed to a skewiff street sign on the wall opposite. "Look at that and then look further down the road; I'll hold onto your legs." Hugh was levered out the window so that he could see the building at the end of the row being demolished, then he was hauled in.

"Damaged," he said simply.

"Yes, unstable from the war, and that's not all. See these holes in the window frame?" Hugh put a long wand hand into one and shuddered.

"Fire."

"Actually, a bullet hole. The street sign there has never been adjusted, and I think it's almost like a hidden memorial. A subconscious one that has been deliberately left. You see, Hugh, there was once a great war here, over thirty years ago, and no-one talks about it. Don't you think that's odd?"

Hugh nodded vigorously. It was indeed odd. There were wars all the time in Fei world, and it was talked about proudly, all the time. People tended to get maimed a little; some ran off howling to sulk, but it was all in the nature of Fei experience. Hugh had told Ben all about warring in a cheerful conversation, a while back, and Ben had added it, in a section called 'Skirmishes', to his study of Fei cultural life. What he did note early on in his conversation with Hugh was that the so-called wars involved more posturing than fighting and rarely any killing unless it was accidental.

Ben turned away from the window to start preparing a salad in the kitchenette, giving Hugh the opportunity to adjust the expression of horror on his face prompted by the mention of the particular war thirty years ago that Ben had mentioned. Hugh knew all about it, because he had been in it as a most effective warrior. It certainly wasn't news to him and though it had been a terrible occasion, he hadn't felt so bothered about it before, but now his feelings on the matter seemed to have changed. Now, all he felt was panic, and despair, like towering black wings of misery had started to descend on him. He had a premonition that he would soon be marching off into a very different version of that war with not-so-good outcomes for himself. He watched Ben, slaughtering the lettuce, caught in his own, lesser, battle and Hugh turned to him, determined to steady the flight impulse that had taken a hold of him. In the interim, the lettuce had become pulped.

"Is there problem, Ben?" Hugh stroked Ben's now long hair away from his face; they had become like two mirror images, but one dark and one light.

"Yes, a broken promise or, perhaps a lure, and it won't leave me alone. Right at the start of my journey I read the words,

'*Tempus Omnia Revelat*,' in bold, and it means time reveals all.
I held onto those words, because they seemed so hopeful, just
like precious gems. Especially for people like me who feel very
overlooked." Ben stared down at his knobbly wand finger. "I
always believed that history is kind of bogus. There are truths
out there, covered up and that's why I responded to the call of
those words. I know I've learnt a lot, but so much is unanswered.
I don't understand how the humans can forget such important
global events as a war, and I still don't know why there's a statue
of Kosmo in the town centre. It bothers me."

"Ben still cares about Kosmo?" Hugh's words were flat and
sullen. Ben pulled him close, arms around his waist.

"Don't be daft, not in that way. He's a friend and I'm
worried." Hugh moved away, picked up a big red book and
flicked the pages.

"Ben has learnt many things and travelled to Fei. Time did
reveal much?" he suggested.

"Yes, and I will always be grateful for that. I'm more Fei than
Human. My identity is bound to Fei sphere." Ben put his hand
on the book's front cover and traced the curves of his own name
clearly embossed on the book. "I belong here," he said dreamily.

"The book?" Hugh was a little startled. He had a typical
Fei's suspicion of books and words. He looked at the book
distrustfully as if it could open up, drag him in and pulp him up
into something else.

"Perhaps I'm nothing else but a textual key," Ben continued,
"- a device to open up a story."

"You are Ben Sopher and real. It is enough." Hugh was a wise
tree.

"Yes," said Ben brightly, "I know I'm important in my own
life, but I'm really a small player in the big scheme, a means to
an end. Kosmo and Ensley are the really important ones. Trouble
is..." he stopped, "they're both a bit unworldly don't you think?"
His words came out in a rush. "And Hugh, how would you feel

about joining them, where they are? I mean, to keep an eye on them, and help them out." It was a fictitiously light appeal that had the effect of putting Hugh on the spot. If he said no, Ben would go anyway, somehow – at some point in time. Hugh looked at the book and without knowing how to read, he knew it was written. He felt the future come close again, with himself mute and powerless. It could only have been love that made him speak his next words, and he chose these carefully.

"I always happy with Ben... whatever."

"Wherever?"

"Of course." Hugh let himself be corrected, but he really felt 'whatever' was the word that could more aptly describe the volatile future that he felt sure he was walking into.

"Well, that's settled then," said Ben, as relieved, he looked around him. I don't think I'll take much." He looked at his dusty rucksack, which hung on the door. "... Just chocolate, in case we miss our mark and end up in Fei."

Hugh lifted up Ben's wand hand which was fizzing with unused power. His lover had been quite tempestuous of late and there were scorch marks on the wall. He needed to do some magic that would test his powers a little more.

"It not likely we miss. We go and we arrive, just as you say."

"Glad you've got faith in me."

***

The faith was well-placed, and it was also very lucky that the sole operative burrow was the one that could take them near to where Kosmo and Ensley lived. That was how the next day, but over forty years earlier, Ben was walking through an arcade with Hugh towards a cluttered corner shop. Kosmo was lounging on a swing chair outside talking to a young girl beside him who was rocking it very fast with her feet against a box.

"Can you please stop that?" Kosmo said. "It's making me

sick." He looked up at Hugh and Ben, "Ah! Great, we were expecting you." He started to bang Ben on the back and then got him in a playful stranglehold. "Great to see you, friend." Hugh stood shyly behind him, but Kosmo reached around and pinched his arm.

"Did you read about us coming in the book?" asked Ben.

"What book?" said Ensley and Kosmo together, making Ben realise that the book did not yet exist in that time.

"I just thought you'd catch up with me somehow Ben," explained Kosmo. "You're a bit determined." Ben was a little taken aback by this and didn't know quite what to say.

"I've heard so much about you," said Ensley, smiling at her guests.

Ben realised that a strange behaviour was overtaking Hugh, who had dropped to a low curtsey which then segued into a bow. The whole thing looked a bit messy.

"Your Royal Highness," he rustled, and on straightening up, started to pick lint in a very embarrassed way off his jacket, the one that had formerly been Ben's.

"Oh, we don't stand on ceremony here," said Ensley and Hugh, much to his delight was introduced by Kosmo as Ben's new partner. "Hey," she said suddenly. "Is that a nineteenth-century scythe you've got?" she reached out. "Ow!"

"Watch out, it's very sharp," said Ben, with a bit of redundant advice, at the same time holding it away from her.

"Yes, I know now." Ensley watched, perplexed, as blood bubbled up out of a deep cut in her palm."

"For crying out loud," said Kosmo, grabbing a first aid box. "Do you always have to touch things?"

"Yes," she said, firmly, "I do. Why have you brought a scythe with you, Ben Sopher?"

"Ben, please," said Ben wondering why everyone always emphasised his surname. "It was left to me in a will by a man named Hippy Phil."

"Couldn't he have left you money?" Kosmo said, laughing like a drain. He now understood how important currency could be, and often made jokes about it. Ben was a little taken aback with how ordinary Kosmo seemed in his new world. However, the vivid glamour that always set him apart did, definitely, clash with his easy conversational tone. Ben decided to carry on speaking as if there was a seamless break with the old Kosmo.

"Well, here's the thing: a solicitor gave it to me with an accompanying note from Phil explaining that once he reached extreme old age, he became aware the scythe had a significance he hadn't remembered before. Phil remembered that his life depended on having it, so it was extremely important and not just an ornament, as he always thought. That's why Phil said he always kept sharpening it, for years and years, though he never knew exactly why before. It was emphasised in the will that I should take it with me if I ever left town, as Phil would undoubtedly need me to hand it over at some point."

"Didn't you say he was dead?" Ensley enquired. "How can it save his life?"

"Well, I suppose I have to give it to him before he dies to stop him from dying earlier, if you see what I mean?"

"Yeah, but in that case, where did the scythe come from in the first place, him or you?" Kosmo frowned.

"I'm not even going to attempt to figure out these time loop things, said Ben. It gives me a headache. I just accept stuff and move on..." he stretched up and yawned, "... never worrying about a thing anymore."

"How very Fei of you," said Ensley, smiling. They shared a look and Ben knew they would become great friends. A crash was heard from the rear of the shop where bored Hugh had decided to 'free' a piece of rosewood that had been made into a lamp. The lamp was now wandering blindly in a circle, the pom poms on its shade shaking in anguish. Ensley reached up lazily and restored the lamp back to a non-sentient state. She had come to realise recently that she did have power after all, albeit a very minor, everyday sort. She didn't count the three or four wishes thing. "Do you think you can do my hair?" she asked Ben. "Kosmo said you're a hairdresser, and it's gone all bristly." Ben peered at her and grabbed a hank.

"It's like a horse's tail," he said, and it's very sticky.

"That's the asses milk, I think," she said. "I'm getting self-care hints from historical figures. Apparently, Cleopatra did it."

"Just stick to shampoo," he said, raising an eyebrow, and for the first time, Queen Ensley of the Fei and All the World to the Margins of What She Chooses to See understood sarcasm. They all laughed, even Hugh.

Chapter 24 Fictions and Facts

On the second from last page of the original edition of the red book (now sadly revised to include, well, quite sad things really...), the editor in chief justified including an actual full-page photograph of the characters: Ensley, Kosmo, Hugh and Ben. This was despite opposition from the book's other contributors who lodged a complaint prior to printing, on the basis, they argued, that it would break the powerful flow of the fictional narrative. However, the editor opined that if a case were to be made that fairies are real, it *is* important to portray them in a realistic context engaged in real-life activities. Indeed, there are no ornate scrolls, illustrated words, or pictures of fairy folk doing cute things or sat on toadstools at any time; except on the first page. (Oona's pictures are reserved to depicting social interactions in a very unflowery, mundane way. She calls it "Constitutional Art" and it's very greyish.) Some of the original readers found this all a little disappointing. Regardless, an executive decision was taken that the moment in time, captured in the photo, had importance in the ongoing scheme of things,

"Even," said the editor, "If the plot trajectory in future volumes did make the photo's significance somewhat redundant in the eyes of some readers. This is why the photo is being reported about now, because it may be that a select, few readers can still see some symbolic significance in it that they can later recall and refer back to. Then again, that might not be the case because what is significant to some and not others *is* such a subjective matter. All the authors did actually agree on this point of fact. Magical, fantasy timelines are very tricky things and meanings are nebulous creatures that hide or broadcast themselves – just like the Fei in fact. It takes a vigilant reader to spot these and pin them down. A lot of people say that fantasy fiction isn't serious literature anyway and has nothing to do with serious intention." Oona, who was leaning over the author's shoulder as the words were written and spoken aloud, just said, "Phooey to that!" She's also threatened to kill anyone who argues with her about it, so watch out!

The contentious photo was taken outside a bar in Kensington, some time after the four friends first met, at Ensley's shop and it is a poor, damaged print. One could wonder why it was chosen in the first place! There are two brown spots on it, one on Hugh's chest and another on Kosmo's shoulder, and they look almost like coffee splats. Ben has grown a beard again; Ensley is laughing and pointing at the camera as if she knows the photographer well. All four are dressed in shorts and tee shirts indicating both their assimilation into mainstream culture and the fact that it is summer. Despite this, the table parasol throws a deep shadow over them all, creating a dingy effect, and even the cafe window, and the awning, have an odd brown-ness to them. So much so, it is clear that someone has taken the initiative further and enhanced the outlines of the characters with sepia, giving an odd, almost Victorian, effect to the photo. The book's earlier boast of, 'time (being able to) reveal all' accretes paradox if the reader doesn't even know what moment in time they are being orientated to. The editor responded with, "Well that's the problem with time, isn't it? There are loads of things to uncover in different epochs that are still relevant today... anyway, we were glad to be able to raise this mind-boggling issue to public attention." Some online complaints were swiftly received from early reviewers. One said she was rightly confused by the whole 'time' issue and wondered if it were deliberate. Also, the story made no commitment to plot resolution. 'I feel a bit short-changed by the short-cut tactic of using a photo to round things off,' she mentioned. Another wrote the contradictory statement of how he was disappointed that, 'The dirty grittiness of the photo combined with the casual, contemporary dress of the characters sabotaged their mystical, fictional presentation in the book, even though one of them still grows twigs and three of them have wand hands.'

"Told you so," said the book's anonymous co-author, to anyone who would listen, but the editor was intractable in portraying as much realism as possible at the end. A closer inspection of the photo reveals further naturalistic elements: a waiter can be seen, hovering to the right of the table in the murk, and there is water beading on Kosmo's glass of lager. The cafe they are at was indeed real and eventually closed in 2017. The participants in the photo are oblivious to the furore their photo might cause; they are just four friends enjoying a day off – caught, quite happily, in the moment. Inner calm reigns and time is subdued for once, if only for a fleeting moment. It really is like that in the sunshine - sort of, hopeful, despite appearances.

***

'Don't like it,' thought Sarah, 'creeps me out - don't think it seems hopeful at all.' Sarah felt she was being emotionally manipulated by a book that engineered uncertainty, and she disliked the clumsy symbolic shadowing caused by the parasol. "Why?" she whispered into the flyleaf not really expecting a reply in print or otherwise. It's a wilful book, like them, Sarah realised, shutting it firmly, though when she looked around her with clear eyes and viewed the bookcases about to be installed in her very own bookshop, she understood how she'd gained by it all.

"I think I've had some manifesting ointment put in my eyes," she told a workman.

"Eh?" he said.

"I think I've personally benefitted from the fairies," she mused. "I can see now that wishes can come true, even though we don't know what we're wishing for at the time... until much, much later," she added. Without missing a beat, the workman said,

"Alright, love. Uh, do you want me to take the flooring right underneath the bookcase?"

"Oh yes, please, easier to move them later on if need be."

Still, Sarah found the text ambiguous, and she wasn't the only one. Stomping through the gap in the doorway, held up by an RSJ, entered Izzy, with a thunderous look on her face... In her hand was a big, red book.

"Stop right there!" yelled Sarah. "You can't come in without a hard hat on."

"It's bullshit, all bullshit," Izzy commenced, allowing Sarah to plonk a bright yellow hat on her. "Look, look," said Izzy, and the book slipped out of her hand onto a pile of wood shavings.

"Slow it all down," Sarah calmed, at the same time trying to pick Izzy's heavy copy back up with some difficulty. She still had her own book in her right hand. "I know," she said, "It's all a bit misleading. Not sure about the cafe ending myself."

"I'm not talking about that," interrupted Izzy. "How can I tell people that I'm reading proper books now if this one hasn't even got the writers' names on the front."

"What?" Sarah hadn't noticed this; she'd been pretty involved in the book's volatile plot and hadn't bothered to look at the front cover for ages.

"Look!" Izzy said again, grabbing it back off Sarah and pointing to the embossed words on the front cover. These were certainly very strange as the authorial credits were somewhat incomplete, the words saying:

... And Ben Sopher
Illustrations by her most Royal Highness Queen Oona

Izzy moaned. "I can't tell people, I'm reading a big, fat book by No-one and Ben Sopher and a mad old bint called Oona who does the drawings, can I?"

"It's amazing that she even deigned put her name to it." Sarah said, quite distracted, "It changes everything really..."

"What does?"

"The drawings. Don't you remember? Every illustration in The Almanac has to be truthful. Add that to the fact that Ben is acting like a non-fiction writer, and the book becomes very authentic. The book becomes more serious, even though it's a fairytale."

"Yeah, but we know they're real people anyway, because we've seen them in real life. So, in that case, why can't we know who did what and when in the end? What's the big deal?!" With her finger acting like a demented woodpecker, she tapped her version of the book, but then the thought occurred that she might actually be interpreted in the book as something she wasn't; an angry, stupid person. She'd had enough of all that. Izzy suddenly stopped, met looks with Sarah and waited for her to say something to help her out. Sarah did.

"Is it easy though Iz? Everybody always argues about versions and who does what, don't they? Everybody always believes that they have ownership over everyone else's' lives and what happened. It's not true," she said her words quiet but sure. "My own life is so, so unlikely... no-one would ever believe me..." She tailed off. This confession had the effect of making Izzie feel very uneasy and she spent a while staring at her boots whilst nibbling the quelled fingers of her right hand. Sarah thought a little bit about her own situation and how it could be summed up as a fiction. Was there another ghostly version of her doing something quite different at that moment in accordance with the omnipotent perception of someone else? Would she be written up, even confined by that author stating, 'this is the 'real' Sarah and this is what she *really* did.' Could it even be taken one step further? Were there in fact actual, different timelines where an unknown version of herself was behaving in a way she didn't want to sanction? Sarah had a cold presentiment that the universe really did have distinct timelines that intersected and wandered off like Bettina Esterhazy's crazy knitting. The thought that there could be a different author or authors - reading her, anticipating her, directing her... recording it for posterity in the far-off future made her feel she could be scrubbed out of existence altogether. For a moment she stood on a metaphysical precipice and a shock of cold horror poured into her legs, freezing her to the spot. She looked again at the front cover. Perhaps the hidden writer of the Forgotten Folk didn't want to actually be so controlling. In that case he or she was taking a backstage role in letting everyone figure things out for themselves. That *was* a nice thing to do.

"Petey said there was no such thing as time anyway," she said a little wildly, so perhaps nothing that happened is really real or solid too; but sensible Izzy, ever straightforward had had enough.

"Don't be daft." She pointed to the piles of books around her. "Look, evidence that real shit happened once upon a time. It's all we've got and anyway it's a starting point. We can build on what's happened and just... Oh, I don't know, just go on."

"So, a book isn't just a book after all...?" she quoted

"Yeah, alright, I knew you wouldn't let that one go." Izzy grinned but she didn't like the reference back to the person she once was, in a queue, in another time. Her smile was more a grimace. Anyway," she said going back to her original contention, "How are we supposed to find out what happens to them then and who the writer is, if it *is* serious stuff? I mean, we're all in it now, aren't we? We're captivated. If we want to be," she added looking Sarah straight in the eyes and Sarah knew that Izzy meant the text had some kind of hold on them all in a very fateful way. They both wanted to be in on it though, she knew that.

"I suppose we buy another book," she said, "the next one; that's what it all seems to be leading to. I wonder how it will all end?" she mused to herself. This particular book seems to want to resist endings.

"What?! Another book?" Izzy was roaring mad. "Are you bloody joking? Another hundred quid - no way! I'm not doing it... conned... flippin' rip-off!" Izzy's rant was drowned out by hammer blows and a circular saw. When the workman paused, she said in a quieter, thoughtful little voice,

"Well. I might, I suppose. Do you want to go halves? Do you think they'd let us?"

Sarah just laughed.

Tempus Omnia Revelat